LOVE IN A SANDSTORM

ZOE YORK

WWW.ZOEYORK.COM

We don't always get what we want, but we can make what we get something worth wanting

For Marie and Diane

CHAPTER ONE

May
Pine Harbour

THE DIRECTIONS from the diner on the edge of Pine Harbour had been clear. Back onto the highway, head just north of town, take the first left.

Such a mundane instruction for a potentially life-altering drive, Jenna Kowalczyk thought.

Five minutes, tops, the waitress had said. Sean would definitely be there. She'd leaned in and with a sympathetic sigh confided that he hadn't left his older brother's house since Dean brought him home four weeks earlier.

Of course he was at Dean's place. Those Foster brothers always had each other's backs.

Jenna had heard all about Sean's family in the two weeks they spent together in the south of Spain. When she'd fallen in love with a soldier and let him promise her the moon.

It had only been three and a half months since they'd clung to each other and said goodbye in the Urfa airport.

Eight weeks since she'd last heard from him. Six weeks, give or take a few days, since he'd been injured in a mortar attack on a convoy.

An attack she hadn't known about.

She took the turns mechanically. Instead of the overwhelming emotions she'd expected to feel, there was just a stiff numbness.

The final turn, onto a gravel lane, was marked by a pair of weeping willows. Past those trees she found a sweeping lawn leading to a well-kept sprawling home with a wide porch and a three-car garage to the side, the house Jenna knew Sean's oldest brother had recently bought and added a recording studio at the back for his fiancée.

She knew all about these people, but she feared they had no clue she existed.

She slowed to a stop in front of the house. Her heart hammered in her chest and she took a full minute to compose herself before she pushed herself out of the car.

The Bruce Peninsula was overcast and rainy, and the unseasonable cool felt even colder given where she'd just come from. She grabbed her jacket.

When she knocked on the door, it wasn't Sean that answered. She recognized Dean from the photos Sean had shown her.

He didn't recognize her in the least, though. He gave her a tight, blank up-and-down glance before speaking. "Can I help you?"

She nodded slowly. "I'm looking for Sean Foster."

"I'm his brother, Dean."

She gave him another nod as she tried to make sense of this moment. Her brain was spinning hard, but there was no sense to be made. Only one thing to do—rip off the bandage. "Is he here?"

Dean crossed his arms and lifted his chin. "What do you want with him?"

She swallowed hard. "I asked at Mac's. The diner?"

"I'm familiar with it."

Heat rushed to her cheeks. "Of course. They said he was staying here."

"He's asleep right now."

In the middle of the day? She instinctively looked past her husband's brother's shoulder, seeking out the man who occupied her heart.

"Maybe it would be best for you to come back another time."

"Right." That wasn't happening, though. She was here now and she needed to see Sean. But first…if Dean didn't know who she was, there was only one explanation. And that was step number one. "Maybe we should talk, anyway."

"Us?"

She gestured for him to join her on his own porch.

He glanced behind him before stepping outside and closing the door. "What do we need to talk about? If you're looking for Sean, you should know he's not in great shape right now."

Something in the way he said that turned her stomach. She'd known that was a possibility, maybe even a likelihood, but anger—at being left behind, at being ignored—had fuelled her to this point. She'd needed to think she'd been wronged, somehow, in order to keep her wits about her. To keep working when she wanted to curl up in a ball and let her heart just be broken. Of course when she'd realized he'd been injured, she'd feared the worst—but the media reports had made it sound…

Well, whatever it was, better to deal in facts. She

squared her shoulders and tightened her mouth. "Then it's all the better that I'm here."

"And why is that?"

She shoved her fingers through her hair, ignoring the way they shook, and glanced to the side. "I guess he didn't tell you."

"Tell us what?"

Spit it out. She sighed and held out her hand. "I'm Jenna. Sean's wife."

It took agonizing seconds for Dean to glance down at her extended fingers, then back up at her face. Process her words and weigh them.

He didn't take her hand, though.

She left it stuck in the space between them. She had nothing to apologize for. She had a ring and two weeks' worth of stories and photos that proved she wasn't insane, even though right now, in this moment, she felt totally crazy.

Slowly, he extended his arm and shook her hand. It wasn't the warmest handshake she'd ever experienced, but it wasn't booting her off his porch, either. Small miracles. "Say that again?" he said carefully after he released her hand.

"We met in January at a transit camp in Turkey. Just before he went to Spain on his long leave. We traveled together. I was in the room when he called home." She'd been curled up against his naked chest, but that wasn't a detail that needed to be shared with his brother. "And then, at the end of our holiday together, we got married."

She swung her bag off her shoulder and dug into it for her phone. Sean's brother didn't say anything as she tapped in her password and clicked into her saved photographs. She didn't have many since Spain. A couple of selfies she'd sent Sean, nothing indecent, and the group photos she took with her Doctors Without Borders colleagues the night her replacement arrived, and she left the camp.

When she said an abrupt goodbye to her life's plans and her planned out future.

All to chase the missing pieces of her broken heart.

She found the end of their trip. The twenty-four hours in Gibraltar. Their wedding pictures, as simple and unassuming as they were.

Fingers still shaking, she handed over the phone.

Dean flipped back and forth, then swore under his breath before glancing up at her and swearing again, this time louder. "Well, I'm sorry for being suspicious. You're right, he didn't tell us."

She'd known that from his initial who-the-heck-are-you expression, but the confirmation still hurt. And when she opened her mouth, nothing came out.

"He's not himself." Dean likely provided this as some sort of justification, and she got it.

She wanted that explanation too. Needed to cling to it because if he were, this would be extra awful. The man who'd seduced her, thrilled her, loved her couldn't do this. Couldn't go cold and silent just like that.

"Can you tell me what happened? The news reports were sparse, to say the least."

He shook his head. "Not my story to tell. But you should come in. We'll give you some space to speak to him on your own."

———

SEAN HEARD voices downstairs and hauled another

pillow over his head. He could handle the ringing, or the spinning, or the nausea. Any one of those things were manageable. But all three together filled him with the worst kind of impotent rage, because there was nothing to be done. Even the medications he'd been prescribed didn't work. They didn't touch the dizziness or the tinnitus. Sure, they helped with nausea, but so did being unconscious.

He closed his eyes and willed himself to fall back into the broken sleep he'd been riding when the noise had started again.

But instead of quiet, he got a knock at the bedroom door.

"Go away," he growled in the cold, hard voice he still didn't recognize as his own.

His oldest brother didn't listen, because that wasn't his way. Instead he pushed the door open. *Creak.*

Sean moved the pillow that was in front of his face out of the way and found Dean looming in the doorway. "You've got a visitor."

"Not up for it."

"Not an option for this visitor."

"Someone from the unit?" Definitely not up for that, then. He was no fucking hero. He'd been dodging visitors the entire month he'd been home, and that wasn't going to change any time soon. "If it's the padre, tell him to fuck off."

"It's your wife."

For two weeks in the military hospital in Germany, he'd imagined those words. At first, he'd wanted, needed to hear them. Tried to ask the nurses to get in touch with Jenna, but his words had been all fucked up, and they'd ignored his badly written notes.

He'd dreamed of her. Futile, frustrating dreams, of

falling asleep in her arms, only to wake up and she was gone.

He'd dreamed of his late mother, too. Hadn't done that in years.

Then the doctors started to talk about his rehab and transitioning out of the army. He'd been reminded at every turn about the ever-present threat of another stroke. Of disability and accommodation. Faces grew sympathetic and voices softened.

Did he want to go to a rehab hospital far from home?

No.

Would he have adequate support if he was discharged? It wasn't a lie to say yes. His brothers would do anything for him. Of course he hadn't allowed them to. He'd hissed and growled and snarled until they gave him space.

And as he struggled with the transition back in Pine Harbour—as he realized just how well and truly fucked he was, not for a short time, but maybe forever—he couldn't stomach the thought of having one of them reach out to her. Couldn't bear the thought of her pitying him, too.

Better for her to be angry and righteous. To move on and leave him behind.

He'd resolved himself to that plan, deciding it would be better for her that he be nothing but a memory.

But she was here.

Now.

His stomach heaved.

He lurched to his feet, ignoring the way the room twisted obscenely around him, and shoved past Dean. There was no way for him to keep the floor from coming up to meet his face. It was only absurdity that drove some part of him to keep trying, like on the three-hundredth try, mind-over-matter might finally work.

It didn't.

Dean hauled him up and half-carried him into the bathroom, where he lost his lunch in the toilet.

Silently, his brother handed him a damp towel.

His whole life, Dean had been taking care of him. Ten years older and endlessly wiser, he'd been shoved into a parent role before he was ready, but he'd stepped up anyway.

And now he was doing it again, his new life with Liana on hold because Sean was a mess.

Sean swiped angrily at his face. He didn't look in the mirror. He hated what he would see if he did. Gaunt cheeks, scruffy beard. Too long hair, sunken eyes. He didn't need to see himself today to know Jenna couldn't, ever. "Make her go away."

"I'm not going to do that."

"Then what the fuck good are you?"

"I honestly don't know." Dean growled under his breath. "You got married?"

That was before.

It hurt so much, a bright, sharp regret in his chest.

"We had a fling." The words turned sour in his mouth. A lie. It had been so much more than that. He'd been the luckiest man in the world.

Had been.

Past tense.

Like everything else in his life, the idea of having a wife was now done. Broken. Impossible and shoved deep down lest it destroy him to think about it.

"She's downstairs." Dean kept pushing that fact in front of him, like he wasn't covered in a cold sweat already.

"I can't."

"You don't have a choice." His brother opened the bathroom door. "Liana and I are going out for an hour to give you some space. I'm telling Jenna you're up here."

No. It was a wounded, pathetic cry, and he swallowed hard not to let it out.

He wouldn't beg.

If he needed to do this, he'd do it. He'd find a way to tell her this was a mistake. Her coming here, them getting married, the whole thing.

He stood there, in front of the sink, and listened to Dean's heavy steps descend the stairs. Murmurs, then silence, followed by noisier murmurs. Dean had gone to get Liana from her studio—interrupting her work—so they could get out of the way.

His chest tightened. It was too late to move—not that he could on his own. Too late to try and look good for her —not that he deserved to preen.

As the front door clicked shut, his pulse pounded loud inside his head. It added to the disorienting cacophony of sound in there that made it so hard for him to think.

Fitting.

All of his fucked-up brain stuff should make it hard to hear things, but if anything, it heightened his sense of sound. He heard her downstairs. Shifting on the spot. Restless, worrying.

If she'd stood there any longer, that knowledge would have twisted tight enough inside him that he'd have tried to move. Tried and failed, like all the other times, but he was close to lurching forward when she took her first step up the stairs.

Tentative.

Creak. Another two steps, and a pause. Then a sigh and a resolute return to climbing, step by dooming step, until she appeared in the doorway, wearing jeans and a jacket, her Chucks still on her feet, like she knew he wouldn't let her stay very long.

Her eyes widened and her perfect mouth, sweet and soft, pulled into a surprised O. "Sean?"

"You shouldn't be here," he said, his voice rough. His knuckles hurt from how hard he gripped the sink to keep himself steady, but what was another layer of pain?

Her eyes flicked down, then dragged up his body, her gaze searching. He stood there and let her hunt for any answer that would satisfy her curiosity. Any answer that would reassure her he was nothing like the man she'd married.

Nothing like the man who'd loved her for too brief a time.

She took a shuddering breath as her eyes met his again, and his chest cracked open in a hard, wrenching twist. "And yet I am," she whispered.

CHAPTER TWO

February, four months earlier
Urfa, Turkey

JENNA RUBBED the heel of her hand against her closed eye as she shoved her feet blindly into her clogs. Her pager was still going off when she stood, still unsteady from not enough sleep.

It was too early for this. But *this* was what she lived for—middle of the night births, endless days of caring for women and children in the most desperate situations.

Making a difference.

So it didn't matter that her eyes burned like they'd been rubbed with sandpaper or that the inside of her mouth tasted like—

Okay, no, that mattered. Blech. She stumbled to the makeshift sink in the corner of the military-grade tent and quickly brushed her teeth. She'd been in Turkey for almost four months, and she still had a lot of moments where the fact that she was here felt surreal. Working overseas as a midwife with Doctors Without Borders had been her goal for more than five years, and yet the reality was jarring.

Although not nearly as jarring for her as it was for the refugees in the transit camp.

She took a deep breath and squared her shoulders. Outside her tent, it would still be pitch black. It wasn't far to the freshly-constructed field hospital set up in the new NATO-protected transit camp, but it was cold, and she'd only managed an hour of sleep before she got the heads-up that three women had gone into labour, and one was progressing quickly.

It wasn't going to be a night for sleep.

If she was lucky—if those mamas were lucky—it was going to be a night of beginnings, of hope, and just enough innocence to keep them all going.

She pulled a scrub top on over the long sleeve t-shirt she'd fallen asleep in, strapped on her headlamp, and darted into the chilliness.

Milly met her halfway down the path and gave her a quick rundown on what to expect. Jenna triaged the cases in her head as they walked and came to the same assessment as the veteran Australian nurse by her side.

The most quickly progressing labour was a fourth time mom. If she hadn't delivered by the time they got to the hospital, she would soon enough. That gave them two labours to watch over the course of the early morning. Manageable even with a full clinic, although there would be lots of apologizing for the interruptions.

At least she'd have help. Mariya, the Jordanian-British midwife who was going to cover Jenna's vacation time, had arrived last night. She'd let the replacement sleep until the two first-time moms were closer to transition.

"I bet your handsome prime minister will enjoy

meeting these new babies tomorrow," Milly teased as they presented their ID badges at the hospital entrance.

"I'm sure he will." A week ago, they'd received a heads-up that a Canadian diplomatic delegation would be stopping at the camp on the way to visit front-line Canadian troops at a base in Northern Iraq. Yesterday it had been leaked that the group would include Gavin Strong, the prime minister, who was quite handsome.

Jenna had never met him, but he was the Member of Parliament for the riding next to hers back home in Vancouver, and he'd had a meteoric rise to national leadership—and international popularity.

"I'll need to get a picture with him…" Milly kept talking, but Jenna hadn't had enough sleep to process anything other than the clinical responsibility of her patients.

She scrubbed up as she entered the delivery ward then found the labouring mom in the bed closest to the door. It was a far cry from the hospital and birth centre she'd worked at in Vancouver. Basic cots and random blankets, but they made do with what they had.

She dropped to her knees next to the woman and murmured gently as she did a visual assessment. Her contractions were right on top of each other now, and good and long.

"You're ready, aren't you Assala?" Jenna whispered. The woman nodded. Her English was limited and Jenna's Arabic was basic at best, but the tone mattered. And speaking to her helped, even if the words didn't mean anything. "You've done this before. You're a pro."

Behind her, the door quietly pulled open then one of the local nurses greeted her before switching to Arabic. A quick greeting to the patient, then she glanced at Jenna, ready to do double duty as a translator.

"It looks like she's starting to push a bit on her own. Let's see if she wants to switch positions." Jenna refocused on the patient. "Assala, would you like to get up on your knees?"

As soon as that was repeated in Arabic, the mom shook her head and moaned, her eyes still squeezed shut.

"Okay. Not yet. I'm here, we'll wait." It was the most powerful lesson in birthing she'd learned here. She'd known this kind of patient waiting in the darkness as a privilege back home, a path chosen rather than dictated. But here on the edge of war, it was almost the only option. They had surgeons and an operating suite, but for many reasons that was the absolute last resort. There would be no rushing Assala.

There was little else for Jenna to do in the interim. She made a quick loop through the eight-bed ward, checking on the other two women, but they were both dozing, with inconsistent contractions.

When she got back to Assala's bed, the mother was moving more, pushing her hand against the edge of the cot.

"Ready to get up?" Jenna asked, and that didn't need to be translated.

They helped their patient onto her knees. She leaned back against the nurse as Jenna touched first Assala's knee, then her thigh, before lifting the long gown out of the way.

First, Jenna replaced the soaked pad there with a clean towel from the basket she had at the ready. With each step, she carefully explained what she was doing and why, pausing for the nurse to translate before continuing. She crouched low, visualizing the birth field. The baby's head was right there, and with the next contraction, mom started to push her child into the world.

"Slow, good, breathe…"

The head came out on the third contraction, the baby's wee little face scrunched tight just like mama's. Then the shoulders, quickly followed by the rest of the baby, slippery and wriggly.

Jenna checked the cord, then between the baby's legs as she lifted him up and handed him to a shaking Assala. "It's a boy!"

With a weepy sigh, their patient sagged back against the nurse, who settled in for a bit of a sit as they waited for the placenta to be delivered. Jenna kept an eye on the baby, who was fussing nicely after a lusty cry, and mama, who was moving her gown out of the way to bring him to her breast.

It wasn't always this easy, but when it was, she said a prayer of thanks.

For the refugees, small miracles made surviving that much easier. A safe arrival of a new child was a wonderful thing, and there would be much celebrating.

It took another hour to get mom and baby settled back in bed, both resting after a well-deserved snack.

Speaking of snacks…Jenna's stomach growled as she added a detailed note to Assala's chart. She pressed a hand to her stomach then glanced up. Milly was already pointing in the direction of the food tent. "Go on. I'll page you if anything changes, but everyone is sleeping now."

"I might actually sit and eat today."

Milly laughed. "No you won't. You're still too nervous for that."

Jenna hated that she was that transparent. "I'm working on it."

"You're a great midwife. Focus on that. Nobody is chill about this environment, not ever. And especially not on a first rotation."

"I know." But it was easier said than accepted. For more than a year, Jenna had planned for this job. She'd sold most of her furniture in Vancouver, getting her worldly possessions down to two suitcases she carried and four boxes stored in her college roommate's garage back home. The plan had been to couch surf when she was done with this six month placement and sign up for another. Then another, and another, until her wanderlust led her home for good.

Then she'd arrived in Turkey and from the first shift, she'd felt like all of her planning had just barely prepared her for the unrelenting pace. Now her new goal was to get to the end of the rotation without having a breakdown where she privileged her own weakness over other people's suffering. And even though Milly—and Sami, their medical director—promised her everyone had a rough adjustment, she wasn't sure she believed them. She'd had such lofty goals for herself that the hard landing in reality had bruised her emotionally.

Deep down, she still wanted this to be the first of many rotations with Doctors Without Borders. It was just that on top of that still-ardent goal was now piled a lot of doubt and fatigue.

Maybe food would help.

Since they didn't have a real residence yet, and were still living in tents, the local NGO coordinator had arranged for them to use the mess hall provided for the peacekeepers and visiting military personnel.

Hall. Everything here was either in a tent or a sea

container. Or in the case of the mess hall, both. The kitchen was in a sea container, and the tables in an adjacent tent.

She had her meal choices down to a simple but reliable routine. For breakfast, she liked coffee, first in the crowded self-service line, then she grabbed a slice of bread and a packet of peanut butter. Fruit was at the end of the line. Today the bananas looked dodgy, so she reached for the only apple on the plate.

She wasn't alone in her assessment of the shiny Granny Smith fruit being the right choice. Her fingers collided with a man's hand, which quickly retreated.

"All yours," the hand's owner said in a familiar accent.

She picked up the apple and twisted around, glancing over her shoulder. She found a tall, broad-shouldered Canadian soldier, his mouth curving into an easy, charming smile that lit up his entire face, crinkling the corners of his eyes. He looked like someone who was used to getting what he wanted, from an apple to…whatever.

"Thank you. I'd be happy to cut it in half if you'd like some?"

Sharing was a huge currency in Urfa. She'd offer the same to anyone who wanted it. But now she found herself actually hoping he'd take her up on it, even though she had women in labour waiting for her and she should prob-ably eat quickly, because this guy was something else. Tall and broad and pulsing with a happy energy, she found herself unable to look away.

There weren't any Canadians regularly stationed here —the only constant military presence were the peace-keepers protecting the camp—but every so often someone wearing a maple leaf on their uniform would transit through, because of the proximity to the airport a kilometre away. And with the arrival of the diplomatic delegation tomorrow, she'd see more of them, she was sure.

But it wasn't just their shared nationality that drew her to him. There was something else, a brightness maybe, and it was like she suddenly realized she'd been deprived of water and here was a fresh stream of hot, happy... soldier? She wasn't sure. She still couldn't decipher military rank badges, and it didn't help that they had a regular in-and-out flow of attaches and liaison officers from all the major NATO countries, so she didn't bother to try to guess. Better to just introduce herself.

"I'm Jenna," she said. "Fellow Canadian. I work in the field hospital."

"Sean. Canadian Forces, as you can tell." He stepped out of the food line, and she followed. "And you can have the apple. But if you've got time to sit and have a coffee...?"

He leaned in a bit as he said it, his smile revealing a dimple. He was flirting with her, and doing it with ease. She'd forgotten what that was like, and experiencing it out of the blue in the middle of filth and destruction was a bit disorienting. Not unwelcome, though. Not unwelcome at all.

"Company is always good," he added, since she hadn't answered him. Well, she couldn't be blamed for that, she was operating on one hour of sleep and he was uncommonly hot. It was distracting.

"Definitely." She pointed to a table. "We can sit there."

He chuckled. Good, he thought her moronic statement was a joke. She'd play it that way, even though it came from sleep deprivation and hot-guy brain stuttering, rather than a good sense of humour.

He'd grabbed sausages and eggs and toast with his coffee.

Hot and flirty and brave.

"The sausages are pretty spicy," she warned.

"Good to know, thank you."

She didn't mention that she wasn't sure what meat was in them, either. He probably knew that, and from personal experience, having someone raise that doubt just before you were about to chow down was a definite appetite ruiner. And really, the food was cleared for consumption. It was fine.

Mostly fine.

She couldn't wait for her upcoming vacation. She'd always thought of herself as a foodie, but life in the camp had tested the bounds of her adventurousness.

She bit into the apple and sighed at the burst of juice against her tongue. Tangy and sweet, even if the fruit itself was a bit mealy.

"Tasty?" Sean asked, his eyes flicking up from her mouth to meet her gaze.

"Definitely more than edible."

"Ah."

She responded with a smile that said all the things one didn't say in this conversation. They were never as good as apples back home.

Everyone gets homesick, she'd been told. She hadn't believed it would happen to her, because she'd longed to travel the world for as long as she could remember. And yet she'd still had a little cry after a week when the hot water wasn't working in the showers. Another one last month when Christmas dinner had been mediocre at best and her only gifts were eBooks from her bestie that appeared on her e-reader when she synched it up before bed and an emailed gift card from her mother and sister.

"What do you miss the most?" Sometimes it ached in her chest to play this game, but not right now. Right now she was simply curious about this man in front of her, with the easy smile and the sparkle in his eyes.

"The forest," he said without hesitation. "Especially when it rains."

"That's a good one. Where is home for you and this forest that you're missing?"

"Ontario. Do you know the Bruce Peninsula?" When she nodded, he continued. "There's this amazing trail that runs through our town, and all the way up and down the peninsula. I ran it almost every day. Now I run laps around camps and try not to breathe in too much."

"But you still run, that's impressive." She hadn't done any physical exercise in four months. Working sixteen hour days was enough.

He shrugged. "Just something I've always done. How about you, what do you miss the most—other than fresh apples?"

"Bubble baths." She laughed. "And chocolate, although I brought a decent supply with me. I couldn't bring a bathtub with me, and after a long shift, there's nothing quite like sinking into hot water."

He glanced at her scrubs. "Are you a doctor?"

"Midwife."

"Did you work in Canada first?"

She nodded. "For five years. But this was always my goal."

"It's different, eh?" He didn't say it glibly. It was different, and not just in the tools they had at their disposal.

"More than I expected to be honest."

"Same for me. There's only so much you can do to prepare for the realities on the ground." He gave her a ready smile. "But you deliver babies. That's pretty cool."

And right on cue, her pager went off. Damn it. She could have sat and soaked up Sean thinking her job was cool for a lot longer. She glanced at the display and folded her bread into a sandwich, protecting the peanut butter. "I'm sorry, I have to go."

"Don't forget your coffee," he said, standing and picking up her cup at the same time.

Right. She definitely needed that, although caffeine didn't do anything for the emotional fatigue she'd been suffering from lately. She flashed him a quick smile. "Thank you. Maybe I'll see you around later. Are you here overnight? Curfew is seven, and then it's pretty quiet unless..." She gestured to her pager. "Something happens."

"I'll be around. I'm here until tomorrow night."

CHAPTER THREE

FROM THE MOMENT he'd landed at the transit camp three hours earlier, Sean had had a mental countdown going on —forty-eight hours until siestas, sangria, and hot Spanish women. Two days until he could take off his uniform for two weeks, stop being Captain Foster, and recharge his batteries. Like any other soldier on a tour of duty, he'd been looking forward to a break after three months of non-stop stress and pressure that went hand-in-hand with frontline infantry military service.

Now Spain was the furthest thing from his mind. All he could think was he had roughly twenty-four hours to make an impression on one woman.

Jenna the Midwife, who liked apples so much they made her blush.

The last thing he'd expected was to meet a woman like her as he transited through Urfa on his way out of Iraq.

Halfway through his tour there as an infantry intelligence officer, he had seventeen days of leave burning a hole in his pocket. The fun was supposed to start in Spain, not here. Not in a mess hall he was never supposed to be in.

He was only here because the Prime Minister of Canada was making a surprise visit to the region tomorrow, and Sean had been looped in to the classified information since his transit plans put him near the camp at the same time as the PM. Sean's commanding officer asked him to adjust his leave dates to give the Canadian Forces a representative on the ground while the young, brash, and charismatic leader took his first tour of the Middle East. From here, Gavin Strong would travel to the NATO base where the Canadian Forces troops were based, and then he'd be the CO's problem.

Although everything the guy touched turned to gold, so not likely to be a bad problem. Just an enthusiastic one. Sean's CO had put the bug in his ear that the PM tended to expand his itinerary at the last second, and could use some corralling.

He took a deep breath. Right. Job first, woman second.

He grabbed his plate and headed in search of the Canadian government advance party, because standing in the way of any attempt to get to know Jenna better were a politician with lofty ideals and an entire refugee camp of patients. He couldn't do anything about the latter, but he could do his damnedest to make the former's visit work to his advantage.

It didn't take him long to track down an officious communications officer and get a copy of the PM's schedule for the next day's visit. It came attached to a six page memo. He glanced at the itinerary then shoved the packet in the pocket on his pants leg. "Do you have a computer I could use to log in to the DWAN and email my HQ?"

After updating his CO that he'd arrived and all was on track for the PM's visit, he checked his personal email. There were messages from all three of his brothers. Baby pictures from Jake, a new-house update from Dean, and Matt gave him the low-down on the gossip from their reserve army regiment back home.

No email from their father, not that he'd opened the last one the Colonel had sent. It was the only message from his father in the last month and had been a forward of a news article with the subject line, **"Worth a read"**. *Sure, Dad, I'll get right on that.*

He'd never understood his father's sporadic attempts to reach out. They were never personal, always forwards like that, leaving Sean to guess at the intent behind the messages. He didn't need any motivation, if that's what it was about. And if it was a cautionary tale; or just a jaded, pessimistic bit of bullshit…well, he wasn't up for those, either.

To be fair, there wasn't anything his father could send his way that would land properly. All his life, Sean tried to make sense of why that was—why he struggled so much more than his brothers did with the Colonel's gruff, removed parenting style.

Maybe it was because they all remembered, at least in small slices, what it was like to have a more loving parent.

Sean scrubbed his hand over his face. As he always did when thoughts of the mother he'd never known slid into his head, he pushed them away. It wasn't helpful to be maudlin. He knew who he was, and why he lived his life the way he did. That was all that mattered. That was how he could honour her sacrifice.

This week that meant ensuring his nation's leader's

arrival on the edge of a war zone was as smooth as possible.

He headed to his bunk in the NATO barracks. He'd been given a shared room as they didn't have any officer quarters available, which didn't matter to him in the least.

He wasn't planning on spending any time there except to rack out.

Right now, he needed to get a better visual on where the delegation would visit tomorrow. His role would be mostly as a quiet observer, and to report an all-clear to his CO at the end of the visit. But there were always unforeseen problems, as well as opportunities. Best to get a good lay of the land and be prepared either way.

He changed out of his uniform and put on his nondescript PT gear. He stuck his ID into a pocket inside his sweat pants, made sure his dog tags were hidden beneath his t-shirt, and headed back outside. The sun was higher in the sky now and the air had lost the biting chill he'd been surprised by when he landed. Now it was almost warm enough for him to run in just a t-shirt and shorts. He was looking forward to getting in some long runs in Spain.

He set off on an easy lope around the perimeter of the NGO compound. As he reached the southwestern most point, he could see through the fence to the regional airport less than a kilometre away. That airfield was why this camp had popped up here in the last year. It was secure enough for Western nations to fly in planes to pick up vetted refugees, and there were some civilian flights, too.

That's where the Canadian delegation would land. This would be the new prime minister's first impression of the effects of war. Sean visualized his own arrival earlier that day, the bumpy drive to the camp in the early dawn. He'd been eager to get this shit over with then.

He wasn't in any hurry to leave now. He had to figure out how to engineer some opportunities to see Jenna the Midwife again.

With a quick wave up at the peacekeepers in the tower at the compound corner, he turned his back on the airport. According to the itinerary the last stop on the PM's tour the next day would be the field hospital, but it was the first place Sean wanted to scope out. Not exactly professional, but there was something about Jenna that made him want to break the rules.

And Sean was checking out everything on the itinerary.

The PM would also spend time out in the camp itself, meeting Syrians in the process of applying for refugee status with Canada, then he'd have lunch with the camp director and NGO coordinator.

So Sean next ran to the checkpoint between the NGO compound and the camp itself. He introduced himself to the guards and presented his ID. He accepted their normal caution about traveling in a group, but he wasn't wearing anything on him identifying himself as a soldier.

And he could out run and out last anyone.

He stuck to the wider main "streets", avoiding the narrow lanes between the rows of tents where women did washing in plastic basins and men beat out sleeping mats. He'd often hear a crying baby, a toddler's shriek of joy, and think of Jenna. How many babies were born here? How many couples lay together, knowing the risk and still taking it—either because they wanted to start or grow their family no matter what, or maybe just to have that intimacy, damn the consequences.

On his third figure eight loop through the camp, he came across a line of people in front of a trailer he'd passed before, but which was now open.

Health Clinic, a sign on the side read.

His heart jumped a little in his chest, which was ridiculous. But his hopes of seeing Jenna were rewarded as he slowed to a stop. She was just inside the doorway, holding a clipboard. He watched as she worked with a translator to go down the queue of patients, writing down some of their names and pointing others to the side of the trailer.

He hung back, erring on the side of not wanting to interrupt her at work. It gave him a chance to look at her, too, which was a sweet pleasure in itself. She was golden and bright, her smile constant and her gaze kind. He found himself imagining the shape of her body beneath her scrubs. High, round breasts, a long, slim torso. Limbs that might fly like the wind. Did she run? Hike? Climb? Camp? He had so many questions for Jenna the Midwife.

And when she straightened up and looked around, as if she could maybe feel his attention, he couldn't help but move toward her.

She had a smile for him too.

So damn bright.

"We meet again," he said as he stopped beside her.

"I see you weren't kidding about the daily run."

"Nope. It's more than a hobby for me."

"Do you race?"

"Yeah." Although that had obviously taken a backseat in the last three months. He'd done two triathlons in the fall during work-up training, but since arriving in the sandbox he'd been limited to laps around the base. This wasn't much different, really. A different kind of noise and congestion. He longed to take off into the desert, but he wasn't that reckless, not even in an allied country.

He gestured to the trailer. "This is interesting. Is it like a walk-in clinic?"

She nodded and gestured for him to follow her inside. She made her way to the back, where she pulled a cardboard box off the shelf. She set it on the counter and flashed him a quick grin. "In the morning we come out here to do non-emergent care at these clinics. It reduces the number of people queuing at the gate to the hospital." She opened the box, revealing a neat collection of wrapped bundles. "And sometimes we hand out routine supplies. Do you want to help?"

He picked one up. "Definitely. What are we handing out today?"

"Sanitary napkins."

She said it deliberately cool, like it was no big deal—which was true, it wasn't. Sean didn't care that he was holding pads, and not just because he wanted to impress a midwife. Although he did want to impress her. No point pretending otherwise. "One bundle per person in line?"

She grinned. "One per woman. You can give them to the girls, too, even if you aren't sure they're old enough to need them."

"Got it."

"If you'd rather, you can carry this and a nurse can hand them out."

He picked up the entire box. "I'm good. Unless you think they'd rather receive them from a woman?"

She shook her head. "It's fine." Her gaze lingered on his face as her expression softened and bloomed into something else. "Thank you."

"It's the least I could do," he said, and he meant it. He

didn't want her to think this small decency was a big deal for him. He wanted to impress her with big things. And yet the look on her face made him greedy and ready to accept the unearned praise.

The line outside the trailer was shorter now, but as soon as he started handing out the bundles, it grew again, like a whisper had skittered through the camp that supplies were being handed out.

"Lil nisa," he said in rough Arabic. *For women.*

The bundles flew out of his hands. Mothers sometimes took two, handing one off to a daughter.

One young woman, a girl really, reminded him of Dani, his best friend growing up and now his sister-in-law. Long, coltish limbs, wavy dark hair. A fierce expression on her face. She pushed forward, taking a bundle almost roughly from him and he wanted to tell her he got it—he was sorry she couldn't go to the drugstore on her own, or get supplies from a mother or sister or friend.

He had a flashback to Dani getting her period in grade nine and hiding in the bathroom on the second floor of the high school. The teacher, thinking Dani was upset, sent Sean after her. His friend had been mortified when he'd insisted she tell him why she was hiding, and when she finally confessed that she needed a pad, he'd almost died.

But then he'd gone to the office and told the secretary what Dani needed, and where, because that's what friends were for.

Friends also never brought up moments like that ever again, and he hadn't remembered it in years. Now it flashed through him like a physical memory. There was nothing impressive about embarrassing a young woman, so Sean let the Syrian woman glare at him. And then as quickly as she appeared, she was gone again.

"All done?"

He turned and held out the empty box. "Yep."

Jenna took it then waved at the nurse in the doorway of the clinic. "I'm done here. I need to get back to the hospital."

"Can I walk you?"

She blushed. "Of course."

"I could carry the box back."

She shook her head. "I'm not bringing it...." She trailed off as they rounded the corner then she pointed up ahead to where a group of children were playing. "I think they'd like to turn it into a car or a space ship or something."

Again he was struck with a memory—him and his brothers playing in the boxes after Christmas, and his father grumbling that he should have saved his money on the toys that came inside them.

He shoved that away, too.

When they neared the kids, she waved, and they came running. She handed over the box as they shyly looked at Sean.

Strange man with their friend, maybe. Strange man in general.

He carefully dropped into a low squat and smiled. Up to them if they wanted to interact with him more than that.

He got some giggles then they took off with the box.

"How many children are here?" he asked as he straightened up again.

Jenna shoved her hands into her pockets. "A thousand, give or take."

More than half the population of the camp. "And more are born every day?"

She gave him a sharp look. "Some. Not many. Don't judge them for that."

He held up his hands. "I'm not, promise." The military-NGO relationship was a difficult one at times. Aid organizations needed to be neutral, always, in order to be granted safe passage—or as safe as possible—by both sides. But damn it, he was one of the good guys. "I was just wondering. I didn't get a thorough briefing on the camp. It's new, right?"

She nodded and gave him a small smile. "People have been here for a year at least, but NATO provided the protected space and peacekeepers six months ago."

"How long have you been here?"

"Four months."

"Where were you before?"

"The greater Vancouver area. That's where I'm from. Never left home before this, so…culture shock. I'm learning a lot."

He nodded. "Yeah, this is my first overseas tour, too. I'm halfway through."

She gave him a surprised look. "Really?"

"Yeah."

"You seem pretty confident." She dragged in a deep breath. "I'm still sorting out my own thoughts about all of this. It's endlessly complicated."

That was the painful truth of it. He nodded solemnly. "We do what we can, though."

"And yet, it's never enough." They approached the gate to the NGO compound. She waved her pass at the guard and Sean dug his ID card out as well. "It was nice to run in to you," she said once they were through. "And thank you again for the help."

"My pleasure. I was looking for an excuse to find you."

She stopped and turned, looking up at him with surprise. "Really?"

"Yeah." He searched her face. "So it worked out perfectly."

"And now I need to get back to work," she sighed, her regret tugging at something deep inside him. "But…"

"But?" He grinned. "I like the sound of but. But has promise."

She laughed, her cheeks tinging pink. "There's a… movie night tonight. I think they're showing Jurassic Park."

Roaring dinosaurs had serious promise. "That sounds fun."

"We do what we can." She shrugged and glanced away, suddenly…shy?

Warmth bloomed in his chest, and he leaned in just enough for her to still hear him as he lowered his voice. "I meant watching a movie with you. That sounds like a lot of fun to me."

She looked at him and a relieved, pleased smile burst across her face. "To me too."

Damn. That twenty-four hour clock was ticking pretty loud in his head. A refugee camp was no place to tumble headlong into an infatuation, but what did he know about the right time and place for such a thing? His life plan had been for this to never happen.

Ha. Joke was on him, clearly.

He cleared his throat. "So, what time is the movie tonight?"

"Seven thirty." She gave him directions, and promised to meet him there as soon as she could. "Sometimes things come up at the hospital, but it looks like it's going to be a quiet night. Relatively speaking."

———

THE COMMONS TENT was located behind the hospital, and served as a communal living room—with rugs on the ground instead of couches. There was a microwave which someone was using to make popcorn, and two hot plates on which another ex-pat was making Turkish-style coffee. A makeshift screen and a laptop hooked up to a projector completed the theatre set up. A dozen accents filled the space as people joked and laughed. Italians, Americans, Australians…

And then the netting covering the doorway swung wide, and in stepped the Canadian he'd been looking for.

Jenna the Midwife had changed after her shift.

Sean had liked her hair pulled up in a ponytail, with those long strands of honey-gold silk trailing over her cheeks, just begging to be rubbed between his fingers. And he'd like the way she looked in a scrub shirt, too.

But now her hair hung loose in long, damp waves down her back, and she'd changed into fitted jeans and a soft scooped-neck t-shirt. She looked feminine and touchable, but he didn't miss the tired shadows behind her eyes.

He grabbed two cups of Turkish coffee and made his way to where she stood just inside the tent entrance.

"Long day," he said quietly, holding out one of the cups. Not a question. He knew better than that.

"Three new babies came into the world today." She smiled as she wrapped her hands around the mug, and her fingers brushed his for a second. The cool slide of her skin against his was nice. Really nice. Want-more-of-that kind of nice.

"I bet that never gets old."

"Never." She said it softly, reverently. "It's worth every second of lost sleep."

"And tonight? Is it busy?"

She shook her head. "And I'm hoping it stays quiet."

He lifted his coffee cup. "Here's to hoping. I'm really looking forward to watching a movie with you."

"It's not the most exciting thing to do."

"Wouldn't want to be anywhere else." And he meant it.

She laughed gently. "Nowhere?"

"Not even a beach in the south of Spain."

Another laugh, this one a rich, ringing peal, and her gaze caught and held his. "Liar. Is that where you're headed?"

He nodded. "I've got a few weeks of leave. I ended up staying here instead of just catching a transport plane out because of the PM's visit tomorrow."

"Your loss is our gain."

"I'm not complaining, I promise." He gestured to the makeshift viewing area. "Do you have a favourite spot on the carpet for movie night?"

Her cheeks turned pink as she shook her head. "Wherever you'd like."

They settled on the back corner of the rug closest to the entrance, and at seven thirty right on the dot, they killed the overhead light and started the movie.

It had been years since Sean had sat in the dark and felt his heart pound in anticipation because of a girl. Jenna was no girl, but this still took him back to high school. To clammy hands and wondering if real girls were anything like the secret pictures he'd seen in magazines one finds in a house filled with testosterone.

Now he wondered what Jenna was like. No comparison, just faint whispers of things he'd be happy to do with her if circumstances were different.

Another few months and maybe he'd find her again. If

she went back to Vancouver, he could visit around a west coast race.

He turned his attention back to the screen. Any second now, they'd see a dinosaur, and if he had any luck at all—

Jenna gasped and leaned closer.

Man, he had more luck than he deserved.

He stretched his arm back and wider, opening up the side of his body so she could fit herself against him.

She leaned in, and each gasp brought them closer together. So too did some yawns, and by the second hour of the film, she was nodding off. He shifted his hand back a bit, so she wouldn't fall forward, and he watched her doze. Every few minutes, she'd make a valiant effort to open her eyes, and she'd mumble an apology, but he didn't care.

He was enjoying her napping leaned up against him way more than he should.

By the end of the movie, his pulse was heavy with awareness. Her body felt just right, her slim, soft curves moulding around his hard edges. But all good things must come to an end.

He stood first and offered her his hand. He'd take any excuse to touch her even if she didn't need help, and she hung on to his fingers for a few beats after rising, so he was pretty sure he wasn't alone in that desire.

Before he could offer to walk her back to her tent, someone called her name, and she twisted around. Then she gave him a tentative look. "Can you hang around for a minute? I won't be long."

"Of course." He grinned. "I was going to offer to walk back with you."

"I'd like that." She grinned back. "A lot."

She crossed the tent to speak to the man who'd called

out her name. As they spoke, she shot Sean a quick glance, then another. Her lips pulled together in a thinking frown then she nodded.

When she returned, her steps were slow. Distracted.

"Everything okay?"

She nodded. "Yes? I think so." She hesitated then shook her head. "It's late. We should get going. The morning will be here before we know it."

Well damn, she'd piqued his curiosity, but whatever it was, it wasn't his business.

He let her lead him outside, but despite her change of subject, she wasn't moving quickly. She stepped to the side, letting most people get ahead of them before they started walking. With each step, their arms brushed, and after a minute, she just took his hand.

He squeezed her fingers gently. "Thanks for the movie invite. I had fun."

She looked up at the night sky first, before dragging her gaze back down to earth, and him.

Then she smiled. "Me, too."

The tent lines where the workers slept were only a short walk away, so too quickly for his liking she stopped again and dropped his hand. But then she turned to face him, her smile growing, and at the same time, they both went in for a hug.

He folded his arms around her, hyper aware of people milling about. They weren't alone, not really, and this wasn't the place for anything more. But damn, Jenna felt good with her cheek pressed hard against his shoulder, her breath warm on his neck.

He squeezed her tight before reluctantly letting her go. "I'll see you in the morning?"

She nodded and rubbed her hands together. "Yes,

bright and early. Actually..." She glanced around. "Our vacation scheduling here is constantly in flux because it depends when we can get a replacement. Back at the community tent, that was my medical director, Sami. He's secured someone to cover me for the next two weeks." She looked back at him and smiled. "So I'm on holidays as of Friday."

He didn't even need to think about it. "Come with me." That had better be where she'd been leading with that. Hope sparked in his chest that tomorrow might not need to be goodbye. "I'm going to Spain, but that's flexible. Wherever you want to go, we could do the backpacking thing. I've got some reservations, but I'm sure they're changeable. We can do whatever you want."

"Spain sounds fantastic." She nodded again. "I want that."

He wanted too. In a big way.

"Because life is short," she added.

He grinned. "Yeah, I like that answer a lot."

"Is this crazy?"

"Definitely up there on the list of never-thought-I'd-suggest-this ideas."

She laughed. "But..."

"But life is short," he echoed. And this felt right. He laced his fingers through hers. "We can talk more about this tomorrow. I have a loose plan for this leave, so we'll figure out if any of that sounds good to you."

"Like what?"

"The Rock of Gibraltar. Siestas and sangrias." And now one hot, amazing woman.

Click. Just like that, something slipped into focus for Sean.

"That sounds perfect."

He leaned in and brushed his fingertips against her cheek. He wanted to tell her he'd stay here until her leave started, but his CO would have his head for loitering around a refugee camp. "I fly to Naples day after tomorrow. I can wait there until you arrive, and then I can get you a seat on my flight to Seville. I promise not to do anything fun until you arrive."

"No, have all the fun for both of us." She smiled at him. That smile was something else. Full of promise and nervous excitement.

They had two weeks together. All of a sudden, he felt light as air. "I'll see you in the morning."

"Bright and early."

Every time she smiled, he wanted to kiss her. The curve of her lips, the way her cheeks turned into pink apples and her eyes danced—it was all irresistible. But this wasn't the time or the place. So he shoved his hands in his pockets to keep himself from touching those cheeks, that hair, or the long stretch of her neck. He nodded as he stepped back. "Until then."

She swayed side to side. "Just a few hours."

"Sweet dreams." Another step back, but he didn't turn. He couldn't stop looking at her, at her mouth. Fuck it, he should just—

"You too." She raised her hand and, with an unsteady shift of her feet, she spun away.

It was a small comfort that she'd had just as much trouble ending their awkward good night as he had.

But a kiss would have been better.

He stood at the end of her little lane and watched as she quickly made her way to a tent halfway down, her head ducked low.

Tomorrow. He'd kiss her tomorrow.

CHAPTER FOUR

SEAN MISSED the comparative simplicity of planning a reconnaissance raid against insurgents.

At four the next morning, he was woken up by the communications officer who had the good grace to look chagrined as he handed over the expanded itinerary that had just arrived from Ottawa.

"It's the middle of the night," Sean grumbled as he pulled on his shirt.

"Not back home."

Sean sighed as he scanned the document. More media were on the plane than originally anticipated, and they all wanted their own angle on the story. Sean's job had just gone from keeping an eye on things to actively mediating four different competing interests.

"So now there will be a camera crew visiting the hospital with the PM right after breakfast? Has anyone given the clinic staff a heads up about that?"

"As you say, it's the middle of the night. You were my first stop."

Sean resisted the urge to point out that he was barely

attached to this mission and to the best of this guy's knowledge had no reason to be the person best suited to delivering this news. Except he knew Jenna, so…fine.

He glanced at his watch. "Two hours until the PM arrives." One hour after that for him to meet with the camp administrators over breakfast, which meant in three hours, the hospital would have the eyes of a nation on it. "I think the hospital staff would appreciate being informed of the change before he's on the ground. Excuse me."

He grabbed a headlamp and headed for the door.

————

JENNA MADE it through the night without an urgent page, but she still woke up at an insanely early hour. She lay in the dark for a few minutes, willing herself to go back to sleep, but the combination of seeing Sean again—she should have kissed him last night, damn it—and the professional stress of having a political delegation at the camp today made for a lot of complicated, very awake feelings.

It was never too early to review cases, though.

At the hospital, she found she wasn't the only one up. Sami, the Egyptian-Canadian medical director, was already in the office.

He didn't look up from the charts he was working on. "Sabaah al-khair." *Good morning*. He must think she was one of the local staff.

"Sabaah an-noor," she replied carefully, proud of herself for remembering the appropriate response.

He jerked his head up and laughed. "Morning, Jenna. That sounded pretty good."

She laughed. She hadn't picked up much of the

language yet, to her frustration. The women she saw either spoke English—and were eager to practice it—or turned immediately to the translator. Nobody was keen for her to struggle through a medical conversation in a language she spoke like a toddler, and she didn't blame them.

Plus almost everyone in this camp was resigned to the reality they wouldn't be returning home, and their future almost certainly lay in a far-away, English-speaking country like Canada.

"You're up early," she said, going to the hot plate to make herself some coffee.

"Couldn't sleep. I'll be happy to get today over with."

"Mmm." She yawned. Maybe she should have given sleep more of a chance before coming in. "Are you nervous about meeting the prime minister?"

He wrinkled his nose. "Nervous isn't the right word. I want to say all the things that need to be said. I guess I'm worried I won't get a real chance to speak to him."

She nodded. "I've met—"

A loud knock interrupted them. The staff office was just inside the entrance to the trailer complex, and Jenna had locked the door behind her.

Sami was on his feet and running to the door before Jenna put down the coffee pot, but it wasn't a medical emergency. Milly must have hustled from the other direction, because the next thing Jenna heard was, "Hey, mate! We're closed, you know? Don't be banging on the door like that. Patients are sleeping."

Jenna grinned. Milly was bad-ass. The wards were on the other side of the clinical space, so the knocking surely didn't wake them, but whoever the offender was, they'd think twice next time. The veteran nurse didn't take bull-shit from anyone, from doctors to military personnel to patients. But under all her gruff bark, the woman had a heart of gold.

Jenna wanted to be Milly when she grew up.

"My apologies," said a familiar voice, and now Jenna was running, because oh my God, it was Sean.

She skidded to a halt in the doorway.

He was in uniform already, although his hair was sticking out at funny angles from under his beret. "Captain Foster of the Canadian Armed Forces. I'm looking for the clinic staff."

Sami introduced himself with a quick handshake. "Sami Bahar, medical director, and this is Milly Anderson, a senior nurse."

"Who is going back to take care of patients, if you've got this," Milly said, sniffing to make it clear she didn't care for the interruption, she didn't care who Sean was.

Sean gave her a bashful smile that went a long way, Jenna was sure, then pulled a rolled up piece of paper from his pocket and held it out to Sami. "There's a revised itinerary for the PM's visit today. It's more extensive than previously understood."

Jenna groaned, and Sean swivelled towards her. "Morning," she said with an apologetic grimace to Sami for interrupting. "A change in the itinerary?"

Sean nodded. "Sorry to be the bearer of unexpected news."

Sami finished reading it over, then handed it to her without saying a word.

That wasn't a good sign.

She took it and skimmed the page. She didn't have Sami's tact. "Seriously?"

When she glanced up, Sean gave her a rueful smile. "I thought it might be worth a middle of the night visit."

Instead of a quick stop at a clinic in the camp mid-afternoon, the Prime Minister of Canada was now bringing reporters and a camera crew to her hospital. Right after breakfast.

"Thank you." Sami glanced back toward the rear trailer. "I need to go prep the nursing staff."

"Is there anything I can do to facilitate this?"

Jenna shook her head at the same time Sami held out his hand. "No, but I appreciate the heads up," he said. "We'll manage with the visit however it pleases the delegation."

Sean waited until Sami left then he stuffed his hands in his pockets. He'd done the same thing the night before, and again she was struck with the urge to tug them out and weave their fingers together. "Will there be any problems with the media? Anything I should know? If anyone might be uncomfortable on camera. Patients, maybe?"

"Sami knows how to manage that. We'll pick a couple of cases who don't mind being interviewed."

Sean nodded. "And if you need anything, just give the secret signal."

She laughed. "We don't have a secret signal."

"We should definitely come up with one." He winked, which did dangerous things to her insides. He was both funny and kind, trying to ease this change in plans for the hospital staff, but also her individually.

She gave him an appreciative smile as she reached for the door handle. "Go away. I need to brush my hair and find a nicer shirt."

He let her herd him out of the hospital in the chill early dawn.

It was extra brr this morning. She wasn't exactly looking forward to the weather heating up since it would quickly get to oppressive and sticky, but the few days that it would be balmy and spring-like would be nice. Right now she was grateful for the worn hoodie she had on over her scrubs.

"Tap your forefinger to your thumb."

"Sean, we'll be fine."

"I know." He hopped off the steps and into the hard packed dust. "And your hair is perfect, by the way."

She'd braided her hair before bed, so she left it like that when she woke up. It was a mess. But the way he looked at her didn't feel polite. "Thanks," she whispered.

She needed to go see her patients. No more flirting.

Why weren't her feet moving?

He took a few steps backward, a grin growing on his handsome face. Square jaw, bright eyes. She could lose herself in him if she weren't careful. "I'll see you later, Jenna."

She lifted the paper he'd handed her in the air, something eager bouncing in her chest. "In an hour and a half, in fact."

He flashed her another brilliant grin before nodding and turning on his heel. His uniform pulled tight across his shoulders and narrowed to his hips in an exaggerated V shape that woke her up better than coffee. Hello again, Captain Hottie. What nice long legs you've got.

She dragged in a shuddering breath before shutting and locking the clinic door.

"Are you done flirting with the handsome young man?" Milly asked as they scrubbed up.

Done? She'd barely started. "For now," she said with a smile. "He's transiting through. Leaving tomorrow."

"Heading into Iraq?"

Jenna's grin stretched so wide it hurt her cheeks. "To Italy, actually. He's on leave for the next eighteen days."

"Is that a fact?" Milly chuckled. "Any chance you're going to meet up with him when you take your own flight out of here?"

"Maybe."

"You sly hussy!"

Yep. Her cheeks were aching. "It just sort of…happened."

"I bet it did. That one's a looker, he is."

She sighed happily. And in a few days, he'd be all hers.

"But—"

She held up her hand, cutting Milly off. "I know. Be careful. We're just having fun."

That was true, although there was more to it than that. Fun didn't really encapsulate all that Sean promised.

The last four months had drained Jenna's emotional well. A trip to Spain with Sean would be both adventure and attention, a chance to take two weeks to refill her soul. Yes, there was a little voice in her in the back of her mind that warned her, again, that she could lose herself in this man. That it might become more than adventure and she needed to be careful about that.

If there was any lesson she'd learned growing up, it was that she needed to be careful around men—and that her future would be of her own making.

Her mother had been dealt a bad hand. Eve Kowalczyk found herself pregnant and alone at eighteen, then again at twenty-seven when she was just starting to get ahead a bit. Two ex-boyfriends who didn't want to be fathers. A host of others who weren't interested in being step-dads too.

Jenna's mother didn't get a partner in life, but she did

get two dependents, and not a lot of opportunity handed to her to make their life comfortable.

Jenna had been adamant she wouldn't fall into the same trap. She wouldn't want too much, and she wouldn't get carried away by impossible dreams. She could have adventure, as long as it fit inside her responsible career.

She hadn't been prepared for how draining the placement would be. So yes, she was going to have some fun. Reset her expectations so when she returned, she could do the job that was needed. Give herself a good shake.

And that was all that would happen in Spain, no matter what.

———

IF SEAN HAD WORRIED about the hospital staff's ability to be camera-ready in an hour, his fear was misplaced. When he escorted the prime minister and the Canadian delegation to the hospital after breakfast with the camp administrators, Sami and Jenna were both waiting. They both wore broad smiles, their statements smooth and rehearsed.

The PM had clearly prepped well for this, asking smart, pointed questions of both Canadian practitioners. The conversation flowed smoothly, and cameras clicked steadily. Sean was startled to feel a stab of irrational jealousy at the way Jenna looked at the handsome, young prime minister. The leader of their country had a magnetism that was...well, at the moment it was annoying.

But once the initial meet and greet ended, she slid Sean a quick look that was entirely different. A look that had nothing to do with work, and everything to do with anticipating the next two weeks.

He didn't have any reason to be jealous of another man.

For the next part of the tour, the prime minister went with the medical director, and Sean let the comms officer follow them so he could go with the camera crew that joined Jenna for a walk through the maternity ward.

She introduced them to a slight woman, her face covered with a niqab, who had delivered a new baby the day before. "This is Assala, and her son. Adnan is her fifth child, and they're both recovering well from the birth." She paused for the translator, then continued. "Adnan has a bit of jaundice, so we'll watch him for the next day, but he's already feeding well, isn't he, Assala?"

After pictures with the well-baby care package Assala would take home once Adnan was discharged, the tour continued. Jenna didn't stop to talk with any other patients, and when she arrived in the medical office near the entrance again, she explained that Assala was the only patient who consented to be interviewed.

The reporters led her through a wide range of questions, first about Assala, then women's health in general.

Jenna leaned in to each question, giving them clear, to-the-point answers, then adding more context and shading around that. She talked about the need for increased education around birth control, but also praised the community's response to their outreach efforts. "When I arrived, we did maybe one or two IUD insertions a week. One of the key tasks assigned to me by the medical director was to work with the local Turkish staff to share the benefits of family planning, and we've worked really hard to do that in a way that makes sense to this population. Now we're averaging a dozen insertions a week most of the time, and word is spreading. We want to support families, and we understand how they value children. Babies are our future, their future. But too many, too close together…it's not healthy for women. You need to protect mothers if they're going to have all the children they want, that's what we tell them."

"It sounds like you're directing that message at the community at large," one reporter noticed.

Jenna nodded. "And probably more so than in Canada, although we always start from what they want. I'm careful that the caution isn't coming from me, but from someone who shares their culture. It's the only way to have the conversation. I can only offer medical care they want. In Canada, the midwifery model is one of informed choice versus informed consent. I follow the same principles here. Sometimes it requires more conversations to ensure my patients are as informed as possible."

"Can you speak to the differences in care?"

"Of course." Jenna launched into an explanation about how she did more general emergent care here than she had previously in Canada.

The conversation wrapped up when they heard the prime minister's group return to the front hallway of the hospital, and everyone started to pack up their stuff.

Sean casually shot Jenna a glance, and did a double take when he found her tapping her fingers together, a small smile playing across her lips.

CHAPTER FIVE

SEAN WAITED for everyone to leave, then quietly closed the door on the office as the group headed outside. He'd find them in a minute.

He stepped forward and lowered his voice. "Is everything okay? Do you need something?"

She grinned up at him. "Just wanted to have a second alone. Did that go okay?"

"More than okay. You were fantastic."

"Oh, good." She pinked up with pleasure. "I could talk endlessly about that stuff."

"And they'd have listened, I'm sure. You had them wrapped around your baby finger. Me too."

She blushed further and glanced to the side as she breathed in roughly. "So…we should discuss Spain a bit more."

"Yes, we should do that."

"Later?"

"Definitely." He caught her fingers gently in his and rubbed his thumb over her skin. "See? The signal is always a good thing."

Her pupils dilated and her lips parted. "Okay, I promise I'll trust your instincts next time, Captain Foster."

He leaned in. "Dangerous promise, Ms. Kowalczyk."

Her eyes lit up. "Are your instincts…impure?"

Hell yes, they were.

He dropped his gaze to her mouth at the same moment the door handle rattled behind them, and they jumped apart.

She rubbed her cheek, now hot and red, and he stepped backwards again, staying between her and whoever just opened the door so she could compose herself.

"I'm sorry," a not-sorry-at-all Australian accent said. He turned around to see Milly, the nurse, grinning at him. "I need Jenna."

So did he, but his need would have to wait. "She's all yours," he said with a smile. "I'll be back later."

The rest of the day flew by. Sean saw Jenna briefly in the camp, at the clinic, and that reminded him of the spot around the corner where the children played. While the PM sat down with local staffers to hear about the refugee vetting process on the ground, Sean went hunting for road hockey sticks and a rubber ball.

Thank God for duct tape. As soon as Gavin Strong saw the gear, he rolled up his shirt sleeves and took off his tie. "Who are we playing?"

Fine. So the guy had appeal for a reason.

"I can't take off part of my uniform," Sean said good-naturedly as he led the PM to the playground.

"I can't give you permission to do that?"

"Afraid not."

"But you've got better footwear," the PM said, comparing his oxfords to Sean's combat boots.

"Fair enough."

And his shoes did give him an advantage, but not enough of one to best the PM and his team of eager boys and girls. The game ended after twenty minutes, with Team Strong winning three goals to Team Foster's two.

"Thanks for that," Strong said quietly as they headed back to the media throng. "Most fun I've had all day."

"My pleasure, sir."

It was a little thing, but word spread quickly, and when Jenna found him at the end of the simple but well attended potluck dinner, she had a teasing grin on her face. "Heard you impressed the PM. It was all the talk at my end of the tent."

"We had fun. He's got a pretty wicked aim."

"You'll take athletic competition wherever you can get it, won't you?"

He laughed. She wasn't wrong. "I even play basketball on the base, and I hate basketball."

"Oh?" She arched one eyebrow. "I played all the way through university."

"In that case, it's my favourite. We'll have to find a chance to play one-on-one."

She laughed before glancing around. "Is there something you need to be doing right now? Or can I take you somewhere?"

The PM would be leaving in a few minutes, and Sean had already said goodbye to the delegation. "You can take me anywhere you want."

She touched his arm, a gentle, guiding touch, and then it was gone as she brushed past him.

He followed her out of the mess hall. The sun was setting, but he had his headlamp in the pocket of his uniform pants, and Jenna had a sweatshirt on for the night chill.

"Over here," she said, pointing to an alley. He followed her down the narrow path, twisting left and right, until they came to a row of sea containers. From the shadows between two of the metal boxes, she pulled a ladder and leaned it against the side of one container. "Up we go."

He stepped closer and wrapped his hand around the edge of the ladder. "Ladies first."

She gave him a quick smile before brushing past him, scampering up the rungs. She was nimble and lean, with a narrow waist and endlessly long legs. Even in jeans and a hoodie, she was something to look at. But when his gaze got tangled up around her, it wasn't just about beauty. He found himself wanting to look deeper, know more. There was something captivating about her that tugged at him deep inside.

When he pushed himself up and onto the roof, he found her standing, arms crossed, looking out across the buffer zone between the NGO compound and the refugee camp. Lights dotted the tent lines. They were lucky to have good electrical supply here, if nothing else. Two days ago, all he would have seen was a scruffy ditch between them and a world of chaos and despair. Now he saw potential and hope, too.

He knew the other side of things. The war zones that drove people away. But this was something else. This was hope and despair twisted together, a promise wrapped in barbed wire.

Literally.

From where he'd come from, though, he understood the dangers. Knew why there was barbed wire and armed guards protecting Jenna, protecting this hope.

It was damn fragile.

He'd been raised a military man. Raised jaded and sharp, ready for a fight. And for all the downsides of that childhood, it served him well. Mental resiliency, they called it. His father would call it being tough and hard.

And two days seeing this through Jenna's eyes had given his perspective a new dimension, although not enough that he wasn't grateful for the protections around her.

"I should have asked you earlier for the best vantage point to see everything," he said quietly as he joined her. "That's some view. Do you come up here a lot?"

She nodded and swayed toward him. He touched her arm, and when she slid her hand toward his, he laced their fingers together. "It's not what I thought it would be." She cleared her throat. "That sounds more naive than I mean it to be."

"What were you expecting?"

"More movement. It's a transit camp. I thought there would be…transiting. But most will wait here for years. The babies born yesterday will grow up to play soccer— and maybe road hockey—before they're accepted some- where else. The crawling pace is disheartening."

"It's one thing to hear about it on the news, and another to see it with your own eyes."

"Was it the same for you?" she asked quietly.

"Everyone's experiences are different." That was the diplomatic answer. In reality, Sean had been training for this mission, specifically, his entire adult life. And more generally, since he was a child. "Your humanity is not a weakness. At all. There's strength in how sensitive you are."

"So it didn't rock your confidence," she said dryly.

He chuckled. "No. But you seemed pretty confident this morning."

"Mmm. It's in the quiet that doubt slips in. When I'm doing the job, it's fine."

He knew all about that. Just because he was confident didn't mean he didn't have moments of vulnerability. Everyone did, it was human nature. "Three weeks after I arrived in Iraq, I experienced my first sandstorm. It was crazy watching this wall of sand roar toward you like a tsunami. I knew not to be frightened of the approaching storm. We took cover, and I was fine. Until it got dark. Not just dark. Pitch black. And suddenly I felt upside down. I wasn't—we were hunkered down and it was fine. But I honestly couldn't tell up from down, left from right, and it was disorienting."

"What did you do?"

"Nothing. I just waited. And eventually, it passed."

She turned toward him, her entire body, and his free hand went to her hip out of both instinct and desire. She sucked in a breath as he made contact with her then pressed in closer.

"So eventually, this will pass?"

She meant what she'd shared about herself. He nodded, his head feeling thick all of a sudden. "Yeah. All storms eventually calm."

"Good." She gave him a faint, sweet smile. He'd barely known her two days and it felt like he'd waited a lifetime for this moment, for her to lift her face to his and her lips to part in invitation.

He lifted their tangled fingers to his mouth and kissed her there, first. His lips brushed her knuckles as he watched her expression shift and soften.

"Jenna," he said as he released her hand and reached for her face. Every bit of her was soft and yielding.

"I didn't lure you up here to steal a kiss," she whispered.

He bent over until her breath puffed warm against his lips. "But now that I'm here?"

Her soft mouth pushed against his. He could feel her smile as she started to pull away, and he wrapped his arms around her waist, hauling her back in.

"You got one," he said. "Now it's my turn."

———

THE FIRST TOUCH of Sean's mouth, when she kissed him, had been wonderful. Firm and warm. The second press of his lips against hers, when he took over and kissed her back, was something else. Wonderful times a hundred. His kiss exploded her senses and had her scrambling to touch him, pull him closer, grab on anywhere she could because his mouth promised a wicked, demanding ride.

His hand squeezed against her hip, sending a skitter of sensation up her spine. She wanted his touch under her shirt, on her waist, then higher. She wanted to touch him, too.

As he kissed her, she traced the lines of his neck. Strong tendons, flexed muscles. Even in the cool night air, his skin was warm. He radiated strength and virility, two things she hadn't been drawn to in the past, but right now—very drawn.

She ached for more, but their position was hardly private.

"Just a few more days," he whispered, reading her mind. "Then we can do that again."

She chased his lips for another soft press before relaxing into his arms.

"Show me more of what we came up here for," he whispered into her hair.

"Who's to say it wasn't for that kiss after all?"

He laughed then lowered himself to sit with his legs spread. Her breath caught in her chest, didn't even make it to her throat, because while she burned for the chance to kiss him again, *this* was what really appealed to her about Sean. The way he looked at her, like he wanted to know her just as much as taste her. The way he offered her his body to lean on just as much as press against.

It was exactly what she didn't know she needed.

She joined him, leaning back against his chest, his thighs bracketing her on either side. He was solid and stable, and for the first time in months, she felt like maybe she could unburden herself of the fears and doubts she'd been keeping inside. Sure, Milly saw through her, but it was just as important to Jenna that she be seen to be brave, too. Uncertainty was normal. Wallowing was not. And one's co-workers were not the people to burden with your confessions.

Probably neither were your potential lovers, but Sean had already shown her that he understood.

"I've been planning this for a long time. Since my training programme, really. I thought I'd go somewhere chronically under-serviced rather than a war zone, maybe. But still, the principles are the same. We're responding to a need. I'm needed here, and I know I'm helping."

"But?"

Hard, unyielding sadness pushed against her chest from the inside. "It's hard."

He laughed. Gently, and not unkindly, but still, he laughed. "Well, yeah, no shit."

"That's not what you're supposed to say." Except the way his chest shook behind her felt good. And if he was chuckling, then he wasn't judging her for being a whiner. She relaxed further into his embrace as he pressed his cheek against her hair.

"You knew it would be hard," he said quietly. "You just said that much. So how is it different than what you'd expected?"

She searched the chaotic memories of the last four months, trying to tease out the points when it got overwhelming. "It's not fair. Don't laugh."

He didn't this time. He squeezed her tighter, because of course he knew just how unfair war was.

"Any of them could be me," she finally said. "I see myself in every educated woman who comes through the clinic. In every girl who had a dream to go to school, have a career, and now she lives…" She gestured toward the camp. "In chaos. And it will take years for them to be resettled. Their homes have been bombed to smithereens. There's nothing to go back to, right?"

He cleared his throat. "Eventually the war will end. The caliphate is on its last legs in Iraq. Syria has a different road ahead, but—"

"Girls don't have time to wait for eventually." She squeezed her jaw tight, then puffed out a frustrated breath.

Sean smoothed his hand over her hair. "You see them having babies, too?"

Her chest tightened. "Yes."

"I'm sorry."

"Be sorry for them."

"I am. But I'm sorry for you, too. That's hard to see."

"I know they'll be fine." She swallowed hard. It was more hope than knowledge.

"So will you."

She blew a raspberry, and he laughed again as she sighed and dropped her head back against his shoulder.

"Can I confess something?" he asked in her ear.

"Please."

"I see myself in them, too. It happened yesterday. I think that's normal as long as we manage our feelings on our time." He squeezed his arms around her.

She nodded. "Thank you."

"Any time."

Not any time. They'd have two stolen weeks together, and then they'd go their separate ways. But for now, she could lean on him—in more ways than one.

"I'm not one to make a big deal about milestones," she said slowly, figuring out how to voice a half-formed thought. "And I'm not here because I turned thirty—that just happened to correspond. But maybe there was something about facing the end of my twenties... I don't know. And now that I'm here, I worry it was for selfish reasons."

He stroked her arms. His fingers were warm and a little rough, calloused from work she could hardly imagine. "There's a school of thought that everything we do has a selfish component." He took a deep breath then let it out slowly. "We can do things for our own reasons, and still benefit others, too."

"Damn, I was hoping you would say no, as we get older, we get kinder and wiser."

He laughed. "I wouldn't know."

"You're plenty kind."

"Maybe. But..." He chuckled as he kissed the side of

her head, then he curled around her, bringing his lips to her ear. "I may not have hit the thirty milestone yet."

She froze for a second, then groaned. "Jeez, how much am I robbing the cradle by?"

"I turned twenty-seven a few weeks ago. Rob away."

Heat filled her cheeks then poured down her body. "Well, in a few years, you can find me and let me know how it goes for you."

He chuckled. "It's not a big deal, is it?" He turned her arm over and rubbed his fingers along the inside of her forearm.

"No," she whispered. Not when he touched her like that.

"Tell me more secrets."

Her head was spinning and she was strongly considering making out with him like teenagers on the top of a sea container, but she didn't think that was the type of secret he meant. Plus it was getting cold and late, and he had a flight first thing.

"I've never been to Spain," she said quietly, twisting her head so she could see his profile.

"Neither have I." He smiled faintly as he looked out across the camp. "A lot of firsts for me this tour."

"Yeah." She turned more, her entire body shifting now, and he kept his arms around her as she burrowed into him. "I'll add a first vacation fling to the list. Wasn't expecting that."

He grinned. "A fling with a sexy younger man, too. Might as well get bonus points."

Good. They were on the same page, then. A fling.

A sexy fling.

It sounded perfect.

She wasn't sure where the secret sharing fit into that,

but he didn't seem bothered by it, so she wouldn't over-think it.

"We should head back," she finally said, letting her lips rub against his neck.

"Soon." His voice caught in his throat. "You're going to need to stop rubbing up against me before I can be seen in mixed company again."

And whoosh, there was more heat again. It almost made up for the freezing metal beneath them. Almost, but not quite.

Four days until her holidays. She could be patient.

They sat there for another half hour, then he walked her to her tent, where he promised to find her in the morning to say goodbye.

He did just that, meeting her at the hospital. They stole a few minutes in the office, and he kissed her until she was breathless.

"I'll just be a short plane ride away," he whispered. "Waiting for you."

CHAPTER SIX

May
Pine Harbour

JENNA WAS SHAKING. She could feel it, in her hands and legs and inside, too. Every inch of her vibrating with panic, because he didn't want her here.

It turned out, when your greatest fear roared to life, you could still stand there and take it.

Not that Sean was any kind of threat. He leaned heavily on the bathroom sink, and he didn't move even as she stepped into the bright space.

He looked miserable.

She took another step toward him, her instinct to wrap her arms around him, but he flinched.

He flinched.

And he'd said she shouldn't be there.

She wasn't going to ask him if he was okay. He obviously wasn't. But all her carefully practiced lines vanished when she opened her mouth.

"I worried you were dead." Her voice cracked, but

even that didn't stop the barrage of words from flooding out. "It didn't make any sense, because there was no notice about a dead Canadian soldier, but it felt like the only explanation. I died inside as the days turned into weeks and I still didn't hear anything. From you, from anyone else. No news. And then I find out, from a co-worker, hey, heads up…that guy you'd flirted with? The one you went on a carefree adventure with, had a *little crush on?* He's been injured and sent back to Canada."

He winced repeatedly as she talked, but when she stopped, he didn't say anything.

She dragged in a rough breath and crossed her arms. "So, I'm glad you're not dead. That's good news."

His mouth tightened, and her gaze was drawn to his beard—of sorts. Scruffy hair covered his jaw, but it wasn't groomed like a beard. He wasn't groomed at all. His hair stood on end, and his clothes looked like he'd been sleeping in them for days.

If he wasn't going to talk, she wasn't going to bother pretending she wasn't curious. She was curious as heck. And concerned, too, as she looked him over.

He'd lost a lot of weight. His t-shirt hung off his shoulders where it would have stretched broadly across his chest before. He—

"You cut your hair." His voice cut into her observation.

She gave him a confused, surprised look. "A bit."

"It looks good." But he wasn't saying that to be kind. It had a hard edge to it, and deflection was a classic trick used by patients. He was saying that to distract her from the fact he looked like he'd been to hell and back, and was barely hanging on.

"You don't have amnesia, do you?" She licked her lips

nervously. "Do you remember… everything?" *Do you remember us?*

Another flinch, this one wracking through his entire body. "No amnesia. I can't concentrate worth shit, and that includes remembering details, but I know…" He worked his jaw hard, not quite looking at her. "I remember. But it doesn't matter."

How could it not? They'd made promises to each other.

He took a careful step forward. His face tightened up and he stopped.

"Can I help?" It was the wrong thing to say, she knew that as soon as the words were out of her mouth. Nothing she could offer would make this easier for him.

He huffed a laugh at that and took another step closer to her. Her heart lurched as she held herself back from reaching for him. He'd made it painfully clear in his few, terse words that she wasn't free to touch him. *You shouldn't have come. It doesn't matter.* She didn't matter. But that self-deprecating laugh was so familiar, and it hurt, like a punch in the chest.

She took a clumsy step backwards, then started to turn, but stopped when he cleared his throat.

"Wait," he said, and her pulse picked up. He groaned then swore under his breath. "I…I can't walk well."

Oh. Pain lanced through her. Pain for him, for how awful it must be for a man whose feet had been faster than the wind to be dealt such a blow.

"I have vertigo. It's the least of my problems in a lot of ways, but it's pretty severe. I can't…"

She nodded, understanding now. He couldn't walk to her, or even past her. He was a captive there, in front of her, until she left him alone. "Does the room spin?"

"The world spins." The words dragged, hoarse and raw. "And there's a lot of other shit. Brain injuries."

She nodded, even though she didn't like where he was heading with this.

"We—I—made a mistake. Rushed into something without knowing the consequences."

We made promises, she wanted to scream. "It doesn't change anything for me. Your injuries, I mean."

He stared at her, incredulity twisted all over his face. "It changes everything for me," he said, his eyes boring into her. "You don't know what it's been like."

No, she didn't. But she would know if he'd sent for her. "I would have come to you."

He gave her a hard, cold glare. "No."

She swallowed around the lump in her throat. "I'm here now. Maybe we could—"

"I'm not the man you married." He said it in a way that didn't invite any argument, but she wanted to fight like heck. She wanted to push and scream and throw things.

Fuck. She wanted to rage at a broken man. What was wrong with her?

"Yes you are," she finally said.

He shook his head as if her words meant nothing. "He's dead. Best you just forget me now."

"I can't do that," she whispered. "Not ever." Her eyes were hot and scratchy. She'd start crying in a moment, and she couldn't do that to him. "I can go for now. But I'll be back. I'll wait for you, remember? We promised that to each other."

They'd said a lot of things, but that was all she could remember right now. His lips pressed against hers, his hands in her hair. His confident assurance that he'd be waiting for her. And then she'd made him the same promise, too.

That commitment had given her strength in the long nights before she arrived here. It didn't matter that he was changed. It didn't matter if he was broken.

She was going to keep her promise to him, no matter what.

She turned, dragging a ragged breath into her lungs as she hit the dark hallway. Blink. She'd vowed to love this man in sickness and in health. Well, they were here now. Her eyes refocused and she pivoted toward the stairs. With each step, a hard resolve grew inside her.

She wasn't going to cry over this. She'd been wrong. This hadn't been the worst case scenario.

It was fucked up, but he was alive, and he didn't hate her.

He might hate himself, and God only knew if she'd be able to get through to him, but...he didn't hate her.

That was something.

She dug in her purse for her keys. They felt strange in her hand. She fumbled with the unlock button on the fob, and when she finally got herself into the driver's seat of her rental, she realized she couldn't focus her attention properly. Maybe she wasn't crying on the outside, but she was freaking the crap out on the inside. She forced herself to take a deep breath and closed her eyes.

Let it out, too. She needed that reminder.

Tears threatened again. Another ragged breath, another exhale. She was cycling through freak-out, false-calm, gutted-sadness, and back to freak-out so fast it was making her brain hurt.

A tap at the glass jolted her out of her deep breathing and made her scream. How long had she been sitting there? She pressed her hand to her chest as she rolled down the window.

Dean gave her an apologetic look and leaned in, bracing his forearm against the door. "I didn't mean to scare you."

"It's fine."

"Did you talk?"

She nodded. "He doesn't want me here."

"That's just the injuries talking."

"I know." That didn't change the ache, though. "I'll come back tomorrow."

"Good." He looked back toward the house before slowly turning his attention to her again. "He is getting better. Slowly. And I'm glad you're here, even if you did throw us for a loop. He's been…not himself. Even around family."

Family. Right. They had a huge, tight-knit group here. That was going to take some getting used to. She nodded woodenly.

Dean softened his voice. "I know this had to be hard for you, too. It can't be what you were hoping for."

She forced herself not to dwell on that. "I appreciate you letting me speak to him in private."

He sighed. "I'd like to say it'll be easier tomorrow, but that might be a false promise. Where are you staying?"

She gestured in the direction of the highway. "Owen Sound."

He frowned. "At a hotel?"

"Yeah." She rubbed her hands together, suddenly cold. "I'll find something closer in a couple of days."

"You're going to stick around?"

What part of wife did this guy not understand? "Yes. Of course I am. I didn't think this would be easy." She hadn't thought it would be *this*, either. But that didn't matter.

He gave her a hard look, searching her face for some kind of confirmation that she was serious. He must have found it, because he nodded. "I have a place where you can stay."

———

SEAN LISTENED for the sound of her car starting up then he lowered himself to his hands and knees and crawled back to his room.

He felt wrung out, like he'd been running all day.

Now he could barely handle a few trips to the bathroom and a complicated, emotional conversation.

She'd looked so good. And so hurt.

He was a raging asshole.

But then he'd had to crawl to his fucking bed, so it wasn't like he had any other choice.

What they'd had was a fantasy. He'd let himself get caught up in magical promises of love and hope and forever, and that wasn't ever going to happen for him.

The universe couldn't have used a blunter instrument to show Sean that he didn't deserve Jenna.

Just like he didn't deserve a mother.

He'd always thought, growing up, that he was more okay with his mother's death because he had never known her. He'd been too young to remember her, and as he got older, he didn't know the difference. His reality was being raised mostly by Dean and occasionally, judgingly, by the Colonel.

It wasn't that he doubted that he'd had a loving mother. He knew that. There were pictures of her all over his father's house. Pictures of him as a baby, in her arms. She'd loved him so much. She'd doted on him even while she was going through treatment, while she was sick and dying.

His father made sure Sean knew that the last thing she ever did was cuddle her two year old son to sleep. There was a picture of Sean sleeping in the hospital bed they'd set up in the living room. Curled up against her side.

And in the morning she was gone.

He didn't remember any of that—he'd been too little— but he knew he'd been loved by this woman so much, it sapped all of her energy and stole her last dying breath. And the Colonel never forgave him for it.

And now here was Jenna. The most amazing, bright, wonderful woman, who thought she loved him and wanted to take care of him. But he couldn't do that to her. He couldn't sap her energy, too.

And he can't do that to her. He can't sap her energy. Because he had no doubt if he were to try to cling to her, something worse would happen.

Something might happen to Jenna.

It was enough that his life had been fucked up, but if something bad happened to her, he would die.

No, if he was going to be a drain on somebody, let it be his brothers. They could all share it.

Or better yet, he didn't need to be a drain on anyone at all.

———

JENNA FOLLOWED DEAN INTO TOWN, her heart still pounding and her head reeling from having seen Sean. He led her to a residential street lined with small bungalows and parked in front of one in the middle of the block.

She got out and stood nervously as he hopped out of his truck. Liana Hansen, Dean's fiancé, jumped down from the passenger side. Jenna remembered Sean telling her about his brother's whirlwind romance with the country music singer.

"One minute he was all, 'she doesn't need a bodyguard, I'm not sure why I have to go on tour,' and the next he was like an alpha wolf protecting his queen. We all knew he loved her before he did. Staged an intervention at the Toronto airport and sent him right back to her. Dumb idiot."

She'd laughed at the time, but man, she understood the whole idiot thing now. Love was scary.

And this was a hell of a way to meet a famous sister-in-law, too. They'd said hello when she'd first arrived at their house, but she'd been distracted with thoughts of Sean.

Now that those thoughts were busy re-categorizing themselves after having seen him, she pushed them aside to give some attention to the fact that she had this big, extended family to meet.

None of whom knew her in the slightest.

"Hi again," she said shyly as Liana approached. "Sorry about before."

"You've got nothing to apologize for, sweetie," the petite brunette said, reaching out to touch Jenna's arm. "Let's show you inside. I love this place, it's just adorable."

"What every man likes to hear about his house," Dean grumbled. The fondness between them was obvious, though, and it made Jenna's chest hurt.

She took a deep breath and re-focused. "I really appreciate this offer."

"It's the least we could do," Dean said. "It's a small

way to soften what has to be a pretty awkward welcome to the family. And we do mean that, by the way. We want you to feel welcome here."

He opened the front door, which wasn't locked. He gestured to a key on a hook just inside the entrance. "That's the house key. It'll open both front and back doors. If you lose it, our friends Rafe and Olivia live directly behind and have a spare." He led her through the small space. A living room in the front, then a hallway with a bedroom and a bathroom, then a bigger bedroom at the back, beside the bright, sunny kitchen that looked over the back yard. He pointed to a partially erected fence. "That's the Minelli house. The fence came down in a wind storm last year and their daughter likes to run back and forth between the two houses. If that's a problem, we can fix it up for you. We just had other priorities."

There were power tools piled on the kitchen counter.

He pointed to them. "I'll take those out to the shed."

"Oh, I can—"

Liana touched her arm again. "How about I show you where the towels are? We left a few things here so the guys could clean up after a work party."

Numbly, Jenna followed the other woman. It was a nice house, and as if from a distance, she noticed the renovations were gorgeous. Restored hardwood, new trim, crown moulding, and the bathroom was stunning. Done in the same white tiles and yellow paint as the one she'd just left Sean in. "If Dean is getting this place ready for sale," she said faintly, "maybe it would be better if I stayed somewhere else."

"I think he was really hoping one of his brothers would want this place, so this works out well, don't you worry." Liana opened a cupboard and clapped her hands. "Good, there's lots of shampoo in here. I wasn't sure. And there's a stack of towels. The laundry is in the basement, where Dean's stashing his tools. It's rough down there, so we'll need to bring a laundry basket over for you. And lord only knows if there's anything in the fridge. There's a small grocery store in Lion's Head, across the highway, and we do our bigger shops in Wiarton or Owen Sound."

The names were all vaguely familiar, but Jenna was certain she wouldn't retain any of it. "I might just get takeout from the diner tonight."

"Mac's is great. I should warn you, though—it's gossip central. You stop in there, everyone in town will know who you are within the hour."

Jenna grimaced. "I was there two hours ago."

"Well, we'll do our best to head off the curious mob, then." Liana stopped her bustling and gave Jenna a searching look. "And you are welcome at our house any time. Don't let Sean's bark scare you off."

"I'll be back tomorrow." And the next day, and the day after that.

After Dean and Liana left, Jenna walked through the small house feeling shell shocked. This wasn't one of the dozen scenarios she'd run through in her head. Honestly, she hadn't properly pictured just how small and remote Pine Harbour was. She was grateful for the place to stay, rather than driving back to the nearest city, but she was also feeling off-balance at the instant acceptance by Sean's family.

She'd been raised to be suspicious of newcomers. To worry about what they wanted and be on guard for their inevitable departure. She wouldn't leave Sean, ever, but they couldn't know that yet. They didn't know her.

A commotion in the back yard drew her attention, and

she stepped onto the deck. A small blur of dark hair and pink cotton streaked across the yard toward her, skidding to a halt when the little girl realized the body on the deck didn't belong to a person she recognized.

"Uh oh," the little girl said. She was small, maybe one or two, with big brown eyes and a sweet, round mouth.

Behind her hurried a pretty, curvy brunette who was wincing. "Hi!" She stopped just behind her daughter. "You must be Jenna."

Jenna ignored her racing pulse and nodded. Might as well put on a brave face, even if she just wanted to run screaming into the house and hide in a blanket fort. "Word travels fast."

"Yeah, I'm sorry about that. I'm Olivia Minelli, and this is my daughter Sophia. We live just there."

Jenna glanced at the little girl. Pudgy hands and sweet, dark curls. Jenna liked kids, and right now, she knew that looking into the eyes of an innocent would be way easier than seeing knowing sympathy gazing back at her. She dropped into a squat. "Hi."

"Hi," was the whispered response.

"Do you know this house?"

She got a nod.

Well, if every single person—big and small—in this little town was going to trust her based solely on her connection to Sean, she'd do her best to live up to that expectation. "Do you want to come inside?"

Another nod, then the girl ran up the stairs and reached for the just-a-bit-too-high door handle.

Olivia moved after her, lifting her daughter up so they could open the door together. "There you go…"

Jenna took a deep breath and followed them inside. As much as she wasn't ready to deal with the larger-than-life cast of Pine Harbour friends and family Sean had told her about, it probably would be easier with some noise in here. The last thing she needed right now was to be lost in her own thoughts.

"I don't know what I have to offer you…" Jenna said, opening the fridge door. "Ah. Beer." There was quite a selection. She grabbed a craft IPA—thank you, Sean's friends and family, for having good taste in drinks—and turned around, holding it out to Olivia. "Would you like one?"

The other woman gave her a faint smile. "I'm good."

"Do you mind if I…?"

"Please, go ahead." Olivia's smile grew a little bashful. "I'm pregnant. If I wasn't, I'd totally be splitting a beer with you right now."

She wasn't showing yet, so maybe it was early days still. None of her business, but there was something about that little tidbit that set Jenna at ease. She could talk to pregnant women for days. She gave Olivia a more natural smile as she twisted the cap off the beer. "Congratulations. And who said anything about splitting?"

Olivia laughed. "Thank you. Most people don't know."

"Would you like water or…" She cast about the strange kitchen. "Whatever else your husband and his friends have stocked this place with?"

"I'm fine, but thank you." Olivia took a few steps into the hallway. "Sorry, I should keep an eye on the dancing ballerina. I also need to give you a heads up. You might have visitors."

"Visitors?"

"Liana called and said that the word is out. Ten bucks says Dani is already loading food into her car. Brace yourself for casseroles. My mother-in-law will almost certainly bring baked goods. And I'm not sure we'll be able to keep Matt away."

"Matt? Sean's brother?"

Olivia smiled fondly. "He's a big personality."

Jenna raised her beer bottle and shook her head. "So there really are people about to descend?"

"Yeah. Sorry." Olivia laughed weakly, and Jenna joined her. At least the beer was cold, and there was more of it. "Do you want to…talk?"

"No?" Jenna laughed at the way the word came out as a question. "Not yet."

"Okay."

"Any chance your friends coming over are bringing cake with them? Chocolate cake?"

"I can make chocolate cake happen."

"That would be great. I'm going to take a shower because I've been on the road for hours." She opened the fridge door and grabbed another beer. "I'll be back in a bit. Feel free to let people in."

She drank the second beer in the shower. It was the most frat boy thing she could imagine doing, and she kind of hated herself for it. But on the other hand, the shower felt good and the beer felt better.

When she got out, she could hear voices in the living room.

It took all of her internal fortitude to get dressed.

It wasn't a horde of people, thankfully.

Just Olivia and a taller, slimmer brunette who had a baby in a car seat at her feet. Sophia was kneeling in front of the baby and playing with his toes.

"Hi," Jenna said, stopping awkwardly in the doorway.

The new woman flew across the room and threw her arms around Jenna. "I'm so sorry," she whispered in

Jenna's ear. "I can't imagine how scared you must have been. I'm so, so sorry. Sean's a fucking dickhead."

From everything Sean had told her, only one person would say that.

"You must be Dani," Jenna murmured, shell-shocked.

"Yeah." The other woman stepped back and propped her hands on her hips. "Nice to meet you, by the way."

Jenna nodded. "Likewise."

"I understand you just arrived today. I bet he was a bear to you. He's been insufferable. We're here for whatever you need. Chocolate cake is in the kitchen."

"Okay. Wow, I was kind of kidding about that. I mean, thank you, I want it. But this is really overwhelming." Jenna shoved her hands through her damp hair and tried to process everything. She couldn't. This was too much. What she needed was a bit of space.

"How about some coffee?"

Yes, coffee was easy. "Sure. Thank you."

"We won't stay long," Dani continued as she led the way into the kitchen.

Thank God.

"Just wanted to bring you food." There were takeout coffee cups on the counter, along with a tray of cookies, a container out of which Dani cut pieces of chocolate cake, and a few boxes of crackers. "I've stocked the fridge with some easy to heat up things, as well as cheese and grapes."

"Wow." Jenna accepted one of the cups of coffee and added some sugar and milk to it before sitting heavily at the table.

"This is a lot, we know," Dani said, joining her. "But we all love Sean, and he loves you, so ergo, we love you."

She wasn't sure he loved her. So instead of saying anything, she took a long, slow sip from her coffee. "Thank you," she finally managed. It was the truth. She was grateful.

"He's going to get better," Dani said softly. "And when he does, he'll be so glad you're here."

Time would tell, but as of that moment, Jenna wasn't willing to take that bet.

CHAPTER SEVEN

THE NEXT DAY, she headed back to Dean's house mid-morning. Liana let her in, and made enough small talk that Jenna realized Sean wasn't up yet.

"Should I come back later?"

"No, it's fine. He's just prickly about being woken. He doesn't sleep well."

Jenna nodded, when really what she wanted to do was race up the stairs and climb into bed with him. Was he having nightmares? Muscle spasms? Headaches?

"We don't want to get too involved," Liana said carefully, moving down the counter to set her hand on one of the thickest medical charts Jenna had ever seen. "But Sean told Dean to leave this out. He said you'd know how to read it."

A shiver ran through her. He'd told her yesterday about the vertigo. He'd meant it to scare her off, and she had no doubt this was another volley. But she'd seen people survive unimaginable horror. She wasn't easily frightened.

She nodded. "I do."

That didn't mean she wanted to read it all in stark, medical language, though. She wanted to curl up next to Sean and have him run his fingers through her hair as he told her what happened. How awful it had been, but hey, now it's in the past. Hurray, they were together again.

Except they weren't, and it wouldn't go like that. The chart practically yelled that at her. It was thicker than a textbook. So big it had changed him.

And now he wanted to frighten her with the reality of what had happened to him. She didn't understand why— if he thought he was doing this for her, or for himself. Either way, she needed to know what he knew so she could find a new path for the both of them. Together.

Dragging in a breath, she flipped the folder open and began reading.

SEAN LAY in bed and stared at the ceiling.

He didn't like anything about his current miserable existence, but if he had to pick something that was tolerable, it was this moment, before he moved. His head didn't spin, and the ringing in his ears hadn't yet been complicated by other noises.

And then he heard her, and for a second, he was back in Spain.

We could stay in bed all day. Isn't this the best?
You're the best.

You're just saying that because you want to get lucky.
I'm already lucky. I woke up beside you, didn't I?

He hadn't known how good he'd had it, that it would all be taken away.

And then another thought. Not a memory, but a recrimination. *She's right downstairs.*

He wasn't so self-centred that he didn't realize, theoretically, that he had another chance here. Her showing up could have been the bright light, the shining hope he'd desperately wanted when he first landed in the hospital in Germany.

She laughed at something either Dean or Liana said, and he twisted his head to catch more than just the edge of the sound.

And the world hurtled sharply.

Whoa. No sudden movements, dickhead. Vertigo rule number one.

He shut his eyes, but the swirling disorientation didn't stop, and the ringing in his ears ramped up alarmingly. He gritted his teeth and grabbed the pillow, trying to block everything out.

Deep breaths sort of worked. Enough to keep the rise of bile back. Throwing up on himself would be a fine fucking way to start the day.

No, he wasn't selfish to want to protect her from this. She deserved more than two weeks of bliss, then a lifetime of playing nursemaid to an invalid husband.

He rolled onto his side, then his front. His legs pulled up easily under him. Fucking irony. His body worked just fine without his head.

Taking a deep breath, he pushed up onto his hands and knees, keeping his head pressed against the pillow until the last possible second.

A knock sounded at his door, followed by Jenna's voice. "Sean?"

Fucking hell.

He knew what he needed to do. He needed to push her

away. *God.* He didn't know if he was strong enough for that, but he'd damn well try. "Go away."

She hesitated, then sighed. "Dean and Liana have gone out. It's just me."

Just her. She said it reassuringly, like she had any clue what was on his side of the door. Like anything they'd shared could prepare her for the fact he couldn't get out of bed without assistance.

At least yesterday she'd found him standing. This? On all fours, unable to lift his head without tossing his cookies? No.

His chest ached. *Jenna, please,* he wanted to beg. But that wouldn't work. He needed to be hard about this. He'd left her his chart. Couldn't she see what he'd become?

"Go away," he said again. "I don't want you here."

His voice broke on the last word, and he hated that show of weakness.

It took her a long time to respond. "I told you yesterday that I will go, but I will also come back. You might as well see me first."

It wasn't *seeing her* that was the problem. It was *her* seeing *him.* "I'm a mess."

"I don't care," she said softly. Then she raised her voice. "I mean, I care. I'll wait here as long as you need me too. But I'm okay with messy."

This was a stupid conversation to have through a door. And more to the point, it wasn't working.

He carefully slid off the bed. He hated the silver walker in the corner, but if Dean wasn't here, it was either crawl or use the assistive device.

And he wasn't fucking crawling in front of Jenna.

He made his way to the walker, then hauled himself

up. He hated how his arms shook. Hated how he had to find a new focus point before he could take each step.

When he opened the door, she was standing in the middle of the hall, wearing jeans and a t-shirt and looking perfectly perfect. Giving him lots of space. Plenty far away, really, but still too damn close.

"I need to…" He pointed to the bathroom. She stepped aside, but he didn't want her to watch him hobble, either. "You could sit in my room. There's a chair."

Too late, he realized that his desire not to stumble in front her had also been an invitation for her to sit.

Damn his fucking useless head.

The guest room had a whole sitting room area, and that's where he found her when he returned. He'd scrubbed his face and brushed his teeth. Still looked like a homeless hobo, but he didn't smell like one.

"Morning," she said softly as he stepped toward her. Step, lift, clunk. Step, lift, clunk.

His snail's pace gave him lots of time to soak up how good she looked. She'd braided her hair today. Even though she'd cut it, it was still long enough for that. A thick twist with loose strands spilling out of it. She'd kicked off her shoes downstairs, too, like she was planning to stay a while.

She was sitting in the arm chair, so he took the couch. As soon as he was down, he kicked the walker out of the way.

"I read your medical file." She pressed her lips together for a second, and he didn't miss the tremor in her cheek. "You had a stroke?"

"So they say."

"Sean…"

Fuck, he didn't want her to worry about him. He

wanted her to run screaming, not crying. "I'm getting better."

"I can see that." She curled her legs beside her and rubbed her hand up and down her calf. "It sounds like it was really touch and go at the start."

He'd been there. It had been awful.

"Since your speech returned so quickly, hopefully—"

"I'm getting better in a not-going-to-die kind of way," he bit out. "Don't confuse that with any hope for further improvement."

She dropped her gaze to the floor.

"The key parts of the file were on the top. Chronic tinnitus, vertigo. Migraines, nausea, balance problems. Short term memory gaps. None of that is going to get better. My brain was put in a pressure cooker. This is the new me."

She didn't say anything, just kept her gaze averted.

He sighed. "You shouldn't have come—"

"I'm not sorry." She said it quietly, softly, but there was steel in her voice, and it shut him up. "I should have come sooner."

"No." Jesus, no. He couldn't have handled her. *Selfish.* "How much did this screw you up for work?"

"It didn't. That's fine." She pushed to her feet, still not looking at him. She started to pace. "I'm sticking around for a while."

"You wanted—"

She jerked her head, finding his gaze, and he shut up. "When I found out, you were... here. With your family. So... I gave notice. I'm fine. It's fine. I waited until they got a replacement for me."

He sagged back against the couch in relief. She could go back. She could get another contract. She was only staying for a while. Maybe he could handle that. They could wrap up their affairs, so to speak. "Dean told me he set you up in his place. You…" He swallowed back the invitation for her to stay here. It wasn't his house to offer, and he wasn't sure he could handle it if she accepted, anyway.

She resumed pacing when he didn't finish that thought. She moved with an effortless grace that stayed him. He hadn't told her enough how beautiful she was. He'd missed so many opportunities in those two weeks to be a better man. He couldn't let his head swivel to track her as she paced, but each time she moved into his field of vision, his heart seized up, and only relaxed when she slipped away on the other side.

It was fucked up, how much anxiety she caused in him just by being in his presence.

No, that wasn't fair. She didn't cause it. He let himself go there, let himself get wound up and worried about shit he couldn't control.

She stopped beside him and sat on the couch.

His pulse jolted.

She wasn't touching him, but she was closer than she'd been the day before. It made him want all sorts of things he couldn't have. He'd tried to think about this—about being well enough to hold her, to kiss her. To do everything he'd missed.

But his body wouldn't cooperate. Hadn't cooperated when he'd thought about it, and now that she was actually here, in touching range, he was still a dysfunctional mess.

She waited until he turned toward her. Slowly, carefully. Weakly.

Then she smiled, so bright it hurt to look at. "So here's the thing. I'm going to have hope for the both of us. You can tell me that's foolish. But the Sean Foster I fell in love with wouldn't have thought it foolish. He taught me a lot in our two weeks together, about taking risks and finding joy. *You* taught me a lot. So I'm not going to push you, but I'm going to be around, because…" She took a wavering breath and her smile trembled, but she kept going. "Because I love you."

She hadn't heard him at all. He rasped her name, a warning, but she was already leaning in. Her lips brushed against his, the barest, sweetest touch he'd ever felt in his entire life, and then she was gone. Standing up.

"I'll be back tomorrow." She pulled a piece of paper from her pocket. "This is my new phone number. I also left it downstairs. If you want anything, need me for any reason, I'm just a call away."

———

SHE'D EATEN the rest of the chocolate cake for breakfast, and after that emotional visit with Sean, Jenna deserved something good, so she went to Mac's.

It was a little early for the lunch rush, if Pine Harbour had such a thing, so the place was almost empty. She had her choice of counter or booth, and after some consideration, she went with the booth. It might look a little odd eating by herself, but this way she wouldn't have to make small talk with the waitress beyond the niceties exchanged when she placed her order.

"Coffee, sweetheart?"

"Yes, please." Jenna set the menu down. "What pie do you have today?"

"Apple, strawberry-rhubarb, and pecan."

"Strawberry-rhubarb, please. With a scoop of vanilla

ice cream. And…" she glanced at the menu. "What's good for takeout?"

"All of it." The waitress crossed her arms. "Sean's favourite is the meatloaf."

She filed that away for future reference, and hated the pang of envy that she hadn't already known that. "It's just for me," she said evenly. "I'll take the lasagna for when I leave."

As she was stirring a sugar packet into her coffee, and trying to convince herself she didn't need it, the door chimed and in came a wave of people. Jenna watched them all, curious about her new neighbours.

One of them was particularly interested in her, too. Tall, good-looking, with a ready, camera-perfect smile, and tousled brown hair… he had to be a Foster brother.

He veered toward her and slid into the booth without waiting for an invitation. "You're Jenna."

It was like she was wearing one of those HELLO, MY NAME IS stickers. She took a deep breath that did nothing for the butterflies in her stomach and held out her hand. "I am. And you must be Matt or Jake."

"Matt. The good-looking one." He gave her a grin. "Or so people say."

She could just imagine what people said. "Nice to meet you."

"I was told I couldn't show up on your doorstep yesterday, but this doesn't count, right?"

She shook her head. "I suppose not."

"Do you mind if I join you for lunch?"

The door dinged again, and another wave of people entered. Dani Foster was among them, her baby in a wrap on her chest, and she was with a pretty blond woman with short, choppy hair.

The two women bee-lined for them.

Dani gave Matt a hard look. "Hey, there, mister. What are you doing? Hi, Jenna. Nice to see you again."

He turned and gave the two new women the exact same big, goofy, flirty smile he'd given her. "Getting to know my new sister-in-law. How are you, Chloe?"

The blonde winked at him. "Hungry. You're in my seat. Move."

"I was going to have lunch with Jenna."

"Well she's in hot demand as a lunch date, we're claiming her. Sorry. You can try again another day."

Matt shrugged at Jenna as if to say, *what are you going to do?*

An excellent question.

"Fine. I should get takeout anyway. That was my plan before I saw Jenna." He turned back to her and gave her a wink. "I'm sure I'll see you around."

"Yep," Jenna said.

The blonde took his seat and leaned in. "Hi. I'm Chloe Dawson, the librarian."

"And defender of town newcomers."

Dani, who'd stayed standing because she was bouncing the baby, laughed. "Yep. She's also good for book recommendations, and awesome for splitting a giant pot of chilli or stew with."

"Now you're talking my language. What kinds of books?"

"Pretty much anything."

"You have any good ugly cry books?"

"Heaps." And bless her soul, Chloe didn't ask why Jenna wanted them. Or maybe it was obvious that she hadn't cried yet, couldn't cry, and was so damn brittle if she didn't do something, she'd break into a million pieces.

Chloe grabbed the menu. "What are you having for lunch?"

"Pie."

"Sounds *great*." When Jenna's pie arrived a minute later, Chloe and Dani both ordered the exact same thing.

"So you want some books?" Chloe asked after they'd stuffed their faces.

"Sure. I could come in to the library and get a card."

"Oh yeah, definitely do that. But I've got tons at home, too. And if I bring you some, then we can also cook up a big batch of stew to split, and then we avoid having to run the Matt Foster gauntlet. I'm surprised he didn't hit on you."

"He knew who I was, so I guess I was saved. He was perfectly nice."

"So he clearly hadn't gotten to grilling you about their precious baby brother, then."

Sean wasn't a baby anything, and Jenna didn't have anything to hide. They could bring on the grilling if they wanted to, she didn't care.

"They mean well, but they'll want to both protect Sean and warn you off of having any expectations."

"I don't have any expectations."

Chloe nodded. "Good." But she said it like she didn't believe Jenna.

"I don't," Jenna insisted.

"I literally just met you," the librarian said. Well, at least she acknowledged that fact. "So I shouldn't weigh in on that."

"But?"

"But you've flown around the world to stake your claim on him. I should hope you have some expectations. And you deserve some. He married you, and now he's holed up in his brother's house feeling miserable and sorry for himself."

"He almost died." More than once. Cold, slick fear rolled over her as she remembered his medical file.

The librarian reached across the booth and touched Jenna's hand. "But he lived."

"Excellent point, Chloe-who-I've-just-met."

Chloe-who-she'd-just-met smiled.

Jenna laughed. "Okay. I'm trying my damnedest to manage my secret expectations. How's that?"

"Better. Say, do you know how to make stew?" Chloe gave her a wicked, beaming grin. "Because I don't. At all. So really, I'm good at grocery shopping and providing reading material in exchange for cooking."

"Yeah, I can cook."

Chloe held out her hand. "Then you have a dinner date for tomorrow night."

Jenna took the proffered hand and shook it. "Deal. I'm staying in Dean's old house."

"I know. And conveniently, I live just down the street."

"This really is a very small town, isn't it?"

"The smallest. But we've got the biggest hearts."

CHAPTER EIGHT

February, four months earlier
Seville, Spain

HER FIRST FLIGHT of the day, into Naples, had been rough, with zero frills. There weren't any flight attendants on a C-130 Hercules. But it was better than an eight-hour bus ride to Ankara, so Jenna was grateful for the travel advisory which meant as an NGO she was given a spot on the US Air Force transport instead of being expected to make do with ground transport to the nearest international airport.

Sean had been waiting as promised. He met her at the gate with a wide grin, his arms out, and as soon as she was close enough, he'd pulled her in tight for a hug, and then a sweet, stirring kiss.

Jenna nodded off after takeoff on their flight to Spain. She dreamed of stripping Sean naked and rubbing against him, and when she woke up, she was twisted around him for real, her face buried in his chest. Even worse her hand was under his shirt, her palm flat against his flexed, hard abs.

"Sorry," she whispered, straightening up.

He caught her wrist and held her against him. "Don't be," he murmured back. "You feel good."

She nestled closer and let her eyes drift shut again. He felt good, too. So good.

"I'm getting used to you nodding off on my shoulder," he murmured. "Don't worry, I booked us rooms close to the airport for tonight. By the time we pick up the rental car, it'll be nearly dinner time, and I know you're zonked."

Her eyes popped open. "Rooms, plural?"

"I didn't want to assume." He grinned at her as he ran his fingers through the ends of her hair.

Since they'd been reunited, he'd been touching her almost non-stop, and she loved it. Right now his other hand rested gently against her knee, and when she returned his smile, he leaned in and kissed her.

"We've got two weeks ahead of us. I'm not in any hurry."

Jenna was, though. She wanted to climb Sean like a tree and that scared her. If she rushed into something here, she might fall so far, so fast, she'd never see the heartbreak coming until it smacked her in the face. She reached for him and caught the front of his t-shirt with her fingertips.

He glanced down at where she was touching him and groaned under his breath. "Okay, that's a lie. But I'm trying to be chivalrous."

Why did his being old-fashioned surprise her? He'd been nothing but kind and attentive since they'd met.

It was a good reminder they were still strangers. Strangers with chemistry and affection for one another, but still two people with a lot to learn about each other.

To be fair, they hadn't discussed room sharing. And this wasn't how Jenna normally went about dating. She'd never been with anyone who wasn't a friend first, for quite a while. Her love life had always rolled out in an orderly fashion, usually after a spark followed by a frank discussion about sex and boundaries.

Healthy, but not...romantic?

And there was something really romantic about Sean. If he wanted to be chivalrous and take his time, she would sink into the anticipation and enjoy it.

"Okay," she whispered, kissing his cheek just as the captain informed them they were about to start their final descent.

They were both traveling light, so they didn't need to wait for baggage. Sean took her hand as soon as they were off the plane and he held it all the way to the car rental counter.

"Do you want coffee?" she asked quietly after he handed over his license and reservation number. She pointed to the cafe at the end of the hall. "Something to eat?"

"Maybe something cold. Coke?"

She grabbed them both pop, and picked up two sandwiches and a fruit tray as well. There was no way she was waiting until the Spanish dinner hour to eat—if she even stayed up that late. Her cat nap on the plane hadn't done much to dull her ever-present fatigue.

Now she was glad Sean had booked a hotel close by instead of driving to Arcos de la Frontera, where Sean had rented an apartment for the next ten days. She'd have only fallen asleep in the car, and she didn't want to miss any of the adventure.

When she returned, the car rental paperwork was

almost complete. Sean's gaze locked onto her and he leaned in, his hand settling on the small of her back. She had all of his attention, and she loved it. It was the most delicious kind of foreplay.

"Here is your key. The car is located through those doors. Please follow the signs, and you will find it."

"Got it," Sean said, his gaze never leaving her face. "Thank you."

Always polite, even when distracted. She was in such delicious trouble.

They found their car easily, and as Sean moved the seat back and adjusted his mirrors, Jenna typed the hotel address into the built-in GPS. The controls were in Spanish, but the interface was intuitive enough she figured it out.

It wasn't the fastest, though. The screen took forever to load, and once they set off, there was a bit of a lag as it updated to their changing direction. But they found the hotel easily and Sean quickly spotted an open parking space in the crowded lot.

"Eagle eyes," she teased him, and he gave her a quick grin and a kiss before hopping out.

The lobby was crowded, too, and when they got to the counter, the desk clerk couldn't find their reservation. "Foster, Foster," he kept repeating, and Jenna's stomach dropped each time he stretched out Sean's last name. Sean didn't seem fazed. Jenna was super fazed. Or super tired, probably. Also, hungry. She wanted to devour that sandwich, then lie down and not get back up again for twelve hours.

"Ah." The desk clerk frowned. "For two?"

"Yes."

"We apologize. It was set aside. Yes, here it is." Set

aside? In a computer? Whatever. As long as they had it, that was all that mattered. "Mr. Sean Foster, reservation for two. Your room is in the north tower. One moment."

Room? Not rooms? Not that she cared.

But Sean did. "A single room? I reserved two rooms."

"A room for two, sir. That's how we have it recorded. Perhaps there was some confusion."

"Perhaps." Sean's voice stayed level, but from the way his jaw flexed, Jenna knew he was annoyed. So Mr. Steady and Calm had limits after all.

"It's fine," she whispered. "If it's fine with you?"

He twisted around so his back was to the clerk. "Are you sure?"

"Yeah. Of course." She held up their bag of sandwiches. "I'll even buy you dinner before taking advantage of you."

He laughed, his face softening. "You have a deal."

A surge of desire pushed her fatigue to the edges again, and when he looped his arm over her shoulders, she leaned into him. If anything, she was relieved not to be saying goodnight at a door tonight.

Her heart thumped in happy anticipation as they headed to the north tower. The room was big, with a king-size bed, and a small couch and table filled the far corner.

She jumped as the door clicked shut behind them, but Sean was moving ahead of her and didn't notice.

Pressing her hand to her belly, she forced herself to be normal. Chill. Food might help. "Hungry?" she asked as he stowed his bag in the corner.

He turned slowly and gave her a sexy grin. "Yes."

Gah, her insides turned to mush and heat flooded her cheeks. She hadn't meant it like that, but that worked too.

Carefully, she set the bag of food on the table then

dropped her backpack. Sean watched, his gaze hooded, as she closed the gap between them and fisted the front of his shirt. A shiver ran up her arm as her fingers curled against the hard, broad expanse of his chest. Every time she thought she was getting used to the bigness of him, to his strength and virility, her body surprised her with another visceral craving for him.

He was gorgeous.

And they were finally alone.

She pulled him closer, the gentlest tug on his shirt, and he came readily. Big and strong and broad as he pressed against her, seeming to know she wanted an all-consuming, thought-scattering kiss.

His mouth covered hers, his lips immediately questing for more access. She opened for him and surrendered to his tongue, letting him taste her. He gathered her in his arms and plunged his fingers into her hair, wrapping her in his embrace as he deepened the kiss. Harder, faster. He devoured her, and her pulse skipped and leapt along.

Yes, yes, yes.

When he eased back, he did it reluctantly. She could feel the tension vibrating through his arms, hard as steel around her. He caught her lower lip between his teeth and tugged, just for a second. Just enough to make something heady tug hard inside her.

More.

Breathing hard, he pressed his forehead against hers and tightened his hands in her hair. "Food. We should eat it."

An out-of-control giggle burst forth from deep inside her. "Yes. We should."

He kissed her again, hard. He nipped and pulled, and

she pushed up onto her toes because she wanted more of that. "Sean…"

"Mmm." His lips softened against hers, then he pulled himself back and cleared his throat, a faint blush colouring the tops of his cheeks. "Come here."

He pulled her to the couch, and they sat next to each other as they ate their sandwiches. When they finished the last sips of their pop, he tugged her into his lap again. This time their making out was slower, more exploratory.

But before they went any further, she really needed a shower. Reality was so unromantic. And she wanted to shave her legs. It was probably too soon in their whirlwind romance to do that in front of him. "Do you want to take the first shower?" she finally asked as he kissed his way down her neck.

He shook his head as he patted her hip. "Ladies first."

The old-fashioned thing was definitely working for her, especially when he was flexible about it.

"You sure?" she asked as she reluctantly eased off his lap.

He hung on to her hand as she stood. Maybe he was reluctant for their contact to end too. "Go on. You've earned that hot water."

After four months of tepid water and horrible pressure, the shower felt like heaven itself. She stood under the heavy spray for a minute, letting the heat get into her pores as she tried to tamp down her excitement for this adventure to a reasonable, healthy level rather than the off-the-charts thrill ride it currently felt like. She needed to keep her attention focused on the travel and not so much the sex, although they were going to have sex, and she had no doubt it was going to be amazing.

Incredible, even.

Sean's kisses promised a lot for what would come next.

But she needed to keep the fling casual, because it had a very definite end-date. And more to the point, she needed to return to work re-invigorated, not mopey about losing access to ready orgasms and easy, soul-warming smiles.

And she had no doubt Sean understood that—because he was in the same boat.

She grinned as she finished scrubbing her skin. Yes, they were going to help each other a lot over the next two weeks. Restore all sorts of positive energy. Humming, she did a double dose of conditioner on her hair before shaving her legs. Only when her fingers turned pruny did she reluctantly turn off the water.

After dressing in the basic grey lounge pants and black t-shirt that she'd brought for pyjamas, she stepped back into the hotel room and gave Sean a ready smile. "All yours."

He gave her a slow, warm once over that made her shiver, then grabbed his own bag. "I won't be long," he said and he gave her a kiss on the cheek as he moved past.

She stretched out on the bed, luxuriating in how big and soft it was compared to her cot. Had a pillow ever felt this good? She rolled her face into it and closed her eyes.

SEAN ROUGHLY TURNED the bar of soap between his hands, working it into a lather. It matched how he felt, although no amount of scrubbing could clean his filthy thoughts when it came to Jenna.

This wasn't a one-night stand. It didn't feel like a

friends-with-benefits thing, either, although he sure as hell wanted to be Jenna's friend.

And he wanted all the benefits.

He rolled his neck under the hot spray of water before turning around to rinse his front. The sting of heat against his junk did nothing to slack his erection. He was so hard for her it hurt. The little sounds she made as he hauled her close echoed in his ears.

When he soaped up his balls, just that touch nearly sent him through the roof. Fuck. He didn't want their first time to be over before it started. He wanted to take his time and make it the best she'd ever had.

He took himself roughly in hand and jerked. Three strokes and he was done, spilling his pent-up release. With a shuddering breath, he leaned against the tile and closed his eyes.

The things Jenna made him feel were strange and new. Why was he putting so much pressure on himself to give her some kind of perfect romance? She hadn't asked him for that. But as he finished showering, he couldn't shake the thought that he wanted it for himself.

He'd come halfway around the world in service to his Queen and country. For himself and his career too. But he'd found something else. He'd found Jenna and the spark she lit inside him, and he *wanted her*, fiercely, on a whole different level from anything and anyone he'd desired in the past. From the second she'd looked up at him, her fingers wrapped around that apple, he'd been a goner.

Need at first sight.

He wasn't crazy enough to think about the l-word. But two weeks of something special?

Yes, he wanted that.

He wanted romance, and he wanted it to be magical. He wanted to remember this time with Jenna for the rest of his life.

And his first orgasm since he'd met her had been by his own hand while she waited.

What the hell was wrong with him?

In the end, it didn't matter. He realized even before he rounded the corner that Jenna had fallen asleep. His shower had taken less than ten minutes, and she'd probably passed out the second he left the room.

He leaned against the wall and watched her slow, even breaths. Damn, she looked sweet.

And exhausted.

In the two days that he'd been at her camp, she'd probably had a sum total of six hours sleep between the two nights. If that was standard, she'd probably sleep like the dead until morning. He had when he'd landed in Naples. Now he was adjusted to vacation-time, and she deserved the same transition. He wasn't going to try to wake her.

He pulled a paperback from his bag and stretched out on the other side of the bed.

The romance could start in the morning.

CHAPTER NINE

—————————

IT WAS STILL DARK out when he woke, although he'd left a lamp on. His book was gone, having fallen away maybe. In its place, he was holding Jenna—definitely an improvement, although his sleeping self had taken some liberties with her body. He was plastered against her back, and he'd cupped her breast under her shirt.

Her nipple was hard and tight and growing against his palm.

He was pretty sure he'd been groping her in his sleep. Hot embarrassment crashed through him, but before he could extract himself and apologize, she covered his hand with hers and squeezed.

"Don't stop," she whispered.

Well, hot damn.

"Nice way to wake up," he said, his voice thick with equal parts sleep and lust.

"The best."

He bowed his head and kissed the bare skin where her neck met her shoulder. She tugged her shirt up, baring more of her chest to his fingers, and he resumed his caress, exploring her naked flesh for the first time. Soft, responsive flesh that pebbled under his touch. He traced a path of goosebumps all the way around her breast then swept his circles in tighter and tighter until he got to the peaked, hard nipple in the middle, standing proud from her body.

He pulled it between his fingertips, and she sighed.

"Like that?"

"Little harder."

He pinched her gently, then not so gently, and she pushed her hips back against him.

"I fell asleep on you last night." She twisted in his arms and he shifted with her, climbing on top of her as he stripped off her shirt.

He grinned. "You were tired. And it's still technically last night."

"But after those kisses…" God, she was sweet, the way she gave him a wide-eyed look that said she'd known he wanted her and she didn't want to disappoint.

She never could.

Because he was a dirty dog.

"You got me worked up, all right." He pressed his hips into her, rubbing his erection against her core. "Want to know a secret?"

Her breath hitched. "Always."

"I was so ready to jump you that I had to jerk off in the shower. Three strokes and I was done." There was no shame in telling her that. He wanted to tell her all sorts of confidences he'd never shared with anyone else.

"You didn't!" She gasped in delight then reached for him, palming his erection through his boxer briefs. "Because you wanted to last longer?"

"Of course." He leaned in and brushed his lips against hers. "I wanted to last all night."

"But I fell asleep."

"I'd let lust cloud my judgement. You needed your rest."

"I'm awake now." She grinned like the cat who'd caught the canary.

He pushed his dick into her hand. "So you are. And I took that edge off earlier…"

She squeezed. "You said that. Super hot, by the way. I want to watch you next time."

Sweet hell. "Yeah?"

She dragged her fingers up his body, lighting a path of sparks across his skin in her wake. "Definitely."

He lowered himself against her, catching her mouth for a thorough kiss before he tangled his fingers into her hair and gave her a serious look. "I got a box of condoms in Italy."

She gave him a matching solemn look. "Excellent."

They both burst into laughter and he rolled onto his side then sat up, pulling her into his lap. She straddled him, both of them naked from the waist up, and she held his head as he kissed her collarbone, then lower, over the skin he'd explored with his fingers. He loved the way she shivered, so sensitive, but rose up on her knees eagerly at the same time and pulled his hair like a warrior goddess eager to fight for what she wanted.

"Get back here," he growled, tugging her hips back down. He craved the firm press of her thighs against his legs, her sex against his cock. Instead of her rising up to meet his mouth, he bent her back, leaning over her to capture her nipples in his mouth.

He couldn't sort out which got him more worked up— the scent of her, the taste of her skin, or the breathy sounds that kept sliding across her gorgeous lips. His name, pleas for more, and when he opened his mouth wide and swallowed as much of her flesh as he could, a single, beautiful, "Yes…"

He needed more.

He pressed his face into her chest, then replaced his mouth with his hands there and kissed his way back up her neck. Biting, licking, sucking. His appetite for Jenna was growing by the second, turning him ravenous.

He'd been starved, clearly. Deprived of this woman his entire adult life.

"I want to taste all of you," he said as she grabbed his hair and pulled their mouths together.

She whimpered into their hot, open-mouthed kiss, and he took that for her consent.

Another flip put her on her back beneath him again.

Sex with Jenna was a workout, and he loved it. He wanted them to roll and twist and fight to be on top, on the bottom, sideways and upside down.

But right now, he wanted her to hold still for him because he didn't just want to taste all of her, he wanted to see her, too. Consume her with his eyes, his fingers, his mouth.

"Let me make you feel good."

She shivered beneath him, and he slowed his caresses. He kissed her neck and tasted the sweet dip above her collarbone. With each unsteady breath, her chest rose and fell against him, and he put his mouth there again, but not for long.

Her pussy waited for him. He told her that, and she groaned.

"Is that a yes?" He moved lower, rubbing his nose along the waistband of her soft cotton pants. "Do you want more?"

"I want everything," she whispered.

He hooked his fingers over the waistband and tugged them down, finding her bare beneath. Her hips, like the rest of her, were lean and muscular, curving into her thighs. Her belly had a soft, sweet swell that dipped just above her mound. He kissed her there and the delicate scent of her swirled into his brain and made him stupid.

He whispered her name in awe as he shouldered his way between her thighs. She moved languidly now, like she knew he was going to worship her. He liked this side of Jenna, too. A queen who knew her own worth.

And worship was exactly what he wanted to do. He stroked the insides of her thighs and the sensitive crease where legs met torso. Then with the tips of his fingers, he got acquainted with her swelling sex.

She felt amazing, soft and wet, and as responsive here as she was with her breasts. When she began to move against his hand, he let himself taste her, too. Each lick, each inhale of her scent, drove him a little further out of his mind. He wanted to bury himself between her legs and never come up for air, and that was crazy, because there was so much more sex still to be had.

Later.

He was busy right now.

He found a pattern she liked, his thumb on her clit, his tongue sliding everywhere else—up and around and down, then back again—and when she asked for more, he was happy to give it.

"You want my fingers?" he asked, teasing her entrance.

She answered by lifting her hips and pulling his index and middle fingers into her up to the first knuckle.

Fuck, she was tight. And hot. He pressed inside,

matching the speed of his thumb, still rolling lazily over her clit. They were in no hurry.

She chased him again with her hips.

Correction. He was in no hurry. *She* seemed mighty eager to come on his face and fingers. He was a fool to not get her there as quickly as she wanted. Later, he could play. Tease her and stretch it out, make it even better for having waited.

Now, he gave her what she wanted. He curved his fingers and tightened his tongue, finding all the spots that made her shiver and shake. When she lifted her legs and wrapped them around his head, he doubled his efforts, until she found the crest of her orgasm and every part of her tightened and trembled.

Beautiful.

"God, that was good," she breathed, flopping back against the bed.

He rose onto his knees, and she reached for him.

"My turn," she whispered, kissing his mouth quickly before she pushed him back against the bed.

She didn't need to, he thought as she tugged down his boxers. He hadn't gone down on her expecting reciprocity. But his heart was going to leap out of his chest, so oh God, yes please…

Her mouth covered the head of his cock. Hot, wet, sucking perfection.

He rolled his head back and groaned. "Yes, Jesus, that…" His hands flailed in the air then he dropped them to the bed and fisted the blankets on both sides.

She grinned up at him before bobbing down again, and he was powerless to hold back. His hips pumped on their own accord, thrusting his dick in shallow, desperate little begs for more. *Lick me, suck me, kill me dead.*

It didn't take long for her to do just that. Her nimble, clever fingers wrapped around the base of him, teasing his balls as they pulled tight to his body. He groaned then reached for her. He was going to come. "Jenna…"

"It's okay," she whispered, her breath hot on his cock before she sucked him deep again.

The edges of his vision started to dance and he let himself go. With another pull of her mouth and a tight squeeze from her hand, he came so hard he saw stars.

She slid away from him, and he heard water running in the bathroom, then she returned, sipping from a glass. "Want some?" She held it out, and he pushed himself up to lean back against the headboard.

"My legs are like jelly," he admitted, and she beamed.

"Excellent."

He took the water from her and she climbed back onto the bed. His gaze tangled in her bare legs and the sway of her breasts, turning his thoughts into single, simple words. Want. Need. Perfect.

She sat beside him and leaned her head back against the wall. Before he could address round two, she yawned, and he tamped down that desire for more. Taking one last sip of water, he handed her the glass, and she drained it.

"Back to sleep," he told her, and she turned her face to give him a tired smile.

"That was really hot," she whispered as she leaned in to kiss him. "Best vacation ever and we haven't even left the hotel yet."

They turned out the light and Jenna lay down on her side, pulling him against her back. He lifted his head and watched her lace her fingers through his. She tugged his hand back to her breast, where it had been when they'd woken up.

"Mmm, yes. Just like that. I want to wake up the same way in the morning," she said softly, her eyelids drifting shut.

He squeezed his arm around her. As if there were any chance of him letting go.

———

INSTEAD OF ANOTHER round of exploring their bodies, the morning brought loud thumping and yelling from the room next door. Sean resigned himself to more sex not happening until they arrived in Arcos de la Frontera later that day.

"Do you think they heard us last night?" Jenna whispered as she packed her pyjamas into her bag.

"We weren't that loud." He was pretty sure, anyway. She blushed in a way that made his blood redirect, and he pulled her into his arms. "They'll never see us again, but if it makes you feel better, the next place is a private apartment. Lots of space. Very thick walls. And I can motivate you to be quiet."

She laughed and kissed his cheek. "I wasn't thinking about me, Mr. Groaner. But that's a good idea. I'll make you cover your face with a pillow the next time I go down on you."

If she kept talking like that, he'd be shouting like their next door neighbours, damn the consequences. "Tease."

"Come on," she whispered. "Let's go drive through some mountains."

Before he'd had a taste of Jenna, he'd had the crazy idea to spend the day in the national park south of Seville before going to Arcos.

Now he just wanted to haul her back to bed.

Not that spending time out of bed was any kind of hardship.

She was funny and sexy and patient with their glitchy GPS. They stopped in the first town they passed and bought a more detailed road map as a backup, and she carefully folded it out on her lap as he climbed one precarious hill after another. The drive was pretty epic, made even more so by her oohs and ahs over the scenery.

They stopped for a quick lunch, then got back on the road and decided at the last minute to take a scenic detour from the national park to Arcos, a decision he was regretting three hours later when they were climbing what felt like an endless hill. The GPS was glitching more often than it was working, and he had a sinking feeling they weren't actually as close to Arcos as the device promised, because they'd already hit two dead end roads and needed to double-back.

"It should just be over this hill," Jenna said as he slowed even further. The switchback was getting tighter and tighter. Not the worst thing he'd ever driven, but pretty narrow.

It would be fun to drive if he weren't starving for dinner and the woman beside him, in whatever order she preferred. He'd had an epic day, but he was ready for it to be over.

"Okay, the GPS says there's one more turn and then there's a straight cut down the hill."

Sean twisted the car around a bend of trees, gunning it a bit to make the climb. But instead of the crest of the hill, he found a tunnel—gated off and not passable. Another dead end.

The GPS was a damn liar.

Beside him, Jenna shook with silent laughter as Sean

braked hard and swore under his breath. "Where the fuck is this place?"

On the screen in the dashboard, it looked like they were nearly there, but…they were nowhere.

"Come on, let's get out and stretch our legs," she said, patting his thigh. Her fingers were light and nimble, and it was so damn unfair they weren't in their apartment yet, because he wanted to feel them on his bare skin.

He caught her hand in his and turned it gently, kissing her fingertips. Her gasp was quiet, but still like a match that lit a flame inside him. He glanced at her face. "We could stretch our legs," he said, his voice gruff. "Or we could sit right here for a minute."

She shifted closer. "Right here sounds good."

One good thing to be said for a dead end at the top of a secluded foothill…it was damn private. For the first time all day, Sean didn't feel like he had to hold back.

So he didn't.

Her lips parted for him and he took the invitation with greedy abandon. She tasted like lemons and warm sunshine, like happiness wrapped in the sexiest laughter he'd ever heard.

He kissed her until they were both breathing hard. Then he kissed her again, tugging on her hair because he wanted to hear another gasp, and when he got it, he rewarded her with his mouth lower, on her neck. She tasted good there, too.

"Sean…" She made an adorably frustrated sound and pushed him away, only to chase him again for another kiss on the mouth. When she pulled back, she was grinning.

He dragged in a ragged breath and tried to think non-X-rated thoughts so his brain would unscramble.

"Come on," she said, her breath brushing against his

cheek as she stretched before leaning away from him. "Let's get out for a minute."

He grabbed the paper map and followed her out of the car. She turned in a slow circle. "This definitely isn't it."

He laughed. "No."

"So where are we?"

He unfolded the map onto the hood of the car and she crowded close. When she brushed against him like that, he didn't care where they were. He just wanted to press her against the car and kiss her again, over and over until she begged him to take her to bed.

Right, a bed. That's why they needed to find Arcos de la Frontera. They had a bed waiting for them. Two of them, in fact, but he really hoped they'd only muss up one of them.

"This road should continue," she said, tracing her finger over the faint line the GPS had sent them down. "Although…" She ran her fingertip back and forth over the switchback. "This doesn't look as sharp as what we just climbed, does it?"

It didn't. Sean darted his gaze over the map, looking for another hill climb. "There." He stabbed at the map. "We turned too soon."

Jenna nodded, then twisted around, shielding her eyes from the sun. "I bet the town is just over that ridge, then."

"Only one way to find out." He took her hand and pulled her toward the rise. She laughed and sprinted past him.

CHAPTER TEN

THEY MADE it to Arcos by early evening, and the instructions for accessing their apartment were blessedly straightforward. After parking their car in the designated spot just off the narrow street, they climbed to the top floor of a three-storey building. Keys were waiting for them in a lockbox with a number pad that Sean knew the code to from his email instructions.

Inside, they found a spacious apartment that faced the town on one side, and had a private terrace that overlooked the valley on the other.

It was beautiful, and private, and Jenna couldn't believe it was all theirs for the next ten days.

She twirled on the tile floor in the living room, then grabbed Sean's hand and pulled him into the bedroom. They made out like teenagers before he slowly undid her jeans and reached inside, not even bothering to tug them down her legs. She writhed against his hand, letting him get her close before she reached for him.

Two could play the hand job game.

He was hot and hard in her hand, his shaft heavy as she stroked him.

"Tighter," he urged her. "God, you feel good. Come on, come for me…"

She squeezed her hand and held on tight as he pumped his hips, rocking into her fist as she rode his hand, and when she came, fast and furiously, he rolled onto his back. She followed, watching as he covered her hand with his and changed the pace. Her eyes gobbled up all the details she'd missed the night before. The veins that stood out in stark relief from his washboard abs. The paler skin across his hips that didn't see much sun.

He was impossibly good looking, and all hers, in this gorgeous apartment in the South of Spain. She wouldn't pinch herself, not ever, because this was almost certainly a magical dream.

All the muscles in his body tensed up as he neared his climax, and his face twisted in concentration, then abandon. She sat back on her heels as his legs twitched on either side of her. He laughed. "Damn, that was good."

She should get him a washcloth. She would. In a minute. Right now, she was taking him all in. "So good," she whispered, and when he caught her gaze, something heavy tugged between them.

So very, very good.

———

JENNA FELT Sean get up the next morning, was vaguely aware of him kissing her gently and whispering that she should stay asleep.

He was going for a run, he said, and the idea of that was so crazy she blissfully went back to slumberland.

When she woke a second time, the room was bright and the street below sounded busy. She crawled out from under the crisp white sheet and blushed as she remembered what they'd done the night before, both before and after a late, simple dinner.

And what they hadn't, yet...but would soon.

Sean Foster was definitely a man to have sex with. Repeatedly. Twelve days in a row, in fact.

There was a note stuck to the mirror in the bathroom.

YOU'RE **extra cute when comatose. Went for a run. Feel free to go find breakfast without me if you wake up hungry.**

RIGHT ON CUE, her stomach growled. She quickly showered, then loosely braided her hair and pulled on clothes. She sent him a quick text that she was awake, had read his note, and would text again when she'd found a cafe.

The restaurant on the corner where they ate the night before wasn't open yet, so she hung a left and descended the narrow street. It didn't take long to find a cafe in the centre of the old town. She texted Sean the address and he replied that he'd meet her there in fifteen minutes.

Instead of getting a table right away, she ducked into a discount shop across the way that had sundresses hanging in the window. Ten euros each, the sign promised, and since Jenna didn't have anything other than jeans and t-shirts, that sounded perfect.

Ten minutes later, she emerged with a shopping bag.

"What did you buy?"

She whirled around and found Sean sauntering toward

her, freshly showered. He'd changed into cargo pants and a white t-shirt that stretched across his chest enticingly. Her heart fluttered in her chest as the sun caught some blond highlights in his hair. "A dress," she said breathlessly. "Well, two dresses, because I couldn't decide. And I thought…dinner here seems a bit fancier than jeans and a t-shirt…"

He grinned. "I like your clothes. But if you want to ask me out to a fancy dinner, I won't object."

She laughed and gestured to the cafe. "Speaking of asking you out, can I buy you breakfast?"

He rubbed his flat stomach, the shirt catching a bit as he moved his hand. She tried and failed not to lose her attention to that slice of skin he revealed. "I'm starving," he said, and she knew the feeling.

She was famished, suddenly, and not just for food. She wanted to drag Sean back to their apartment and feast on his body. Lick the ridges of his abs and then lower, exploring him again with her mouth before—

"Jenna," he growled, and she guiltily jerked her gaze back up to his face. His expression was serious now, hooded and hot. "Don't look at me like that if you want breakfast."

"Breakfast might be optional," she whispered, heat swirling through her torso.

He reached for her, tugging her close—and then closer still, until she was plastered against him. "Maybe we just didn't say good morning properly," he whispered as he brushed his lips against hers.

If he thought a kiss would quench her thirst for more of him, naked and at her bidding, she was going to—

Go along for the ride. All it took was one teasing touch of his tongue, a barely-there lick to the soft swell of her lips, and she was all in. "Good morning, Captain Foster," she breathed as he kissed the corner of her mouth before returning front and centre.

He sank into her, his lips electric against hers, sending sparks of awareness shooting through her body as he kissed her with everything he had. It was a kiss to make her blush, to turn her on, but also a kiss big enough to satisfy her cravings for now.

A main course kind of kiss.

Like he saw that she was hungry for him and he knew just how to fill her up—and buy enough time that they could eat actual food, because she might be able to survive on kisses and orgasms, but he couldn't after a run.

He kissed her mouth one last time then brushed his lips against the tip of her nose. "Breakfast."

She nodded. "Right."

"Then sightseeing."

Hadn't they done enough of that yesterday?

He grinned, wicked and cool. "And *then* siesta."

Oh, the Spanish had it right. "My favourite part of the day."

He led her into the cafe, where they had coffee and toast. Jenna went with the most basic version, thick, crusty Spanish bread drizzled with olive oil. Sean had his with crushed tomato and ham, which looked so good, Jenna ordered a second plate to go with their second round of coffee.

Then they set out for a long walk around the old town, hand in hand.

They talked about everything and nothing. Sean bought postcards for his brothers. "They'll give me shit if I don't, so it's good to get it out of the way."

"Are you close?"

"Yeah." Sean paid the clerk then led her out of the store as he expanded on that answer. "Dean's the oldest, and there are ten years between us."

"You're the youngest?"

He nodded. "So I was only eight when he left for college, but as soon as he finished his police training, he came back. Jake never left Pine Harbour, except for an Army tour a few years ago. And by the time Matt left for college, I was nearly grown and giving Dean and Jake a headache more than anything. I was a shitty teenager."

"Aren't we all?"

"Maybe. My two oldest brothers were practically born boring adults, so they don't see it that way."

She laughed. "So far you don't sound really close."

"It's a deep bond that defies reason." A fond smile twisted over his face.

"That sounds really nice, actually."

He laughed and nodded. "It is. What's your deal with your sister?"

"We get along better now that we're both adults. The first time she texted me to say, *whoa, is Mom always this controlling?* I knew we were good. But there's such a big age difference between us that we were always at a different developmental stage growing up."

"And is your Mom always that controlling?"

"More concerned than controlling, but to a sixteen-year-old, it's one and the same." Jenna sighed. "Annie's twenty-one now."

"And your mom…"

"Still worries about *me*, so I think Annie's got a little ways to go yet."

She changed the subject as they climbed the narrow, twisting streets to the top of the hill. Sean knew a lot about the Moorish history of southern Spain, and took a lot of pictures of the architecture.

She took a lot of pictures of Sean. She couldn't help it. He was beautiful.

When they reached the castle and church that soared above the town, in the Plaza Del Cabildo, he took her phone. They pressed their cheeks together and Sean stretched out his arm, taking a picture of them together with the buildings in the background. And when she led him out onto the terrace at the edge of the plaza that had an even more breathtaking view of the valley below the town, he wrapped his arms around her waist and hugged her tight against him.

"Which way is Gibraltar?" she asked, holding out her hand.

He slid his arm along hers and adjusted her angle. "That way."

"Do you know as much about it as you do about the Moors?"

He chuckled in her ear. "Maybe even more."

"Is a day going to be enough time there?" She twisted and kissed his cheek. "I didn't realize how much you were going to geek out on this history stuff. We could spend more time there if you'd like."

"What do you want to do?"

"Have hot showers and sleep through the night." She turned back to the amazing view. "And see more things like this."

"Then we'll do exactly that."

———

AFTER THE SIMPLE BREAKFAST, Jenna was in the mood

for a big Spanish lunch of shared plates, and as they looped back toward their place, they stumbled across the perfect restaurant.

"Do you like tapas?"

"I don't know that I've ever had it."

"It's just shared plates. Little bit of this, little bit of that."

"Whatever you want to get is fine. Food is fuel," he said with a shrug. "But I like good fuel."

She poured over the menu posted on the wall. "I want to try it all."

"Then let's get everything. If we don't finish, that's okay. Do you think they do doggie bags?"

She giggled. "No. And I don't want to be wasteful."

"We're on vacation. Live a little."

"I'm living plenty already." She rolled her lower lip between her teeth as she tried to make a choice. Nope, she couldn't do it, too hard. "I'll let the chef pick, maybe?"

"Sounds good."

They moved into the patio, and they were quickly seated by a waiter who took their drink orders, then left them to peruse copies of the menu they'd looked at outside.

Sean frowned and dug his phone out of his pocket. "Sorry. It won't stop vibrating."

The waiter returned as Sean scrolled through his messages. She slowly explained what she wanted—"We would like six or eight dishes. Chef's choice. Whatever goes together, okay?"—and he repeated that back with a beaming smile.

When she looked back at Sean, his face was twisted in a weird expression.

"What's wrong?"

"Nothing." He laughed. "There's a picture of me playing hockey with the prime minister. Now that he's returned to Canada, the publication embargo has been lifted and the stories are flooding the papers. I'm anonymous in the picture, but my family is having a field day in my text messages."

"Show me!"

He handed over his phone. "If you scroll through that article, there are some pictures of you too. Feels like a lifetime ago already."

"My mom will get a kick out of that." She flicked her gaze up to his face. "Can you forward this to me so I don't have to search for it?"

"Sure."

She handed the phone back and he tapped out a quick message. Her own phone vibrated in her pocket as their first small plates to share were delivered to the table.

She smiled. "I'll send it after we eat. Tell me more about your running. You take it seriously. And you said it was more than a hobby."

"Did I?"

She laughed. "Yes. In Urfa."

"Good memory." Sean leaned in and watched as she served him a bit of everything. He pointed to a piece of meat. "What do you think that is?"

She shook her head. "No idea." She popped a piece into her mouth. "Mmm." She swallowed and smiled. "It's delicious. Try some."

He laughed and took a bite. "It is good. Wow."

They cleared the first round of plates and then she leaned back in her chair.

"Do you run marathons? I've run a 10k race a couple of

times, but I'm always impressed by people who can run for hours."

His eyes lit up. "I wouldn't want to miss an opportunity to impress you."

"So that's a yes?"

He grinned. "A marathon is a light run for me."

"Shut up."

"Okay, that's an exaggeration. But yes, I run marathons. A bunch of them a year. And longer distances, too. It's actually something I do semi-professionally."

"For real? Is that your job?"

"It's one of my jobs." He leaned back and took a slow sip of his beer. "It just sort of happened. I'm fast. I always have been. I went to provincials every year in high school. I used to joke that it came from having three older brothers chase me. I had to get fast enough to out sprint them. But really, something happened in university. I ran my first marathon, and I realized… I could have kept going. Others hit a wall somewhere around three hours of cardiac exertion."

"But you don't?" She couldn't imagine what that was like.

"I do, but I push through it. Every time I hit a wall, I bust on through, and I get a second wind on the other side. And I like the science of fuelling my body on the go." He shrugged. "That dovetailed with my military career, and suddenly a whole new world of competition opened up. Races that had pretty significant purses attached to them. Some low-level sponsorship stuff. It all adds up to a decent part-time job, and with the Army reserves, I keep busy."

"Do any of your brothers run?"

"Only with me for training. None of them are competitive in the same way. They're more career-oriented."

"What do they do?"

"Dean's a security consultant now. He was a cop for a long time. Jake's got his own construction business. Matt's a paramedic. They're all in the military, too, but I'm the only officer." He snorted. "It's ironic, really."

"How so?"

Tension flashed across his face for a beat. "That's a story for another time."

More food arrived then, and it was a good distraction. Sean was so open about everything—for him to shut down like that had to be for a good reason. And while she was curious about every part of him, she had to respect his boundaries.

Some limits would be good, she told herself. It was dangerous how much of this man she wanted to consume. His history, his likes and dislikes, his family details.

She pointed at his plate. "That's octopus, I think. It's delicious."

He didn't miss a beat. He speared the morsel with his fork and popped it in his mouth. His eyes lit up and he slowly chewed and swallowed.

She could watch him eat for hours, and hopefully would.

The second plate in this next round was eggplant. It wasn't her favourite food, but it was done perfectly, and they cleaned that off, too.

The third plate made Sean laugh. "Those are hash browns."

"But they're Spanish hash browns." She grinned. "Fried potato is universal."

"It is." He took a bite, then leaned in and gave her a curious look. Her turn to be on the hot seat. "Are you going to tell your mother you know the soldier playing hockey with the prime minister?"

Her fork froze in mid-air. Slowly she set it down. "Uh...."

He waved his hand. "You don't need to answer that."

"No..." She took a deep breath. "It's not because of you. My mom and I have a complicated relationship. She'll be thrilled I met the prime minister, but also obsessed with how I can leverage that into something important. Something to..." She winced and made air quotes. "Take me to the next level."

"Are there levels of midwifery?"

She laughed. "Not like that. It's just...Probably one of the reasons I went into health care was because it's exactly the opposite of the type of career my mother dreamed of for me."

Sean pulled a face as he reached for his beer. "Parents. Ironically, my story for another time is the same thing. Well, the opposite thing." He took a long slug. "My father is—was—an officer. And we don't see eye-to-eye on anything. So it's a big, weird thing in our family that I went that path. He sees it as following in his footsteps."

"And it's not?"

"Fuck no. I just like being in charge."

She probably shouldn't find that sexy, but with all the chemistry sizzling between them, it was impossible not to. "In all ways?"

He grinned, right there with her. "Not with you. Not unless you wanted to play that way."

She shrugged. "I could be convinced it might be fun."

He lowered his voice as his smile grew. "That wasn't what I meant. When it comes to sex, I'm usually pretty laid back."

"Usually?"

"With you, everything is different." He held her gaze as he said it, and her chest grew hot.

More plates of food arrived, but something had shifted. Everything was different with Sean too.

And she was totally ready for their seista, thank you very much.

AS SOON AS the door of the apartment closed behind them, they were all over each other. Shirts off, mouths together.

It was hard to grin and kiss at the same time, but somehow Sean made it work.

"Let me see you."

He turned her around, carefully, reverently, his hands never leaving her body as he unzipped her jeans. She wriggled out of them and then his hands returned to her hips to tug down her panties. His mouth dropped to her shoulder, her neck, his breath hot against the spot behind her ear. He wove his fingers through her hair and twisted it out of the way so he could lick the top of her spine.

Having all of his attention was heady and intoxicating.

So too was feeling the press of his erection against her, feeling the urgency in his touch, even as he took his time stroking and caressing her body.

This man wanted her on a whole different level.

She took his hands in hers and tugged him toward the bed. Seduction and play could happen another time. Later, after dinner. Tomorrow, when they woke up.

Right now, she wanted something simpler, more elemental.

She wanted Sean inside her.

He had a condom already. He pressed the foil into her hand as he kissed down her body, and she ripped it open as he went down on her.

"Sean. Now." But it came out as more of a plea than a command.

He rose above her, gloriously hard and sculpted, and she rolled the condom down his length before pulling them together. He followed, bracing one hand beside her head as he spread his legs wide, his knees planted on the bed. Her own legs rode high on his hips as she rubbed him against her clit, then lower.

She loved the way his eyelids fluttered at the first tantalizing feel of his erection against her entrance. Yes. Oh, God, yes. That was…so good.

He let her play, stroking him up against her sex, then back down to where she was slippery and ready. His cock pulsed in her hand, but he held himself still and just watched as she rubbed against him. She watched, too, her breath catching with each jolt of feeling. Spark, fire, gasp, repeat.

"Look at you," he whispered, smiling in a lazy, feral way as he held himself above her. "That feel good? Sure looks good. Feels damn sweet to me, too."

"I want you so much," she breathed.

"Then take me."

She rolled her hips, bringing them together again, and this time, she wasn't teasing. This time she let go, and he pushed inside, stretching her with a steady, sure thrust.

Crying out, she arched her body at the perfect intrusion. Yes, yes. She breathed his name and he did it again, filling up space inside her she hadn't known to be achingly empty. Now she knew, though. Now a brand-new need clawed at her. For him to push again, to stretch and fill and *be* inside her. "Slow," she pleaded, wanting him to stay there when he was as deep as he could go.

"Like this?" He stroked down her body and hooked his arm over her hip, spreading his hand wide across the curve of her bottom. He lifted her up as he pumped his hips then held them together before repeating the delicious motion.

"Yes." She pushed her arms up above her head, finding the headboard to get some leverage. "Just like that." The words felt weak, not big enough to describe just how good, how right it felt.

When the headboard wasn't giving her what she needed, she twisted her hands to grip the pillow, but that wasn't… "Fuck." She flailed her arms out, needing to ground herself on something.

"Shhh…" Sean caught her hands with his and laced their fingers together, pressing her fists into the mattress as he moved over her. "Hold on to me."

Her heart wobbled and caught against her rib cage as she pulled against his hands. Yes, again, yes. He grinned down at her and she wrapped her legs tighter around his waist. His gaze darkened, turned molten, and she flexed around him, inside and out. She held on tight.

"I want you to come, Jenna." Those dark eyes pierced right through her as he surged forward. "Let go and let me make you feel good. Or use me and make yourself feel good. God, you're so gorgeous right now. I want to see you come apart. Gimme that secret, angel."

She could feel her eyes go wide, but his dirty sweet words did the trick. The tightness that had bound her in a restless, panicky energy started to dissolve in the face of her mounting pleasure. "You, too," she breathed. "With me."

"Want to make this last," he said, his voice husky.

Oh, the idea that he craved more of her tugged in all the right places.

"Slow…next time—" Her words caught as he shifted his angle, nudging a new spot deep inside her that set off technicolour explosions in her brain. More, yes, there.

And suddenly it was too much to look up at him. His hot, hungry gaze burned her skin. She twisted her face and tugged her hands free. "Turn me over. I want… from behind."

He dropped his face into the curve of her neck and groaned. "God, yes." He slapped her hip lightly and she flipped herself over as he slipped out of her.

Shameless, she dropped to all fours and pushed back against him, desperate to have him fill her again. Aching for that sweet stretch, and eager to feel it like this. Deeper and harder.

Less intimate and more instinctive.

But it wasn't any less intimate when his hands covered her hips, hot and wide and strong, and tugged her up. He revealed her completely, pressing her shoulders down to the bed before thrusting into her again. She shouted from how good it felt, and he growled at her.

"Whatever you want, Jenna. However you want it. Tell me and I'll make it yours."

"You," she panted. "Just you. Like this. So good."

He slammed into her.

Her need was coiling now, twisting tight. Her legs started to shake and she reached for her clit, but he was already there, his fingers pressing on either side. Just enough pressure to drive her insane without tripping over the live wire that was her out-of-reach orgasm.

"More…"

"More what?"

Everything.

She licked her lips and shook her head, trying to think straight. She flexed her fingers, and Sean leaned into her, over her, pressing her down. Once again, he linked their fingers together, their left hands pressed against the pillow together now. His other hand wrapped around her and pressed against her clit, and as he buried himself inside her again, she came in a spectacular, shuddering climax that took her by surprise.

"Oh…" It was all she could say, her voice stolen by pleasure and other more deceptively simple feelings she didn't want to explore.

Like how good it felt when Sean held her hand during sex.

How crazy, out-of-this-world good that felt.

He rolled away from her for a few seconds. She glanced down when he rolled back. Condom gone, taken care of. "Did you…"

He kissed her so softly it cracked her chest. "Yes, I came. Hard, and deep inside you. Best fucking feeling in the world."

"I didn't notice." She was out of breath and out of complex thoughts, too.

He chuckled and folded her into his side.

What the hell had just happened?

They'd fooled around repeatedly. Blow jobs, hand jobs, all the jobs… And it had been awesome. Sexy good times fun.

But none of it had prepared her for having him inside her.

She needed to be careful and remember what it was they were doing—and what they weren't.

Two weeks of magic. Two weeks of sex and friendship.

Then it was back to reality and no more dreaming.

CHAPTER ELEVEN

THE NEXT FEW days sped by in a blur of food and laughter and sweet, dirty sex. For the first time in a long time, Sean was a ridiculously happy man.

Some afternoons, they even used the siesta to have a real, honest-to-God nap. They explored the younger vibe in the new town, and stayed out late dancing a lot and drinking a little.

Jenna kept plying him with new and interesting foods, and he dragged himself out of bed most mornings to get a long run in before she woke up.

A few times he skipped the run, though, because she was soft and sweet to laze next to in bed.

The day they were planning to go to Gibraltar was one of those days when he just couldn't pull himself away from her, so he let himself drift, not really asleep but in a warm, muzzy state, until she stirred.

She made the best pleased noise when she realized he was there.

"I could get used to waking up like this," she said, her

words soft and only half-awake. "I've never in my life slept so well, or so long."

"It's easy to impress someone who hasn't slept through the night in four months."

She smiled and burrowed tighter against him. "True. But this is still the best feeling in the world."

Yeah, it really was.

He liked his space, he liked his quiet.

But Jenna didn't crowd him, she complemented him. She gave him something to hold on to. She grounded him.

It had only been a week, and he already knew he was going to miss her like hell.

"It's been a long time since I've slept next to someone other than the guy in the next cot. You are a definite upgrade in that regard."

"Same. Well, not army guys. But it's been a long time."

Up until now, they hadn't talked about their past relationships. It was as if they had an unspoken agreement that doing so might unmask *this* for a relationship, and given what they were both heading back to, that felt…complicated.

He also knew he'd burn with an unfamiliar jealousy if he heard about some other guy sharing Jenna's bed, even if it was in the past. Because other guys could do this with her again, and he couldn't.

They only had two weeks together, and one had already sped by.

He hugged her closer, and she twisted in his arms. They'd started sleeping naked, with a bowl of condoms handy. But she wasn't reaching for his half-erect cock. Instead, she walked her fingers up his chest as she looked at him, curiosity all over her face.

Ah, shit. He grinned at her. "You want to ask more about this, don't you?"

"I admit I'm curious. You're an interesting guy. Hot, kind, funny. Quite talented in the sack." She winked at him. "How come it's been so long?"

He took a deep breath. "Life? Work, mostly. Not a lot of women are interested in being third on a list of priorities. Nor should they be."

"Damn." She leaned in and kissed his jaw, her lips catching on his overnight stubble. "I knew there had to be a catch. Because otherwise, you're totally perfect."

He nipped the end of her nose with his teeth. "Definitely not that. Anyway, I wasn't thinking about a woman when I said that. I was thinking about sharing beds with my brothers, and how grateful I was when I finally got my own room."

"Tell me about that."

He'd rather make her scream his name, but the way she asked, he could hardly refuse. "My father has a big, rambling house. But four boys in three rooms meant I shared with my brother Matt. He's two years older than me, and..." It was hard to explain. He cracked his jaw before continuing. "I had nightmares when I was really young, and my oldest brother would be the one who'd come to me. So when I got big enough, if I woke up scared, I'd just go to Dean. I'd wake him up by kicking him. In hindsight, I don't know why he put up with a preschooler crashing his bed every night. He would have only been about fourteen."

"Why didn't you go to your parents?"

"My mom died when I was two. I don't remember her."

"Oh." The shock in her voice sliced against his skin. "I'm sorry."

"It is what it is."

She swallowed, and he imagined she was shoving down the next question. *What about your father?* Yeah, that was a good one. And way too loaded for this morning, although he would tell her, in time. He'd tell her every-thing, because opening up like that with Jenna hadn't felt bad at all.

She kissed his jaw, then his neck, nestling close, and he squeezed his arms around her. It had felt damn good, actually.

"What should we do today on our way to Gibraltar?" she asked quietly.

"Find a sherry bodega and get tipsy. Sleep it off under an orange tree." He rolled her onto her stomach and kissed his way down her spine, until his breath brushed the tops of her hips, and she rocked up against him.

———

THEY ARRIVED in Gibraltar mid-afternoon and checked into their hotel for the night. Instead of cramming it all into a day trip, they were going to stay the night, tour the Rock in the morning then head back to Arcos in time for a late dinner.

He'd wanted to cram so much into this trip when he'd first planned it, but now that it was under way—now that he was doing it with Jenna—he was enjoying the slower pace. Maybe next time he'd do the rock climbing and wind sailing he'd originally planned.

Although maybe next time she'd be on this side of the

pond, too, and he'd want to do more lazing in bed again. So far, that had proven to be his best vacation idea ever.

"Do you think you'll sign up for another rotation through a camp?" he asked Jenna as they sipped coffee at a cafe in town.

She nodded. "I think so. If you'd asked me when we first met, I'd have said maybe I couldn't hack it. But this trip has done wonders for my spirit. And there's always a need for trained medical staff. That's hard to ignore. Next time, I'll go into it with the experience from this time, and I'll plan for a break like this in the middle." Her lips curved into a brilliant smile and her eyes softened. "Not that this, or you, can be replicated."

Damn straight. "I was just wondering if maybe it could. If when you signed up for another contract with Doctors Without Borders, I might be on this side of the pond at the same time."

"That would be something, wouldn't it?" Her eyes unfocused and he wondered if she was thinking about some distant point in the future where they might hook up again.

Except, it didn't have to be that distant.

"It'd be great to stay in touch before that. We'll be heading back to Canada around the same time, I think."

She nodded. "I'm back in June, for sure."

"I'll come out west and visit you."

Her eyes widened and refocused on him. "Oh." A myriad of emotions played in her expression as she schooled her face. "Okay…"

That wasn't the reaction he'd been hoping for. He cleared his throat. "That doesn't sound like a good okay."

"Just surprised, that's all." She licked her lips. "I was thinking that we were focused on this trip. And afterwards, we'd go back to…" She gestured east. "All the things that consume every moment of every day. Being an officer and a midwife on the edge of a war zone."

Ah. She didn't want any distractions.

She didn't want him, and his promises of future hook-ups, to distract her from the thing she'd worked so hard towards. He could appreciate that. Her hard work, sacrifice, and determination were big parts of what he found so attractive about her. So he'd be an ass if he tried to persuade her to focus on him instead.

The temptation to be a selfish ass was strong.

He tamped it down. "That's fair."

She gave him a warm smile. "I like the idea of doing this again, though."

As long as it was a theoretical fantasy and not an actual plan. He nodded. "Me too."

And if he was disappointed, if his stomach twisted at the thought of saying goodbye in the Urfa airport and not knowing when he'd see her next, that was a problem of his own making.

The next morning, they were the first people on the cable car to the top of the giant rock that gave Gibraltar its unique purpose and identity, and they spent hours exploring the caves and tunnels. There was a display dedicated to the Canadian engineers who helped dig the tunnels during the Second World War, and they took turns taking pictures with the sign pointing toward Ottawa.

"Would you like a picture together?" asked a British tourist, and Jenna handed over her phone with a shy smile.

Sean wrapped his arm around her waist and held her tight as they said cheese. "Send that one to me," he said after they said thank you and continued along their way.

Over the last week they'd exchanged dozens of texts and pictures as they each compiled a record of their trip together. Another reminder that once they said goodbye, they'd be going their separate ways.

But he could still reach out. As a friend, if nothing else. Say hi; find out how she was doing.

She might not know now that was a good idea. But walking away? That wouldn't work, either. He knew it deep down. He may not have been in Jenna's master plan, but plans could change. He wanted to be around if she decided she was ready for something more complicated than a vacation fling.

Back at the base of the rock, they found their car and drove back across the border into Spain. It was a warmer day than they'd had to date, so they rolled down the windows and put on their sunglasses. Sean told Jenna to find him a scenic drive back, and she sent him through the hills again while they traded stories about the stupid shit they'd done when they were younger.

"I was a bit of a shithead, to be honest. Sullen and angry, full of hormones. Running was good for me." He slowed down as he crested the top of a ridge, shifting gears as he started the slither down again into a valley. "So was the military, although it took me a few years to get my head on straight and focused on getting overseas."

"That was a big moment for me, too," she said. "Realizing that I could work with an NGO. I knew I'd need at least five years of work experience, with immigrant communities, too. So when I graduated, I got serious about finding a practice that would give me that. And I loved it."

"That was in Vancouver?"

She nodded. "I did a placement in a rural practice my

second year, which I loved, too. But the urban setting was important for the multicultural experience."

"Where was the rural placement?" He was so curious about everything she'd done, everywhere she'd gone. He wanted to greedily soak up all the details of her life, so when he headed back to Iraq, he'd have this fully formed memory of her, layered with so much more than just their heady attraction and combustible chemistry.

"Vancouver Island, so not that far afield." She pulled out her phone and took a picture of the view out the front window, then a picture of him. "You look good behind the wheel."

"I like driving. I haven't done it for a few months. I miss my truck."

"Of course you have a truck," she teased him.

"Have you ever made out in one? They beat a car, hands down."

"Can't say I have."

One day he'd show her. One day he'd make her moan his name in the cab of his truck, and all would be right with the world.

She took another picture, then leaned back in her seat and started flipping through stuff on her phone. When she groaned, he knew she'd gotten another email from her mother.

He couldn't quite sort out their relationship. It wasn't as antagonist as his deal with the Colonel. Sometimes Jenna talked about her mother with awe, and other times she had to grit her teeth before replying to an email.

Today it was the latter.

He must have glanced over enough times that she knew he knew what she was reading. She sighed and rolled her head back. "My mom is blowing up my phone again about the PM photos. 'There's a real opportunity here,' she keeps saying. No, Mom, there isn't. Stop chasing rainbows. I swear, if I ever have kids, I'm not going to pressure them to do anything with their lives. If they want to be beach bums, that's totally fine by me."

He could picture her on a beach, teaching a kid how to surf. Golden brown hair whipping in the wind, beaming, proud grin when they figured out how to jump up from a crouch. "Those would be lucky kids."

She laughed. "Well, we'll see. Lots of adventuring still to do, first."

"So your biological clock didn't start ticking when you crossed thirty?"

She shot him an amused look, one eyebrow curving high. "No."

"Back home, everyone is having babies." He didn't know why he was sharing that. "I'm an uncle now. Officially. I was one unofficially last year…" He found himself telling her about Rafe and Olivia Minelli, and their daughter. About Dani and his brother Jake, and how he hadn't yet met his little nephew in person, but he'd seen lots of pictures. "I spoiled the shit out of him at Christmas. Thank God for online shopping."

"Is *your* biological clock ticking?" She asked with a sweet laugh. No judgement, just poking at each other's secrets.

He was surprised to find himself not thinking no, but instead, not yet. Maybe.

Maybe he could see himself teaching a kid to surf.

———

WHEN THEY GOT BACK to Arcos, they had a nap that

was seventy-five percent rest, twenty-five percent arousing snuggles. Sean kept drawing lazy circles on her side, and finally Jenna rolled onto her back and pushed his hand between her legs. He followed with his mouth, and once she got off, he rose above her and stroked himself until he came in messy spurts across her naked torso.

Then he cleaned her up, and they actually fell asleep for a bit.

Jenna was going to miss siestas so much.

She glanced from his face to where his fingers tangled around hers. His already tan skin had darkened over the last week. Had it only been that long? Every inch of his body was now familiar to her. Every expression.

Was it only yesterday that she told him they shouldn't talk about what came next for them? She was kidding herself if she thought she wouldn't think of him every day they were apart.

They would write. He'd said they had wifi on his base. She'd email him and when he could, he'd email back.

And then he'd come and visit her. She could play coy all she wanted, there was no denying she'd be counting the days until that reunion.

Once it was dark, they got dressed up and headed to a restaurant they'd already visited twice before. The waiter recognized them and welcomed them with a big smile, arms wide. "You weren't here yesterday!"

"We went to Gibraltar," Sean said as they sat at what she'd started to think of as their table.

"Ah yes. You had said that. We missed you, but you had good weather for it. Can I get you drinks?"

Sean looked at her, and Jenna shrugged. "Beer? Wine?"

They'd mostly stuck to beer, because Sean only liked to

have one drink most nights, but tonight he grinned. "Let's do a bottle of wine. Do you want white or red?"

They settled on a bottle of Spanish red that the waiter said would complement what was coming out of the kitchen tonight. He set two glasses on the table before uncorking the bottle. "Did you see any weddings when you were there?" he asked as he poured them each a small amount to taste.

"In Gibraltar?" Sean handed her the first glass, then lifted his own.

"Yes, yes. It is known for… how do you call it? The shotgun wedding."

Jenna blinked at him in surprise. "Really?"

"Indeed. They have the easiest rules in all of Europe. Here, there are so many rules. Waiting time, translations. So people go to Gibraltar and it is done in a day."

"It's that quick, eh?" Sean tipped back his glass and she watched his throat work. His eyelids hooded his gaze as he lazily picked up Jenna's hand. "Something to think about."

Energy zinged up her arm.

When she lifted her gaze to his face, the look was one she'd learned intimately. Yearning. She swallowed hard and squeezed his hand.

She felt it, too. Big feelings. She could see Sean being the one, which surprised her. But it didn't scare her, and that was surprising, too.

Her stomach flip-flopped hard.

"Too bad," she offered, her voice low and husky. "Missed opportunity, maybe."

Sean made her feel things she'd never experienced before. Nothing like the puppy love of her first adoration in high school, or the safe affection of her relationships since.

She thought falling in love would feel like a tumble down a cliff, something scary and big, the fall taking some time. Bumpy, maybe. Terrifying, definitely.

Who knew it could be simple and quiet, like a drop of water in a still pond?

Plink.

———

SHE DIDN'T TELL him that night. She showed him, though. She loved him so thoroughly they fell asleep in a pile, all arms and legs and full hearts.

And in the morning, she woke before him for the first time and just watched him, her Adonis at rest. Had she fallen in love with him because he was beautiful?

Maybe a little. There was no denying the physical attraction. She traced her finger, feather light, along the straight line of his nose, then over his perfect lips.

He blinked his eyes open.

"Sorry," she whispered. "I woke you."

"It's okay." He gave her a crooked, sleepy smile. "I never do this. Sleep in."

"We could stay in bed all day. Isn't this the best?"

"You're the best."

"You're just saying that because you want to get lucky."

"I'm already lucky. I woke up beside you, didn't I?"

She didn't tell him then, either, although the words almost slipped out on their own.

They got up and went for a long walk. Their hands just slid together now, Sean's fingers wrapping around hers.

They stopped at an open-air market and he bought her a tiny wooden box. "To put your secrets in when I'm not around," he said as he flipped the lid up and down.

She hadn't shared with him as much on this trip as he had with her. She didn't have that many secrets, really. But she'd share anything with Sean.

Her heart swelled, and again she thought, *I've so fallen for you.* There was a secret she could give him, since he seemed so hungry to know her, inside and out.

And yet something still held her back from saying it out loud because it was way too soon.

"I should get you something," she said as they wandered through the stalls.

"So you admit you want me to remember you," he teased.

Her heart tripped over his words. "Yes."

"Can I ask again about visiting you?"

She nodded. "Yes."

"Okay." He grinned, and she laughed.

"Aren't you going to ask?"

"No, you shot me down last time. I'm going to wait until you're feeling all soft and mushy towards me, and use that to my advantage."

She blushed. "That's all the time."

"Really?" His eyes lit up and he pulled her close. "Lucky me."

She wondered if he'd bring it up again. She waited for it all day, her secret growing inside her. *I've fallen for you.*

He waited until they were reading in bed that evening. "So..."

She grinned and closed her book. "Yes?"

"In the summer, I might be out west. If I were to look you up..."

"I don't want to wait until the summer," she said, surprising both of them with her candour. She sat up and took a deep breath. "I know I said things, but I was wrong. I...you..."

He took her hand and waited.

"If you want to stay in touch, I want that." Her heart squeezed. Fortune favoured the bold. "Actually, I want more than that, but we can take things slow."

"Slow has never been my speed. I'm an all or nothing kind of guy."

She was learning that. She leaned in and touched his face, tracing the lines at the corners of his eyes and around his mouth. "Let me be the brakes to your runaway train, then."

He caught her hand and kissed the tips of her fingers. "I don't know what I did to deserve you, but God, am I ever grateful."

And just like that, she was in. All the way in, whatever he wanted.

"I love you," she whispered. "I know it's too soon, but—"

He rolled her onto her back and loomed above her, his eyes bright and his smile crooked. "Say it again."

"I love you." This time it floated on a breath.

He leaned in and kissed her, his lips light and teasing. "I love you, too," he murmured. He kissed her again, then his smile grew. "Marry me."

She didn't answer him. She kissed him instead. Brakes to his runaway train.

That didn't stop him from asking again the next day. "We could go back to Gibraltar. We missed an opportunity there, you said it yourself. So let's make another chance."

Jenna smiled. "We can't just get married."

But Sean wouldn't be deterred.

And each time he brought it up, the less sure she was about her answer being no, when really, it was secretly not yet.

———

AS THE FINAL days of their vacation counted down, they started eating more meals in the apartment. It was like there was an unspoken agreement that their time together was precious, private, and to be protected.

Four more days.

A lump formed in her throat as she reached past him to stir the sautéed vegetables. Four more nights.

He ran the tap until the water was cold, then filled a glass. "You want some?"

She smiled and took it from him. "Always."

He grinned at her as she drank some of the water, then handed it back.

Always.

Could it be that simple?

He hadn't asked her yet today.

Maybe that was important, too. That he'd given her a bit of space to think about it.

Always.

"Yes," she said, and his eyebrows pulled together.

"Yes?"

"Yes." Her heart leapt at the rightness of the answer. "Yes. Let's get married."

"Really?" He hadn't asked her today. His eyes leapt, bright with excitement. "Yes?"

She nodded and he pulled her into his arms, kissing her hard before he pressed his lips to her temple. "Thank

God," he said, his voice barely above a whisper. "I was seriously starting to wonder if I'd have to kidnap you."

"We might not have enough time, though." She leaned back and gave him a stern look. "You can't be disappointed if we need to wait until we're back home."

"We can try." He caught her hand and lifted her fingertips to his mouth. "You make the impossible possible. I have faith we'll find a way."

She wasn't so sure, but they woke up early and headed back to Gibraltar. She wore one of her new sundresses, and he wore his only buttoned-down shirt, a blue Oxford, with his cargo pants and freshly polished boots.

They crossed the border just in time for the wedding registry office to open. They were given the application forms and a list of local notaries who could authenticate their ID, and told to come back before the end of the day and they'd be fit in for a quick ceremony.

"Surely it can't be that simple," Jenna whispered as they left.

Sean just grinned, and took her hand. Instead of starting down the list of notaries, he led her to a cafe, and once they'd ordered coffee, he asked the waitress which notary she'd heard good things about. Which one was the most romantic? She wasn't sure, but their conversation attracted the attention of a couple nearby, and before too long, Sean had flashed enough smiles to the locals that he had a name. A man was known to be sympathetic to soldiers in a hurry to marry their loves.

So off they went, Sean holding her hand the entire way. They had their passports and a collection of other identification. Sean's military ID card, Jenna's letter of employment.

They had a compelling story and enough euros to sway anyone not romantic enough to see they needed to do this.

Her heart squeezed tight.

They did need to do this. Before they headed back, she wanted to make a promise to Sean.

And she wanted him to make one to her.

The office was empty when they entered, but they could hear someone moving around in the back. Then an older man appeared and introduced himself as the lawyer they were looking for. He didn't look like a romantic. Jenna was suddenly seized by panic, and she wondered if she had any more cash in her purse she could shove across the counter as Sean did his slick introduction.

"We're hoping you can help us. We want to get married, but we're tight on time." He set his passport on the counter, with his ID card on top of it. "I'm a soldier, and I'm leaving in two days." He shifted his hand, and Jenna saw the neatly folded stack of bills under the passport. "If there is any way you can help us…"

The lawyer glanced at Jenna, then back to Sean. He picked up the passport and ID. "You are Canadian?"

"We both are," Jenna said, handing over her own passport. "We met here in Europe."

"Are you staying in Gibraltar?"

They both nodded. They'd booked a hotel room again for that night. She held her breath, but he didn't ask any more questions.

He looked at Sean's passport, then Jenna's. Back and forth. Finally, he nodded. "I can help you. Come back in one hour, and I'll have your documentation notarized. In the meantime, you can search the streets for your two witnesses." He also named a fee higher than the bribe Sean had already paid, and Jenna was quite certain it was significantly higher than the stated rate for document notarization, but she didn't care.

"Thank you," she breathed.

Sean extended his hand. "Thank you so much, sir. We greatly appreciate it."

Back outside, Sean swung her around in a circle and kissed her twice before putting her down again. "Let's go find you a bouquet."

She laughed. "He said witnesses, not flowers."

"And a ring," he continued, undaunted. He took her hand and headed down the street. "There was a jewellery shop I saw when we were here before."

"Sean," she tugged on his arm. "I don't need a bouquet, or a ring. Let's just find some witnesses and call it good enough."

He let her slow him down, but only so he could sweep his arm around her waist and kiss her temple. "Good enough is not acceptable."

"I think it is when your wedding is planned in a few hours."

He just grinned and waved ahead at the shopping street. "Let's see what we can find."

Because he had a golden horseshoe up his butt, there were both a jewelry shop and a florist in close proximity. They hit the florist first, who agreed to make a small bouquet.

"We'll be back in fifteen minutes," Sean said as Jenna paid the clerk. "And if you'd like to come to our wedding, we'd be honoured."

He made the same invitation at the jewellers, where they bought simple matching white gold bands. Sean had to choose between a band that was too big or one that was too small, but Jenna's was almost a perfect fit. The jeweller started to say that he couldn't close up, but then his son arrived to work for the afternoon, and they had their first witness.

They went to the florist's again, to collect the flowers, and that clerk was free to join them, too.

So they had two witnesses, and a wedding parade, too, because the florist told everyone they passed what was happening.

By the time they returned to the registry office, documents clutched in Sean's hand, a bouquet in Jenna's, there was a small crowd with them. It felt weird. Jenna thought their wedding would be private, just the two of them—which showed she really had no clue how this worked, because she hadn't considered the witnesses.

But it was a good kind of weird. Celebratory oddness. The jeweller took Jenna's phone and promised to take excellent pictures.

Sean completed the business of receiving their license and paying the fee, then the registrar showed them into an anteroom where he performed the shortest wedding service perhaps in human history.

They started with a simple declaration, facing each other, holding hands with her bouquet resting on top.

"Are you, Sean Edward Foster, lawfully free to marry Jenna Ann Kowalczyk?"

The look of pride on Sean's face made her knees weak. "I am."

The registrar asked her the same question back. She nodded. "I am."

"Then please repeat after me…" The registrar's voice dulled to a buzz as Jenna zeroed in on Sean's mouth, and the curve of a smile.

"I, Sean Foster, take thee, Jenna Kowalczyk, to be my

wedded wife." His smile grew as he was prompted the next line. "To have and to hold, from this day forward. For better, for worse, for richer, for poorer, in sickness and in health, as long as we both shall live." She let out the breath she hadn't realized she'd been holding, and gave him a shaky smile of her own. He held her gaze for a long beat before saying the last line. "This is my solemn vow."

Tears welled up in her eyes, and she blinked them away. This was more emotional than she'd expected.

Then it was her turn.

"I, Jenna Kowalczyk, take thee, Sean Foster, to be my wedded husband. To have and to hold, from this day forward. For better, for worse, for richer, for poorer, in sickness and in health, as long as we both shall live." She squeezed his hands. "This is my solemn vow."

They quietly exchanged rings, then kissed twice, once politely and the second time a little less so—because holy hell, they'd just gotten *married*—and then they signed the wedding registry book on the desk in front of them.

And that was it.

The florist cheered. The jeweller took their picture. They shook the registrar's hand, and then they left the office, husband and wife.

CHAPTER TWELVE

May
Pine Harbour

THE NIGHT after they met in the diner, Chloe showed up with a big bag of groceries and a bigger bag of books.

Jenna led her back to the kitchen. "I'm drinking my way through the beer left behind by the Foster and Minelli men. Would you like one? We could put some of it in the stew, too."

"Fancy." Chloe unpacked the groceries. "How was your day?"

Jenna shrugged. Shitty. She'd gone over to Dean's, but Sean had been tired and obviously in pain. She'd suggested they sit outside, and he'd fallen asleep on a lounge chair, so she'd read for a bit. But when he woke up in an even worse mood—disoriented and grumpy—she accepted his broad hints and came back here. But all of that was private. "I started to pull together what I need to register with the Ontario midwifery college."

"Productive."

"Yeah." In that regard, it had been. "How about you?"

"I worked at our branch in Wiarton, hence the groceries. Pine Harbour isn't big enough to have a full-time librarian, so I'm a floater across the county system on my off days."

Jenna started cooking as Chloe told her about life on the peninsula. Once the stew was simmering, they took their beer to the deck and sat out there, talking about books and food.

They didn't talk about Sean, or his extended family, and Jenna was grateful for the gift of a normal night with a new friend.

When the stew was ready, they listened to a stand-up comedy show as they ate. Then they packed up the copious leftovers into individual containers.

"Lunch for a week at least," Chloe crowed.

"We could do this again next week." Jenna was eager for that. "This was a lot of fun."

"For sure. And if you want to just grab coffee or whatever, give me a call. I'm usually around in the evenings."

After Chloe left, Jenna wandered through the too-quiet house and turned off all the lights. Then she climbed into bed and wished again that Sean was there. That he'd been there for dinner, and she felt guilty for not having thought of him while she'd been cooking.

But it had only been three days.

Since she'd arrived, she'd lost control of her feelings a bit.

She needed a long-term plan. Needed to think further out. What was her goal for the end of the summer? Where did she want them to be by Christmas?

She'd promised him forever.

One summer was nothing in the grand scheme of things.

In Spain, he'd been ready to marry her in an instant, and she'd slowed him down. He'd been right, but she'd put the brakes on anyway. She knew all about patience, about being careful.

She'd slow down. Way down. And she'd show him that patience was more than a virtue. Patience could be a blessing and a gift.

———

ANOTHER DAY, another pounding headache.

But when Sean heard voices downstairs, his first reaction wasn't fear, and that took him by surprise.

Yesterday had been a shit show. He'd thrown up his meds the night before last, which meant he'd woken up with the full force of his nausea and vertigo in play, and he hadn't been able to stay awake. It had been a shame, really, because he'd gone to the effort to sit outside with Jenna, but when he woke up, he'd felt worse than how he'd started the day.

Last night, he made sure to take his pills slowly, and then not move around much after, all in an effort to do better today.

So yeah, he had a headache. But the rest of him felt okay. New normal okay, which was still debilitating if he thought too much about it. But he could deal.

He got himself upright then grabbed the walker, which he'd left right next to his bed. Time to get over his stubborn self.

"Morning," he hollered down the stairs.

"Morning," Jenna called back.

"I'm gonna take a quick shower."

"No rush. Liana's going to show me her studio."

Sean hadn't even seen that. It was the furthest point in the house, and frankly, the thought of walking that far made him want to go back to bed.

He sat on a temporary medical bench in the tub and turned on the water. It felt good to scrub himself down. There was something cocooning about the shower curtain and the steam. Like it gave his brain enough near points to keep itself properly oriented.

He was learning some tricks for managing the vertigo. Keeping his head pressed against something worked well. That's how he got in and out of the shower, with his head pushed into the tiles. Closing his eyes sometimes helped—but sometimes it sent him into a panicked spiral, it really just depended on the situation.

He'd learned the hard way not to dry his hair too vigorously—nothing a bruised brain likes less than being shaken around inside the skull. So he hung his towel around his neck, letting his hair drip into it, as he carefully dressed in sweatpants and a t-shirt.

Jenna came up the stairs just as he opened his door again.

"Squeaky clean?" she asked. She had a tray of food, too. "I haven't eaten yet, so I brought brunch with me."

"I don't have much of an appetite these days." Even to his own ear, his response sounded surly and sullen.

"Liana said that." She gave him a bright smile that promised she didn't care. Hope enough for the two of them was going to kill him. "What can you stomach?"

He glanced at the tray. Strawberries, cheese, fruit bread, coffee. "Yeah. That looks okay."

She pointed at the towel around his neck. "Do you want me to put that back in the bathroom?"

"No, it's collecting the drips from my hair."

"I could dry your hair for you."

"It hurts." He pointed to his head. "The jostling."

"Oh. Sorry." She bit her lip and he felt bad.

"It's just…one of the many new lessons I've learned."

"Okay." She reached for the milk and put a splash in his cup, which he'd noticed she hadn't filled all the way. So she'd noticed that his hands shook. He felt both a flare of embarrassment at that, but also a small pulse of appreciation. That was dangerous. It would be easy to slip into her caring for him, when he couldn't reciprocate.

But he could do something for her. "How would you feel about driving a truck?"

"Pardon?"

"I've got a perfectly good truck in storage. I can't drive it. You might as well return the rental and we can get it back up and working for you." He cleared his throat. He didn't want to be too kind. "Just while you're visiting."

She held his gaze. "You don't need to do that."

He lifted one shoulder. "It's stupid for you to pay for a rental when you can drive my truck free of charge."

A long silence stretched before she agreed. "Okay. Thank you."

He took the mug from her and took a long sip. It was good. "I guess I should thank you for breakfast, too."

She glanced up at him from under her eyelashes as she fixed her own coffee. "You guess?"

The corners of his mouth twitched involuntarily.

"And that was…almost a smile. Are you in…almost a good mood?" She grinned at him. "Hey there, stranger. I was wondering when I'd see you again."

"Jenna…"

She nodded. "Warning duly noted. I'm just making small talk. I thought we could play cards today."

"That sounds like a play straight out of a physiotherapy handbook."

"How about that? I noticed you don't have any physio currently on your social calendar."

"It doesn't work."

"Bit early in your rehab to say that, don't you think?"

"No." He knew his body better than the average person. He was—had been—an elite athlete, for fuck's sake. He knew what his limits were, and what training would work and what would be a colossal waste of fucking time.

She didn't argue with him again. Instead she leaned back in her chair and pulled her legs up so she could balance her plate of fruit bread on her knee as she ate and watched him.

"We never talked about cards and board games," she finally said. "What do you like?"

"No. And I don't."

She curved one eyebrow high in disbelief. "None of them? How did this not come up?"

Because his former self had better things to do than sit around and discuss card games. He could run and dance and make a woman scream. Make Jenna scream. But that was in the past now. He wanted to growl, but instead he sighed and forced himself to be less of an ass. She hadn't told him she liked card games, either. "Do you play cards?"

She shrugged. "Sure. Some. I can kick my own butt in solitaire, and hold my own in a game of Go Fish."

"I don't know if I can remember." That wasn't entirely

true. He knew the rules of Go Fish and it wouldn't be hard for him to play a hand or two.

And he knew she saw right through him. "Let's give it a try anyway."

So he moved to the edge of the couch, where he could reach the coffee table. But it was a mistake to agree to play, because every time she didn't have a card, she'd lean forward. The v-neck of her t-shirt would show him the shadow of cleavage between her high, round breasts. Heat pooled low in his belly and he found himself remembering, for the first time since the accident, what that skin had tasted like. The sounds she would make when he licked her there.

My wife.

Two words he hadn't said out loud since being back on Canadian soil. Two words he'd banned from his head, in order to keep his sanity.

"Sean?"

He cleared his throat and glanced at his cards. "Sorry, what were you asking for?"

"Do you have any jacks?"

"No. Go fish."

Another glimpse made him groan, low and painfully in his throat.

She glanced up at him, freezing with her arm outstretched. She searched his face before giving him a small smile. "Getting tired?"

"Yeah." His head was swimming, but not with fatigue.

He still wanted her. Or at least…he wanted to want her. Even as a fire burned in his chest, even as he wanted, suddenly, her skin under his tongue, her cries in his ear, even then, he got no reaction in the place where it mattered most.

His dick was broken.

"Do you want to keep playing, or should we stop?"

"I'm okay." His cards blurred in front of him. "Do you have any sevens?"

"Yep." She handed over a card, and he put the pair down.

If he couldn't get a fucking hard on over his gorgeous wife, at least he could play a mean game of Go Fish.

Fucking hell.

They finished the game, but she didn't push a second one, and he was grateful for it. He wanted to lie down and be one with his self-loathing.

She shifted around the coffee table as she tidied up the tray, and when she finished, she was standing next to him.

"Thank you for humouring me," she whispered.

"Yeah." He knew his voice was gruff, but not gruff enough. He needed to try harder, because otherwise she'd read this as a step forward when he knew better.

She was close enough he knew she wanted a hug. Pain lanced through him as he turned away, a physical manifestation of a soul-wrenching ache he didn't want to examine. He shifted his walker toward the bed. Step, lift, clunk. He didn't deserve her softness, and she didn't need any false promises.

When she left, he dragged himself through almost every night in Spain. No amount of thinking about how their bodies had twisted together got him hard.

The only day he couldn't bring himself to imagine was their wedding, and the afternoon and night that followed. He wasn't sure he could handle it if that didn't raise a reaction, so he locked that memory down.

No replaying the best day of his life, knowing he'd never get that back.

Loathing swept through him as he lay on his bed, useless and empty inside. No more cards. No more kindness.

He needed to be clearer about the fact they didn't have a future.

She could stay for a while, but he needed to redirect her focus to returning to her life. To moving on and forgetting him.

———

JENNA WASN'T sure she could try the card game trick again. Definitely not two days in a row. So the next morning, she stopped at Mac's and picked up pie—almost certain to have healing properties—and a copy of the *Toronto Star*.

She had fond memories of doing the crossword puzzle with her grandparents, and it was the same kind of brain work as playing cards.

But Sean wasn't in the mood.

He picked at the pie, and gave her monosyllabic non-answers when she tried to draw him into working on the crossword with her.

"Do you prefer numbers?" She refolded the section of the paper to show him the Sudoku puzzle instead.

He batted it away.

Shocked, she let it fall to the floor.

"Stop pushing me," he growled.

"I hardly think pie and the paper is a challenge."

"Then you're hardly thinking. It is a challenge." He swore under his breath and grabbed for the walker.

She watched, horrified, as he visibly reeled. She moved toward him and he pinned her with a glare so cold it froze her in her tracks. "Sean…"

"I told you. I'm not that guy. Go romanticize someone else's recovery, because this is my fucking life." He planted his feet and with a frustrated roar, he surged to his feet, head weaving through the air on his way to being upright.

He was right on one front. He didn't need her hovering. This was awful for him. She knew that.

Why couldn't he see that she *knew that*?

She was a medical professional. Sure, she usually stuck to women and babies, but she knew the human body was capable of amazing things. Of recovery and compensation. And it was early days.

She grabbed her paper off the floor and swept out of the room.

Downstairs, she found Liana writing on the couch. The other woman gave her a surprised look—because Jenna had only been upstairs for twenty minutes, tops—but something on her face must have given off a warning, because Liana kept her mouth shut.

"See you tomorrow," Jenna muttered.

Then she went to Mac's and bought another slice of pie, because she'd left her first one in Sean's room, and she'd hardly eaten any.

The next day, she didn't bring cards, or the paper. If he didn't want her to push him, she wouldn't.

"Morning," she said as she poked her head around the open door to his room.

He was stretched out on the couch, staring at the ceiling. "Hey."

"Dean said you already ate breakfast."

"Yeah."

"I could bring you another cup of coffee—"

"Are you flying back to Vancouver?" He didn't look at

her as he asked the question. "Or are you thinking about doing another rotation overseas?"

Neither, but the weird, aching feeling in her gut told her the honest answer wouldn't be well received. "I haven't decided yet."

"What did your mother say about you coming here?"

"I haven't told her yet." She sat in the chair. She didn't know where he was going with this, but she was making herself comfortable anyway.

"That's smart." His voice was cold, clipped.

Was it? Jenna was pretty sure it was cowardly. And she didn't like the barbed way Sean had said that. She changed the subject. "What are you doing?"

"Taking a nap. Or trying to, anyway."

And being a passive-aggressive asshole, too. She should praise him for his multitasking. "I'm not in any hurry to go back overseas," she finally said quietly.

His face twisted. "Don't sacrifice your dreams for me."

He was no sacrifice. He was her dreams. But she couldn't tell him that.

There had been a time—a short, fragile time—when he'd wanted to know all her secrets. Had practically begged to get inside her head, under her skin. And now he was acting like he couldn't care less.

And maybe he couldn't.

She knew brain injuries could change personalities. She wasn't so naive she hadn't considered that. But there had been a few moments when they'd been playing Go Fish, that she'd thought she'd glimpsed her husband inside this stranger.

No, he was her husband no matter what. Until he outright asked her for a divorce, she was committed to him.

Even if he was being a sullen jerk.

Was this what he was like as a teenager? No wonder it was a trying period for his brothers.

"Anyway," she finally said, standing up again. There was no point in trying to continue a conversation with his profile, no matter how handsome it was. "I'm returning the rental car. I'll be back tomorrow. I'll speak to Dean about getting the truck in order."

"I'll tell him," Sean muttered, not looking at her.

"He's just downstairs, I can—"

"It's my damn truck. I'll tell him. He doesn't know what needs to be done to it, anyway. And neither do you."

Great. Their first fight was over car maintenance. How romantic.

She bit back a snarky response—which would be as much out of her character as this sullenness was out of his. They didn't both need to contribute to a downward spiral.

Instead, she just left.

CHAPTER THIRTEEN

SHE WENT home and called the car rental company to figure out where she could return it.

While she was on hold, she wandered into the backyard, and as soon as she stepped onto the deck, Sophia streaked across the lawn.

"Jenn-ah!"

"Hey, Sophia. What's up?"

"Play-doh." The little girl held out a grimy fistful of bright pink dough, dotted with grass and dirt.

"Awesome."

"Eat it?"

Jenna chucked, some of her tension easing. "No, sweetie. Thank you, but I'm good."

Sophia pointed at the phone pressed against Jenna's ear. "Talk?"

Jenna held out the phone so the little girl could hear the on-hold music. Sophia wiggled her diaper-covered butt in a little dance, and that made Jenna feel good too.

But her grumpiness returned when the rental company customer service person came on the line and blandly informed her they would charge her a ridiculous return fee for a pickup anywhere near the peninsula.

She groaned and hung up. "I guess I'm driving to Toronto this afternoon," she said regretfully to Sophia.

"No," said the little girl.

"I know, right? I wish I could say that." Jenna waved at Olivia, who was making her way across the lawn.

"Sorry. She slipped over here while I was hanging up laundry on the line. I didn't notice she wasn't playing behind me."

Jenna shrugged. "That's why both yards are fenced, right? It's all good."

Sophia shook her head. "No."

Jenna laughed and replayed their conversation for her neighbour. "So now I'm driving to the city."

Olivia gave her a sympathetic look. "How will you get back? Do you want Rafe to follow you? He's got three days off starting tomorrow."

"No, I'm good. I'll grab the bus back. But maybe he could pick me up from wherever it stops?" With her luck, that might still be somewhere far-ish away from Pine Harbour.

"Of course. Just text me when you're heading back and someone will meet you."

"Chloe could probably do it…"

Olivia made a humming noise that told Jenna it would probably be a Minelli who showed up.

"Thank you," she said, truly grateful for the kindness.

"Of course. Okay, Sophie-Dophie, time to say *see you later* to Jenna."

Sophia shook her head solemnly. "No."

"Story of my life." Olivia sighed and hoisted the

toddler onto her hip. "Here's hoping she's out of this *no* phase by the time I'm as big as a house."

———

JENNA TOOK advantage of the long drive and the car's built-in Bluetooth to make some long overdue phone calls.

Jenna's mother answered on the third ring. "Hello?"

"Hi, Mom." Jenna swallowed hard. "How are you?"

"Jenna." Relief poured into how her mother said her name, but just as quickly, she bounced out of it. "Busy with the usual. How are you? What time is it there?"

About that… "I'm not in Turkey any longer. I'm back in Canada. Ontario, specifically."

"My goodness." Jenna heard a clatter in the background. Whatever her mother had been working on had now been set aside and she now had Eve's full attention.

Great. "I'm looking for work here, actually." Not a lie.

"So you're not working right now?" That was always her mother's fear, and Jenna understood the reasoning behind it. As a single mom from day one, Eve had always lived close to the edge of not having enough to make ends meet.

"I'll be fine."

"It's a slippery slope if you start to dip into your savings."

"I know. I'm living pretty low-cost at the moment, and it'll only take a few weeks—" maybe months "—to get registered with the college. Then I'll be able to pick up work quickly. And I'm staying in a friend's place, so it's fine."

"A midwife friend? That girl in Toronto?"

Maybe deep down, this was why Jenna had waited to

call her mom. Because now she wasn't lying. "I'm on my way to the city right now, and I'm going to try to see Grace tonight. But no, I'm not staying with her. I'm up in cottage country." Tell her, tell her, tell her… "I, uh…I met a guy."

As expected, that was met with silence, then a long, loaded sigh. "Oh, Jenna."

If she weren't driving, Jenna would have closed her eyes and thunked her head against the steering wheel. She was thirty years old. Why did her mother still have to see her as a teenager liable to get knocked up at any second? "We actually met in Turkey, but he's Canadian, too."

"And he's from cottage country?" Eve didn't need to spell out that she thought Jenna had followed a man to the middle of nowhere for what could only be a stupid reason like lust.

"It's not like that."

Eve made a noise that could have been a snort, but Jenna was choosing to hear it as a laugh so as not to be annoyed. "So…you didn't chase a man halfway around the globe after falling for him in a whirlwind romance?"

Fine, it was exactly like that. Damn it. "His name is Sean. And he's really lovely." Not today, exactly, but in general. "Remember the pictures of the prime minister playing hockey? Sean's the soldier who was the captain of the other team."

"Ah." So much loaded into a single syllable. Ah, well it's your life to gamble with. Ah, well of course you'd be distracted by a handsome man in uniform. Ah, well at least he's gainfully employed. "Speaking of that, did you ever follow up with those media contacts? I saw a doctor on the news the other day—"

"Mom—"

"Maybe that would be a good use of your time in Toronto."

Hardly. A good use of her time in Toronto would be drowning herself in a bottle of red wine with Grace. Jenna decided that was enough sharing for the day. "I'll keep you posted on the job search," she said weakly. "What's the latest from Annie?"

"She's decided she likes boys again."

"She never stopped liking boys, Mom. She's bi."

"I know that." Of course Eve sounded defensive. Jenna wasn't going there, either.

Jenna rolled her eyes. "Okay. Did she find a summer job?"

"Yes. On campus. It doesn't pay much, but they'll work around her summer class schedule."

"That's good. I'll give her a call next." In the distance, she saw a sign for a Tim Horton's coffee shop. "I'm going to stop and get a coffee now. I've still got four hours of driving ahead of me."

"Be safe, Jenna."

She swallowed the retort that desperately wanted to spill out. Instead, she took a deep breath and jammed on her good-daughter hat. "Love you, Mom."

After she re-caffeinated, Jenna called her baby sister. Annie had been another unexpected pregnancy. Their family was unconventional, but they'd made it work. Her mother had made it work.

Jenna didn't tell Annie anything beyond what she'd told their mom—the marriage news could wait for a better time—but Annie's general reception was warmer.

"Is that why you were so vague about what you did on your trip to Spain?"

"Maybe."

"Jenna!" Annie laughed gently. "That's awesome, actually. You're always so responsible. It's good to know that you do impulsive things from time to time."

That conversation gave her the courage to call her friend Grace, who she'd gone to college with out in British Columbia, but who had moved to Ontario for love and was now working in Toronto.

It turned out Grace was free for the evening, so after Jenna returned the rental car, she hopped on the subway and headed downtown.

They met at a bistro on Queen West. Grace was waiting outside, her dark red hair piled high on her head in a bun. She was dressed down, in leggings and a long tunic, with three long silver necklaces hanging around her neck.

She hadn't changed a bit.

"Hey, stranger," Jenna said, holding out her arms for a hug. "It's been too long."

Grace gave her a good squeeze. "I'm so glad you called. I didn't realize you were back."

"I've been keeping it quiet for reasons."

"Ooh, sounds interesting. Come on, let's get some food and wine and you can tell me all about it. Are you staying over tonight?"

"I was going to catch the midnight bus..." She trailed off. She was going to say home. And it did feel like that, maybe. A tentative home, but yes, there it was. A little kernel of attachment to the place, not just the man. In the last week, she'd grown quite fond of Pine Harbour. "Back up north," she finally said.

"Are you in a hurry to get back? You can stay at our place tonight if you want."

"Maybe. Thank you. Let's see how much wine we get into."

They ordered, then once they both had a glass in their hand, Grace leaned back and opened the conversation up with a gleam in her eye. "So...what's up north?"

"A man," Jenna admitted. "But it's complicated."

"When is it not? Do you want to talk about it?"

"Yes." She stopped there, and they both laughed.

"More wine first?"

She shook her head. "I just want to be careful about how I lay the story out."

Grace waved her hand. "How about I promise not to make any judgements? You tell me everything you want to tell me. I'll just listen."

Jenna shuddered, and it wasn't until that moment that she realized how much she needed that. "Well...so...I met this guy. In February. He was kind, and smart, and tall." She smiled as she remembered their first meeting in the food tent. "Really, really good looking. And we ended up travelling together. We went to Spain, and Gibraltar, and... we got married."

Grace didn't blink. She didn't gasp, or drop her jaw, or freak out. She just waited.

Jenna's heart hammered in her chest. "I fell in love," she whispered, as the happy memories slid into the rougher ones. "And then he was injured."

The rest of the story spilled out, between sips of wine and tugs on her hair. When she reached the bottom of her glass, Grace silently refilled it.

"And now I'm here, and he wants me to leave, but I know that's the injuries talking." That sounded thin, even to her own ears. "Well, I'm pretty sure it's not what he wants, deep down."

"Is it what you want?" It was the first time Grace had spoken since Jenna started.

Jenna gave her a startled look. "Being in Pine Harbour?"

"Yes. Are you where you want to be right now?"

She was where she needed to be. Want didn't enter into it. But then she thought of how much she liked sharing a yard with Olivia and Rafe. Of cooking with Chloe, and how everyone—Dani, Dean, Liana, Matt, and the entire town—had taken one look at her and claimed her as one of their own.

She nodded, surprising herself. Yes, she was exactly where she wanted to be.

She missed working, but when she thought about returning overseas or finding a position locally, again her answer was surprising. She wanted to stay on the peninsula.

"Then don't worry about what he wants, or thinks he wants. As long as you aren't unhappy being there, let it play out. Give him space if he needs it, but it's a free country. Even if he doesn't want you in his face, you can share a town."

That hurt her heart. "I…it's hard to stay away from him."

Grace leaned in and took her hand. "I can see that. You must love him a lot."

"So much. It's crazy, really. We only had two weeks together."

"But then you had that time after you got married, when you thought you were coming back to Canada to build a life together." Grace squeezed her fingers before letting go to empty the wine bottle into their glasses. "We're going to need another one of these."

Like magic, the waiter appeared with their food, and promised to return shortly with more wine.

"Have you thought about counselling?" Grace asked after they took a few bites.

Jenna shook her head. "He won't go."

"For you."

She jerked her head up and looked at her friend in surprise. "Oh. No."

"You should. You were traumatized, too."

"I didn't even know about the injury until weeks after it happened." Three weeks in which she'd worried and fretted, but generally carried on with her life.

"But when you found out, it was new and raw for you. And I bet you didn't get any chance to process that properly."

"No, I guess I didn't." Sadness swelled again as she thought about the dead ends and road blocks she'd run into every time she'd tried to find out information about him, to get in touch and let him know that she was coming. In hindsight, the weeks after she found out, before she could leave the camp and fly to Sean's side, had been deeply traumatizing—and she still couldn't let herself relive that panic. "I really want to be strong for him through this."

"It sounds like you are doing just that. Which is great. But everyone has a breaking point, and you can't help him if you hit yours."

"I know," she whispered.

"Then take care of yourself while you give him the space to heal."

"That's…" Jenna played with her dinner. "Really smart advice." She laughed. "I guess I needed to hear it from someone else."

"Always the way. Now tell me more about this

delightful little town. It sounds like quite an adventure, really. Small town living for the big city girl."

Jenna told her about Mac's, about meeting Chloe and Dani and Olivia, and all the Foster and Minelli men. She found herself waxing on about the landscape of the peninsula, too, and as she talked, she realized that yes, it was an adventure. Maybe not as exotic as Turkey or Spain, but wasn't charging in to Pine Harbour, not knowing what she'd find, just as daring?

Her wanderlust had taken her to some strange and wonderful corners of the Earth this year. Pine Harbour was simply the least expected of those corners.

By the time they finished the second bottle of wine, and were weaving their way back to Grace's apartment, Jenna had a Pine Harbour travel pitch down pat, and Grace was promising to visit towards the end of the summer.

Grace's partner Alex was waiting up for them. He'd made Jenna a bed on the couch, and she passed out as soon as she lay her head down.

———

SHE DIDN'T WAKE up until noon the next day.

Oh, her eyes hurt. She squeezed them shut and—

Was it possible that she had invited random strangers on Queen Street to visit Pine Harbour?

With a groan, she rolled off Grace's couch and stood up. Yep, definitely hung over.

"Good morning," Grace said quietly from the kitchen behind her. Jenna turned around and waved gingerly as Alex silently held up a carafe of coffee.

"Yes, I need that, please." She dug out her phone. No messages, not that she'd been expecting any.

As Alex poured her a cup, she checked the bus schedule and then squinted at the time. "There's a bus I can catch in ninety minutes."

"Perfect," Grace said. "I can drop you at the bus station when I head uptown to check on a client this afternoon."

They didn't talk about Sean again, and Jenna was grateful for that, too. She'd appreciated Grace's listening—and advice—more than she could say, but there was something lovely about the normalcy of just drinking coffee and making small talk with an old friend.

But her husband wasn't far from her mind—nor was the fact that, since she'd slept over in the city and the bus home was the milk run that stopped in every small town, dropping off packages at the same time as they picked up people, it would take eight hours to get back to Pine Harbour. She wouldn't get in until ten o'clock at night, and Sean would be passed out for hours by that point.

She didn't know why she felt guilty about missing a day of visiting. He probably didn't care in the least.

———

SEAN'S TRUCK sat out front all day, but Jenna didn't show up.

That burned at him, even though he knew he deserved it. So he was an asshole to Dean and Liana, who didn't deserve it. Especially not Liana, but not Dean either.

His older brother pushed him up against the wall and told him to be nice to his wife or else. Sean understood. He may have only had a wife for two months, but she'd been his everything. And now he couldn't be anything to her.

He went back to bed.

When he woke up in the morning, nauseous and seeing

auras from a migraine, he realized he'd forgotten to take his medication the night before. After he threw up, he told Dean Jenna couldn't come over.

She did anyway, and he pretended to be asleep. She lay down on the couch in his room, and at some point, he drifted off for real.

When he woke up, she was gone.

He ignored the ache in his gut.

The next day she brought him breakfast, and he couldn't bring himself to be a jerk again. It was exhausting.

"Driving a truck is interesting," she said.

As far as conversations went, it was deliberately benign. He didn't miss that. She wasn't pushing him—as he'd requested.

He still bristled. "How so?"

She took a long sip of coffee before answering. "Well," she said dryly. "I'm much higher up."

"And that surprised you?"

"Jesus, Sean," she snapped. "It wasn't a serious statement."

He blinked at her.

"Sorry."

"Don't be," he said. Because he knew she was.

Something he'd noticed since the accident was that his voice didn't sound right to his own ear. Nobody else had said anything about it, but he always felt a weird distance when he spoke. Like he was listening to someone else.

She gave him a tight smile. "Want more coffee?"

"I'm fine."

"How's your head?"

"Better today." He tried to make himself stick to the two word answers. They were safer.

"I'm going to Owen Sound. Could I pick anything up for you while I'm there?"

"No." He hesitated. "Watch the speedometer. It sticks right around the speed limit."

Eight extra words to an answer and her face softened. "Thanks."

Damn it. She was unrelentingly sweet to him. Even when she'd just snapped at him, it hadn't lasted.

He hated that her pity overrode everything else.

Hated that she didn't look at him the way she had in Spain.

God. He missed that desperate way she'd needed him. The way her gaze had gone lusty and hazy. Horny Jenna was the most beautiful vision in the world.

But he'd never get that look from her. At some point, the sweetness would fade, and in its place would be resentment. And he couldn't handle that.

What a selfish thought, jackass.

Although, it wasn't selfish to want more for Jenna than brittle conversations about cars and coffee. He could give her a little more. It was the least she deserved.

"I'm..." He swallowed. "My brothers are forcing me outside today."

She lifted one eyebrow. *Oh?*

He sighed. "Jake's coming to pick me up. They're trying to trick me into walking more," he grumbled, "by making me needlessly get in and out of his truck and push my walker to his front porch."

Her eyes crinkled as she laughed. "I'm sorry."

"Gotta give them something." He refused to go to outpatient physio, which was an ongoing bone of contention, with his brothers and his family doctor. And he'd liked sitting outside with Jenna.

Fresh air was as much of a compromise as he felt like giving them this week.

"That's the spirit." She winked. "And I really do think it's a good plan. You're putting up with a lot today. Pushy brothers, me snapping at you."

"You're entitled to a bit of snapping with all of this."

She shook her head and gave him another smile. "Okay, I'm off. Good luck with the sunlight and the overbearing brothers."

Getting downstairs was a chore. He went down on his ass, but there was something about his visual field changing so quickly as he descended that made his head spin. So he took his time, even though he was painfully aware that Jake was waiting for him at the bottom of the stairs, baby Calvin fussing in his baby carrier.

Jesus, Sean had more crap than the baby did. Walker, medications, a neck brace for the car ride.

Jake didn't have time for this shit. Between juggling a full time business and a young family, the second-oldest Foster brother had the least amount of spare time of any of them.

"Sorry you got stuck with me today," Sean muttered.

Jake shrugged it off. "We've got all day. I don't have anything to do today but hang out with my boy and you."

They made an odd trio as they slowly made their way out to Jake's truck, Calvin fussing, Jake bobbing up and down to sooth him back to sleep, and Sean slowly plodding along beside with his walker, which he hated so fucking much.

When they arrived at Jake's place, Tom Minelli was waiting on the front step. If it had been anyone else, Sean wouldn't have immediately gone on guard. But Jake and Tom, out of all of their two-family band of brothers, had something uniquely in common. They, too, had been over-seas, in Afghanistan. An ugly, messy tour that had seen many casualties.

Ah, fuck. Well he couldn't just sit in the damn truck. Jake had already hopped out, and had carried Calvin, sleeping in his portable car seat, inside.

When he returned and hauled Sean's walker out of the back of the truck, Sean accepted that whatever awkward conversation they were about to have might as well happen in a more comfortable seat.

He carefully slid out of the truck and made his way to the porch. His shoulders burned by the time he got there. From *leaning*. He was a mess.

Tom had been watching him patiently.

Sean sat and gave his friend a mock-jovial grin. "So. What's going on?"

Jake stood in front of him and crossed his arms. "What do you think is going on? I love you—we all do—but you're being an asshole. This is an intervention."

So they weren't beating around the bush. Fine.

"You were already a pain in Dean's ass before Jenna arrived, and this last week has been even worse. Maybe we should have done this sooner, but it's clear we can't wait any longer. It's time to talk about what happened."

"Says you."

Jake swore. "Yes, says me, you ungrateful shithead."

Sean gave him a deliberately bland look. "You have a way with words."

Tom stood and held out his hands. "Guys, let's do the intervention first before you beat each other up."

"I couldn't beat him up even if I wanted to," Sean muttered under his breath.

Jake leaned in and shoved his shoulder hard. "That

right there. That's the fucking problem. You should want to beat me up, and you could if you wanted to."

"You don't fucking understand."

"Yes, I do." He gestured to Tom. "Both of us do. We've been there, remember? We've done our tours overseas. We've been in the sandbox when everything was going to shit. We've been in the middle of firefights, and we've seen guys die. And when we came back, we put our lives back together and got on with fucking living."

"You weren't injured, though."

"Not physically. But nobody comes out of that unscathed. For fucks sake, you have a wife. We all thought when she showed up that it would be a turning point for you, but not a negative one."

"I didn't ask her to come."

"Yeah, we're all figuring that out. What the actual fuck, man? You made vows to her."

"That wasn't me!" Sean's voice cracked, but something else cracked, too, and he finally heard himself.

For the first time since the explosion that had torn his world apart, he heard himself and he recognized his own voice.

Jesus Christ.

He sounded desperate. Pathetic. Angry.

He hung his head.

"What do you mean, that wasn't you?" Jake said slowly, dropping to a squat in front of Sean.

"I don't know." A lie. He knew. He just didn't want to say it again.

"We're getting ahead of ourselves," Tom interjected. "Sean, where do you see yourself landing? You can't stay at Dean's forever."

He knew that. He didn't want to be dependent on his

brothers. But he didn't have an answer to that question. He couldn't see into the future. He couldn't imagine a future now.

When he didn't answer, Jake threw his hands in the air and again muttered something about having a wife. That word sliced through him like a hot blade.

Tom looked at Sean. "Look, your brothers have their own perspectives. But I'm telling you — you gotta commit to a rehab plan for yourself. Get healthy *for your-self*. You can't do this for Jenna. But you gotta ask your-self, what do you want? Because right now, you're just driving a wedge between you and everyone who loves you."

"I just want to be left the fuck alone. It's all that I want." That rang hollow. It wasn't *all* he wanted. But what he wanted wasn't possible. What he wanted had been stolen from him. In a single, awful, life-ripping moment. His universe had literally exploded, and how dare they expect him to already be trying to put the pieces back together?

It was the worst kind of jigsaw puzzle. There were pieces missing. Pieces torn in half. Pieces crushed into a pile of dust.

It would always be incomplete.

Tom and Jake had no idea what that was like, because their lives were whole again. They may have experienced some of the same fracturing reality, but their pieces hadn't been blown apart in the same way.

"I don't know what you guys were trying to accom-plish here. What I know is that no two circumstances are the same. Before I was injured, I thought I was invincible. I bet Jenna's life on it. I hitched her wagon to mine on the cocky-as-fuck belief that I'd see her on the other side, a war hero with legit swagger. Instead I'm half a man with a fucked-up brain."

Jake stared at him. "And yet she's here, isn't she?"

"I don't know why."

"Then you're an idiot, because she doesn't act like she thinks you made a bad bet."

Tom cleared his throat. "Or you need us to help you see that even though you've done your level best to be an asshole, she's stuck around. She knows what she's up against, too."

She didn't, though. She didn't know how broken he was inside his head.

"I see what you're doing, Sean," Tom said, giving him a sober look.

Did he? Because Sean wasn't completely sure. He felt like he was flailing out in some uncoordinated attempt to fight the world, to fight his new reality. "Oh yeah? What's that?"

"You're trying to isolate yourself."

Maybe he was. He kicked at his walker.

"It's not a plan, though. It's a sign of depression."

"I'm not depressed. I'm angry."

"The two are not mutually exclusive."

Sean looked at Jake. "Tell him I'm not depressed."

Jake gave him a pained look. "You're not yourself."

Jesus. He knew that. He'd never be that guy again. It wasn't a temporary thing. "Traumatic brain injuries will do that to a guy," he muttered.

"That's not what I'm saying." His brother sighed and sat down beside him. "Sean, you're so angry about what happened to you that you're forgetting it could have been so much worse."

"How the hell could it—"

"We could have lost you." Jake turned his head and gave him a hard look, his eyes glittering dangerously. "You could have died. And we are all so fucking grateful that you didn't. Your wife is, too. When are you going to stop feeling sorry for yourself and be glad you're alive?"

Sean stared at his brother. He would have preferred a punch in the face. "Fuck," he finally said.

"Yeah."

Tom sat on the other side of him. "It's okay to miss your old life. But you have a new life that's going to stretch in front of you for decades. Make it count."

Because others had lost that chance.

He *was* an asshole.

He needed to do something. Fix this, somehow. Enough leaning on others. Fucking hell, enough leaning, period.

He couldn't cling to the memory of what had once been. It was time to move forward. It was time for a plan.

CHAPTER FOURTEEN

February
Gibraltar

"WE'RE MARRIED." No matter how many times Jenna said it, that sentence felt foreign and unexpected. Yet oddly right. She squeezed Sean's hand as they walked back to the hotel. "At some point will this feel less surreal?"

"Probably not. But it'll be an awesome story to tell our grandkids." He stopped in his tracks and hauled her in for another quick kiss. "My wife. God, that sounds good."

"How do you want to celebrate?"

He skated his hand up her back, pressing her against him. Maybe she wasn't the only one reeling from what they'd just done, and he needed to hold on tight. "Horizontally?"

"Obviously." She gave him a dopey smile. She wanted him like crazy, constantly, and she knew that was probably painted all over her face. "But what about after that?"

"Whatever you want to do." He nuzzled his nose into

her hair. "We haven't gone out for dinner in a few nights. Maybe we could go someplace nice."

They stopped at the front desk of the hotel and got a recommendation, and a reservation for that evening.

Once in their room, Jenna kicked off her shoes as Sean unbuttoned his shirt. This was easy now. This was sweet and wonderful and familiar, and the fact they were married didn't change that at all.

Except it could.

Jenna twisted her arms in front of her body. "So...we're married."

"You keep saying that."

She stuck her tongue out at him. "Yes, but this time it isn't because of the surreal thing. More of an...administrative detail."

"Oh?"

She swayed closer to him. "So the thing is...I have an IUD. If you've been tested recently, we could ditch the condoms..."

He held out his arms, and she went to him, letting him pull her close. He threaded his fingers into her hair, his eyes hot as he searched her face. "I have. And I haven't had any activity in that regard in a while."

"Same." She swallowed. "I figured our wedding night might be a good reason to bring that up."

"I love you." His hands tightened in her hair and he leaned in. "So much it scares me."

He hadn't admitted that before, and it made her racing heart slow down. She caressed his cheek. "We're still us. This is a promise, not a chain. Nothing's going to change."

He leaned into her touch. "Since we're covering administrative details, we should talk about that—what's going to change, and what won't."

She nodded. It had been bouncing around in her head, too. "I thought some of that might sort itself out once we were home in the summer. I'm not tied down anywhere, and you travel a lot. We can figure out a new normal that keeps us together as much as we want."

"I can move out west."

She shrugged. "Let's cross that bridge when we get to it. I've never lived out east."

"I can't wait to show you my hometown." He kissed her gently, his lips soft and coaxing.

She'd follow him anywhere, she was sure of it.

"We should also talk about the next of kin thing." His voice got rougher as he said that. He twisted his head and kissed the palm of her hand. His jaw tightened, and she let him sort out his thoughts. It didn't matter. She didn't say her vows to get listed on his life insurance.

Finally he dragged in a deep breath and turned back, pressing his forehead against hers. "The thing is," he said quietly. "You could be in danger. You work twenty clicks from the Syrian border. The camp has armed guards for a reason. It's not out of the realm of possibility that you could be targeted as a valuable asset if anyone knew that you were married to a Canadian army officer."

Her heart stopped cold. Oh. He wasn't worried about his life insurance. He was worried about her life. "What?"

"I know that sounds like crazy worst-case scenario talk, but it's part of what I do. I run all the possibilities and plan to avoid the ones that don't work for my goals."

"And your goal here is…"

"Getting my wife back to Canada in one glorious, gorgeous piece. Safe and sound."

Her heart slammed back into gear. She nodded shakily. "Good goal."

"There might be some complicating factors on your end, too. I don't know if you have a duty to report any changes of circumstances. I probably do, but I'd rather beg for forgiveness later."

"I don't think I do." She touched his face again, smoothing her fingers over his brow then running them up into his hair. "I don't want you to worry. We can tell people when we get back to Canada. Although my co-workers know we travelled together…"

"And I'm not going to be able to keep the fact that I've met an amazing woman from my team. I just won't tell them we're married or where you are."

She could keep her ring in the wooden box he bought her. "I can work with that." She pushed off his shoulders and stepped back. "Any other administrative details we need to discuss, husband?"

He grinned. "None that I can think of."

She reached for her bag. "Then I'm going to slip into something special." Her cheeks heated up, but they were no match for his gaze.

"Really?"

She nodded shyly. She wasn't normally the silk and satin type, but it was a special occasion. "I went shopping the other day when you were running, and I bought something silky."

She'd bought it for their last night together, but this was even more special.

He licked his lips, and whoa, that little reaction did some big things to her insides. "I can't wait."

She grabbed the small bag she'd tucked away, and dashed into the bathroom to take off the sundress she'd worn for the ceremony. She didn't close the door, and from the other room, she heard Sean moving around. He took off his boots with two heavy thuds. He pulled back the blankets with a soft swoosh, and her nipples tightened in anticipation.

The lingerie she'd bought was little more than scraps of silk connected by criss-crossing ribbons, and it floated over her body like a whisper. She smoothed her hands over the flat of her belly and then glanced at her reflection in the mirror. Looking back at her was a woman she hardly recognized. No scrubs, no hastily gathered ponytail, and no dark circles under her eyes. Her hair fell in loose waves around her shoulders and her face sparkled with excitement. Bright eyes, pink lips.

Marriage suited her, even as it filled her with nervous energy. She dragged a deep breath into her lungs and reached for her toothbrush. She was delaying now.

And it wasn't going to work.

With a gentle knock, Sean came into the bathroom. He was still in the cargo pants he'd worn for the service, but he was barefoot and bare-chested. He took her breath away.

"I..."

He laughed gently at the toothbrush in her hand, but gestured for her to continue. "It's fine. But I couldn't wait any longer," he murmured, settling his hands on her hips.

She did a quick back and forth on her teeth, and when she leaned forward to spit out the toothpaste, he brushed her hair off the nape of her neck and whispered what were fast becoming her two favourite words.

"My wife."

A thrill raced through her at how unbelievably special that sounded coming out of his mouth. The shivery-good feeling intensified as he kissed her back, his breath warm at the top of her spine.

She filled a glass with water then rinsed away the toothpaste taste.

Sean didn't let go of her hips. He watched her in the mirror, his gaze hot. It was domestic and intimate, and as she wiped a water droplet off her lower lip, he tightened his grip.

Here?

Sure, why not consummate their marriage bent over a vanity? She bit her lip and leaned forward again, bracing her forearms against the counter as she watched him in the mirror.

With quick, efficient jerks, he undid his belt. The chink of metal was followed by a growling zip as he opened his fly.

Her husband.

SEAN TUGGED HER NEGLIGEE UP, baring her bottom, and she pressed up onto her toes. He told himself to slow down, but fuck, there was no chance of him forgetting this.

"I love you," he said as he curved his hand over her hip, tracing her soft skin to where she was both soft and wet. "Is this is okay?"

He caught her gaze again in the mirror. She looked wanton and sexy as fuck as she smiled at him. "It's perfect."

She bit her lip and leaned forward, tipping her hips back, and he was done for.

No more going slow.

She was his, and the need to claim her roared loud and fierce inside him. She gasped as he rubbed against her, and her hand skittered forward to press against the mirror.

She was perfect. Smart and fierce and brave. Humble and kind. Gorgeous. Sexy as fuck.

She'd changed his life in two short weeks.

And now she was giving him this gift, her body, with nothing between them. Her gaze, lusty and aroused, locked on his face in the mirror.

But her gaze wasn't enough. He needed her mouth, he needed her hands on him. Pulling back, he spun her around and lifted her onto the vanity. Her legs went around his hips, pulling him back into her body. Hot, wet, tight heat surrounded him as he surged into her, and he didn't miss the way her breath hitched.

This was affecting both of them on a deep, fundamental level.

He buried his face in her neck as he grappled with his tenuous hold on his self-control. "My wife." It was a chant, a prayer, a promise as he started to move inside her.

She rocked against each thrust, her bare heels digging into his ass. She tugged on his hair, urging him to lift his head up, and he took her mouth in a savage kiss, as primal as their mating. So much better than anything he could have imagined.

Maybe better because he hadn't, really—who could anticipate this? He was lost in her.

She tasted fearless, and when he pulled back, just for a second, just to see her, she looked fearless, too. Her skin was flushed with passion, her eyes endless pools of want as she tugged on him. She looked on the edge of abandon and he was going to follow her right off that cliff.

He hadn't even gotten her naked. That's how desperate he'd been to forge this connection with her. As he skated his hands over her body, over the silk that decorated her curves, a foreign emotion welled up inside him, a need to bare his soul to her. To be tender.

He kissed her again, soft and coaxing, as he moulded her against him. As close as two people could be. Fused in every way. They'd need this moment to get them through the next few months. Need this promise, this vow, as much as the ones they'd spoken out loud.

He loved her with every inch of his body, with his strong legs that powered each thrust, with his arms that held her tight.

She reached between them, and he pushed harder, catching her fingertips as she rubbed her clit. He pressed his forehead against hers as they ground against each other, and he watched her face as she came apart. Then he followed her into the abyss, his brain exploding as he buried his cock deep inside her for his own release.

Holy. Fuck.

She clutched the back of his neck, breathing hard, and he crushed his mouth against hers.

His wife. His. Forever.

"I love you," he whispered, his own breath ragged.

She whispered it back, and it filled him with an intense joy.

He kicked his pants out of the way then carefully eased her back against the mirror. Her legs shook visibly as she watched him run warm water and grab a washcloth. He pressed his hand to her knee, and she giggled.

"That was…"

"Wow."

"Very wow." She sighed and lifted her legs up, pressing her bare feet against the counter. He squeezed the cloth out, then carefully stepped between her legs again. She gasped as he wiped her, but she didn't stop him.

He'd never done that before. It was messy. He liked it.

He washed her carefully, then dropped to his knees and kissed her tender flesh.

He licked her until she was squirming and breathing his name on every moan, and then he picked her up and carried her to the bed. He peeled her out of the silk, then covered her with his body and made love to her again, slow and long and perfect.

———

"DID you always know you wanted to be a soldier?" she asked after, as he spooned her and played with her hair.

"It was a given. We were raised to be soldiers. My father was a career officer. And I didn't mind. All I wanted to do when I grew up was run away from home. I always knew I'd be here, somehow. I didn't imagine it exactly like this…" He laughed as he kissed her shoulder. "But finding you, and falling in love on the other side of the world… that sounds about right. And I bet teenage me would definitely approve of you as part of the fantasy."

"Do you miss your family?"

"Sure." He said it readily. It was true. Just because he couldn't wait to get away didn't mean he didn't also leave a part of himself back home when he flew the coop. "How about you?"

She should miss them more than she did. "I don't have any homesickness." She stretched her arms out and twisted onto her side, pillowing her head on her arm as she looked at him. "I grew up wanting to see the world, and not being able to afford to. This is the first time I've been able to really live anywhere other than the Vancouver area."

He traced the line of her jaw, then picked up a strand of her hair and let it run through his fingers. "When we get back, where do you want to work?"

They'd talked about this already, but getting married changed things. It had changed him—but not his desire to come back and do another tour. He hoped it was the same for her.

She searched his face. "I don't know."

"You said we could try to be together as much as we want."

She nodded.

"I want to be together. Period. I don't want to try to fly back and forth across the country. I want to build a home with you. Wherever."

That got a smile that did wicked things to his insides.

He leaned in and tasted her neck. "Or we don't need to pick one place to live," he whispered against her skin. "As long as we're nomads together."

"Nomads who serve the greater good?"

"That sounds perfect."

She dusted her fingertips over his body, and his muscles jumped against her touch. "You want to do more tours."

His chest tightened, because yeah, he did. But now he had a wife to think about. "If possible."

She nodded. "Me too."

Oh, thank God. He let out a shaky exhale. "Probably should have brought that up sooner, eh?"

She laughed. "Worried I wouldn't have understood?"

"Not when I think about it for a second."

"I understand." She kissed him, her lips gentle and soft. "It's all going to work out. Promise."

CHAPTER FIFTEEN

THEY FOUND Naples cold and wet when they landed for their stopover. It was a sombre reflection of Jenna's mood, but she didn't want to dwell on the weather or the countdown to saying goodbye.

They confirmed their spots on military transport back to Turkey for the next day, then checked in to military lodgings across from the air base.

"I should do some shopping," she said as she stretched out on the bed. "Stock up on chocolate."

Sean nodded as he unpacked his bag. He had everything in a sub-divided container. His shave kit, a smaller bag for socks and underwear, his phone and tablet in a neoprene case that had cable and charger slots built in. Neat, organized. Precise.

She watched as he pulled out the last bag from the bottom of the larger knapsack. His running gear. Sean was the only person she knew who traveled with two pairs of running shoes, and only used them for running. He had an indoor pair for treadmill training, which she hadn't actually seen him use, and an outdoor pair that had seen a decent number of hours given the guy was on vacation.

He held the running gear bag long enough she knew he wanted to get outside.

She climbed off the bed and crossed to him. "If you don't need to go shopping, we could split up. I'll shop while you get a run in."

He gave her a startled look. Did he not know that she saw him, and loved him, for who he was? "It'll be my last chance for a few months," he said, almost apologetically. "You're sure you don't mind?"

"No, of course not." She frowned and tugged on his shirt. "Are you okay?"

"Yeah. Just in a weird mood." He leaned in and kissed her. "I'm going to miss you like crazy."

"Same," she whispered. "I was thinking that the cold drizzle was a fitting backdrop today. You're a little crazy to want to run in it."

"I'm in a run through the cold, wet rain kind of mood."

She kissed his lopsided grin. "I suppose it'll be hot soon, and you'll miss the rain."

"If each day of sweltering hell is another day closer to being back with you, I'll gladly take it."

He got changed, and they headed outside together, where the rain had let up. He took off on a loop around the base, and she watched him disappear around the corner. A minute later, the shuttle bus arrived and she hopped on.

It took nearly two hours to find everything she wanted to take back to Urfa, and she was worried she'd taken too long, but when she got back to the hotel, Sean was still running.

Instead of heading back upstairs, she found a seat on a bench under an overhang and she watched him. He hadn't seen her yet, she didn't think. She'd spotted him as the shuttle approached, disappearing around the far corner of the base, and now he'd nearly completed the lap.

Jesus, he was fast. He didn't even break stride when he finally saw her, just waved. "One more time," he gasped.

It only took him a few minutes. When he stopped in front of her, he was drenched with sweat. But his grin was back.

Back in their room, she stripped down with him, and washed his back as he stood under the hot shower. He rolled his neck as she slicked soap bubbles over his muscles there then leaned forward as she moved down his body. His legs were a thing of beauty, defined muscles and warm, smooth flesh covered in soft, golden fuzz.

He shivered as she swept her hands up the insides of his thighs, then up onto the hard, flexing tightness of his butt. That made her achy in an instant. And suddenly it felt like they hadn't had any time together at all.

She swallowed hard as she stood again and pressed against his back, her arms wrapping around his waist. She opened her mouth to say something, anything, and her voice cracked. It sounded like a cry, and she hadn't meant it to. She wouldn't cry, that was silly.

They'd see each other soon. They'd have all the time in the world together… soon.

"The summer feels so far away," she admitted, her words as jagged as the first rough sound had been.

Sean pivoted under the shower and picked her up, his hands sure and his body strong even after a long run. "We're going to be together again before you know it."

He kissed her hard as he pressed her against the tiles, cold against her back. He radiated heat. He radiated confidence and energy, and she knew she needed to trust him.

"Count in weeks," he whispered into her neck as he pushed inside her. "Seventeen weeks until we're together again."

Could she hold her breath that long? She closed her eyes and pulled him close. She didn't need to make it easier. If she wanted to count in days, hours, minutes, she would. Maybe the prick of panic would feel good. A hundred days. Three thousand hours without her husband.

"We'll write." God, his voice was cracking now, too, just like her heart. If he couldn't be carefree about this, there was no hope for her.

It wasn't fair to find love like this. There was no pause button for how big their feelings were.

"We'll send pictures, too," she whispered.

He cupped her face, kissing her until she smiled. Then he slid his hand down her body, stroking her neck, her breast, her waist, before he hitched her leg up and thrust deeper.

She arched between him and the tiled wall, welcoming him into her body. Her husband. "I love you," she breathed.

He said it back, an echo she didn't know she needed until the words ripped from his mouth and made her cry out. Deep inside her, he swelled, making the final few drags desperate and perfect and everything she needed. A rough, hard, overwhelming push into release.

She wound her legs around him, holding him tight as her body shook. He buried his cock deep as he followed her orgasm with his own, filling her with his seed.

"I love you," he growled again.

She'd hold on to those words, too. And the memory of him running like the wind.

———

THE RETURN to work was easier than expected. It helped that Jenna's expectations were rock bottom, of course. But she'd come back from Spain with a new sense of hope and boundless energy.

Of course she ached for Sean. She dreamed of him at night and woke up reaching for him every morning.

But she filled her days with patient care and her evenings with long, rambling emails to her new husband. Sometimes he was able to reply, other days she knew she'd be sending the message into the void and that was okay. It made her smile to think of him coming back from a reconnaissance mission and finding a few emails waiting.

When he was able to reply, his letters were long and loving and funny, filled with promises for the future. It was hard to believe that this was her life. That this was her love and yet every day that passed proved she wasn't dreaming.

Days turned into weeks, and she counted them down just as Sean had told her to. Sixteen, fifteen, fourteen, thirteen. He warned her that he would have to disappear from time to time, and he did. The first long break was stressful. Nine days went by without a response to her emails but then he returned and sent along some pictures of himself in the field.

Tall, smiling, handsome.

And pink along his cheekbones. He was getting a sunburn.

If she were at home, she would send him a care package with sunscreen. Instead, she was stuck not that far from him in the grand scheme of things, but limited in terms of access and support.

At the twelve weeks to go mark, she found a new normal. A month had passed since they'd said goodbye. Sometimes she walked to the corner of the compound where she could see the air field where they'd stolen one last embrace before she was picked up by a local driver, and he got on a helicopter to take him back to war. But most of the time, she didn't dwell on where he was and how long it had been since she'd heard his voice.

She poured herself into work instead. She was smarter about when she grabbed sleep and what she ate, making sure she had enough rest and fuel to get her through long shifts.

To get her to the end of her contract, and to Sean on the other side.

Their wedding rings were in the wooden box in her locker. She resisted the urge to take them out and put hers on. Most of the time. She celebrated the end of the tenth week out—moving into single digits—with a bottle of beer and a night of wearing her ring as she wrote him a dorky almost-seven-week-anniversary email. Seven weeks married, Ten weeks to go.

They had this.

He sent her an equally dorky note back, promising an "all out bash" to celebrate their twentieth-week anniversary once they were home and together again. All the Granny Smith apples she could handle. He warned he was heading into the field again, and she shouldn't worry.

So she didn't as she fell asleep with her phone pressed to her chest and a ridiculous smile plastered on her face.

———

A WEEK LATER, Jenna nodded as Sami talked about the

new ultrasound machine that had just arrived, but she'd stopped listening somewhere around the details of the soft tissue imaging capability. It was Thursday, and Sean had said they'd be back from the field today.

She felt like a toddler obsessed with a promised activity.

She could hardly stand another second of chatter because she had email to check and—

"Jenna?"

She winced. "Sorry."

Sami just laughed.

Everyone knew she was over the moon about Sean, and she didn't let it affect her work—except for right now. She flushed. "I just…"

"You haven't heard from him in a week." Her medical director shooed her toward the door. "Go check your email. I promise I understand."

Sami's wife was a doctor, too, back in Canada with their two kids. And this wasn't his first placement overseas.

After telling Sami in a rush that she'd see him tomorrow, Jenna ran from the hospital to her tent. She opened her locker and pulled out her phone.

No messages.

The crash of adrenaline slamming into disappointment was enough to rock her back on her heels.

Damn. So much for managing her expectations in a healthy way.

Hands shaking, she carried her phone to her bed and lay down. It took ages for her pulse to stop racing, but when it finally did, she carefully composed yet another uplifting email.

Another week passed. Jenna had sent two more emails

then took a break for a few days. She was starting to sound mopey, and that wasn't what she wanted.

She'd started obsessively reading the news, scanning for any updates about the Canadian mission across the border. No news was good news, she told herself.

Then one day, there was news. And it was awful.

CHAPTER SIXTEEN

JENNA SCRUBBED HER FOREARMS, all the way up to the elbow, then rinsed and repeated. She was dead tired, and so snappy she was afraid she might say something she'd regret to the wrong person—really, anyone—if she didn't get a good night's sleep soon.

Taking a deep breath, she blinked her scratchy eyes as wide open as she could and tipped her head to the ceiling and then to each side, stretching her neck. It was the end of her shift. Sleep was right around the corner.

She wasn't looking forward to going back to her tent, though. It was only April, but the temperatures were soaring. It was hot and sticky now, even at night, and before she could fall into a reluctant, shallow slumber, she'd spend an hour searching the internet for Sean's name.

Nothing ever came up, but it had been more than a month since his last email. Something was wrong. Surely this was too long to go without contact, but... she wasn't sure. And she couldn't ask anyone, not without revealing far too much.

"I think you're clean now," Milly said, bumping hips as she joined Jenna at the scrub station.

"Yeah."

"You were a cool cucumber today. You handled that breech birth like a pro, well done."

Jenna gave her a tired smile. "Thank you."

"Go get some rest."

She nodded and headed for the door, but before she got there, it swung open. Sami gave her a grave look. "Jenna, I need a minute."

Shit. If he was going to jack her up for being a sad, miserable bitch, could he at least wait until she was halfway rested? Her stomach twisted uncomfortably. "Right now? It's just that—"

His mouth tightened into a white line, and she cut herself off.

Silently, she followed him to the front office.

He waited for her to move inside and then closed the door behind her. He gave her another hard look. "I just got off the phone with my wife," he finally said. "There's a news story breaking back home."

He wasn't reprimanding her? Then Jenna's brain caught up to her heart, already pounding, as she figured out where Sami was going.

"It just came out in the last half hour, and I knew you'd see it when you checked the news yourself, but I thought you should hear it from a friend first."

Even as pain and fear exploded in her chest, she felt her face frowning and heard herself say, "Hear what?"

He scrubbed his hands over his face. "Captain Foster was injured. He's now back in Canada…"

A dull roar filled her ears. Sami's mouth kept moving,

and her eyes translated some of his lip shapes to words. Stable. No details. Significant injuries. Recovery.

The next thing she felt was a sharp, piercing pain, and the coppery taste of blood filled her mouth.

"Jenna…" Sami put his hands on her shoulders. "Say something."

"I…" More blood spilled against her tongue. She'd bit her lip.

She needed a computer. She needed to read the news. She wasn't going to process it properly if he told it to her.

She wasn't going to be able to hear a medical report on her husband, her brain couldn't handle that. "Show me," she finally managed to spit out, and Sami handed over his phone.

The article was brief but still shocking enough to make her heave.

Three weeks ago, there had been an incident.

Three weeks.

She'd worked and slept and worried and written him, but she'd never known. She hadn't felt it. Shouldn't she have felt something? She was his wife.

"I know you two were close. I thought you'd want to hear it from a friend."

Jenna blinked up at her medical director. He didn't know they were married.

Nobody knew.

"Yes, we're close," she whispered. *He's my husband.*

All this time, Sean had worried that something would happen to her if they told anyone they'd married. That it would compromise his job.

"I'll need to go home," she finally said, not bothering to acknowledge the look of surprise on her boss's face. "How much notice do you need?"

———

SHE FELL asleep in the office the next morning. Someone had covered her up and pinned her pager to the blanket. When she woke, the first thing she did was reach for her phone in a panic. She'd left it in her locker while on duty for months, but no more.

He hadn't called her. Yet.

But he would.

She hit refresh on the search results page and saw the same dozen articles she'd read the night before. They were basically the same six paragraphs with minor variations. An explosion on base had injured a Canadian Forces captain, a reserve officer from a unit in Wiarton, Ontario. There was a service picture and a brief biography that noted his endurance running career.

At the end, in the most benign of add-ons, it mentioned that Captain Foster was recuperating at home with his family.

His family.

But not his wife.

"How are you doing?" Sami asked when he brought her a cup of coffee. "Do you need anything?"

She didn't know how to answer that. She needed out of her contract, and that wasn't possible, not without putting women and children in danger. She glanced down at the phone in her hand. "I can't find anything about his injuries online."

Sami hesitated before leaning back in his chair. "I'll see what I can find out."

"I can't ask you to do that."

"You didn't. I offered. And I won't do anything under-handed. I'm going to call his commanding officer and express my concern, having met Captain Foster on his transit through this camp."

She let herself imagine that would actually work.

But she was bitterly disappointed the next day when Sami shook his head. "Tight-mouthed over there. No details. Just that the news reports are accurate, and they appreciate our concern." He hesitated before adding, "I've put in a request for a replacement for you. But it might take a few weeks."

Mariya and Milly covered for her as much as they could, and when she was needed, she worked harder than ever, driven by guilt and fear and some unspoken negotiation with a higher power that if she did what she could here, someone else would take care of Sean back home.

Prayers were all she had, because he didn't reach out.

For all she knew, he had amnesia.

She'd already tried to contact him. His phone number didn't work, and none of his family members had listed phone numbers. Oh, for the straightforward days of landlines and phone books.

The military was no help, either. She called again and again, only to get the same brick wall of no information.

"I appreciate what you are saying," Jenna said through gritted teeth. "But I have a marriage license that promises I do know him. I'm happy to fax it to whoever needs to see it. And I'm not asking you to tell me anything about his condition, just to pass a message on."

"Ma'am, you will need to contact the Canadian Forces member yourself, directly. And as this is not the first time you have contacted us, I need to remind you that everyone has a right to privacy. You are not an authorized next of kin for any member of the Canadian Forces. I cannot help you."

The line went dead, and Jenna almost threw her phone across her tent. There went another twenty dollar phone call that had done her no good.

She wiped a lazy drop of sweat from her brow and swallowed back the tears she refused to let fall.

Her pager went off, and she stuffed her feelings down, deep inside. This was the only way to get through the day now. She'd turned herself in an automaton. She took a quick look at the message, then washed her face and headed for the hospital.

Sami was coming out as she approached the front doors. "I was coming to see you," he said, his expression not giving anything away.

"Yeah?" She stopped abruptly, dust kicking up around her.

"I've secured a replacement midwife. She'll be arriving in two weeks." He searched her face. "It's the best I can do, Jenna."

She nodded numbly. Two more weeks. She just had to survive fourteen more days of work, and then she was going to be on a plane back to Canada.

To Sean, and whatever the hell was going on in Pine Harbour.

Because she'd made him a promise. She was his wife, no matter what.

CHAPTER SEVENTEEN

June
Pine Harbour

THREE WEEKS after her arrival in Sean's home town, Jenna had to face two unhappy truths: she was zero help to her husband in his current mental state, and the pie at Mac's was no longer an acceptable form of therapy.

She could deal with the latter point more easily than the former. She found a therapist in Wiarton who could see her once a week, and she started walking every evening. Sometimes Chloe or Olivia came with her, but often she walked on her own. She explored every street in the small town, and figured out the fastest way to get from Dean's little house to the still-freezing-cold beach where the town dipped down to the natural harbour on Lake Huron which gave the town its name.

Grace checked in with her every few days too. Jenna clung to her friendships with these women, to the new routines she was forging, because after a week of decent visits with Sean, everything between them had gone downhill.

And counting in weeks had been reassuring when she first arrived, but now they were nearing the twelve week mark post-trauma. She'd been here for four weeks. Pretty soon, she'd be counting in months, and that shift felt depressing.

She focused on work to distract herself. By the start of June, Jenna had her documentation submitted to the provincial midwifery college. She had to take an online course while her registration was being transferred from British Columbia to Ontario. In another month or two, she'd be registered and able to apply for local jobs. She was purposefully keeping herself from doing any active job hunting, though, since most positions were further afield than she wanted and the lure of that escape would probably be attractive to her at this point.

Very attractive, if she let herself admit how frustrated she was getting with Sean.

The closest they'd come to a real, meaningful conversation had been weeks ago. In the time since, he'd been cold and hard to her, and some days, hadn't been up for a visit at all. She'd gotten used to his cryptic texts. **Today's not a good day.**

She hated she couldn't do anything to relieve the migraines.

She hated that her visits taxed him. She didn't want to be a drain in any way. She wanted to give him room to recover, but she also ached to see him for the twenty-two hours a day she was away from him. Stretching it to forty hours between visits physically hurt her.

And in the crazy yo-yo swing between feelings, she'd come to resent going to Dean and Liana's house to see him. The beautiful home Sean had turned into a voluntary prison.

Anger surged through her, unexpected and harsh.

He obviously didn't want her to meddle in his care. It wasn't her place. She told herself to be respectful of boundaries and understand he could choose the care he wanted—or didn't—and he was smart enough to be making good choices.

She told herself a lot of bullshit.

He needed something else.

And his brothers, as well meaning as they were, weren't helping.

She took a deep breath and marched up the porch. She knocked loudly on the front door, then stepped back and propped her hands on her hips for a second before clasping them behind her back.

No need to be confrontational.

But when the door swung open, her mouth opened and words poured out.

"I'm here to collect Sean and bring him back to my place. Your place. Your old place, I mean. This isn't the right environment for him, with you doting on him."

Dean gave her a long, slow blink. "Hey, Jenna."

She swallowed hard and nodded. "Hi."

"So you…willingly…want to live with the grumpiest man on the peninsula?"

Want wasn't the right word. Needed, maybe. "It's the right thing to do."

"I'm guessing you haven't suggested this to him yet."

She flushed with guilt. "No."

Dean grinned. "That's the Foster way. Come on in." He stepped out of the way and hollered up the stairs to Sean. "Yo, bud! Your wife is here!"

That had stopped embarrassing Jenna somewhere around the fourth visit, but it hadn't stopped making her feel funny in a different way, deep inside. There was a long stretch of silence. Then they heard a grumble, followed by, "Yeah. Coming down."

What? Jenna started for the stairs, but stopped when Sean rounded the corner on his own. Well, not totally on his own.

He was holding a cane.

Using it, even.

He didn't look at her. His gaze was fixed on a point on the wall high above her. She could only imagine how much concentration it took for him to ignore the swirling disorientation that was his constant vertigo.

But he was doing it. Step, step, step.

He stopped at the top of the stairs and switched the cane to his other hand before grabbing the bannister and with a lot more grace than she expected, he sat down.

It was a little thing, really.

But he sat down fluidly. No hesitation. Was he aware he'd done that?

She beamed at him as he took the stairs on his bottom, and when he stood in front of her, he rolled his eyes. "Don't look so proud."

She could scarcely believe what she was seeing. Proud didn't even touch the surface of how she felt. "I am," she said, her voice cracking. Damn feelings.

His jaw flexed as he switched the cane again and leaned against it.

"You've been practicing behind my back." She smiled to soften that statement. "How? Here?" Maybe she was wrong about this being a bad place for him to recuperate. He'd made more progress than she'd ever have suspected.

"Here. Owen Sound for physio. Some strength training, too."

How had she not seen it? She looked at him through fresh eyes. He was standing stronger, and his face wasn't pinched in pain, either.

Dean cleared his throat. "Jenna was saying—"

"Nothing important," she interjected.

Sean's brother gave her a confused look.

Now wasn't the time to change his routine. Not when he was finally on the path to recovery.

"It can wait." She pointed toward the kitchen. "Okay, Mr. Mobile, offer me a coffee or something."

———

SEAN WATCHED Jenna eye the fancy cane sugar cubes Liana liked. She looked at them three times, each time convincing herself she didn't need them. She'd been cutting back, he'd noticed. His old self would have understood, and encouraged her.

Now he had to keep himself from reaching out and putting one in her cup for her. Life was too damn short to deprive oneself of a sugar cube in one's coffee.

"What was Dean talking about before?" he asked when she finally lifted her unsweetened coffee to her lips.

She sipped slowly.

He waited. He'd caught the edge of their conversation, something about the right thing to do. Depending on who you asked, that could be a lot of different things.

She couldn't leave. That wasn't right.

He couldn't keep her here, though. That wouldn't be fair.

Fair and right weren't the same thing anymore, though. Not in his new normal.

For months, he'd buried the memories deep. All the things he'd said to her. All the promises he'd made. He hadn't known jack shit when he'd been spouting that nonsense. Thought he could offer her the moon when really, all they got were a few dances in the moonlight.

Borrowed magic. That's what they'd had.

"You seem like you're doing a lot better now," she finally said, softly.

His chest tightened. *Let her go.* That had been the plan, but now that it was here, now that she might be done…it hurt. *Selfish at every turn.* "Yeah. Well, I'm motivated." Her eyes lit up. He couldn't have that. There was no room for hope. "I need to get out of here."

"Really?" Her eyes got brighter still. "I wondered if you were happier with everything your brothers were doing."

"I don't want to rely on them," he said tightly, and then to drive the point home, he added, "Or anyone."

Bam. Direct hit. He put that light in her eyes out like a fucking pro, like an emotional sniper, and his stomach turned.

"Good," she said softly, glancing back to her coffee. "That's great." She didn't look at him. She played with her spoon. "So…are you more mobile now? I mean, I feel kind of horrible for not noticing the improvement over the last month."

"There wasn't much change, at first." He gave her a rueful smile. "I did my degree in kinesiology. I should have had more faith. But I wasn't sure it was going to work. I didn't know what else to do, but I was pessimistic."

She lifted her head, her eyes wide as she searched his face. "Did you worry I would be too optimistic?"

The question startled him, and he answered before he could stop himself. "Maybe. Yes."

"Oh." She nodded slowly. "I understand that."

"The real breakthrough came last week. And then I really was exhausted the next day when you came over." He hadn't needed to lie to her as much as he'd thought he would.

And he'd found himself increasingly uncomfortable with that plan, anyway.

"So how mobile are you?"

"It's a lot faster than with the walker. I haven't started testing myself on distance, but I can move around the house no problem."

"That's amazing." Damn it. Nothing could keep her hope dimmed for more than a minute or two. She fiddled with her spoon as she looked at him. "How would you feel about…"

When she trailed off, he leaned in. "About?"

She pressed her lips together. Her eyes shifted, like she was re-categorizing her thoughts before continuing. "Come over for dinner. I…I go for a walk most nights now. It's been a soothing routine. And the sidewalk in front of Dean's old place is easier to walk on than the gravel drive here, I bet."

"Dinner."

"No pressure. Would lunch be easier?"

"Dinner's fine," he heard himself say.

Was it fine?

It was something.

Definitely not part of the plan, that was for sure.

But he found himself struggling to find a good reason to shut her down again.

————

NOT ONCE IN her early relationship with Sean had Jenna felt nervous. Excited, yes. Shy, a couple of times. Overwhelmed with want…constantly.

But nerves hadn't played a role in how they started. There'd been no expectations. What was there to be nervous about flirting with a man who was going to disappear from her life? And then by the time they were travelling together, they were friends and lovers, and the time for nerves was past.

Their wedding day, maybe.

She pulled out their rings, carefully stowed in the small wooden box he'd bought her in Arcos. She tried to remember that day, but it was cloudy now, fogged up by all the frustration and fear since.

Definitely something to talk to her therapist about. Not something to dwell on tonight. Sean would be arriving soon. Dean said he'd drop him off around four.

She looked at her phone. Five minutes to the hour, and her stomach was a riot of butterflies.

When she heard the growl of a truck out front, she forced herself to go to the kitchen instead of racing to the front door. If she was too excited, that would stress Sean out. They both knew she wanted this desperately. She didn't need to highlight it for him with sparklers and a neon sign.

When the knock came at the door, she counted to three —and then the door opened.

"Hey," Sean called out, letting himself in.

She stepped into the hallway. "Hey."

They stood there, exchanging nervous looks for a moment. Then she laughed and pointed to the living room. "Want to sit?"

He gave her a tired smile. "Yes. Thanks."

Out the front window, she spotted Dean pulling away.

Sean followed her gaze. "I told him he wasn't allowed to come in. I didn't need a chaperone."

"He worries about you."

"We get on each other's last nerve."

"That too."

"Last time I was here, we were having a house party," Sean said as he eased into the corner of the couch. "Dean was away, falling in love with Liana, and Matt's apartment was too crowded. That feels like a lifetime ago."

Jenna curled up in the arm chair and frowned in confusion. "What about your place?"

"I was staying at the Colonel's house. I was gone so much that maintaining a separate apartment here stopped making sense."

"But..." Sean despised his father. Spending any amount of time together didn't make any sense, either. Jenna still hadn't met the man. He was the only Foster who hadn't actively sought her out, and Pine Harbour was a small town. Not having met yet meant the man was avoiding her, which she didn't care about—except in any way that affected Sean.

Sean gave her a lopsided, tired smile. "Yeah. Looking back, that seems like a weird choice. I don't know. We both seemed to like the antagonism. I wouldn't do it now. Couldn't. When I was injured, he didn't even offer to take me in. I think it was just understood that Dean would do it."

"Have you seen him a lot since you've been back?"

"No. A few visits in the first week or two. But his thing is that he likes to have us all over for dinner every so often. So far we've only managed one, just before you arrived, and it was at Dean's house. I think the old man is waiting until I'm mobile again to rally his sons around. That's what he likes to do, summon us."

She'd promised him no pressure. But a regular family dinner raised all sorts of questions. She took a deep breath and changed the subject. "Speaking of dinner, what would you like tonight? I've got salad stuff, stew in the freezer, and chicken breasts."

"I'm easy. Can I help?"

"Sure. But we've got some time first. Do you want a drink?"

He shook his head. "Thanks."

So polite. So shallow. Small talk might just kill her.

"Nice weather—"

"Do you want to watch something—"

They stopped at the same time and laughed. Sean gave her a lopsided grin. "So how about that sports team?"

"Right? Really slaying the ball stats this year." She groaned and rolled her head to the side as she laughed with him.

He pointed to her tablet on the coffee table. "Have you been listening to anything new?"

"Yeah. Actually, I got a new album." She reached for it and swiped into the music player. "Folk rock, a little bit country, a little bit blues. Good for walking to."

"You said you were walking after dinner. How far have you explored?"

And just like that, they slid into a real conversation about Sean's home town. They laughed together about the house painted purple and teal, and she filled him in on the latest gossip she'd overheard at Mac's—and he in turn explained who the gossip was about, since a lot of the names were still unfamiliar to her.

After a while, she stretched her arms and declared it cooking time. He excused himself to the washroom, and she went to the kitchen to get the prep started.

As she chopped vegetables, she listened to him move through the house. The thunk of his cane, the squeak of the wood floor as he slowly walked down the hall. She smiled to herself. She liked the noises of having Sean here.

Barely five weeks. They were still in early days, and if only for a meal, she had her husband back. If she squinted, she could see this as their future.

"What did you decide to make?" he asked from the doorway.

"Stirfry," she said, glancing at him over her shoulder. Just a second, just enough to soak up the sight of him filling the doorway. Did he know he was standing taller lately? She even liked the beard. He needed a haircut, but she'd let him figure that out on his own. "Would you rather rice or noodles?"

He scratched his belly, pulling up his shirt a bit, and she had a visceral flashback to Spain. She turned back to her cutting board lest he see the desire in her eyes.

No lusting after her husband. Not yet.

"Rice sounds good," he said from behind her. "What can I do?"

"Set the table? The rice will take twenty minutes, and then it'll be time to eat."

"I can do that."

Baby steps. She smiled again to herself. One thing at a time.

———

FOR SEAN'S next rehab session, Jake and baby Calvin picked him up and drove him down the peninsula to the hospital.

Jenna hadn't pushed back on his preference to do this without her. She'd just smiled and wished him luck.

It wouldn't be, though. It never was. He hated the circuit of exercises they put him through. Balance and orientation stuff designed to retrain his brain, but all it did was make him so tired he always passed out on the drive home.

He knew they worked. He was using a cane, wasn't he?

That didn't mean he liked them, though, and on a day-to-day basis, they hurt more than they helped.

He had to get his attention back on the long term goal. Independence. Getting to a place where everyone around him could stop watching him like he was an invalid.

Speaking of his independence…

"Do we have time to stop and get me a new cell phone?" he asked Jake when his brother picked him up.

Jake looked at Calvin, sleeping in his car seat. "Yeah, of course."

The phone he'd taken overseas had been lost in transit back to Canada. Some of his personal belongings had shown up, but not others. And in the weeks after he'd returned home, he hadn't cared, hadn't wanted any contact with the outside world.

But it was ridiculous that Jenna—or anyone else, not that anyone else did—had to contact him through Dean and Liana. That needed to change.

The clerk at the store set it up for him on the cell

network, but as soon as they left, he turned it off and put it in his pocket. One thing at a time. Phone acquired. Check. Didn't mean he had to use the thing.

"I'm gonna rack out for the drive back, if you don't mind."

Jake just squeezed his shoulder. "Of course."

The most common refrain his brothers said to him now. Sure, Sean. Whatever you need. Of course.

It had been what he wanted after coming home. But now it was starting to chafe, and that was his own making, wasn't it?

CHAPTER EIGHTEEN

JENNA NOTICED a pattern emerge over the next week. On the days that Sean did rehab, he needed an early bedtime that night, and food was invisible to him.

But the next day, he was ravenous, and those days, she claimed him, and not just for dinner. She started picking him up earlier and earlier, even if he protested that he'd just nap the afternoon away. That was fine by her. She didn't need to be Suzy Homemaker, with small talk and a formal dinner on the table every night. They weren't playing some fantasy version of house.

She just wanted to be together, alone. Or as alone as they could be in a town almost entirely populated by people he was related to by blood or marriage. So she had to share him a bit when Sophia saw Uncle Sean sitting on the back deck, or when Matt popped in for a cold one. And she'd backed down on her righteous indignation that he needed to live with her—that had been rushing things.

It was rewarding enough to see him wander into the kitchen and grab something. To watch him graze on food that filled him up, all day long, on the days that he had energy to eat.

Something had shifted between them. Sean wasn't pushing her away, wasn't angry. She didn't quite trust the peace, but that didn't stop her from enjoying it.

And their new friendship wasn't all she was enjoying, despite her best efforts to keep things platonic. The summer heat had settled in, bringing with it basketball shorts instead of sweatpants.

Not that she'd minded the sweatpants. They had a certain appeal, too, when they rode low on Sean's hips.

But she liked the shorts a lot. The way they slid up his thighs as he napped, for example.

One afternoon she found herself standing in the living room, just watching him sleep. He was stretched out on the couch, his arm thrown over his eyes, his shirt rumpled and pulled up above his waist.

His legs were bare, long and muscular, but leaner than before. All of him was thinner, but still so familiar. The golden hair on his legs, and on his belly, where it decorated the remnant of a tan from his shirtless runs in Spain. Her heart leapt into her throat as she looked at him.

She knew this man intimately. But not *this* man. He'd shown no interest in her in that regard, and she knew he wasn't well, but...how could he be so different? The intimacy they'd shared in those two weeks now seemed like a dream. It wasn't the first time she'd had that thought, but this time she didn't push it away.

She just stood there, and let herself remember.

It hadn't been a dream. It had been amazing and special and very, very real.

She'd become pretty adept at ignoring her attraction to

Sean, which hadn't abated any. Fallen secondary to concern at times, but it was always there. The tease of his broad shoulders. The tight, warm skin of his neck and his forearms, just begging to be touched.

And now her head swirled with the reminder of how that line of hair ran south from his belly button.

A knock at the door startled her out of her remembering, and she quickly hustled to get it before Chloe knocked again.

She eased it open and pointed around to the back. "Sean's sleeping," she whispered. "Come around to the other side."

This afternoon, Chloe brought the fixings to make cold salads that worked as full meals. One pot to boil some pasta, but everything else was chopping and mixing and waiting while they drank lemonade.

When she checked on Sean an hour later, she found him still snoring.

"He's still fast asleep," Jenna said. "I'll leave him a bit."

Chloe nodded as she crumbled feta over the pasta. "I'll pack up my portions and head home. I've got a date with Netflix tonight."

"What are you watching?" Sean hadn't shown any interest in television, but maybe she could suggest a movie. Or a show…shorter episodes might be easier to follow.

"I like to listen to stand-up comedy. Lets me do something else at the same time, because I don't need to keep my eyes on the screen."

Jenna snapped her fingers. "That's genius."

"Right? The laundry mountain can't best me and my clever mind."

She laughed. "You win. But I also mean for Sean. It

would be great for him to listen to something, because the visual stuff is annoying."

Chloe did a little dance. "Even better. I do enjoy being helpful and making smart suggestions. Go Chloe!"

"How are you still single?"

Chloe sighed. "I know. It's a tragedy. Except… I love my life, and who needs a man? Other than you. You need that man." She pointed toward the living room. "But that's different and special."

Jenna laughed. "Fair point. Did you get enough of the chickpea salad?"

"Yep." Chloe spooned some of the pasta salad into a takeaway container. "And now I've got some of this, too, and I'm gone." She disappeared out the back door, the same way she'd come in.

Jenna was tidying when Sean woke up. He was getting pretty quick with the cane in general, but he was slow when he first woke up. Tap, step, tap, step.

He stopped in the doorway of the kitchen. "Hey."

She turned around and leaned back against the counter.

"You getting ready to make dinner? I can help."

"All done, actually. You've got your choice of pasta salad or chickpea salad. And there's watermelon for dessert."

"You've been busy."

"Chloe helped."

"She was here? I didn't hear her arrive. Or leave, I guess, for that matter."

"You were out cold." She found herself smiling at him, in a flirty way, and she couldn't help it. "I came to wake you up earlier."

He didn't notice the flirting. "Yeah, I was dead to the world."

I know, she wanted to say. You always are the day after rehab. You just eat and sleep and recover, and that's okay. I see you. Don't worry.

But he didn't want her to care too much, so she kept that to herself.

She pulled two plates out of the cupboard then got the salads from the fridge. "Which one do you want?"

"I'll try both."

She already had the spoon of chickpea salad ready. "Here you go."

He shifted his cane to his other hand and carefully took the plate. By the time she joined him at the table, he had a forkful of pasta salad speared. As soon as her butt hit the chair, he shovelled it into his mouth and made a groan that pleased her more than words could say. "Man, this is good. You're going to make me fat with all this food."

She shrugged. "Or strong."

"Is that your plan?"

"I wouldn't call it a plan. That sounds certain and deliberate."

"And what is this?" He stabbed his fork at the pasta again and she had to swallow a grin.

"Something between a wish and a prayer."

He gave her an inscrutable look as he pushed the food into his mouth. "It's good. As dinner. Crap as a plan."

"Gee, thanks."

"If you want to bulk me up again, you could make steak."

Was that right? "*You* could make steak."

"Maybe I will." He glanced toward the deck. "We'd need to get a barbecue."

We.

It wasn't devouring kisses or even heated looks, but Jenna fell on that single word like it was a gift from heaven. "Sure," she said smoothly. "That sounds like a great idea."

And just like that, her desire to have him move in roared back to life.

———

TWO WEEKS after Jenna's first dinner invitation, Sean woke up to a text message from Dani. **Up for a visit from me and Calvin?**

It was the first social call he'd received on his new phone, and it startled him. Was he such a miserable cur that it had taken this long for anyone to reach out to him?

You could have texted someone. Anyone, really.

He scrubbed a hand over his face. Yeah, he could do a lot more than he had. He was still dodging visits from the regiment, too.

Dani first, though.

For sure, he typed back. **Do you want to pick me up and we can hit Mac's, just like the old days?**

Now a visit to the diner meant grabbing a high chair for his nephew on the way in—and feeling like a champ for managing the chair in one hand and his cane in the other.

Not quite like the old days.

But the burger and shake was the same. And so was Dani's nosy, accept-zero-bullshit attitude about his life. She didn't fancy it up by calling it an intervention, though. She just wanted to give him shit.

"What's with this pick you up business?" She grinned

at him. "We're not twenty, and you have a perfectly good truck."

"Jenna's using it. And I had a truck when I was twenty."

"Which I had to drive half the time because you were drunk."

He snorted. "Yeah, I was a shithead. So what's your point?"

She gave him an unexpectedly soft look from across the booth. "It was my turn to hassle you. What I really want to say is that you've come a long way in a short period of time."

"We can stop talking about me now," he said gruffly, his cheeks flushing as he reached for his milkshake. He wasn't sure he deserved much credit for any of that. Jenna was the one who'd been feeding him well, re-fuelling him after gruelling physio sessions that left him gutted.

"Can we talk about your wife?"

He choked on a mouthful of chocolate shake. "Sure," he said after clearing his throat.

"She's lovely."

Dani had no idea. "That she is."

"And you didn't tell anyone."

"It was..." He rubbed at his temple. "At the time, it seemed like the right call. I didn't want her to be in any danger."

"And then once you were hurt?" Dani's eyes flashed in anger. "I can't imagine Jake being injured somewhere and not being told."

Sean wanted to tell her that was different, but he wasn't sure it was. Not at the time, anyway. Now...now he didn't know what he was to Jenna. A friend, maybe. "I tried," he admitted quietly. "At first. But they couldn't understand me. And then it seemed like it was for the best that she wasn't there."

Dani nodded. "I know it was awful." And she was a paramedic. Sean knew she wasn't just saying that. Dean may have been the one to fly to Germany and sit at his side, but his entire family had received updates—

Not your entire family.

He shoved his plate away.

"Do you want a doggie bag?"

He blinked at Dani.

"Let's get everything. If we don't finish, that's okay. Do you think they do doggie bags?"

Jenna laughed, soft and bright. "No. And I don't want to be wasteful."

"We're on vacation. Live a little."

"I'm living plenty already."

Instead of answering his friend, he lifted his hand. When the waitress came over, he asked for a box for his food, and then asked what pies they had today. "I'll take a slice of each of them, please. To go." He looked across the booth at Dani, who was beaming at him. "What?"

"Jenna likes pie."

"I know. How do you know?"

"We have lunch sometimes."

"Sometimes?"

"A few times."

Jenna hadn't said anything about *that.* "Please tell me you haven't pulled out any naked baby pictures. Of me, I mean. Feel free to show off Mr. Calvin here." He tried to give his nephew a French fry, but Dani swooped in with mom hands and snatched it away.

"No fries."

"Spoilsport."

"Yep." She gestured to his lunch. "Come on, pack up. I'll drop you off on my way home."

"I'm going to Jenna's next."

She gave him a weird look. "Obviously."

"Is it?"

Dani just laughed. "Oh, Sean."

He didn't know what that meant, but he wasn't digging into it now.

Jenna was reading on her iPad when he arrived. The way her forehead was scrunched together, he knew it was work-related, so he waved the takeout bag at her and kept on going to the kitchen. She joined him as he was putting on coffee.

"Chloe's arranged for me to have access to some medical journals through the library," she said as she grabbed two mugs from the cupboard. "So I've been catching up on some reading I didn't have time to do in Turkey."

"What's new in the field of midwifery?"

She laughed. "A fair bit, actually. Lots of shifting opinions about the importance of giving birth in your own community." Twin slashes of pink cut across her cheeks. "Something I wish I'd spent more time reading about before going to Urfa, really. I knew it was difficult for those women to be displaced, but…" She let out a sharp breath. "Well, when you know better you do better. It's fascinating reading, really."

"Tell me about it." He gestured to the counter. "I just had lunch with Dani, and there was pie. I had to share it."

"Cool. I can totally take a pie break now. Then I need to

dash to the library to load more articles on my iPad. The journal subscription is restricted to the library network only." She took a careful look at the four slices he'd set out. "This is *a lot* of pie."

"I may have gotten carried away," Sean said, suddenly feeling a bit wrong-footed. Had he overreached?

She slid him a sideways glance and smiled. "I wasn't complaining."

She picked the strawberry rhubarb, and he grabbed the apple.

"Tell me more about this new way of thinking," he said, and she did. She leaned in and between slow bites, she spilled everything she'd been reading and thinking.

She had his whole attention. He was engrossed as she told him about a study done by Inuit midwives in the north.

But too soon, the pie was gone, and an unwelcome yawn forced its way out of his mouth.

"I should go to the library," she said.

He opened his mouth to protest, and another yawn slipped out. Fucking hell. "I'll just grab a quick nap," he said quietly. "I'll be recharged by the time you get back."

He was asleep before she left. He'd stretched out on the couch one second, and the next he was being dragged out of his unconscious stupor by a series of knocks at the front door.

Bleary-eyed, Sean dragged himself up off the couch. Once the room stopped spinning, he carefully made his way to the door, where a delivery driver stood filling out a missed-delivery notice slip.

"Oh," the guy said. "I didn't think anyone was home."

"Can I help you?" Sean wasn't interested in small talk.

"Registered letter for Jenna Kowalczyk."

Sean nodded and took the envelope. He scrawled his signature on the driver's digital pad then closed the door. He checked the clock. He'd slept for an hour.

He slowly made his way into the kitchen and set the letter down on the counter. He stared at the return address and logo in the top left hand corner. *The College of Midwives of Ontario.*

His brows pulled tight. What was Jenna doing? He poured himself a glass of water and downed it in five steady gulps.

He'd just refilled the glass when she returned.

"I'm in the kitchen," he called out when the door opened.

She came in and set her tablet on the counter. Her skin was flush and her hair had a bit of a humid curl to it.

"Hot outside?"

"Little bit. I walked over." Her eyes darted to the water glass in his hand.

He held it out. "You want some?"

Instantly, he had a flashback to Spain.

Always.

Her eyes widened. Was she hit with the same aching jolt of deja vu?

But she just smiled and twisted around to grab her own glass.

"You got mail," he said as he shifted out of the way. He tried to be casual about it, tossing it over his shoulder as he headed back into the living room. "It came as a registered letter to the door and I signed for it."

"Thank you." Behind him, she didn't move. He heard her drink, and kept moving.

"It's from the College of Midwives of Ontario."

"Oh, excellent!" Now she was following him, ripping the envelope open. "That was faster than I expected."

His heart pounded in his chest as he sat down on the couch and looked up at her. "You're going to start practicing here?"

She stopped mid-rip and glanced at him, giving him a cautious look. "Yes."

"You didn't tell me that." He tried to not make that sound petulant. *Tell me more secrets.* He knew less about her now than he had after knowing her for two days. She'd stormed ahead with some plan here and not breathed a word of it to him.

She searched his face. "It just didn't come up. I mean, you didn't ask. And I need to work—"

She cut herself off, and shame twisted Sean's gut. Of course she did.

He couldn't.

He grimaced, and waved her off. "I get it."

———

CRAP.

Jenna felt like a heel.

In her dogged optimism that they'd find their way back to each other, she'd forgotten that he lost most of his identity in the explosion. No more career officer. No more running.

She'd pinned all his happiness on a return to being her husband.

How would she feel if the situation were reversed?

She set the letter down. "I should have told you. This is

probably confirmation of my application for registration. I sent in my degree and work records from British Columbia a few weeks ago." *When you were giving me the silent treatment*, she wanted to add. "I haven't pursued any jobs yet."

"But you want to."

In the long term, she'd need to, but she wasn't going to point that out again. "I do."

He gave her a hard-to-read look. "Are there jobs around here?"

"I don't know. I haven't…that hasn't been my focus." She moved around the coffee table and joined him on the couch.

"You could go anywhere."

"I could. I'm not going to." *Not unless you wanted to move.* There was still a lot of stuff that couldn't be said between them. But it didn't matter if she couldn't voice that truth out loud; it was still the truth even if it was a secret. Even if at the same time, she resented that he no longer welcomed her secrets. That he actively hid from the deeper, darker bits of her. She'd once thought she might follow him anywhere. Now she knew that to be absolutely true. She'd follow him no matter what.

"You're really not going," he said quietly, and the fact he'd still thought she might give up on him sliced into her like a scalpel.

"I'm here to stay," she breathed. "I thought I'd made that clear."

"You probably did."

"Keeping my college registration from you wasn't deliberate, I promise."

He nodded, but there was a tightness to his jaw.

Maybe she needed to re-examine some of the accidental things she was doing, too. Like not sharing how she was coping. She took a deep breath and changed the subject. "I've been seeing a therapist. Talking stuff out. I thought you might want to know."

He gave her a guarded look. "Stuff about me?"

"A bit about us. Mostly about me."

"Is it helping?"

"Yeah. It's good to have an outlet."

He nodded. "I've been seeing Jake and Tom."

Her lips twitched. "About…?"

"Mostly about how I'm a jackass."

———

SHE LAUGHED, but it hadn't been a joke. He was a jackass. He'd been so tangled up in himself he hadn't noticed she was laying a foundation to work here. Live here.

Therapy, friendships, job hunting.

Jenna was planning to stay.

He'd been a complete ass to her, repeatedly, and she'd registered with her professional college.

He'd frozen her out of his rehab, and she'd made friends elsewhere.

She'd been struggling with her feelings and had needed to turn to a professional to have someone to hear her out.

Meanwhile he'd done his damnedest to show her that he didn't need her, and she'd somehow twisted that into a regular dinner date between equals.

He didn't deserve her loyalty. Or her kindness.

But he was done being blind to it. "Everything you do comes from a good place," he finally said. "I promise you that I see that." No, it was more than that. He took a deep breath. "And I'm proud of you." The words rushed out of him. "You don't need to hide work from me. I know you said it wasn't deliberate, and I see that. But I want to hear more. I want to hear about the research and the job hunt and everything else that goes with shifting gears like this. I know this wasn't your plan."

"I've learned that plans need to be flexible." She gave him a half-smile. "And I need to be patient."

That's why she hadn't said anything. Fuck. She'd told him she'd have hope. He just hadn't heard her.

"Why are you being so good to me?"

She lifted one shoulder in a small shrug, her face soft. "Because… you were good to me. Good for me. And I know that if the situation was reversed, you'd take care of me."

A pang shot through him. He hadn't thought of his mother in weeks. As he'd gotten on top of some of the more painful symptoms, the panic and fear that had accompanied them had drifted away, and he'd seen those thoughts as irrational worries. But there it was, a little tug. He shoved it away. Jenna. He needed to focus on her.

"I'm not the same now," he said. "I can't compete with that guy."

She reached for his hand, and he let her take it. Her fingers were cool and comforting as she squeezed them tight around his. "You don't need to."

"I do. You deserve him."

She was quiet for a while, but she didn't let go of his hand. "You know," she said. "You're way more annoying than he was."

At first he wasn't sure he'd heard her correctly, and then she grinned.

His mouth dropped open, and her eyes lit up.

"You're a much bigger pain in the ass," she added, growing bolder. "Grumpier, too."

He laughed, because she was right. "I'm fucking tops at that."

"You win at scowling. And pessimism. You sweep the entire category." She shifted closer and bumped her shoulder into his. "Don't sell your best qualities short."

"Clearly I was just looking at this the wrong way." Except he hated that she saw him as those things. It was the truth. He just didn't care for how he looked in that light.

"I like this guy," she whispered. "Don't underestimate his appeal."

Like. Not love. She'd loved the old Sean. Fell for him in a single easy grin. Now nothing about him was easy and she still liked him.

He shouldn't want that. Should know better than to hook his hope onto leftover crumbs. Love had faded and been replaced with something pale and paltry.

But it was also all he could handle right now. Like.

What an odd word to fill him with unexpected joy.

"I like you, too," he said roughly.

She smiled. "That's something, then. As good a place as any to start again."

His stomach tightened up. Start again? No. That was—

"Don't freak out," she said, her voice soft and her eyes warm. "No pressure. Promise."

What was the point of starting again when he wasn't sure what he could offer her?

Of course he was freaking out. She deserved so much more than this.

But his plan to push her away had failed, because deep

down, he didn't want her to go. And where they were right now wasn't a permanent solution, either.

As good a place as any to start again. That was scary as fuck.

It was probably time for her to pressure him a little.

His hand shook, and he tightened his fingers around hers. "Have you thought about what that might look like?"

She shook her head, then stopped, and nodded. "Yes, actually. But I don't want to pressure you."

Maybe it was time for a little pressure. "Try me."

"There are two bedrooms here," she said faintly, almost smiling. The deja vu was weird.

But where she hadn't cared about separate rooms in Spain, he grabbed on to the offer like it was a life preserver. "I could spend more time here."

Her smile grew, just a bit. "You could."

He went back to Dean's house that night, but it was the last night he slept elsewhere. When Dean brought him home after rehab the next day, it was to the little bungalow.

His brothers moved fast. All of his stuff had been moved over while he was gone.

Jenna had dinner and Netflix cued up.

"Hey," he said.

She gave him a quick smile before turning back to the salad she was tossing. "Good session?"

Not really. "It was fine."

"Tired?"

"Yeah."

"We'll eat, and watch a thing, and call it an early night."

He was exhausted when he finally lay down. Not so

wiped that his brain didn't swirl around how weird it felt to be one room over from her—not the goal, to be sure, but something. A place to start, she'd said.

It was weird.

But it was something. It was a start, and he hung on to that as his last thought before sleep consumed him.

CHAPTER NINETEEN

HIS NEXT TRIP to Owen Sound after moving in with Jenna was a big one. Two appointments, on the same day, a doctor's visit as well as his physiotherapy. She'd offered to take him, but he asked Dean to drive him instead, as he knew he'd be a bear by the end of the day.

He wasn't wrong.

"How have the last two weeks been with the disorientation?" the doctor asked as he had Sean turn his head left and right, up and down. His vision wobbled then righted itself with each movement.

"The new dosages seem to be helping."

"Have you tried driving yet?"

"No."

"There's no reason not to. You're capable of assessing and managing your own function there."

"I'll try soon."

"There are assistive devices that can be installed in a vehicle to limit the amount of head twisting you need to do. Better mirrors, rear view cameras. I can refer you to occupational therapy for an assessment."

Another layer of therapy. "Maybe next month."

"Sure, I'll make a note to revisit it then. How's the sleep?"

"Shitty."

"Are you still napping during the day?"

"Yeah."

"That's not the worst thing in the world—I'd rather you get the sleep in pieces than not at all—but ideally, we want you to get a good chunk of unbroken sleep at night."

"I hear you, doc."

"And how's your sexual function?"

Sean froze.

The doctor didn't miss a beat. "Decreased sexual function is a common side effect. We haven't touched on it yet because we had other, more pressing concerns, regaining your walking and balance. But I can—"

"Please don't say you can refer me to someone for that."

"There are great therapists. We can discuss it again at a future appointment."

"I'd rather we didn't."

The doctor rolled back on his stool and crossed one ankle over his knee. "There are options that work for most patients."

Sean gritted his teeth. "Doesn't feel like that to me."

"Are we talking about decreased function or a total absence?"

The paper on the exam table crinkled beneath him as he shifted. Sweat beaded on his forehead. "Nothing."

"All right. We'll work on that. Do you have access to material?"

"Material? Are you asking if I have porn?" He didn't need porn. He had Jenna, lithe and sexy and smelling like sweet oranges. Nothing could be more arousing, if arousal were possible.

"Some people find pictures or videos easier to respond to, initially, than a partner."

His skin turned hot beneath the cold sweat. "I'll take that under advisement."

"It's normal."

Sean could know that in his head. Had known it, had reconciled it for himself, in a pessimistic way.

Of course the doc would bring it up now.

Like Sean needed his... dysfunction underlined. A reminder that no part of him was going to magically start working again.

He wasn't ready for dick rehab, too.

"Try driving," the doc said. "The independence will do you some good."

"Yeah, maybe."

He meant, yeah, no, not yet, but after physio, Dean stopped at the dealership to pick up a new spare tire for Liana's car. Sean was tired, but there was a truck with a big slash through the sale sticker that kept drawing his attention. When Dean didn't immediately return, Sean climbed out and made his way over to the shiny red pick-up.

"See something you like?" A salesman joined him.

"Maybe." No. He didn't have a job. His disability would run out at some point, and then his savings would have to last him for a good long while. Until he figured out what the fuck he could do with his life now that everything he knew was out of reach.

And he had a truck.

Jenna was driving it.

Maybe he needed to get her a smaller car.

Maybe he needed to drive down the street for a hot minute before thinking about a second vehicle.

"What are you doing?"

Sean didn't need to turn around to hear the scowl in Dean's voice. He put a matching one on his own face and twisted around, ignoring how his head pulsed. "Looking at a new truck."

"Is that a good idea?"

"Is there some law against looking?"

"Guess not." But Dean said it in a way that made it pretty clear he didn't approve.

Fuck him. Sean clambered into the truck and slammed the door behind him.

As soon as Dean was in the driver seat, Sean set him straight. "The doc said I should start driving again."

"Driving. Not buying a truck you can't afford."

"You don't know what I can afford."

"I know you're living in my house rent free."

"You want me to pay you rent? Because I will. I'll buy the damn house from you if that's what you want."

"I don't—" Dean swore under his breath. "What the fuck has gotten into you?"

"I'd ask you the same fucking question. I was just looking at the damn truck. I'm not going to buy it. Why would you assume I was?"

That shut his brother up, and Sean slouched hard in his seat. He closed his eyes. Let the jerk think he'd fallen asleep, because that's all Sean was good for. Being an invalid. Being cared for. Being weak.

He didn't want to acknowledge that he was still encouraging that coddling, in a way.

The tense silence lasted all the way home. When Dean pulled up in front of the little house Sean was apparently mooching off him, Sean grabbed his backpack and his cane.

Fuck. He cleared his throat. "Thanks for the ride. I appreciate it."

Dean just raised his hand and exhaled an exasperated noise that might have been something like goodbye.

Jenna wasn't home, so he sat in the shower for a long time, until the hot water turned lukewarm.

When he got out, she still wasn't back, so he dried off and stretched out on his bed, his wet hair on a towel. He wanted to have a nap, his usual post-physio rack out, but the doc's advice echoed in his tired brain.

If he didn't have a nap, maybe he'd sleep better tonight.

He groaned and reached for his phone. Maybe he could just have a short nap. He'd set an alarm.

No. He should stay awake.

Think about Jenna. Try to jerk off.

It wouldn't do any good, but that wasn't the worst idea. He palmed his junk. The best he could get was a desperate, heavy want in his gut, and some normal thickening from direct stimulation.

Two words that weren't fucking hot in the least—direct stimulation.

He squeezed harder. Think of her tits, the taste of her skin. He'd spent two weeks licking her all over, because she tasted like sunshine. Why didn't he want that now?

He did. He was just tangled up with also wanting something he couldn't manage. To be hard for her, to be on top of her. He pictured himself railing her. Let his thoughts get filthy, and it just made him angry.

Beside him, his phone beeped. An email notification.

He'd never been a big device guy, and he was even less so now.

Do you have material?

Porn. His phone could be used for porn.

He picked it up and opened a browser window. He typed in **hot athletic sexy woman**, and images filled the screen. They were mostly hot, and they were all athletic and sexy.

Nothing. He clicked through to a free video site, and scrolled through the options. Cheerleaders, blow jobs, gang—nope. Blow jobs, maybe. He clicked on a video where the woman looked like Jenna. Long golden hair, ready smile. Wet mouth. He could remember it all, but putting the pieces together felt like an impossible task.

He slid his boxers lower on his hips and reached inside to cup his balls.

There was something clicking in his brain, a secret, dirty want, but it just couldn't connect properly.

Frustrated, he shoved his phone away and rolled over. At the end of a long day wasn't the time to experiment.

———

JENNA CAME home to the sound of gentle snores. Sean's door was closed, but even through it she could hear he was passed out cold.

She doubted he would wake up, so she didn't bother making anything for dinner. Instead, she wrote him a note telling him to call if he woke up, and she headed out the back door to see if Olivia wanted to walk to Mac's.

"Are we getting pie?" the other woman asked as she wiped Sophia's sticky fingers. "There you go, all clean. Go find Daddy. Rafe! I'm going out for a walk with Jenna!"

"I haven't had dinner yet."

"So that's a yes to pie?"

"Of course. Sean's asleep, and I don't feel like cooking for one. Pie for dinner is totally acceptable. It's pie as therapy that's dangerous."

Olivia gave her a smile that said she wanted to ask how that was going, but would be polite and keep it to herself.

"Did someone say pie?" Olivia's husband stalked into the living room and swooped his daughter up and into his arms. "Is Mommy going to bring us back dessert?"

"I can do that," Olivia murmured, pressing up onto her toes to give Rafe a kiss.

He looped his arm around her waist and held her tight as Sophia horned in on their smooch.

Jenna ignored the pang of envy that shot through her at the sweet, casual affection.

"Don't forget your phone," Rafe murmured as he let his wife go. His gaze stuck to her as they waved goodbye, and Olivia wiggled her phone at him before sliding it into her purse.

"He was even more overprotective with my first pregnancy," she whispered.

Jenna laughed as they turned off the front walk and onto the sidewalk. "I can imagine."

Olivia blushed. "I'd had every intention to space the kids out a bit more, but…"

"These things happen." Jenna had seen back-to-back pregnancies more frequently than Olivia might guess. "You've got a decent spacing, really. What will there be, two years between them?"

"Almost exactly. Twenty-three months."

"You're fine. Official midwife stamp of approval."

"Speaking of that…I mentioned to my doctor that a

midwife was living behind me. I'm not comfortable with the idea of a home birth like Dani had, but…"

"If something were to happen, you could call me up. Any time. And Dani's midwives also do hospital births. I've met them now, a few times." Jenna filled Olivia in on the job hunt. "So I can't just hang out my shingle, it's not that easy, but I bet by the fall, something will click into place. And emergency hollering is always acceptable."

"Good to know. Rafe will be relieved."

"He's really quite sweet."

"You say that now. Wait until he's texting you questions four months from now."

"I promise I won't mind." They'd reached Main Street, and Jenna pushed the button for the town's only cross walk lights.

After they crossed, Olivia gave her a sideways look. "It wasn't always easy for us. Rafe is extra attentive because of that."

Sean had told Jenna about Rafe and Olivia's first marriage in broad strokes. They'd married young, and divorced maybe too hastily. Two years passed before they found their way back together.

Jenna normally didn't consider herself a nosy person, but she found herself craving the story in Olivia's own words. Like she might find some clues there to shore up her patience with her own soldier who was locked inside himself. Maybe help her maintain healthy and reasonable expectations for progress.

Hell, she'd settle for a double-dose of false hope at this point.

"How did you find your way back to each other? Can I ask that?"

Olivia threw her head back and laughed. "I'm

surprised you haven't asked sooner. We have no secrets, really." She touched her belly. "Including this one, since I've already popped out, and nobody is shy about guessing whether or not I'm knocked up."

Jenna didn't bother to point out that Olivia had told her the so-called secret within a minute of meeting her. It wasn't just Rafe who was besotted with their little family. And Jenna kind of adored them both for it. Their love was sweet and innocent and inspiring.

But before Olivia could dig into the story of her marriage—and re-marriage—they were at Mac's, and suddenly not alone.

Matt and Tom were on their way in too, and Matt wanted to talk to Olivia about the annual Canada Day party, so their party of two became a working dinner for a party of four.

Romance inspiration would have to wait.

"How's Sean doing?" Tom asked quietly after they placed their food order.

Jenna's default answer to those kinds of questions was polite deflection. Non-answers that protected her husband's privacy.

But Sean had told her he was confiding in Tom. She could answer the question honestly without giving away too much, and maybe in the process let the other man know how grateful she was. "He's asleep right now," she said. "Physio day."

"He's still sleeping a lot, eh?"

She nodded. "It's good for him. As are your chats, by the way."

Tom gave her a surprised look. "Yeah?"

"He said…" she laughed. "Well, he said you called him a jackass. But he appreciated it—because men are weird."

"That was Jake, but yeah, we can be."

"Thank you for being just the type of weird he needs."

Tom nodded. "Any time."

"His best days are two days after physio, by the way."

"Is that so…" Tom leaned back and tapped his fingers on the table between them. "Good to know. Thanks."

———

WITH HER REGISTRATION with the provincial college officially in progress, Sean watched Jenna start her job search in earnest over the next two weeks. She took Canada Day off, and they went to the town party, which was laid-back and almost fun—as much fun as one could have on a one-beer limit and while watching all the pick-up sports games from the sidelines.

And then it was back to the daily grind of rehab for him, and job searching for her. She threw herself into it, and he was damn impressed.

He was proud of her. He hadn't been lying about that.

But it still felt weird to watch her leave for the day—to meet midwives within driving distance, to interview at hospitals, and sometimes just to explore the area—and leave him behind.

He needed to get his shit together. He'd gotten the all clear to start weight lifting on his own while at physiotherapy, because they had a full gym, and he might as well take full advantage of having made the drive in. His brothers were game to work out with him, too. They always had been.

He was lucky.

He knew it.

But he didn't feel it, still, and he felt like shit about *that*, too.

The one part of rehab he'd been avoiding was talking to the psychologist. He wasn't interested in talking about his feelings. He didn't need a shrink to work out new life goals or some shit like that. And since he was definitely being medically discharged, thanks to the stroke, he didn't have hoops to jump through to stay in uniform.

Maybe if he was special forces, they'd have pressured him to do more medical clearance. But a reserve officer? Nobody cared that much.

So fuck it. No talking.

But he'd been an elite athlete long enough that his stupid brain did a lot of the talking anyway.

Before he was injured, he'd thought the tour would be the first of many. He'd liked extreme racing, but it took a toll on his body. And the military gave him the same adrenaline rush, but for a greater good.

Now he was twenty-seven and his plans for the next fifteen, twenty years had literally exploded into a million broken pieces.

Except if he was being honest with himself, those goals had shifted the second he met Jenna.

He'd forgotten that in the chaos that followed the explosion. His life had shifted on its access two months earlier, too, and he'd rolled with that no problem. From the first night in Spain, he'd been thinking about some kind of forever with her.

That nebulous want, forever, quickly coalesced into a clear idea of the future. He'd wanted to be a husband, a father. Ideas which he'd never considered before. Never.

Now those wants seemed impossible again.

But as he lay in bed, listening to Jenna wake up, get the

shower going, whistle in the bathroom, he couldn't tell himself he didn't want her.

He blindly grabbed his phone and lifted it in front of his face. Not twisting his head quickly had become second nature to him, and the vertigo and tinnitus were now background nuisances more than overwhelming distractions.

It was seven in the morning. He hadn't been up this early in weeks, not since he'd started sleeping more or less through the week.

If Jenna was up, that meant she was heading out for the day.

He'd been planning on heading into Owen Sound with Jake, to work out and do physio, but maybe if Jenna was heading in that direction, she could drop him off.

He hauled himself out of bed and grabbed his cane as he closed his eyes and tried to reset his brain. Three, two, one… He blinked his eyes open again and started moving. She was still in the shower, so he went to the kitchen and put on coffee. He'd been reading a bit about vertigo, and some people swore it got better if you cut out caffeine. He wasn't there yet, but it was on his radar as something to try.

The shower cut off, so he put toast on and walked to the hallway. Tap, step, tap, step.

He leaned against the doorway and crossed his arms, waiting. He pictured her in the bathroom, drying off. They hadn't taken enough showers together in Spain. He should have washed her hair. Drawn her a bubble bath and scrubbed every last inch of her body.

He groaned and swiped his hand over his face. There was no point torturing himself like that when *his* body wasn't reacting. Or at least the useful part wasn't reacting.

His insides were hot and bothered, for sure. The hair dryer turned on, then off again.

He grinned. That was her de-fogging the mirror. She'd done the same thing in Spain.

Now she'd be pulling on her clothes. Panties first.

He glared at his dick. Nothing? Panties. Jenna, naked. Silk tugging up her legs.

It was like his body had forgotten how to redirect blood flow.

And now he was burning up under the collar of his t-shirt, too, which was unhelpful. He needed to think of something else. How to strip a rifle, maybe.

The bathroom door swung open, steam billowing out—because after Turkey, Jenna would probably always like her showers extra hot if she could get it—and Jenna whistled her way into the hallway.

But she wasn't dressed.

She was wrapped in a towel, and it wasn't very big.

"Morning," he choked out, and she jumped.

"Sean!" She stopped in the middle of the hallway, legs wide, eyes wide, hands clutching her towel tight. "You're up."

"I put coffee on."

"Thank you." She didn't move.

His pulse thumped hard at the base of his throat. "I was, uh, wondering…"

She waited, her eyebrows raised.

"Are you heading south down the peninsula today? I have rehab. We could go together. If it was convenient for you."

"Yeah. Yes, I'd love that. I have a couple of errands to run."

He nodded, even though that wasn't quite the right response. He felt slow and flat-footed here.

"I'll just… get dressed." She stepped towards him. Right. Her room was beside the kitchen. Beside him.

He didn't move, and then she was right in front of him, wearing nothing but an itty bitty towel, and suddenly he felt faint.

It wasn't a hard-on, not even close, but there was definitely a blood flow redirect situation going on in his body.

"You should get dressed, too," she said as she stopped in the doorway to her room. He followed her gaze down his body.

Right. He was just in boxers.

She stood there until they both lifted their eyes. Then she gave him a slow, sweet smile before closing the door behind her.

That's when he let out the breath he'd been holding.

Fuuuck… yeah.

It wasn't much, but he would totally take it.

Back in his room, he texted his brother that he didn't need a ride. Matt immediately called back.

"Hey, what do you mean you don't need a ride?"

"Jenna's going to take me."

Silence was not a great response. "For real?"

"Yeah."

"I thought you didn't want her to."

"That was before."

"Before what?"

"Before… I don't know. Just before now. And now it's fine."

"Okay. Just checking that you aren't skipping."

"Thanks, Dad."

Matt snorted. "Speaking of our father, though, a reminder that Friday night is family dinner night."

"Shit."

"Does Jenna know?"

He couldn't remember if he'd told her or not. "We'll be there."

He hung up and scowled at his phone. He didn't want that hanging over the week. He set a reminder in his phone so he wouldn't forget to tell her later.

After shoving a change of clothes into his backpack, he pulled on sweats. He could shower after his workout.

In the kitchen, he found Jenna buttering the toast he'd put on and then forgotten about. "Sorry, did I burn it?"

"Nope, it's perfect." She took a bite of one piece and handed him the other.

Then she licked a buttery crumb off her finger.

His chest tightened. "Good."

———

HIS PHYSIOTHERAPIST PUSHED him hard through a brutal arm workout. "Nothing wrong with your arms, Sean. Do it again. More weight this time. Let's find your fatigue point."

Then he did the circuit of brain exercises, and by the end of that, he had a killer headache. He refilled his water bottle and slowly made his way outside, where he downed some extra-strength painkillers and texted Jenna. **I'm done.**

She replied immediately. **Just leaving the grocery store. Five minutes away.**

When she pulled up, she had a ready smile for him. He walked around the truck, tap, step, tap, step, and pulled himself up into the passenger seat, his shoulder burning from the effort.

"Ready to go home?" she asked as she steered back toward the main drag.

Home.

That sounded so right it hurt. He exhaled roughly. "Yeah."

"How was your session today?"

He shrugged. "Hard. How about you? How was your day?"

She made a face. "Ran into some administrative hiccups. Basically spent the day confirming that there's only one way to practice here, which I knew, but I was hoping there might have been some workaround. So I need to find a practice to join. It's okay. It's just that's different from how I've previously…"

She kept talking, and he caught most of it, but his headache wasn't getting any better. He closed his eyes and pressed his hand to his forehead.

"Sean?"

"Headache." Maybe a migraine. He still wasn't completely sure he knew the difference until he was in the throes of a migraine and on the wrong side of twelve hours in bed.

She stopped talking. At the next traffic light, she dropped her hand to his knee and squeezed.

When they got home, he muttered an apology and patted her on the shoulder before crawling under his covers.

———

HE DIDN'T WAKE up until the next morning.

She'd left a note on the coffee maker.

MADE THIS POT AT EIGHT. **I'm off to Walkerton today, should be back mid-afternoon. Take it easy. XO Jenna**

HE'D ONLY MISSED her by half an hour, and the regret that hit him was solid and intense.

Take it easy.

He'd slept for fourteen hours.

He was so spun over the fact he'd just missed her and the worry that she thought he needed to take it easy after he *had* just taken it easy, thank you very much, that it took him some time to realize she'd signed it with a kiss and a hug.

He hadn't given her either in the six weeks she'd been in Pine Harbour.

He rocked back on his heels, and the kitchen spun around him. He gripped his cane tight with his hands, so tight his knuckles started to hurt, and he leaned against the counter.

CHAPTER TWENTY

JENNA RETURNED, as promised, mid-afternoon. He heard the truck pull up then she called out his name as she opened the front door. "Sean?"

He walked through the hall, his cane part of him now, an extra point of balance and stability he'd finally gotten used to, and he strode almost smoothly to where she was pushing through the front door, and he wrapped his arms around her.

"Oh," she breathed, and it was kind of awkward, because she had her bag slung across her body and what felt like a wine bottle in her arms—now pressed between them—but on her next exhale, she relaxed into him.

And that was so, so good.

"Hey," he said into her hair.

"Hi," she whispered back, and he had a strong sense of deja vu. Something sliding into place. Something suddenly being crystal clear.

It wasn't, not this time. But he remembered that it had been, and he tightened his arms around her.

How did he get to such a place that a hug felt foreign?

"I'm sorry," he whispered against her hair, and she shook her head.

"Don't. Not right now. Just hug me."

He could do that. He wasn't sure what else he could do, but as his PT kept pointing out, there was nothing wrong with his arms. He was strong enough to give her this.

She looked up at him, but didn't move any further. She just stood there, being still.

Her eyes held his own gaze, but she wasn't staring. She was simply being here with him, present and in the moment, like she had been for six long weeks—no matter how hard he tried to push her away.

When the corners of her eyes crinkled up, and a silent laugh bubbled up from inside her, it broke something inside him. A piece of the hard crust around his heart cracked and split away, and with a painful thud, he *felt* again. So much. He started to laugh with her, and then drew her closer.

"Can you drink?" she asked.

Probably not a lot with his meds, but if she wanted to open a bottle of wine, he wouldn't make her drink alone. "A glass, sure."

"Good. Because I'm in the mood but I didn't want to be a jerk if you couldn't."

"I wouldn't care."

She wriggled the bottle of wine free from between them. "That's what I was hoping you'd say. I stopped at the wine store on my way home."

Home. There it was again. He smiled and tapped his chest. "I gathered as much."

"Sorry."

"Don't be." He touched her cheek, and she pressed into

his touch for the briefest of moments before moving past him, her fingers sliding along his arm.

"I'm going to put this in the fridge to chill for a few. Do you want to sit on the deck?"

He followed her into the kitchen. No, he wanted to hug her again.

He waited while she stashed the wine, then dumped her bag on the table, and pulled out a few pieces of paper. She had a mini filing box on the table where she'd been keeping her work stuff, and she tucked those papers into that. It was when she started rifling through receipts that he knew for sure she was avoiding eye contact—and any conversation about the hug.

"Jenna."

"Mmm."

"Jenna."

"Yes…"

"Look at me."

"No." But she smiled, he could see the edge of it, curling in the shadow of her dipped head.

He grinned. "Please?"

She looked up, and her eyes were bright. But then she blinked, and any hint of tears were gone. "I just needed a minute."

That was fair. He'd needed three months.

He held out his hand. He thought about leading her to his room, or to hers, but he didn't want to send mixed messages. He wasn't sure he could perform, and they didn't need to try to go from zero to sixty here. Zero to ten would be an improvement. Hell, he'd take zero to one. Any movement at all.

Instead, he sat on the couch, in his napping spot. He

leaned back against the cushions and tucked his cane away before tugging Jenna into his side.

She look like she wanted to plaster herself to him, and he wanted that too, but she simply sat close. Still too far away, but talking first, cuddling second.

"What's brought this on?" she finally asked, her words a warm rub against his chest.

"Your note on the coffee maker this morning. The XO. I...hadn't realized I hadn't done either of those things." He swallowed hard. "And it's not that I don't want to. But it's...complicated."

She tipped her face up, hope radiating off her—and that didn't freak him out. "You want to?"

He nodded.

She caught his hand and squeezed. "Then it's okay if it's complicated. We'll get there."

There was *we* again.

He tugged her closer. *We.* Yeah, he liked the sound of that.

He cupped her cheek. His heart hammered in his chest as he looked at her lips. Soft, pink, bowed. Sweet, and unkissed for far too long.

Ring.

His chest tightened as the moment was interrupted, and Jenna shifted in his arms.

THAT WAS HER PHONE, in her bag, across the room.

She ignored it.

He was holding her again. He'd been about to kiss her. The world could burn down around them and she wouldn't care.

The ringing stopped and then started again.

"You should see what that's about." He kissed the tip of her nose, and *no*, that wasn't the kiss she wanted, damn it.

But Sean was already pulling away, his face flushing with embarrassment. *No…*

She took a deep breath. Baby steps. "Yeah. I should see who's calling."

When she dug out her phone, there were two missed calls, both from the midwifery team in Walkerton. She'd gone to their offices that morning, as she had a couple of times before, to peer review a couple of client cases.

Tapping the number to redial, she took a deep breath and pressed her hand to her belly to calm herself down.

"Jenna, hi! Thanks for calling us back. This is Nadine. Is this a bad time?"

"No, it's fine. What can I do for you?"

"We'd like to offer you a contract, if you are interested, to cover the rest of the summer."

She didn't even need to think about it. "Yes, I'm thrilled to be considered. Thank you so much."

"Can you come back in tomorrow to shadow Annette in the clinic?"

"I'll be there first thing."

Dazed, she hung up the phone and just stared at it. This was great news. But it also meant she was going to be flat out for the next couple of days.

"Good news?" She spun around and found Sean leaning, as he did now, against the doorframe.

She grinned. "The best. I have a job. In Walkerton."

It was a long drive there, but no longer than getting stuck in Vancouver rush hour.

Sean grinned back at her. "We should celebrate. Do you want to go out for dinner?"

"I…" She exhaled. "You know what I want to do?"

———

AN HOUR LATER, they pulled into the car dealership where the Fosters had bought all of their trucks. Where just a few weeks earlier, Sean had stood in this same spot and quarrelled with his brother.

"Back to see the truck again?" The same sales guy approached.

Jenna gave Sean a curious look.

"Long story," he whispered. "For the drive home."

She smiled when he said home. He knew the feeling.

"Not the truck," he said. He pointed behind him. "We have one of those already." He put his hand in the small of Jenna's back. This was her celebration, and her shopping trip.

"I'm looking for something a bit more fuel efficient," she added.

"But still good in the winter," Sean said.

She smiled at that, too.

Yeah, he was thinking ahead. Surprised the shit out of him, too.

Jenna looked at a used SUV, a brand-new sport crossover, and a few others to cover her bases. But the first two cars she looked at were the ones she kept coming back to, and the ones which she took out for a test drive.

"What's the best you could do on the crossover?" she asked when they were back.

The sales guy named a figure Sean didn't believe for a second.

Neither did Jenna. "Hmm," she said. "Well, the top end of my budget is two grand less than that. If you get something in that price range in, give me a call."

Then she turned and headed for Sean's truck, not looking back for even a second.

"Smooth," he said as they headed north again.

"I can drive this for a few weeks," she said, shrugging.

"I don't think you will be. I'd bet good money he'll call you tomorrow with a deal in your price range."

She gave him a surprised, pleased look. "Yeah?"

"Definitely."

She beamed. "Oh, you were going to tell me what the deal was with the truck?"

Ah. That. "Dean and I were there earlier. He needed to get a new spare tire. So I walked around a bit and looked at that red pick-up."

She whistled. "Fancy."

"I wasn't seriously interested in it." He sounded defensive even to his own ears.

She reached across and patted his knee. "If you were, I'd think that was a good sign."

"Dean didn't."

"No?"

"He gave me a lecture on not being wasteful."

"Huh." She cleared her throat. "Well, I don't see how that's any of his business."

"He made a crack about us living rent-free in his place."

Even in the rapidly dimming evening light, he didn't miss that she rolled her eyes. "Oh, whatever. He practically shoved me in there. And Liana told me he really wanted either you or Matt to move in. So don't let him get to you. Maybe that was about something else, and you were just a casualty."

"I may have goaded him into snapping."

She laughed gently. "For brothers who love each other, you all have a very dysfunctional style of communication."

"That reminds me. We have a family dinner at my father's on Friday night."

She gave him an amused look. "You're not looking forward to it?"

"Never."

She held up her hand and tapped her thumb to her middle finger. "Remember this?"

The signal he gave her in Urfa. "Yes."

"Dinner will be fine. And then we have our out plan."

Good Lord, she was amazing. "You're a genius."

"No, we just make a good pair."

They really did. How had he forgotten that? "I have been thinking about what Dean said, though. My disability pay isn't going to last forever." At some point, probably by the end of the year, the army would give him a lump sum payout to get him off the books. "I need to start thinking about getting a job."

She flashed him a look of alarm across the cab of the truck. "Don't rush it. Your recovery is like a job."

"That doesn't pay for shit."

"Are you worried about me getting a new car?"

"No." And he really wasn't. She wouldn't make a decision that she couldn't afford on her own, and he had savings. He was in a decent position to help her—for now. But those savings wouldn't last forever. "Just starting to think about the future."

"Okay." Her expression eased into one of warmth as her phone rang.

Sean was pretty sure this was going to be the rest of his life, having conversations interrupted by that phone. He couldn't complain, though. She loved her job.

She gestured to her bag, and he pulled out the phone. The screen showed that it was the dealership calling back.

Sean showed her. "Won that bet by a mile."

She laughed and told him to answer it.

"Jenna, it's Pete from the dealership. How are you?"

"Pretty good, Pete. How are you?"

He cleared his throat. "I just talked to my manager. Since your family has been such loyal customers, we can cut you a good deal on that crossover."

She wasn't biting just yet. "How good?"

"I can get that price down to where you wanted it."

She pumped her fist in the air. "We can be back in fifteen minutes to sign the paperwork."

Sean disconnected the call, and Jenna started laughing. "Oh my God, I just bought a brand new car!" She reached for him and squeezed his hand. "Wow. I'm so excited."

Her fingers were shaking. She didn't need his help with the car, or her job. But she wanted him by her side, and maybe she needed something else from him. Something more than help.

———

JENNA WAS LATE FOR DINNER.

He didn't blame her—she'd had to go in to work today, and she'd lost the morning to getting her new car insured and registered.

But since she wasn't there, he was stuck making small

talk with his father, who had all sorts of opinions about how Sean should just harden the fuck up.

The Colonel shared them in small, barbed bursts, in between bouncing his grandson on his knee and praising Matt for how good the ribs looked.

Like grilling skills were more important than crawling back from the edge of death.

"What are you drinking, son? Are you up to having more than water?"

Sean took a deep breath and nodded. "Yep. But I'm good with water all the same, sir."

He got a frown for that, but his father moved on. They were all milling around the big eat-in kitchen. Dani was tossing a salad she'd brought, and Jake was setting the table. Matt's ribs had just been set in the middle, and Liana was teasing Dean that baby Calvin wanted some of his uncle's beer.

It was...nice. He could see, if he squinted, why his family did this, month in, month out.

Then his father made an off-side comment about how some people had worked hard that day, and Sean swallowed a comeback about the old man being retired and how perfectly cutting a diamond pattern into one's lawn hardly counted as essential work.

He wanted to work.

It was time to think about that, for sure.

He'd never been lazy. It wasn't in his nature. Where did his father get off seeing him like that?

"I've been spending some time with Tom Minelli and the Search and Rescue Team," he said. It was a stretch. He'd hung out with Tom at the training facility twice, and they'd done little more than shoot the breeze.

His father snorted. "You can hardly go stumbling around in the woods, though, can you?"

And so much for fucking trying.

Before his resentment could get a full head of steam, though, there was a light, quick knock at the front door. "Jenna's here."

He loved her knock. The quick rap had become part and parcel of the unrelenting sunshine she brought to his life, as she doggedly kept using it to announce her presence in his life, even when he hadn't been well enough to know what to do with her. He was getting there, though. Slowly, and all because of her efforts.

He pushed himself up and got to the foyer before anyone else.

"Hey." She gave him a breathless smile, and he pulled her into his side. He didn't miss her surprised little squeak, but she hugged him back without hesitation.

"Just in time," he said gruffly.

"Everything okay?" she looked up at him.

"It is now." He took a deep breath. "Come and meet my dad."

Even though Jenna had been around for weeks, she hadn't met the Colonel, because it would never occur to him to come over to visit Sean.

Not that Sean wanted his father to come to him.

That would be too weird.

The construct of the family dinner was all the interaction they needed, thank you very much.

"Dad," Sean said, raising his voice as he led Jenna into the kitchen. He didn't call him that often, but it seemed appropriate now. "This is Jenna. Jenna, this is Colonel Foster."

"The original officer in the family. A pleasure to meet

you, young lady." The colonel held out his hand, and Jenna took it.

Her eyes crinkled as they shook hands. "Sean's told me all about you."

"Has he, now?" That got a sideways glance. "He kept you quite the secret."

Jenna didn't miss a beat. "I keep his secrets, too."

That hadn't been what his father had meant, but Sean was pretty sure Jenna knew that.

She was fierce, and pride bloomed hard inside him.

They sat shortly after that, and dinner went as well as it could. The Colonel had lots of thoughts about Jake's construction business, Dean's security jobs, and Matt's office politics at the county EMS department.

He had zero thoughts about what Sean should do next with his life, except to point out what he couldn't do.

Jenna squeezed his knee each time his leg tensed up.

He finished eating before anyone else. Despite his best efforts, his appetite wasn't what it had once been. He stretched his arm across the back of her chair and tried to convince himself to eat a few more bites.

From the floor, where he'd been put down on a blanket, Calvin started fussing. Dani went to get up, and Sean waved her off. "I'll get him."

He carefully moved his chair back. His cane had been shoved out of grabbing range when everyone came to the table, but he managed without it, and once he was down at his nephew's level, it was all good.

"Hey, bud."

Calvin quieted down and gave him a wide-eyed look of wonder. Either that, or the kid didn't want him to steal his rattle.

"It's all good. I'm not going to take your teether. Can

you shake it? Shake it good?" Calvin thumped him in the face with the slimy toy, and Sean laughed. "Good one. Jake, your kid has a mean left hook."

"You'll have to get him into the gym, show him what you've got."

There was a thought. "How about that, Calvin?" Sean whispered. "Can Uncle Sean train you to be fast on your feet and even faster with your fists?"

Dani cleared her throat. "I heard that. No training my kid to be a street fighter."

Sean scoffed. "No street fighting. Calvin is going to be an Olympian."

As if he were completely in agreement, his nephew grabbed two chubby fistfuls of Sean's shirt and hauled himself up to stand on unsteady feet.

"See? He's a champ."

And Sean would know. He'd been a champ, too.

He thought about that as Calvin climbed on him.

He had a lot of knowledge locked inside, about training and resilience and striving for excellence in sport and life.

Coaching had never been his favourite part of athletics, but… it was a possibility.

He'd talk to Jenna about it.

The dinner conversation swirled away from Calvin's Olympic future, and Sean tuned the adults out. He zeroed all of his attention on his nine-month-old future champion. "No pressure," he whispered to the baby. "But whatever you want to do in this world, I'll have your back."

By the time Dean and Liana were clearing away the dinner dishes, Calvin was rubbing his eyes.

Dani swooped him up and settled in her chair, holding her son close as she nursed him.

It was still kind of amazing to him that Dani was a mom. Dani, who'd rubbed his back after all night benders in college. Who'd chased him off the end of the dock and into the freezing cold lake every year to mark the unofficial start of summer.

Everyone's lives had changed so much while he was overseas. Not just his own.

Matt carried in a cheesecake big enough for them all and everyone oohed and ahed.

Even Matt had changed.

Since when did his brother know how to make a cheesecake?

And it was good, too.

Damn.

Sean was surprised to discover he had an appetite for that cheesecake. He took a decent sized piece, and savoured it.

Next to him, Jenna was talking to Dean about her job.

Sean's father interjected himself into that conversation, but Jenna handled him with ease.

"Sean should have brought you around sooner," the Colonel said.

Jenna smoothly countered with an invitation for the senior Foster to come around to their place.

Sean ground his teeth together. His father was playing some kind of passive aggressive game through her, aimed at Sean, and he didn't like it.

Jenna didn't either. Nobody else would be able to tell, because the only sign she wasn't completely at ease was that she was fidgeting her fingers under the table.

Sean frowned. She was tapping her thumb and middle finger together. Just as he noticed, she shifted her hand, setting it on his knee, and she did it again.

The signal.

She wanted to go.

Sean groaned and leaned back against the wall. Seven concerned heads swivelled his way, and he gave them a weak smile. "Sorry, was that out loud?"

Dani tutted, like a legit Mom noise that he wanted to make fun of, except he was pretending to be all tuckered out. So he let her give him a sympathetic look, then he reached for his cane, which he'd moved closer after he'd hung out with Calvin on the floor. It was a good security blanket.

Plus it reminded everyone to give him some space, and he did still need that. A lot.

Jenna may have been the one to silently cry uncle, but he was more than ready to get out of there, too.

"I'm going to need to call it a night," he said. "But this was...fun."

Jenna's lips twitched at the ellipse he couldn't help but insert there. Whatever. She got him. He didn't care if nobody else did.

They made their goodbyes and then they headed out to her car.

"How'd your new baby drive today?"

She winked as she patted the steering wheel. "Like the queen she is."

It only took two minutes to drive across town. Jenna was still talking about her car as they unlocked the house and went inside.

But she stopped mid-sentence and reached for him, although her hand fell short and fluttered back to her side. "Thank you," she said softly. "We didn't need to leave dinner so quickly."

She shouldn't need to thank him. It was what a spouse did.

It was past the time for him to start acting like a husband. "You've been pushing yourself hard. I should have said something sooner."

"I was having fun, right up until I wasn't. But you were quick on the ball." She yawned and stretched her arms. "Do you want to debrief on how that went?"

He laughed. "It went. We'll do it again next month."

She gave him a sleepy smile. "Okay. I should try and get some sleep."

"Try?"

She waved her hand, dismissing the question.

He frowned. "Are you having trouble sleeping?"

"Like you say, I've been pushing hard. Just a lot of things swirling around in my brain."

A lot of those things had the name Sean tattooed on them too. He knew the right answer here. Could feel the words forming in his mouth. They didn't want to come out, though, because they opened Pandora's Box in a big way.

They'd settled into a halfway decent routine.

But he wanted more than decent. Or at least, he wanted that for Jenna, if not himself. "Come and sleep with me."

Her eyes sparked at that. Hope warred with suspicion, though. "Are you sure?"

Jesus, he didn't want to answer that tonight. Because…

No, he wasn't sure. This might be a terrible idea. But he had an idea for a future career, maybe, and he wanted to talk to her about that. Lying down. Side by side. And he wanted to hold her, maybe.

Damn it, he didn't want his reason for finally opening up to her to be selfish.

"I'm not sure," he admitted. "I know that's probably not the right thing to say, but…"

Her gaze stayed glued to his face as her expression shifted again. He couldn't read it, though. His head was spinning from the force of his confession. It had been the wrong thing to say, probably. She needed certainty. Commitment.

She inhaled, a little breath that caught at the top, and she held it there. Then she gave him a half smile. "Do you want me to? Don't offer if it's just for me."

He reached out and caught her hand. "It's not. At all. I want…" He exhaled roughly. "I was worried I was asking for selfish reasons."

Her smile got bigger. "Okay. I'll get my pyjamas on."

———

JENNA BRUSHED her teeth and then put on lightweight pyjama pants and a tank top.

Her heart pounded as she made her way to Sean's room. She paused at the door, pressing her hand against the wood frame.

And he was already asleep.

He was so exhausted, constantly, that he fell asleep as soon as he was horizontal.

He'd left the bedside light on, and a book lay discarded beside him. He was stretched out, taking up most of the bed. One arm was thrown over his eyes, and his chest moved up and down in a regular, steady pattern.

Moving into the room quietly, she picked up the paperback and set it on the bedside table. She went to turn out the light, but hesitated.

Maybe he liked to have it on. Now that she thought

about it, she'd seen a light coming out from under his door most nights. She'd leave it on.

As nervous as if she were a virgin on her wedding night, she climbed onto the mattress.

It was dangerous, how much she wanted this.

You're going to get your heart broken. She knew that. Had accepted it as the inevitable consequence of loving Sean. But she couldn't help herself.

She stretched out, holding her breath as she sank into the mattress. It wasn't the same as before. It would never be. But there was something precious about this moment, for how hard-fought it had been.

And for how innocent it was. Just lying next to him, watching him sleep.

He'd aged in the last five months. Her heart ached.

But it was a warm, soft ache. Surrounded by other, sweeter feelings.

Dangerous feelings that lulled her to sleep before she could explore them in any depth, because she, too, was exhausted.

She woke up in the early morning, overheated and confused. She pushed the blankets off her legs, but most of the heat was coming from behind her.

Sean.

With a jolt of embarrassed awareness, she realized she'd nestled herself right against him in her sleep.

Her heart raced.

This was the opposite of not pushing him.

Frozen, she tried to figure out if she'd woken him up, too. How could she not? But his usually tense muscles were relaxed around her and his breathing was still even.

Carefully she slid back to her side of the bed and rolled

onto her back. It would be dawn soon. Maybe she could turn out the light.

She reached for the switch and out of nowhere, Sean's hand clamped around her wrist.

"Light stays on," he said, his voice thick with sleep.

"I… Okay. Sorry."

He didn't say anything else.

He hadn't let go of her wrist, either.

She closed her eyes and dragged in a breath. She told herself to go to sleep, to calm down. But she was too hot. She was wearing too many layers. It was the height of summer. Sleep pants were unnecessary, but she'd pulled them on so…

Bitter regret pulsed in her chest. So she wouldn't give her husband the wrong idea and think that she wanted sex just because she'd climbed into bed with him.

But she did.

She realized with a sinking feeling that's why she'd woken up. She'd been dreaming of him pressing into her from behind. Hell, maybe it had been real. She didn't know, but…that was risky. She didn't want to ruin the fragile progress they'd made.

She wiggled her wrist. "I think I'm up."

He still didn't let go. "What's wrong?"

Did he really want to know? Now, at five in the morning? She shook her head. "Nothing. Need some water."

He let her go, and she slipped from his bed without looking back. In the bathroom, she filled the water glass sitting on the edge of the sink. Then she downed the entire thing in three thirsty gulps.

CHAPTER TWENTY-ONE

JENNA WENT to her room for a while, but she couldn't get back to sleep. Mostly because she was reeling from wanting to bang her husband, which was an odd place to be, mentally.

She wanted to go back to Sean's room. Claim it as hers, too, and wait for him to ask her what was wrong again.

Eventually she got up and put on the coffee.

Caffeine would help chase away the weird feelings. So would fresh air.

When she'd lived in Vancouver, she'd always tried to do something on her first day off each week. Go for a hike, hit a market, something like that.

Today was her first day off. It had been a big week. She needed to recharge and refill her well.

As the coffee percolated, she moved restlessly through the living room. There was still a row of banker's boxes along the wall from when Sean's brother had moved him in. Papers from his previous life he hadn't wanted to deal with just yet.

He didn't want to deal with anything from his previous life.

Not his papers, not his wife.

Resentment bubbled up fierce and fast inside her. Damn it.

Why was she getting mad about a few boxes?

It's not the boxes. It's the box he's put you in.

She kicked at the nearest banker's box and the lid fell off. Sighing, she picked it up and went to put it back, but the books inside caught her attention.

Big, spiral bound notebooks, stacked face up. The top one was neatly labeled. **2014-2015 Training Log.**

She flipped it open. Each page was a journal entry of sorts, the physical training Sean had done that day. Running, weight training, cross-training, active rest. It was a peek inside the life he had before he met her, before his world turned upside down.

It looked like he'd spent most of the winter that year in Florida, training on the Gulf coast while Pine Harbour was covered in snow. But by the spring, he was back. She flipped through the next few pages. **First swim in the lake —fucking cold! Great for the legs.** She laughed at that, and then gasped when she saw the date. She'd put her toe in the lake now, in the middle of July, and it was still pretty chilly. Standing in it in May was insanity.

From the kitchen, the coffee maker beeped.

Caffeine time.

She went and poured herself a cup, then went back to the boxes. She put the training log away and peeked into the next box. Medals and framed photos.

She'd thought about printing some of their pictures from Spain. Would Sean like a wedding picture on the mantle? Or would he hide that away, too?

She sank into a chair at the table and pulled out her phone. She hadn't looked at the photos in weeks, and scrolling through them now probably wasn't a good idea, but she couldn't help herself.

Sean's bedroom door swung open as she was on the photos from the drive through the mountains.

"Morning," he said quietly.

"Coffee's on," she said without looking up.

Her pulse pounded in her neck as she listened to him move into the kitchen and pour himself a cup. For a big guy, he moved lightly in general, and as he recovered, his footsteps were getting quieter and quieter. Now all she heard was the tap of his cane every few seconds.

He slid into the seat across from her. "You didn't sleep well."

She'd slept great right up until she felt guilty for rubbing her ass against his crotch. "Just woke up early, that's all."

"What are you doing?"

She didn't want to say she'd been looking at their wedding pictures and doing her damnedest not to cry, so she didn't say anything at all. She just sighed and pushed her phone away.

He looked at it, then back up to her. "Bad news?"

"No." She waved her hand toward the boxes. "Why haven't you unpacked?"

He didn't look over there. He'd gotten so good at not turning his head more than he needed to, and she felt bad for pointing to something out of his field of vision.

"Your boxes of racing stuff."

"I know what you meant." His jaw flexed and he took a sip of coffee. "I should put those in storage. I don't need to unpack them."

"Better to keep your history packed away?" It came out sharper than she intended it, and he gave her a look that said, *whoa, pissed off much?*

Yeah, maybe she was.

"Some of it," he said slowly. "The running part. That's done now. In the past."

"And the rest of it?"

He looked at her phone again. "What is this about?"

She bit her lip. The sharp, bright pain felt good.

"May I?" He reached for the device.

She nodded. Sure, why not. She told him the passcode, and watched, heart in her throat, as he scrolled through the pictures she'd been looking at.

"We look so happy," he finally said. "I lost my phone. When I was evacuated, all of my stuff was packed up, but some of it was lost in transit. My phone was in that shipment, I guess. I lost my copies of these."

"I've had them the whole time." And he hadn't asked to see them. Man, she could *not* strip that barbed tone from her voice. Maybe she should head out for the day. Get some fresh air and some perspective again.

He gave her another careful, searching look. "What do you want me to say here?"

I love you. That's what she wanted him to say. Over and over again, until it was the only thing she heard. Until it drowned out all the other shit, like how he couldn't sleep with her and couldn't see a future for himself and couldn't be happy.

If he only admitted that he still loved her, the rest would be bearable. They'd get through it together.

But the thought that he'd only loved her when he was whole, that in sickness or in health had been a lie *for him*... that just about broke her.

Still she kept her mouth shut, though.

No good would come of admitting how much she needed him.

He didn't look away, at least. That was something.

"Those two weeks together were perfect," he finally said.

That wasn't what she wanted to hear. She took a deep breath.

"They were great," she said carefully. "Isn't that the thing about vacations? They're an escape from real life. I don't expect our marriage to be like a vacation."

"I...I think I did." He sighed. "I know, that's terrible. I don't now, to be clear. But I feel like I should confess my stupidity from before, to put us on the right footing going forward."

"Going forward?"

"Yes. God, of course, yes."

"Sometimes I'm not sure that's what you want."

"Even when I wasn't in my right mind, I wanted you."

Wanted her. It wasn't an affirmation of love, but it was something.

He leaned across the table and brushed his fingers over her cheek. "What do you want to do today?"

She wanted to stop wishing things were different. She wanted to be grateful for the progress they'd made. "I want to get outside. Shake off the heavy stuff and get some sunshine on my face." She lifted her gaze and found him watching her. "Want to come with me?"

———

HELL, yeah.

Sean knew he'd fucked up, on more than one level, in more than one way.

Ever since she'd left his bed in the early morning, he'd been rolling over every bit of their short history together.

He hadn't known how good he'd had it. How sweet and precious a thing Jenna's love had been, not even when he lost it the first time. Maybe because she hadn't given up on him, and he'd known that deep down.

He'd been petrified, of course. Of not being good enough for her any longer. Of not being able to love her, physically. Or mentally. Of never again meeting the impossibly high standard set by another man, a reckless daredevil who believed himself immortal.

And yet even as he cowered at Dean's house, on some level he'd known she would eventually come to him.

More cockiness.

More hubris.

And he hadn't been good enough. Hadn't loved her the way she deserved.

He'd ached at the loss of her this morning. Had wanted to haul her back into his bed. He ached and hated himself, and for a good long while, he let that dark anger twist through his mind.

Not good enough.

She's better off without you.

But he'd been down that road, and he couldn't accept it. He wasn't actually that selfless. Admitting to himself how possessive he was gave life to a new realization.

He hadn't tried hard *enough*.

And she'd still hung in there. That was a gift she'd given him.

Gifts needed to be returned in kind.

It was time for him to up his game.

"How would you like to go camping?" The invitation was out of his mouth before he realized he didn't know where any of his camping shit was. Well, they'd find stuff.

"Sure…" The way she trailed off, he could hear the doubt in her voice. Was it a good idea for him to go camping? He didn't know. But it felt right, and that was all that mattered.

"Just for the night. We won't go far. I've got a secret spot."

"Okay."

He stood and moved around to her side of the table. "And we'll talk more. I promise."

She gave him a searching look that cracked his chest open. "Okay."

It would be. He was going to fix this.

They packed enough food for lunch and dinner then checked out the garage.

"Thank God for type-A older brothers," Sean said as he hauled out an over-sized plastic tub clearly marked **camping**. And behind it was pay dirt—Sean's own camping stuff, which was more suited for expeditions like back country hiking or mountain climbing, but would also work for his new normal of a meadow just outside of town.

He carefully divided what they would need between two packs, leaving enough room for Jenna to pack some clothes and her pillow on the top of hers.

They filled up a bunch of water bottles, grabbed the gear, and climbed into the truck.

"You've got your medication?" Jenna asked as he slid his cane between the seat and the door.

"Yep." He forced down the burn of resentment. New normal. It was fine. Meds had replaced gels and jerky.

Maybe one day he'd carry all of them, and go further than a few clicks down the road.

In the grand scheme of things, this was a win. He'd suggested a spontaneous camping trip and now they were heading out the door ninety minutes later. He was a lucky motherfucker that he wasn't still flat on his back at Dean's house.

He directed her out of town. As they passed Mac's, he pointed at the woods behind the diner. "There's a path there that hikes into this spot, but it's easier to drive around. There's an access road off the highway."

Access road was generous. It was an ungraded dirt lane.

Jenna slowed right down as they bumped over new holes that had appeared since the last time he'd driven in to the meadow.

"What is this place?" Jenna asked as she parked the truck at the dead end.

"A secret." He grabbed his cane. "Come on."

The snowmobile and hiking path that snaked all the way up the peninsula cut through the forest right in front of them, and he pointed that out as they crossed it. Their own path, which cut due west toward the lake, was narrower, but clearly marked and relatively easy underfoot.

That didn't mean it was easy for him. The added weight of his pack made the five hundred metre walk tiring enough that Sean felt his pulse increasing as they walked.

Damn it, he needed to start walking with a weighted bag. This was embarrassing.

But that was forgotten the second Jenna caught sight of

the clearing, and it was as if Sean was seeing it for the first time again through her eyes.

"Oh, wow," she breathed.

The dense, scrubby pine trees gave way to lichen-covered rock—large, smooth boulders that formed a natural barrier around the sunken clearing. He grinned as she scrambled forward. The view got even better in a second.

"Oh. Wow. Sean, this is gorgeous!" Jenna laughed and danced ahead of him.

He was looking at her as she looked at the meadow. He couldn't agree more. "Very."

She twirled in a circle. "What should we do first?"

"Head to the right, along the tree line. You'll find my camp site."

She jumped from one rock to the next, her legs warm and golden in the mid-morning sun, and his head spun just thinking about doing that. But he wasn't jealous, which surprised him. Yeah, he moved slower now. But he was moving.

He was *camping*.

Small miracles.

She found his preferred camping spot among the trees at the edge of the clearing, with the well-used fire pit he'd made out of stones, and they set up the tent.

Fatigue nipped at him, and he wanted to push back at it, but it wasn't yet lunch. If he ignored it and ended up with a migraine, ruining his first night outside, he'd be pissed at himself.

"I should stretch out for a few minutes," he said after stringing their food up a tree, inside his pack. "I don't need a nap, but just a rest."

She beamed at him. "For sure. A nap sounds great, actually."

They left the tent flap open, and at first Jenna lay with her head toward the door, watching the meadow. But after a few minutes, she sat up and stretched, then flipped over and lay out on her sleeping bag the other way, her head now next to his.

His eyes were closed, but he could feel her shifting around. Feel her attention on his face, and slowly he blinked his eyelids open.

"Hey."

"I don't want to bother you," she whispered.

"You're not." He reached for her hand and she wove her fingers through his. Something inside his chest tugged.

That's your heart, idiot.

"How are you feeling?"

He was pretty sure she meant physically. That was the longest he'd walked so far, and carrying a pack was new, too. If she meant emotionally…well, he hadn't sorted that out yet. So he went with the easier answer. "That took a bit out of me, I won't lie."

"But you made it." She smiled at him. "That's pretty cool."

"Yeah. I wasn't sure I'd ever see this place again." His voice caught as he said that.

"But you did." Her eyes were bright as she bit her lip.

"It's been a while since I've shared a secret with you," he murmured. "I'm sorry about that."

She shook her head. "In the past. Is this a secret? This meadow?"

"Yeah, sort of." He took a deep breath. "I own it, actually. It's not worth much, because there's no road access, no water or sewer or hydro pick ups. But I didn't care about any of that."

"Sean!" She laughed and squeezed his hand. "That's quite the secret. How cool is that? And I totally get it. You just wanted a retreat."

He grinned. "Yeah, it's a little piece of the world that's just for me. And now you."

He didn't miss how that made her breath catch in her throat. Her face went all soft as she exhaled. "Thank you for sharing it with me."

He pulsed his fingers around hers. "No, the thanks is all mine. You've been a saint these past few months, and I've been hard to be around. I'm sorry about that too. I know this isn't what you signed up for."

"I signed up for you. No matter what."

He rolled onto his back and held out his arm. "Come here." She burrowed into his side, and he brushed his lips against her temple. "We're going to be okay. Do you remember me telling you about the sandstorms?"

She nodded. "We had one just before I left. It was kind of crazy. Almost zero visibility. I slept at the hospital instead of going back to my tent."

"The first one I experienced, that I told you about—that was the worst. Totally disorienting. The world upside down. But there were others, too. And it wasn't always so dense that I couldn't see anything. So you could think... hey, it's not so bad, we could head out in this if we're careful. But it wasn't effective. We learned it was best to wait until the storm passed before launching another offensive. Always."

"Are we in a sandstorm?"

"Is it too clumsy an analogy?"

"No." She sighed against his chest. "I can see what you mean."

"It will pass. It is passing. We'll get there." He wanted to promise her more. But he'd promised her everything once, and fallen far short of that. He wouldn't make that mistake again.

Words were cheap. This time, he was going to show her how he felt. Show her what he could do.

———

JENNA DOZED off in the warmth of the sun-dappled tent, with Sean's hard chest as her pillow. When she woke, the sun had curved past the high noon mark and was now shining in the west-facing flap of the tent and onto her legs.

"Oh, that's hot," she murmured, rolling away from Sean.

He grumbled something in his sleep and pulled her back into his side.

Well, that was hard to argue with.

She relaxed into his embrace and made herself a promise. No more sadness. Not today.

Sean roused a few minutes later, and once he'd stretched and taken his mid-day medication, they set off for a tour of his property.

"It's mostly rock. This meadow in the middle is my favourite part. There's a small pond on the far side, and then the land starts to drop away toward the next road. The lake is on the far side of that road" He pointed west. Thick trees stood in the way, but she could imagine it. "It's not really passable."

She gave him a wry smile. "Which means you've climbed it many times, haven't you?"

"Twice, and we used ropes both times." That led to a mini lecture on the different kinds of rock. Which ones were good for free climbing and which would crumble away if looked at wrong. Jenna couldn't get over how dynamic he was outside. It reminded her of their walks in Arcos, when he talked about Moorish architecture and the history of the region for hours.

"We? Who did you climb with?"

"Tom. He's on the search and rescue team. He's never met a challenging climb he hasn't wanted to master. I didn't tell him this was my land, only that we had permission."

"Where are the boundaries of your property?"

"From the road, where that access point was, to the far side of the meadow. The descent on the other side technically belongs to someone else, but it doesn't even have an access lane."

"Amazing."

"There are neighbours to the south and north, but their houses are closer to the highway, in the woods. I don't think they're even aware I come out here. This is probably the first time in years I've parked a truck in the lane."

"Did you always hike in?"

"Yeah." He tapped his cane on the ground and gazed into the distance. "More often I ran it. The snowmobile trail is great for running."

"The wet forest!" She snapped her fingers. "That's what you said you'd missed the most."

He nodded. "Yep."

Damn it, she'd slid them into some melancholy territory. No more sadness. "And I said—"

"Bubble baths." He grinned at the trees ahead of them. "None of those out here."

"I'll have one when we get home tomorrow."

He turned his whole body around and gave her an inscrutable look. "I like that."

"The bubble bath plan?"

"Sure. But the way you call it home."

She stepped forward, then again, until she was right against him. "That's because it is my home." *It's where you are.* But that would be too much sentimentality for this day.

He gave her a quick hug before he changed the subject to gathering wood for dinner.

Later, after grilled mushrooms and smoky chicken thighs that had the crispiest, most perfect skin she'd ever tasted, Jenna made them makeshift s'mores for dessert as they watched the sun set over the meadow.

Instead of graham crackers, she was sandwiching the ooey, gooey, melty goodness between two chocolate chip cookies.

"I didn't even know we had marshmallows in the house," Sean said as he licked the remnants of his first one off his fingers. "And I will totally have another if you're offering."

"Of course." He didn't eat a lot of dessert. If he had a secret marshmallow addiction, that was good information to file away. "And I just bought them yesterday. Fate."

She made him two more, then set down her official marshmallow roasting stick and sat back next to him on the smooth, worn log behind the fire pit to enjoy her own second helping.

The fire snapped and crackled, and in the distance, an owl cried out. *Hoot.* There were a lot of other forest noises, too. The rustling of little animals moving through the brush, a breeze shifting the tops of the trees back and forth.

All of it was perfect.

"This is exactly what I needed today," she said quietly as she finished her cookies.

She turned her head and gave Sean a grateful smile.

He returned the expression then his gaze slowly slid to her mouth. She could feel her lips tremble under the weight of his attention. His eyelids hooded as he watched her, and her smile fell away.

His own mouth twisted into a rueful grimace. "I don't want to rush anything between us."

"No." Her chest hurt as she nodded. "I understand that."

He reached out and brushed his fingertips against her cheekbone. Light as air, but the simple touch shook her to her core. "But..."

Yes, she loved the sound of *but*.

She shifted closer, and he cupped her cheek. "Jenna..."

"Slow is smart," she whispered. Her heart hammered against her ribs as his lips parted.

"Slow," he repeated. "Slow can also be sexy."

CHAPTER TWENTY-TWO

JENNA GASPED, a sweet little mew, as Sean covered her mouth with his. Her lips were soft and warm and wet. And perfect.

She was so perfect as she broke against him. Her lips parted and he licked into her mouth, taking every inch he could get.

He'd been watching her all day. Wanting her too. Fresh air wasn't a cure-all, but it did damn good things for his libido. There was nothing he liked more than spending a day outside, and sharing this private paradise with Jenna had felt so damn right.

Kissing her did too.

Kissing her made him feel like a man again. He could get drunk on the way she looked at him over s'mores.

He stormed ahead without a plan. In the back of his head, warning bells went off. What next, lover boy? You'll kiss her, and then what?

He could…

There were things he could do.

He could get her off.

His gut twisted selfishly, and he hated himself for that reaction.

Not now. There wasn't any room for self-loathing in this kiss.

He'd promised her sexy, and he wasn't going to let her down. He pulled at her lower lip with his teeth. She smiled and he did it again, until she groaned, and then he dove back in again, tasting every inch of her sweetness. It had been too long. He was almost out of practice, but she was kissing him back. They made magic together. It didn't matter that he was a different man now, that he had doubts and fears about what might come next.

Right now, he had this kiss, and he was going to blow her mind with it.

Soon. Soon he would take more than a kiss, and it wouldn't matter if he…

But right now, tonight, it mattered. Tonight, he only had kisses in him. He needed today to be only good things. Only successes. And if that made him weak and pathetic, he'd live with that. He'd been living with it this long, hadn't he?

He kissed her once more, hard, for good measure.

Fuck, why didn't his body work?

He tried to pour everything into this kiss. He made it desperate, apologetic. Tried to channel into it his regret and longing, his impotent need.

He kissed her until she shuddered, until she pulled away to drag in a ragged breath.

Then he eased back. He didn't let go of her. He stroked her cheek, then tugged gently on her hair.

"That was definitely sexy," she whispered as she dropped her head onto his shoulder.

He slid his arm around her and tried to figure out how to explain what was wrong with his body.

She's a medical professional, she'll understand. But it hurt him to have her think of him as a patient.

"How hot are those coals, do you think?"

He startled at the unexpected question. "Pretty hot."

"Hot enough to make tea?" She didn't move from where she was still leaning against him.

"Yep, I bet we could boil water."

"I might like a cup before bed. You?"

And just like that, the opportunity was gone. "Sure. Thank you."

———

JENNA'S FEELINGS were rioting all over the place. She wanted to climb into Sean's lap and kiss him again, but that was the opposite of slow.

It had been barely fifteen hours since she'd crawled out of his bed feeling confused and frustrated.

Brakes. On.

Tea on too.

Her hands shook as she emptied a water bottle into the sauce pan and careful set it onto the cast iron grill.

Sean's campsite was really well equipped considering it had been abandoned for almost a year. He had two different grills to go over the fire pit, and set back into the forest was a locked shed, inside which were pots and pans, tarps and rope, garbage bags, flares, and a crack-in-case-of-emergency first aid kit.

When the water boiled, she used the oven mitt and pulled the pot off the fire. Carefully, she filled their camp mugs then added tea bags.

"Jenna..." There were a million different ways he said her name. As a caution, as a prayer, as a tease. Sometimes an endearment, sometimes a question. Right now, she didn't know where he was going with it.

"This is chamomile," she said. "Calming."

He chuckled under his breath. "Okay."

She couldn't resist that laugh, though. She turned to look at him.

His brows were furrowed, but he was smiling.

"What?"

"You really want to know?" That was definitely teasing.

"Yes." Her pulse zoomed. No. Yes. *Yes.*

"Do you think..." He trailed off, then cleared a frog from his throat and tried again. "This is going to sound random."

"I like random." Random meant secret-sharing again, and she'd missed that so much.

"I had an idea last night. When I was playing with Calvin. I might like to get into personal training. Coaching, really. Find people who want to get more serious about distance running and help them get to the next level."

That wasn't where she thought he was going...it was way better. "Yeah. That's brilliant. You should totally do that."

"It'll take time."

"We've got nothing but time."

"I meant to tell you last night, but I passed out when I lay down."

Her smile felt warm and real and very big. "You do that."

"You really don't mind, do you?" He gave her a curious look at that.

She shook her head. "I really, really don't. Rest is so crucial to recovery. Normally I'm saying that to new moms, encouraging them to stay in bed with their baby and let other people just take care of them. But I'm sure it applies to you too. When you're sleeping…this is going to make me sound like a creeper, but I like to watch you."

He laughed out loud. "Okay."

"Like if you're on the couch. You're cute."

"Mm hmm."

"I don't stand in your room and watch you sleep." She grinned at him. "Promise."

He held her gaze. "I wouldn't mind if you did."

They bumped shoulders, and he slung his arm around her again as they drank their tea.

Once the fire was out, they climbed into the tent. Sean had zipped their sleeping bags together, and they changed into their pyjamas together in the dark before sliding under the covers.

It was sweet and intimate and wonderful, and Jenna sank into the drowsy loveliness of it all. But she didn't drift off, and after a while, she realized Sean's breathing hadn't changed, either.

"You're not asleep."

"No."

"You usually fall asleep as soon as your head hits the pillow."

"Mmm."

"Everything okay?"

His hand found hers in the dark, his arm brushing against her hip. "Everything is great."

She squeezed back. "Good."

There was a long stretch of silence. "I was thinking about that day. When I was injured."

Her breath froze in her chest. Oh. She squeezed his hand again because words weren't possible.

"You were the first thing I thought of that morning when I woke up. And the last thing I thought of as everything went black."

Oh, God.

She started to shake. That's what she felt first, the tremor. Not the tears. She didn't realize she was crying until Sean was running his thumbs over her cheeks. He brushed her slick skin as he murmured words she couldn't make out, and he pressed his forehead to hers. "Please. God, I'm so sorry. Please, Jenna. Don't cry. Let me fix this. I'm sorry…"

She leaned into him as the dam burst, and he wrapped her in his arms. Arms he'd spent all summer bulking up.

Arms she never thought she'd feel again, not like this.

"I missed you so much," she whispered, her voice hitching as she pressed into him, her face into his neck, her hands sliding around his waist to hold him right back. "I'm sorry. I can't stop—" she hiccupped and squeezed him harder as a new wave of tears fell.

He groaned into her hair. "It's okay. You can cry. It's okay…"

"I haven't been crying." She yanked herself back together and eased back. Sean fumbled in the dark then his phone lit up, the flashlight app shining onto the ceiling of the tent.

She furiously swiped at her cheeks. "This is—"

He caught her wrists and gently stilled her hands. "It's fine."

"It's not." But as she said it, she realized how silly that sounded. Of course it was fine. She exhaled in a wobbly, weak fashion, and blinked up at him, her eyelashes wet and sticking together.

She puffed out her cheeks on the next breath, and he gave her a small smile. "You were holding that in for months, weren't you?"

"Maybe."

"You are brave and strong and so beautiful," he said, his voice rough. "I didn't mean to make you cry."

She shook her head. "Oh, Sean." She kissed him softly. She was still trembling and felt all shaky inside. "We've veered off course a bit, I think. That's all."

"It hasn't helped that we've been avoiding the difficult topics, though."

She nodded. She'd definitely been doing that.

"I'll share more secrets," he whispered into her hair as she pressed her face into his neck. "Like how much I've missed you too."

———

FOR THE SECOND morning in a row, Jenna woke up next to Sean. This time she was cold, and without thinking, she moved closer to him.

As he had the afternoon before, he wrapped his arm around her and held on tight.

Maybe the trick to sleeping together was doing it outside, in multiple layers of wool and flannel.

She felt renewed. Steady and happy and very much in the right place, with the right man.

And holy crap, did she need to pee.

"Sean," she whispered.

"Mmm."

"What are the chances I'll run into a bear if I go to pee in the woods?"

He laughed sleepily. "Not high. Make noise."

"Okay." She didn't move. There was something different about heading out alone into the forest in the early dawn.

"You want me to come with you?"

"Yes, please."

He kissed the side of her head. "Fine. I'm up. And then we can strike camp and go to Mac's for a hot breakfast."

They took their time hiking out.

Sean closed his eyes as he settled in the passenger seat. She leaned across the seat and brushed a kiss against his cheek. "You okay?" she murmured.

"Yep." Which meant no, but she didn't push him. He never complained about the vertigo and tinnitus, but she knew both were background, constant bothers he was learning to live with, live through.

He kept his eyes closed until they pulled into the parking lot at Mac's. Then he took her hand and squeezed. "Breakfast, then home for a nap?"

Her heart might burst from the simple joy of it. "Sounds perfect."

The diner was packed, and there weren't any Fosters present, but the Minellis were well-represented.

Holding her hand, Sean led her to two booths in the corner where Rafe was trying to convince Sophia to try a hash brown—no go—and across the table, Zander Minelli and his step-son, Eric, were showing her how much they loved their breakfast. Sean exchanged handshakes with both men as Sophia threw herself at Jenna for a hug. In the booth next to them, Olivia and Faith, Zander's wife, were sitting with Chloe and Tom.

Sean gave his friend a grin. "You got the good seat," he said.

Tom groaned. "And now Chloe's going to kick me out so Jenna can sit here."

Sean wrapped his arm around her waist. "I was planning on sitting next to her at our own booth."

Chloe protested, and tried to shove Tom out of the booth anyway, but just then the third booth in the row cleared out, and Jenna gave her friend a weak shrug. "What are you going to do?" she said, laughing as she slid into the booth first. Sean joined her on the same side.

"Lovebirds," Chloe muttered as she gave them a thumbs up.

Tom grabbed his plate and swung around to join them in the newly opened up booth. "I'm sitting with you guys now."

"So much for our private breakfast," Sean murmured against her ear.

She twisted to give him a little smile. "Did you really think that was going to happen here?"

"Probably not."

Their chatter paused briefly as the waitress showed up with coffee, which they gratefully accepted, and menus, which they didn't need, and they placed their orders immediately. Mushroom omelet and turkey sausage for Sean, French toast and bacon for Jenna.

Tom asked for more coffee and reminded the waitress of an order he'd previously placed for an urn of coffee to go. He turned back to Sean. "Search and Rescue Team training in the middle of the woods."

Sean laughed. "And you're bringing hot coffee with you. Nice touch."

"Yeah. I'm going to be suggesting something they're

going to balk at, so I'm bribing them. I've got cookies in the car, too."

"What's the new idea?"

Tom sighed. "I'm still working on the language. Basically, I want them to have workout buddies, but if I call it that, it'll be a non-starter. As a group, our fitness level could be lifted, basically. To improve our function in rescues."

Jenna heard a lot of stuff not being said there. She was pretty sure Tom's group was a volunteer organization, though, so maybe his hands were tied.

Sean groaned and waved his hand. "Same problem we face with the unit, right? Barely meeting the minimum standards on a PT test doesn't cut it when you need to haul your team mate out of a fire zone."

Tom nodded. "Or do a rapid descent down a cliff face."

"I feel your pain, brother. The answer is always better recruitment in the long run, but in the short run, there are things you can do to set your current team members up to want to compete to stay on the squad."

"Yeah?"

Jenna took a secret look at Tom. She didn't think this was a setup, which made it all the better because an organic need for Sean was perfect. She slid her glance sideways at Sean, and kept looking at him, eyebrow raised, until he noticed.

"What?" he said, in a carefully guarded way that told her he knew exactly why she was looking at him.

"You could help," she whispered.

Tom leaned in. "What's this now?"

"Nothing," Sean said.

"Not nothing." Jenna squeezed his hand below the table. But she didn't say anything else.

Sean chuckled under his breath as he stared into his coffee Then he slowly lifted his head again and looked at Tom. "Well…I was thinking about hanging my shingle as a running coach. Maybe leverage some of my experiences—"

"Done. Yes. We want to use and abuse your knowledge."

Jenna clapped. "See?"

Sean growled under his breath, but he looked pleased. "Okay. Maybe I can come out to the next Search and Rescue meeting and talk about some running mechanics stuff."

"We'd love that."

As Tom and Sean talked about the team's strengths and weaknesses, Jenna twisted around to poke Chloe over the back of the booth. "Hey, stranger."

"Hey. You've been busy, eh?"

"But it's a good busy."

"We'll need to do another big cook next weekend."

"For sure." She tipped her head to the side, letting Chloe glance past her to Tom, since that's where her gaze seemed to be heading anyway. "Should we invite other people?"

"Like who?"

Jenna grinned. "Tom."

"No." A flat, sharp, quick answer.

Interesting. But Jenna wasn't going to dig into that right now. Not when her French toast was on its way over. "Food time. Talk later."

They dug in, but she only got halfway through her meal when her phone vibrated. She pulled it out of her back pocket.

"Oh!" She grinned as she read the text message. "One

of the other midwives is with a labouring mom, and could use me as a second."

Sean was already on his feet, waving at the waitress. "Can we get some takeout boxes?"

"You could stay and get a ride home with Tom."

He didn't even look at his friend. "This is your first call out. It's kind of a big deal. I'm coming home with you."

Her heart melted. "Thank you."

They shoved the rest of their breakfast into the cartons and waved goodbye to Tom. In the truck, Sean held her phone while she talked to Nadine on speaker.

"I'm just heading home to grab my bags and a two minute shower, then I'll hit the road. ETA to your location, about an hour, hour-ten tops."

"Sounds good. She's progressing really nicely, went from six to eight in the last two hours—" Jenna liked the sound of that cervical dilation "—so it should be a good day for an awesome home birth."

"Oh, yeah! I'll see you soon." Jenna was grinning as she parked the truck. "I'll have to take a rain cheque on the nap."

Sean leaned across the cab and kissed her softly. "Any time."

CHAPTER TWENTY-THREE

AFTER JENNA LEFT in her sporty crossover, zinging with excitement over her first birth on the peninsula, Sean set about to unpack the truck and get the camping gear cleaned and back into the garage.

It took him a solid two hours, but he did it, and at the end, he didn't fall flat on his bed. Progress.

He cracked a beer to celebrate, another first, and he stretched out on the couch.

His brain was churning ideas for coaching. Ways to make it work as a feasible job. He could reach out to the team he'd run with. He'd never been one of their stars, but they knew he knew his stuff.

He wasn't sure he wanted to fly anywhere. But maybe he could organize some trail running retreats. If he was careful with his disability payout from the Army, he could make it stretch out over a few years. Take his time and build a business that worked around his limits.

When he looked back on how angry he'd been when he first came home, he felt a healthy dose of shame. He hadn't handled being injured well.

And the last two days had cast a bright spotlight on the damage that had done to his relationship with Jenna.

His wife.

Jesus, he'd been so stupid to think he could let her go.

His beer was nearly empty when a knock came at the door.

Sean left his cane next to the couch and carefully made his way to the foyer without it.

Progress.

He opened the door, and his good mood evaporated.

"Sir," he said to his father. "What can I do for you?"

The Colonel gave him an unimpressed look. "Invite me in, for starters."

Sean waved his hand—and his nearly empty beer bottle—toward the living room. "Be my guest." He stepped back, letting his father pass. "Would you like a drink?"

That got a grunt which Sean took as a no. He made his way into the kitchen and got rid of his own beer.

When he returned to the living room, the Colonel was standing in the middle of the space, glaring at the doorway as Sean re-appeared. "You're drunk."

Sean frowned. "What the fuck?"

"Watch your language."

"So glad you stopped by, *Dad*. But I'm not drunk and this is my own home, so I'll use whatever fucking language I want." He swore again, this time under his breath, just for good measure. This was already going swimmingly.

"You're swaying."

"I have *fucking vertigo*." And he really didn't need to be making the blood pound in his head like that. He could feel a vein pulsing in his neck as he took a deep breath. He gritted his teeth and gestured toward the couch. "I left my cane there when I answered the door. I spent all morning tidying in the garage and I was having a beer—a single fucking beer—to chill the fuck—"

His father raised his hand. "Point made, Captain Foster."

Jesus. Sean rolled his eyes, even though that strained his brain, and he threw himself into the nearest chair. He closed his eyes and counted to ten. "What are you doing here?"

"I was invited."

When the fuck—oh. Jenna had invited him. Right.

"Jenna was called out to a birth." So run along, old man. Thanks for the headache. Don't let the door smack you in the ass on the way out.

"I came to see you."

"Really?"

"Why is that so hard to believe?"

"Because you never bothered before."

"I wasn't sure I'd be welcome."

He wouldn't have been, until Jenna had issued an invitation—one Sean never thought his father would take her up on. He should have seen this coming, but he'd been busy realizing how much he loved his wife.

Priorities.

"Well, you came, we bonded, now you can check that off your to-do list."

"That's enough attitude from you, boy."

Boy? He'd gone to war and got the brain injury to prove it. Started two careers, lost them both. Found a wife. Nearly lost her. Working hard on finding yet another new path through life.

He was too damn busy for this bullshit right now.

"I'm not a boy. Haven't been for a long time."

"You'll always be my boy." There was an attempt at fondness in his father's voice, but that just made Sean see red.

"You think you have that right?" He pushed himself out of the chair and carefully—no fucking swaying, not now, no matter how much the room spun around him—walked over to his cane. He grabbed it and paced back towards the archway to the hallway. They'd have this out, then he'd show the old man the door. "When was I ever, eh? Colonel Foster was never, *has never* been a caring, loving father to *this man*. So keep your platitudes for my brothers who don't see you as the cold, pathetic shell that you are."

So that's what it felt like for twenty-plus years of antagonism and resentment to boil over.

Excellent. He was all warmed up now. He leaned against the doorframe and sneered. "What, nothing to say?"

His father crossed his arms and gave him a hard look. "This wasn't how I expected this conversation to go."

"What were you hoping would happen?"

"I..." His jaw worked and his eyes glinted dangerously. "I don't know how to talk to you."

"You never did." Sean laughed, hard and sharp, completely without humour. "Because you never cared about me. You gotta care to pay attention. To listen to what a *toddler* needs. You want to call me boy? You should have been around when I actually was one."

"I care about you. I always have."

"You have a twisted way of showing it."

"I admit we've never been close. I'm to blame for that. Your brothers got some time with an innocent dad, who thought he had the world in his hands. You got me. I'm a shitty father, and I know that. But it doesn't change the fact that you're still my boys. All four of you. I..."

"You what?"

"I love you," the Colonel said gruffly. "In my own way."

Sean shook his head. "Why do you have to add that on the end? Like you want to be some kind of hero, but only a little bit."

"I'm no hero, of any kind." His father's face twisted into an ugly mask Sean had seen many times before.

His own anger made him want to feed on that ugliness, to push him further, push him the hell out. Push, push, push.

But there was something else in his father's expression. An edge which now took on a new meaning for Sean. He'd never understood it before.

He'd seen it plenty.

He'd just never read it as anguish before.

But that's what that sharp glint in the Colonel's eyes was, no doubt about it.

Sean had never thought of his father having a soul. He was a hard man, through and through. But right now, there was a bleak, destroyed pain in the other man's expression.

Sean recognized it, because he knew it intimately.

He knew anguish, and he knew loss. He knew what it was to see your dreams evaporate. "You didn't..." His throat felt thick and useless.

All the fight slipped out of Sean and he dropped his head. He couldn't breathe as he tried to make this right, somehow. His father might not deserve much, but he deserved this. "I know I took her from you."

The Colonel froze.

They never talked about her. There were pictures all over the rambling house on the other side of town, but they never spoke of Sean's mother.

"What did you say?"

"I..." He dragged in a breath. "I get it now. Now that I have Jenna. When I was hurt, I told myself it would be better if she left me. I didn't want to drag her down the way I'd—"

His father's face went white. "Don't you dare let her go."

He shook his head. "I won't."

"You didn't take your mother from me," his father said quietly, his voice cracking.

"I was—"

"If she hadn't had you, she'd have just dropped dead. You bought her another two years of life. I'm the one who failed her, son. Not you."

"I tired her out."

"You made her so happy. You brought her joy."

"I don't remember her." Sean lifted his head, knowing he looked just as wretched as his father did.

"She was..." The Colonel walked toward him then stopped.

Well, fuck. Sean paced forward and let his father pull him into an awkward hug.

"She was beautiful," his dad said, his voice muffled. "Endlessly patient with you boys. She found joy in the chaos in a way I never could."

Sean didn't know what to say to that, so he squeezed his father harder.

But the old man wasn't done accidentally slaying him. "She made me promise to be gentle with you." He grunted in what could only be an acknowledgement that the promise had not been lived up to. "I failed her, and I failed you."

It was more words than they'd ever exchanged.

It overwhelmed Sean.

"I'm fine," he finally said.

"You're more than fine." The Colonel's jaw flexed as he stepped back. He clapped his hand on Sean's shoulder and nodded. His eyes were bright, but clear.

And the emotional connection was over.

They were Fosters, after all. Hard as fuck.

Sean would collapse from the weight of this conversation later. When he was alone.

Or maybe when Jenna got home, and he could hold her.

Until then… "Are you sure I can't offer you a beer?"

His father gave him a firm nod. "All right, then."

"And maybe you could come back for dinner sometime when Jenna's home."

That got a smile. "You did right with that one. She's smart as a whip, isn't she?"

"She is."

"Pretty sure she had my number at dinner."

And yet his father came anyway, knowing Jenna could see through him. Sean returned the smile, even though his was still strained. "She'll be glad you came by, and sorry she missed you."

———

JENNA GOT home at ten that night. Sean had fallen asleep on the couch waiting for her, and he jolted awake when he heard the door creak open.

"Hey," he whispered.

She gave him a tired smile as she dumped her bags in the entrance way. "Hey."

"How did it go?"

"Big baby. Took mama forever to find the right position to push him out, but she got there in the end. They're both well and tucked in for the night."

"Amazing." He stood and pulled her in for a tight hug. "What do you need now?"

"A shower, a snack, and bed."

"I'll make you something to eat."

She dressed in her jammies and found him in the kitchen ten minutes later. Her hair was still damp and she'd twisted it into a bun on the top of her head.

He pushed a plate of cheese and fruit toward her as she slumped into a chair at the table. They didn't talk while she munched. He could tell her attention was fading to nothing, and she just wanted to shut down after a long day. A long weekend, really.

When she finished, he pushed her toward the bedroom. He washed her plate as he heard her brush her teeth, then he met her in the hallway and tugged her toward his bed.

Their bed.

"I've got a crazy bedtime story for you," he murmured as he tucked her in.

She was yawning again by the time he got to the beer offer. He skimmed over the fight about his mother. That felt too raw for tonight.

"Did he take you up on it?" she asked, her eyes wide.

"Yeah. We sat on the back deck for a while."

"Wow. What a crazy afternoon for you. How do you feel?"

He looked at his sleepy wife, tucked into his bed. "Damn lucky."

"I meant about your dad." She gave him a soft look. "And that bit about your mom."

She didn't miss anything. He kissed her mouth, then the tip of her nose. "I told you. I'm lucky. I can't change the past. But I can make sure you know how grateful I am for the present."

She snuggled in close, and he tucked their entwined hands against his chest as she yawned one last time and fell asleep in his arms.

———

THE WEEK HAD STARTED with a roar, and early, and it didn't let up.

Each day she was up and out of the house first thing, and by the time she got home, she was exhausted and ready for bed.

On Friday, Jenna left at dawn so she could stop at the hospital and check on a patient due to be discharged after morning rounds.

Sean got up with her and, as she got dressed and brushed her teeth, he silently filled her travel mug with coffee and toasted a bagel for the road.

She took both with a grateful smile, ignoring the way her stomach did look-at-me handstands when he reached past her to open the front door and brushed a quick kiss across her temple.

They hadn't had any quality time all week. She was looking forward to a couple of days off, that was for sure.

For the drive, she cranked up the radio and listened to soul-deep aching country music. When she arrived in Walkerton an hour and twenty minutes later, she was all full of complicated feelings. They were in a good place, but it was hard to quell the rising drumbeat of want inside her belly.

But work was a balm.

In addition to scheduled clinic appointments with existing clients, Jenna had her first intake with a new client. Brenda was thirty-four weeks pregnant and had recently moved to the area. Their appointment ran into Jenna's lunch hour, but she didn't care.

After lunch she sat down with Nadine to do a video peer review—how they managed to keep up with professional development between smaller communities—and they discussed her professional development obligations for the next year. Then she had two more client appointments, and by half past five, she was ready to head home.

She texted Sean and asked if he wanted anything from the store.

He replied immediately. **I've got dinner under control, but we need oranges.**

Okay, will get those.

On the drive home, she changed the radio station. She'd had enough soul-deep ache for a lifetime. It was time to be grateful for texts about oranges.

When she pulled up in front of their little house, she noticed the lawn was mown. The front door was open, with just the screen in place, to let a breeze carry through to the kitchen.

She followed that path herself, and found Sean at the sink. She set the grocery bag on the counter and pulled out his oranges. "Here you go."

He flashed her a quick smile. "Thank you. How was your day?"

"Pretty good. Did an intake for a new client today who's new to the area, so I should have a delivery of my own to manage soon enough. I've missed that."

"Awesome." He turned away from the sink and grabbed a tea towel to dry his hands.

She looked around the kitchen. "What are we having for dinner?"

It was spotless, but also empty of any cooking evidence.

He grinned. "Bring one of those oranges and come with me."

He grabbed his cane and with his free hand, gently took hold of her. His fingers wrapped around hers, strong and warm, and he led her to the back door. She forced herself to ignore the electric currents streaking up her arm from where he touched her.

She had texts about oranges and a mowed front lawn. A clean kitchen and a happy smile.

It was a hell of a lot more than she'd had three months earlier.

Sean pushed the door open and stepped onto the back porch. When he moved out of the way, she gasped, because in the middle of the yard was a rug.

A Persian rug, covered in dishes.

"A picnic?" She asked, her heart thumping against her chest.

"Sort of," he said. He carefully stepped down off the porch and pointed to the back of the house.

She followed him, twisting as she went.

Off the back of the house hung a white bed sheet.

Sean slung his arm over her shoulders and gave her a light squeeze. "We're having a movie night."

"Oh, wow." She bit her lip as she fought not to cry. It was perfect. "I love this."

"Good." He turned his head and looked down at her, his expression heated.

She swallowed hard and tried to tell herself he wasn't thinking about seducing her, but the way he dragged his gaze slowly over her face, lingering on her lips, that made it hard.

He leaned in, and her breath caught in her throat.

"Sean..." She wanted to warn him not to play with her. Not to push her into wanting more than he could give.

"I know. It's okay. Just kiss me."

Just. There was no just kissing him. There were head-first dives into dark, unknown waters. There was swirling chaos that felt better than any drug imaginable.

There were memories so painful they felt like blades against her chest. She blamed the country music that morning, and a week of long drives where she had nothing to do but think about how much she wanted him.

None of that stopped her from lifting her face and closing the gap between them, because no matter the cost, she would always kiss him.

She'd lost this once. She'd never take it for granted again.

He licked along her lower lip before sliding his tongue inside a little, teasing her. She pushed up on her toes, chasing the kiss. He squeezed her shoulders, holding her in place—and that was different. In Spain, he'd never needed to control anything between them.

But it wasn't helpful to compare anything to Spain.

That was in the past.

That was done.

And if he needed to be in control here, she could give

him that. She stood as still as could be and let him kiss her. When he pulled back, his gaze was a little glassy—and she could feel a similar lusty haze falling over herself too.

"Wow," she said.

"I should have kissed you that first night in Urfa," he said roughly. "I wanted to, but we weren't alone."

They weren't necessarily alone now, either. It made her unexpectedly happy that he didn't care.

Because she was his wife, and if he wanted to kiss her in their backyard, he could.

Sultry backyard kisses could be added to the texts about oranges and mowed lawn.

"Can I interest you in another viewing of Jurassic Park?"

And movie traditions.

She was blessed. She needed to remember that. "Yes, please."

He gestured for her to sit on the rug.

"This is really nice. Where did you get it?"

"I sent it home from the base. There were some vendors there, and I liked this particular pattern. It reminded me..." He ran his hand over the pale red, yellow, and cream pattern. "I thought you would like it."

Her breath caught in her throat. "When did you buy it?"

He lifted his gaze to hers, and there was no disguising the tortured look in his eyes. "After I returned to the base. After saying goodbye to you."

"Where has it been?"

"Wrapped up. I'd forgotten about it." He grimaced. "Maybe suppressed is more like it. I found it earlier today when I was over at Dean's."

"Did he help you move stuff back here?"

Sean shook his head. "I drove myself."

"What?"

"Don't look so surprised," he said gruffly.

"I'm...happy. I just thought you didn't want to even try."

He leaned in and kissed her lightly. "There are a lot of things I need to start trying again. No more fear."

But fear was healthy. Fear kept ridiculous hopes and dreams in check.

Fear helped her put the brakes on. "So...a picnic, eh?"

"Popcorn, of course. And apples."

She held up the orange. "I'm sensing a theme."

"Have a seat."

She settled in the empty space behind the food, facing the make-shift screen, and Sean opened a thermos.

"Turkish coffee?"

"Oh, fancy."

"Not sure if I made it quite right..."

She tasted it. Strong and thick and sweet. "It's good."

It wasn't quite the same, but it still brought her right back to that first night they'd met, and she sighed happily as she took a second long, slow sip. Her time in Turkey had been rocky, but she missed the new experiences. And the coffee.

"Do you miss it?"

Her eyes flew to his face. "I was just thinking that. How did you know?"

He grinned and leaned in, brushing his fingers over the corner of her mouth. "You make the sweetest sounds of appreciation when you get something you haven't had in a long time. That apple, for example." His gaze was tangled up around her lips, and she felt a deep, yearning tug inside her. "When we met over breakfast..."

"I remember," she whispered. Of course, after all they'd been through, they knew each other. "What else do we have?"

He broke his attention away and showed her the rest of the food. Meatballs, tomatoes, cucumbers, and cheese, neatly cubed for easy picnic-style eating.

"Shall we start the movie while we eat?" He leaned over and pressed play on a laptop hooked up to a projector.

"Where did you find that?"

"Put the call out." He winked at her. "The projector belongs to the library. Chloe loaned it to us for the night."

Her sneaky friends.

She watched Sean's profile as he looked at the screen, adjusting the picture clarity. Her sneaky husband.

They ate slowly, picking at things here and there as they watched the movie.

All the memories from Urfa washed over her as the film progressed. The moment when she'd leaned into Sean, the way his body had felt. Warm and strong and welcoming.

He was right next to her tonight too and the offer was clear. She shifted her weight and slid her head onto his shoulder. He squeezed his arm around her.

"How long did I last the first time before falling asleep?"

"About half the movie," he murmured. "You were pretty worn out. But beautiful. That's what I remember the most. Thinking that I was the luckiest man in the world to have your head on my shoulder. Just like this."

A lump lodged in her throat.

"I'm not going to fall asleep tonight. I don't want to miss a second of the movie, or the company." She turned her head and kissed his shoulder. "Now pass me the popcorn."

They held the bowl between them, their fingers brushing when they reached into it at the same time. A few times, Jenna swore Sean did it on purpose, the same way his gaze kept travelling down her body to her bare legs beneath the light, floaty sundress she'd put on that morning. By the end of the movie, she was totally distracted with wondering where he was planning on this night ending up.

She shifted onto her knees and leaned in to kiss him. "That was magical."

He caught her lips with his and deepened the kiss for a few seconds before breaking away to turn off the projector. It was all-the-way dark now, and she shivered. Not because it was cold, but because she didn't know what came next.

It was hard not to want everything to come next.

But she would be over the moon thrilled about just a little more. To have *something* more, and even that felt like a dangerous thing to hope.

"I'll, uh…take the fruit in." They'd shared one of the apples. She picked up the remaining one, and her untouched orange, and balanced them in one hand while she grabbed the popcorn bowl with the other.

Behind her, she heard the clatter and ting of metal dishes being stacked neatly.

Sean caught up to her as she tried to open the door, and he leaned his cane against the back of the house, freeing his hand. "Let me."

Her insides rioted at the warm, intimate words. Oh, she'd let him do whatever he wanted, and really he was just getting the door for her, and flicking on the dim lights that ran beneath the upper cabinets.

Of course she read that as mood lighting.

She was hopeless.

Her hands shook as she set the fruit in the bowl on the counter then dumped the remaining popcorn kernels into the rubbish bin. Sean set his bowls in the sink, and she did the same with the popcorn bowl.

"I'll go back and get the—" She cut herself off as she turned around just in time to see Sean grip his t-shirt behind his neck and pull it off in one smooth motion.

Her mouth went dry.

His frame had filled out in the last two months, but it wasn't the same body she'd memorized in Spain. This body had scars and dents, was leaner in some places and bulkier in others.

She loved this new body.

And she *wanted* this new body with a fierceness that took her by surprise.

"The rug can wait a few minutes," Sean said quietly, his voice rough around the edges.

She knew the feeling. Her edges were a bit frayed, too.

He rolled his shoulders, making his muscles flex beneath his skin, but his gaze didn't waver as he looked at her—like he was trying to really, really see her. "I've been thinking a lot this week," he finally said. "About where we're at. About what I told you last weekend, how you were in my heart, constantly, when I went back to Iraq. Jenna, you still are, even though I've made a hack of our relationship. And I know it's going to take some time for you to fall back in love with me, but—"

"Fall back..." She stared at him, dumbly trying to catch

up with what he was saying. "Sean, I never stopped loving you."

"You said…" He searched her face. "You said you liked this new me. And I knew you…I know you love me, but maybe the in-love-with-me part has faded. I'm good with taking things slow, you know? But I want you to know I love you. I still love you. I never stopped, even when I was deep in the middle of…all of that…" He waved his hand, his mouth tightening.

"I don't need time. And nothing has faded." How had she managed to give him that impression? "Not for a second. I'm in love with you, with this new-and-grumpier Sean. I adore you. For who you used to be, and who you are right this very second."

He exhaled like he'd been holding his breath for too long.

She took a tentative step toward him, and he moved, too, closing the gap. He cupped her cheek, his fingers sliding into her hair, and he kissed her.

Now she recognized the vibrating tension in him as he kissed her. He didn't want to control her. He was trying to control himself. Hold himself back.

He didn't need to do that anymore.

When he released her mouth, she hovered her hand just in front of his chest. "May I…?"

He nodded, his gaze suddenly almost shy, and she reached out, grazing the hard planes of his torso with just her fingertips.

The drumbeat inside her got louder.

"I thought I was fattening you up," she murmured as she traced the cut lines of his abdomen.

"I've been doing my best to convert all that to muscle."

"Your best is...exceptional." She licked her lips as he caught her wrist, his fingers a loose manacle.

"Enough," he said in a rough whisper. "I need to kiss you."

She smiled up at him. "I want to touch you."

"I know the feeling. But..." He turned them around and gripped her by the hips.

She gasped as he hoisted her onto the counter. "Sean, don't—"

"I'm fine." He grinned, his teeth flashing white in the dark kitchen. "Just a little boost." He grazed his hands down the outside of her body. "I like your dress, by the way. It's been distracting me all night."

"Oh?" She wiggled against him, her thighs falling open as he moved closer. She'd worn the dress for him, too. It had a row of buttons down the front that begged to be peeled open.

She wasn't above begging. She might explode if he didn't touch her.

And hopefully if he did touch her, there would be explosions of a different sort.

Her desires were a runaway train tonight. There was no putting on the brakes, not the way he was touching her and looking at her and...oh, his lips on her throat, his breath on her skin...

Her head dropped back as he tasted her, too. He sucked on her neck, then licked his way over her collarbone.

She shoved her hands behind her, skittering the fruit bowl across the counter. "Oh!"

Sean didn't stop, not for a second. His lips ghosted down the bare plane of her upper chest until he got to the neckline of her dress.

Her hand slipped again, and this time the fruit bowl toppled into the sink with a loud clatter.

Sean just laughed as he flicked the first button free.

Thank God for talented fingers. His mouth followed, tasting each newly exposed bit of skin until he found her bra, and then he tasted her through that, too.

Hot, wet heat tugged at her nipples through the lace. It lit the live fuse which led directly to her core, and she made an inhuman, wild keening sound.

He groaned in response and redoubled his efforts.

Oh, it had been way too long.

His hands pushed her skirt up as he sucked, and she managed to lift her hips for him, one at a time, so he could strip away her underwear.

Yes, yes, yes. Bring on the explosions.

He breathed her name against her neck as he dragged his mouth up to meet hers again. His kiss made her legs shake, and he dropped one hand to her thigh.

"Sean..."

"I've got you." His voice had never been stronger or more sure.

And as his fingers slid up her bare skin again, she felt herself tumbling. He had her, and she was a goner.

The first touch of his fingertips between her thighs made her jump. The second had her hips rocking forward, ready for more. And the third could only be called a cruel tease of the best kind.

He moved through her wetness, straight to her entrance, but he only circled there with the lightest fingertip before dragging her slick arousal up to her clit.

Oh, that was good. So very, very good. But she wanted more.

She wanted him inside her. "Please, Sean."

He nipped at her lower lip. "Tell me what you want."

She chased the kiss, and they got lost in that for a beat, maybe three. When she broke it off, her head was swimming with delicious heat, and want had loosened her tongue.

"Your fingers."

"You've got them."

"Inside me."

He groaned and obliged, smoothly twisting his hand so he could enter her and still give her his heel to grind her clit against. "I want you to come like this," he said hoarsely. "I want to feel you grip me, tight and hot. God, I've missed you."

That made her shudder, and he pressed deeper, stretching her with another finger.

Heat flooded her body as he leaned over her to whisper in her ear. "Is that good?"

Oh God, his voice was an aphrodisiac.

"So good." She was panting now, writhing on his hand, and the way he was breathing, too, she knew she wasn't alone, but she couldn't think about what he needed right now.

Too close.

Too twisted up.

It was right there, that desperate, clawing hunger. His fingers sped up, thrusting into her with just enough of a curve that he was both stretching her open and rocking against her G-spot at the same time.

"Come on, Jenna. Show me how pretty you are when you let go," he crooned.

She cried out as he pressed into her again, and as his heel rocked over her clit, she shattered for him.

He held her as she shuddered in his arms, and kissed

her, over and over again, and told her that he loved her, until her breathing returned to normal.

When her brain finally worked again, she reached for him. He caught her wrists and lifted her hands so he could kiss her knuckles.

He shook his head, and a little bit of her joy slipped away. Just a little. She frowned. "What about you?"

"That *was* for me." His eyes glittered a warning not to press him again, so she nodded as he leaned in and kissed her again. "This is just the start," he whispered against her mouth. "We'll find our way back."

She didn't need to go back to what they'd had. If this was the start of something new, that was a-okay by her. She cupped his face with her hands and softly kissed him. "We're exactly where we need to be."

CHAPTER TWENTY-FOUR

"WHAT TIME ARE YOUR FRIENDS ARRIVING?" Sean asked as he crowded Jenna against the bathroom counter. She was smoothing sunscreen over her face, and she flashed him a quick smile in the mirror.

"They should be here in an hour. Grace messaged from Markdale thirty minutes ago."

Good. That meant they had time for something a little dirty first.

Two weeks had passed since he'd set up the Jurassic Park screening, and ever since, he hadn't been able to keep his hands off her.

He dropped a kiss to her shoulder as he squeezed her hips, snugly hugged by black spandex. "I like these shorts." He liked the bathing suit beneath them even better.

They were heading up to Tobermory for an afternoon on the water. Snorkelling and swimming.

Sean would stay on the beach.

Small price to pay to see his wife in a bright pink bikini.

Two months ago—hell, a few weeks ago—he'd have wallowed in what he couldn't do.

Now he drew strength from what he could do.

Namely, make Jenna cry out his name like it was a prayer.

"I think you like everything I wear," she whispered as he tugged down the shorts, baring her pink-covered bottom.

"True. And everything you don't too." He traced the line of her bikini bottoms before tugging those down, too. He left them around her thighs, trapping her legs together as he wrapped his arms around her and stroked his fingers up her neck.

"Just like this," he whispered in her ear. "Just like Gibraltar."

She gasped as he eased her forward, onto her elbows.

Jenna bent over the bathroom counter, her pretty pink pussy on display for him between the round curves of her ass—there was nothing sexier in the world.

It wouldn't be just like Gibraltar, though. Sean wasn't the same man.

He stroked her gently at first then filled her with his fingers; one, then two. He leaned over her and pressed his cock into her hip. She twisted her head to look at him face-to-face.

Her eyes were glassy and her lips were swollen and pink. "I love you, my wife."

It didn't matter that it was different. It was still theirs.

Things weren't exactly back to normal—he still struggled to maintain an erection, and he hadn't even tried with her—but he wanted her something fierce.

Orgasms were overrated, he'd come to realize. He'd get

there, eventually, but in the meantime, giving her pleasure was more than enough.

"Don't move, okay?" He grinned at the weak, wobbly groan of consent she gave him. Then he pushed up and just looked at her.

His. Wife.

Fuck, he was lucky.

He lowered himself to his knees behind her and buried his face between her legs.

She cried out, her legs trembling, but she didn't move. She took it. Every lick and swipe and suck. She took it until she couldn't hold back, and as she came on his tongue, he felt himself get hard and stay hard.

Fuck, yeah.

Soon. Soon, they would do something about that.

He pressed his face into the back of her thigh and dragged in a rough, hungry breath.

Time for visitors.

Carefully, he pulled himself back up to a stand, and helped her right her clothes again.

She gave him a mock-scolding look that said heaps. She wanted to return the favour. But the thing was, it wasn't a favour at all. He got a lot out of making love to her with his hands and his mouth, and right now, that was where he was comfortable holding their sex life.

Soon, though.

He took her hand and let her cup him through his shorts. She squeezed the fading strength of an erection, and he pressed into her touch before shifting away to wet a washcloth.

She turned pink as he scrubbed his face, but as soon as he was done, she pressed herself against him and kissed him until they were both breathless.

"That was really hot," she whispered.

"Mmm." He sank into her mouth, tasting her excitement. Promising more of the same later. "I should get changed, too. That's what I was going to do before you distracted me with your shorts."

She followed him into their room, but after he changed into a pair of swim shorts for their drive up to Mermaid Cove, she disappeared into the other bedroom. What had been her room, when he'd been stupid, and where all her clothes still lived. They needed to rearrange some furniture. He had the better, bigger bed, but she'd had the bigger room, without enough space for two dressers.

That would be his project when she went back to work next week.

He'd surprise her one night when she got home.

When she reappeared in the doorway, she was blushing. "Okay, so—I was—"

Blushing and stammering.

"What is it?" He sat back on the bed and spread his legs. She stepped into the space he made and held out her hand.

When he peeled her fingers open, he found a wooden box in her palm.

His heart thumped hard against his ribs. He opened the lid, knowing what he'd find inside.

Their wedding rings.

"Just like Gibraltar," she said haltingly. "Maybe it's time to put these on."

He took her ring out and rolled it between his fingers before he silently took her hand in his. There was a lump in his throat as he thought about what he wanted to say.

"I made you promises with this ring. And I didn't live

up to them. But I will. I've stumbled, but I'm up again. I'm yours again."

She reached for him, and he let her cup his cheek and tug his gaze up to hers. She smiled through bright, unshed tears. "I love you."

That was all he needed. He pulled her into his arms and kissed her, and then he put her wedding ring back on her finger.

Jenna didn't let his hand go very far before she caught it. "Your turn," she said. She took a deep breath. "I made promises, too. And some of them were based on hypotheticals. We didn't know it would be so hard, so soon. Now we know. We are stronger together. We are fierce together. And we are happy together." She beamed at him as she slid his ring onto his finger. "My husband."

He flexed his hand. "Hey, look at that." His ring fit. Where it had been too big in Spain, now his finger filled it almost perfectly. "Good job fattening me up, wife."

She laughed and patted his abs.

Okay, maybe just thickening up, then. He liked this bulkier version of himself. He didn't need to keep his weight crazy lean for running any more. Now he could pack on a bit of muscle—and eat pie from Mac's without any guilt.

"Our life is pretty sweet," he said, squeezing her hand.

She nodded and held his gaze. "It is."

A knock at the front door interrupted the moment, but Jenna's squeal was worth it. "They're here!"

Sean found his cane in the bathroom, where he'd left it before the sex and all it had led to. By the time he made it to the living room, Jenna had their guests inside and was talking a mile a minute about what they had planned.

"And this is Sean," she said, bringing him into the loop as she gestured to her friends. "Grace and Alex."

Grace was a stunning redhead, and her partner Alex was a quiet black man who gave Sean an understanding grin. "Nice to meet you, man."

"Welcome to the peninsula. Jenna says it's your first trip."

He nodded. "I've been to Collingwood a few times for skiing, but never got quite this far. Same with Grace."

"Then you're in for a treat."

They took Jenna's car, and on the drive up to Tobermory, Sean discovered Alex was a distance runner, too.

"You ran Western States 100? No shit." Alex was impressed, and that puffed Sean's chest a bit, he couldn't deny it. "That's hardcore. How'd you get an entry ticket?"

"Lucked into a qualifier win in Colorado. Had my best run ever—in Colorado. I didn't finish Western States."

"No shame in that. I watched the live stream this year."

Sean rubbed his jaw as he thought about doing that. He was surprised that he wasn't twisted up inside at the thought of watching a premier race from the sidelines. "I should do that next year. More and more races are going to the YouTube coverage, eh?"

"Yeah, it's pretty slick."

That gave him another idea for the running coach plan. As they arrived at Mermaid Cove, he pulled out his phone and sent himself an email so he wouldn't forget.

Earlier they'd packed the car with a thick blanket to lay out on the rocks, a basket of towels and sunscreen, plus a couple of snorkel sets. Sean grabbed those, and Alex carried the picnic basket as the girls led the way—which Sean found hilarious, because Jenna hadn't been here before, either, but she was in full county hostess mode.

He loved that she'd taken to the peninsula and made it her new home.

She stopped at the water's edge and turned around. "Okay, who's going swimming?"

———

JENNA WASN'T EXPECTING Sean to set their stuff down, drop his cane, and peel off his t-shirt in that far-too-sexy and super distracting one-handed way of his. "I am."

She swallowed her concern about that plan—because he was a grown up and fitter than her on his worst day.

He stopped as he got to her and lowered his voice. "Don't look so worried."

"I'm not *so* worried. Just moderately, normal-level of worried."

"I won't go out past where I can touch."

And he smirked.

She gasped at him, and he kissed her before stepping into the bright blue water of Georgian Bay.

"Yes," he hissed. "That's the good stuff right there." He rolled his head back and sighed. "You cold motherfucker, I've missed you."

Well, who could argue with that?

Grace stopped beside her and winced. "Is it really cold?"

Alex went in next. "Yep," he yelped, but then he grinned. "Come on in, sweetheart."

Grace shook her head. "I'm going to catch a bit of sun first."

Jenna dipped her toe in, then back right up. "Okay, so sun sounds good."

Grace laughed as they stretched out on the blanket.

"Besides, now I can get right to the real good stuff. How are things going? You look ridiculously in love."

"We are." Jenna didn't care that she was blushing. "I really feel like I've got him back, you know?"

Her friend nodded. "I'm glad for you."

Jenna looked out at the men, who were now lower in the water. As promised, Sean wasn't that far from shore.

"I gotta say, given how you described his injuries, he's doing *really* well."

"He's been working so hard on his recovery. The last two months have just been an explosion of ability. But don't be fooled—he's masking a lot, too." She frowned, then sighed and puffed her cheeks out. "He's just stubborn and independent. And he hates sympathy. Can't handle it."

"Sounds like someone else I know."

Jenna laughed. "Maybe a little."

"So without any sympathy, just friend to friend... how are you doing? Besides obviously getting laid like a queen."

Jenna blushed.

"Damn, girl. Look at you. Zero to sixty in just a few months."

"Zero to thirty, maybe."

"Pardon?"

Jenna looked at the blanket and picked at invisible fuzz. Why had she said that out loud? "We haven't...The intimacy is different now."

Grace didn't say anything. That. That's why she'd said something. Because Grace was a safe listener and Jenna wasn't going to talk about sex with her gentle therapist.

"Don't get me wrong, it's good." Good Lord, her cheeks were hot now. "It's great, really. He's very...thoroughly attentive. But it's in both of our natures not to dwell too much on the negative. That's one way to spin it, anyway."

Out of the corner of her eye, she saw Grace nod. "What's the other way?"

Jenna stuck her tongue out at her friend. "Neither of us is comfortable talking about where it's not going well."

"Why is that?"

Jenna didn't know. She'd never had any problem talking about sex with any of her other partners. And when they were in bed, it was fine—she could talk about sex *during sex* with Sean. Tell him what she wanted and what she liked. "The stakes are higher," she finally said. "They're everything. I think with previous partners, it didn't matter so much if I said the wrong thing, or we weren't compatible. I never saw anyone as my forever partner. But Sean is it for me. I love him. He's my other half, literally for better or for worse. And I don't want to hurt him. I think he probably feels the same way."

"Yeah. That makes a lot of sense." Grace nodded. "And it's probably unhelpful bullshit, too, since it's causing you grief now."

"Hey!" But Jenna laughed. "I didn't want to hear that."

"Yes you did. Otherwise you wouldn't have brought it up. Just talk to him. Avoiding the topic doesn't make it go away. Do you think he's not aware that it's not all hunky dory?"

No. He knew. And he was carrying all the weight of that responsibility when he didn't need to. "Stop being so smart. It's annoying."

"Speaking of annoying…have you told your mother yet that you're actually married to this boy you like in Pine Harbour?"

Jenna threw her napkin at Grace's head. "No."

"You might want to do that some time before the grand babies arrive."

"I regret inviting you up here." But she didn't, at all, because Grace was exactly the echo of reason she needed right now.

It was time to put on her big girl panties and have some tough conversations.

But first, she needed to swim with her love in an ice cold lake.

And then they'd go in search of fish and chips served by pirates.

———

AFTER AN AFTERNOON IN THE SUN, and dinner on the picnic tables outside Castaway Pete's they came home and opened a bottle of wine.

Sean liked Jenna's friends—no surprise—and the conversation flowed smoothly. But something was bothering Jenna.

"What's on your mind?" he finally asked when they had a few minutes alone in the kitchen.

"Grace reminded me that I need to update my mom. About us."

"Ah."

"Time kind of slipped away from me and now it's been a while and…"

And her mother was a mother, and worried. Maybe more specifically than other mothers. Sean didn't know what to say. "Do you want to call her tonight?"

"Maybe."

"Let's go put on a movie. And if you decide to slip

away, I'll know why. Do you want me to be there or would that be more awkward?"

She sighed. "It'll be a whole thing. I'll do it on my own."

So he gave her a supportive smile when she excused herself mid-movie, but after twenty minutes passed, he left Grace and Alex watching in the living room and followed Jenna onto the back deck. Now he was worried she was trapped in a difficult conversation.

When he eased the door open, she wiggled her fingers at him, but the rest of her body was wound tight and stressed out.

So was her voice. "Mom, I hear what you're saying, but —" He sat in the chair next to her and held out his hand. She took it as she exhaled roughly. "I'm thirty. I'm not—"

She gave him a pained look and pulled the phone away from her ear. She pressed the mute button. "I haven't been able to get a complete sentence out for the last ten minutes."

"Offer for us to come and visit her. Or she can come here, if she'd like. We can pay for her ticket."

Jenna shrugged weakly. "Maybe." She un-muted the phone and held it back to her ear. And listened, for quite a while.

"Are you done?" she finally asked. "I kept it a secret because I knew this is exactly how you would react. I apologize for not telling you sooner." Her eyes went wide. "Well, I'm glad you didn't come out here. That would have been difficult when he was recovering. But you could come now, if you'd like. We'd be happy to pay for your ticket."

Sean tapped his chest.

Jenna shook her head, but he nodded. Yes.

She sighed. "Mom, Sean's sitting next to me, and he wants it to be clear that he's offering to pay for your ticket, not me. Although I would, too." She laughed. "I know, I told him no, but he doesn't understand." She looked at him. "Kowalczyk women pay their own way. It's a rule."

He grinned at her. "That's a good rule, but I'm still offering."

"Yeah, that's him. No, you can't speak to him." She rolled her eyes. "Because we are in the middle of an argument, Mother. Yes, an argument. We do not agree that I am a responsible, grown woman who can make her own decisions in life."

Sean tried to fill in the gaps of the conversation from the squeaks of noise coming from Jenna's phone. *You may be a grown woman but that doesn't stop you from making mistakes.*

"Sean isn't—Mom, come visit. Okay?"

"We'll see."

"Or not. Your choice. We can also come to you. Sean loves the west coast." She took a deep breath. "He's run a lot of races out there. And you know he's a fan of the prime minister's, too. Maybe we can visit when the PM is in his home riding."

Sean covered his mouth to keep his laugh from barking out. It had taken her twenty-five minutes, but she'd stooped to emotional manipulation.

Jenna was kind and sweet and perfect, but even she had limits when it came to parental intrusion into her personal life.

Sean approved.

She was grimacing as she hung up the phone. "I'm going to hell for misdirecting her like that."

"But was she suitably impressed by the reminder that I once let the nation's leader kick my ass in road hockey?"

"Let?"

He grinned. "Losers never share their secrets." He pulled her tight and brushed his lips against his ear. "Except with their wives, of course. No, he won fair and square. The guy has game."

"Now I've boxed us into having to go visit her."

"But you were right—I do love the west coast. We'll go as soon as you can get some time off."

"In September, maybe. I have a client due at the start of the month, but I think I can block a week off at the end."

"It's a plan." He kissed her mouth softly. "Anything else on your mind tonight?"

She hesitated before she shook her head. Just for a second, the tiniest of freezes. "No," she said. "Nothing else I want to talk about tonight."

Not exactly the same thing.

Sean stretched his legs wide and patted his thigh. "Come here."

She crawled into his lap and he wrapped his arms around her.

"We should get back inside," she whispered.

"Yeah." But there was something on her mind that she didn't want to talk about tonight. His brain hadn't lost the ability to parse the difference between words. "Soon. I just want to hold you for a minute."

He couldn't, wouldn't push her to talk.

But he could and would try even harder to be all she needed.

CHAPTER TWENTY-FIVE

THE NEXT MORNING, Sean got a text message from Tom inviting him to work out at the search and rescue team's training facility.

He told the others about it over breakfast. "It's a pretty cool space, if it sounds like something you guys might like to do too? They have a rappelling tower with a climbing wall, a ropes course, and a decent weight room."

Alex's eyes lit up at the same time as Grace and Jenna exchanged a look that said *oh goodness no thank you*.

Jenna waved her hand. "You guys go. We'll call Chloe up and see if she wants to come over and make sangria with us."

They were making their guests a meal that night that reminded them of their time in Spain. Jenna had thrown herself into the meal planning, spending the entire previous week tracking down Spanish cheese and sausage and wine, and trial-running different recipes.

"Should I invite Tom back here for dinner, then?"

Jenna's eyes lit up. "Yes, great idea."

Sean drove. He'd ordered in extended mirrors for his truck, and they made a big difference in his confidence that he was seeing all other drivers on the road while minimizing head swivelling.

The Pine Harbour Search & Rescue Team's training centre was located inside the provincial park where Tom worked as a park ranger. Sean gave his name at the gate then drove through to the facility, where Tom was waiting for them.

He gave Alex a quick overview of the facility, but Sean knew what their visitor wanted to do. "You want to head out for a run?"

Alex laughed. "Was it that obvious?"

"I recognize the hungry gleam in your eye." Sean clapped him on the shoulder. "Go. Run like the wind. We'll stay here and I'll kick Tom's ass in the weight room."

As they warmed up, Tom showed Sean the workout he'd planned on the white board on the wall.

Sean made a few suggestions then they ran through three circuits of the first set with ease.

"Okay, for the next one, let's up the intensity a bit. Work to exhaustion each time."

Tom nodded then dropped into a plank. "Bet you can't do more push-ups than me."

The old Sean would have taken that bet. Would have tossed in a race up the ropes as a kicker. "You're probably right."

Tom glared at him. "Seriously?"

"Yeah."

"Fuck off. You've been doing nothing but arm and chest exercises for months. Come on. Show me what you've got."

Against his will, Sean felt himself flex his biceps. He could hold his own, maybe. But he wasn't winning any contests. "I'm getting there."

"Then if I kick your ass today, you've got a goal for next time. Come on. Show me what you've got."

Sean slowly lowered himself to the ground. "Yeah, all right." He did a quick mental scan of his body. All good. He locked out his shoulders and pressed himself up. "Ready? Go."

He couldn't turn his head to watch Tom. He heard the other man counting, though, and they were keeping pace with each other. He passed twenty with ease, but then his shoulders started to burn. Thirty was a nice number to hit, too.

Thirty-five, thirty-six…

He tightened his core until it felt like his entire torso was made of steel. Thirty-nine. Forty.

Forty-one—

"God, I'm done," Tom gasped as he hit the ground.

Forty-two.

Sean held the last one an inch off the ground, then lowered himself. He kept his eyes looking straight, but he grinned.

Fuck, yeah. He dropped his head to the ground and rolled onto his back. "What were we betting?"

"Nothing. Pride. Bragging rights."

"Next time, we'll put money on it."

Tom laughed. "You may not be able to go fast anymore, but maybe there's some value in going slow."

Yeah. But it also wiped him out. "That's probably it for me."

Sweat rolled down his back and his arms shook from

the effort. He'd definitely pushed the limits there, in a good way.

"You mind if I keep going?"

"You mind if I give you pointers on your form?"

"Not at all." Tom grinned at him.

"That was your plan all along, wasn't it?"

"Free personal training from an elite athlete? Sue me for being clever." Tom grabbed onto the rope and jogged backwards.

Sean watched as his friend used the rope for balance and dropped into single leg squats.

Tom's face tightened up as he passed fifteen reps, but he kept going for another five, and when he finished, he gasped and stumbled, shaking his leg out before switching sides.

"Where are you feeling that?" Sean asked.

"Fucking hell, everywhere." Tom laughed then winced as he kept piling on the reps. Again, his face twisted before he pushed out the last few. "Right up the outside chain of muscles. My calf is on fire."

Sean didn't say anything, just swivelled his fingers in the air. "Go again. Push-ups first, then the assisted pistol squats. Back to back, you can do it."

"In a minute."

"In thirty seconds. You're not paying me to go easy on you."

Tom swore under his breath. "I'm not paying you at all." But he grabbed the rope and went again at the thirty second mark. This time when his expression shifted, Sean glanced at Tom's feet. "Did you just shift your weight to the outside of your heel?"

Tom froze before laughing in a strained way. "Maybe. Shit, yeah."

"Earning my keep already." Sean cleared his throat. "Don't do that. Stay on a balanced foot to the point of exhaustion, even if it comes sooner."

"You've got an eagle eye," Tom said, gasping, when he finally collapsed on the grass after six more gruelling exercises, each of them made harder when Sean figured out how Tom was compensating to push himself to more reps. "On form."

"Combination of not being able to let my head move while working out, and my history of having my own form analyzed, I guess."

"You could do personal training in general, not just running coaching."

He nodded. "Yeah."

"Come back tomorrow and kick my ass again."

"Deal."

As they finished stretching, Alex emerged from the woods, his dark skin gleaming with sweat. "Sweet trails up here."

"You know it." Sean shook his hand. "Good run?"

"Great."

There was a pang of jealousy at that, but it was short and mostly a benign flavour of bittersweet.

One of these days, he was going to need to try running —maybe if he fell over or stumbled into a tree, he'd be able to convince himself it was better not to miss it at all.

He started laughing.

"What is it?" Tom asked.

Sean shook his head. "Just thinking of myself careening wildly off trail. It's nothing. This was great, though. I'll be back tomorrow, just name your time."

THE NEXT DAY was a holiday Monday, but Jenna had a birth to attend, so Sean saw Grace and Alex off on their drive back to Toronto, then headed out to the training facility again.

Tom was in his work uniform. "Sorry, had to pull a last minute shift. Holiday weekend and we've got campers galore. But I've got an hour free now, let me just change." He pointed to the locker room, but didn't move.

"Sure, my day is wide open."

"Dinner last night was fun," Tom added. "I like Jenna's friends."

"Yeah, they're good people. It was nice to hang out with Chloe, too." Sean wasn't going to poke too hard, but after Tom and Chloe had left last night—within two minutes of each other—and Grace and Alex retired to the spare room, Jenna had confided that she thought the park ranger and the librarian had a flirtation going on.

Tom just nodded.

Oh, well, Sean tried.

Tom changed the subject. "And Jenna looks ridiculously happy with your grumpy ass."

Despite his best attempts to be nonchalant, the corners of Sean's mouth turned up in a grin. "Helps that I'm less grumpy now. We're getting there."

"Where are you getting to?" Jake asked as he rounded the corner.

Sean waved to his brother and ignored the question. "What are you doing here?"

"We heard there was a free workout session with an elite athlete."

"We?" Sean groaned as Matt and Dean appeared, too. He pointed at Tom. "I will get you for this. I will find a way to hurt you. Pendulum lunges until your quads explode."

"They love you." He winked. "But not as much as Jenna does." He turned to Sean's brothers. "That's what we were just talking about. How your baby brother here couldn't keep his hands off his wife last night. Or last weekend at the diner, when they had twigs in their hair from a roll in the forest."

"We went camping," Sean muttered. "Now are you here to work out, or gossip?"

Everyone but Matt said working out.

"Matt can go up the rope first, then. Up you go, asshole. No rest for the wicked."

By the end of the hour-long session, everyone was groaning and sweat-slicked—even Sean. It was good practice for him to adapt their workout to his own limitations, and he surprised himself by flipping it, too. Some of the things he'd learned in rehab, like the balance exercises, were quite hard for his muscle-bound brothers.

Dean fell out of step twice while trying to balance on one foot with his eyes closed. Sean made a note on his phone, where he had rudimentary notes on each of them.

Whether they liked it or not, his brothers were his first clients, and he was taking this new job damn seriously. Even though he wasn't quite sure what it was.

As Tom tossed protein bars around, Dean sat next to Sean on the wood steps. "That was really good."

"Thanks."

"I mean it."

"So do I."

Dean sighed. "We were rough on each other."

"We always are. But you were right. I was being a jerk,

and selfish. Now I've got my head on straight. I've got a plan."

"Are you going to share it?"

He sketched out some of the ideas he'd been considering. Running coaching, personal training, but maybe also something for wounded vets. He wasn't really qualified to help anyone psychologically—but on a human level, he could relate to the reluctance to accept that kind of help.

Fitness wasn't a replacement for medical help, but it might be a replacement for other things vets had lost. "It needs a better name than this, but I'm thinking something like Sean's Fitness Coaching and Rehab for Reluctant Jackasses."

Dean nodded along. "Bit of a mouthful, but yeah, I like the idea."

"Mmm."

"What's holding you back?"

"It still feels too soon to bite off something new. It's good in theory, good with you guys, but..."

"You don't do anything in half-measures." Dean gave him a gruff nod. "You never have. Why should this be any different?"

Sean hadn't realized until this moment just how much his brother's approval meant to him. "Thanks."

"When it's the right time, you'll launch it with a bang. It's a good plan. Liana might be interested in the running coaching."

"You don't need to—"

"It wouldn't be a pity hire or anything like that. You know she's serious about her running. When we first met, she was almost more interested in your running than in anything to do with me."

Sean bumped his shoulder. "That changed, though."

That got a bigger smile.

"Hey, when are you going to actually marry her?"

"Soon. After her next album releases. You'll be the first to know."

"Hey, speaking of the women we love…" Sean raised his voice. "Jake! Come here. I need your help."

———

BY THE TIME he got home, Jenna had returned from the birth and headed back out again. She'd left a note for him saying she'd gone over to Chloe's with some of the left-over sangria.

He showered, then pulled on clean clothes and texted Jenna. **I'm home. Are you going to be long?**

She replied immediately. **Just poured a glass. Will be a while. Do you want to come here?**

He could, but he had plans for their evening together. **I might take a nap.**

Okay. Rest up.

He was tempted to fire back something filthy in reply, but Chloe was the type of friend who might read her texts over Jenna's shoulder.

Instead he stretched out on their bed and thought about what he wanted to do tonight. Maybe draw her a bubble bath first. He hadn't done that yet, and it would show her that he remembered the things she'd missed the most when she was in Turkey.

Then…

He closed his eyes and thought about her bikini. Her curves. Her smile.

Yes, her mouth.

His brain caught on that and something thick and heady started to swirl around in this thoughts. He tugged his shorts down until the elastic pressed against the top of his groin, and he rubbed his lower abs. Could he jerk off?

What had once been such a simple, fundamental function was now a mountain to climb. He'd made his peace with his vertigo, accepted the faint, constant ringing in his ears. But this dysfunction was hard to handle, especially now that his libido had roared back to life.

He didn't need to come every time Jenna did. Hell, after months without sex, both before and after meeting her, he knew life was more than a quick fuck to a climax.

But...

Jesus, he needed to get out of his head. He grabbed his phone and pulled up the same dirty video site he'd visited before.

Blow jobs. He was overthinking this. Maybe the doc was right. He'd asked about it again at a follow up appointment, and Sean had pushed it off, but maybe he just needed basic sexy visuals to retrain his brain.

Dick rehab. Maybe it was time.

He thought of Jenna's mouth as the video buffered. How wet and sweet and warm it was when he kissed her. He thought of Spain. Of sun-warmed skin and endless days of hedonistic pleasure.

He slid his hand into his shorts and cupped his balls as the video started. No thinking, just watching, he told himself. *Let the lizard brain take over.*

The sounds were better than the visual, really. He closed his eyes and turned up the volume. Appreciative hums, teasing promises. Wet licks and groans that followed.

Then he heard a creak in the hallway, followed by Jenna calling out his name.

His brain had trouble switching gears—one part screaming *Jenna's home, dipshit,* the other happily turned on and lizard-tastic—and before he could get his hand out of his shorts, Jenna pushed open their bedroom door. "I'm back. Do you want to listen to some comedy as we make—"

He dropped his phone, but it was too late. Her eyes went wide, and from where it fell on the mattress, his phone continued to emit the tinny sound of sloppy slurping.

She froze, her eyes wide, and he tried to jump off the bed. The room spun hard around him, and he fell back onto the mattress, landing on his ass.

Fuck.

His stomach twisted in panic as she twisted away.

"Wait!"

She turned back so slowly, so reluctantly, he wanted to die inside.

"It's just—"

She shook her head, her expression unreadable. "You don't need—"

Oh, but he did. "The doctor—"

"Really, it's—"

He swore, interrupting their stream of talking over each other. Every cell in his body twitched from the shot of fear-driven adrenaline his brain had just dumped into his system, and he couldn't think straight. He pushed off the bed, keeping his eyes locked on her this time, and crossed the room.

On auto-pilot, he reached for her, curving his hand around her arm.

Holding on.

She looked up at him as he braced his other arm against the doorway and took a long, steadying breath. "I want to say it's not what you think, except it's exactly what you think." He gave her a weak smile. "But nothing more."

"Okay…" she trailed off, confused. That made two of them.

He dove head first into the probably too-much-information explanation. "My doctor brought up sexual function a few weeks ago, and I didn't handle it well."

"Oh." She pressed her hand to his chest, and he stroked his fingers down her arm, until his palm covered hers.

"But he suggested some basic visual aids, and I've been trying." He exhaled roughly. He leaned in, ignoring the swirl in his brain, and he lowered his voice to an intimate, pleading pitch. "It's just exposure therapy."

God, let her believe him. After all the progress they'd made, let her understand.

Time stretched painfully as her cheeks pinked up, as her eyes roved across his face—and then over his shoulder.

And that's when he realized, through the blood pounding in his ears, that the video was still playing.

"Does it help?" she asked to a soundtrack of an unmistakable blow job.

He opened his mouth but no words came out. He shook his head.

"That's a shame," she whispered. "I'm all for exposure therapy."

Wait, what?

"If it's doctor recommended." Oh, God. She was teasing him. She rolled her shoulders and slid her hands into the back pockets of her jean shorts. "Who am I to say you shouldn't do...that?"

"You're my wife," he ground out. She had every right to say that.

"That's right, I am." She lifted her chin. "And maybe we should have talked about this sooner, but I'm not upset. Just surprised, that's all. Have you been trying this a lot?"

He shook his head. No.

"Mmm." She smiled at him, and deep in his belly, need reared its head.

"Uh..." This was good, right? She wasn't upset. Good.

But he'd lost most of his vocabulary and all of his higher processing skills.

She reached for his shirt and tugged it up, sliding her hands over his waist. "Sean," she said, his name a breathy offer that made his head spin in a whole new way. "Do you want to keep watching?"

"No."

"Okay. Do you want... me?"

"Yes." God, yes.

Her eyes sparkled as she pointed to his phone, and what sounded like an epic fake orgasm from one or both participants. "On my knees, maybe?"

"Uh..." Did he? Yes, fuck yes. But also, no, Jesus, he couldn't.

She licked her lips, and the scales shifted. Just a hair. "Or would you rather something else..." She closed her eyes, and the pink in her cheeks deepened. "Exposure therapy...like maybe watching me?"

Yes. That. He needed that. "On the bed."

She nodded as she moved past him, her eyes blinking open again.

His gaze caught on the sway of her hips, and his brain thudded against his skull. Hot and cold waves rolled over him as he followed her. He leaned heavily on his cane at the side of the bed and watched her stretch out.

Bare legs, denim cut offs, a soft cotton t-shirt stretched tight across her breasts.

And she had his phone in her hands. With a grin, she turned off the video and tossed it aside. "If you want to watch that again, feel free. But I think…" she reached for her button. "I mean, I don't want to rush you. But I think we might be ready for more, yes?"

"Rush away."

Deja vu, fierce and disorienting, slammed into him. *Rob away*. That kiss on top of the sea container in Urfa happened a lifetime ago, but the want he'd felt that night was so fresh he could taste it.

"How would you like me?" Her voice was a breathy whisper as she unzipped her shorts. The denim fell open, revealing pink underwear underneath.

He licked his lips. "Take the shorts off."

She wiggled them down her hips. Then her legs fell open as she ran her fingers over the elastic waistband of her panties. "And these?"

He shook his head quickly. Oh shit, that hurt. He blinked away the pain and focused on her fingers. Nimble and slim.

They would feel so good wrapped around his cock.

Deja vu that, motherfucker.

This was going to work. He wanted to crow. He wanted to punch his fist into the air and yell, but there would be time for that after.

She lifted one leg and stroked her toes up his body

until she hooked her foot under his shirt. "Now your turn. Take that off."

Showing off his torso for her was no hardship. He stripped down then slowly lowered himself to his knees after she got her fill of his chest. He cupped his hand around the swell of her calf muscle and she slid closer, until her knees were bent, her legs hanging off the bed on either side of him.

He kissed the inside of her thigh. "Touch yourself."

She took her time easing her fingers into her underwear, stroking leisurely at first. But he knew the moment her fingers made contact with her clit. He *knew* that gasp, that pleased little intake of air. He jerked his eyes up just in time to see her head roll back against the bed.

And in the next second, she twisted her head to the side and found him watching her.

Her. Not her fingers, not her sex, although that made him hot, too. But her face…He crawled up onto the bed and covered her body with his. He kissed her swollen lips, keeping his eyes open the whole time.

Bare, brushing kisses. Promises. Pleas.

"I don't know what I can do…" he breathed against her skin.

"It's okay." She smiled as her pupils dilated, the heat that was radiating through him obviously affecting her, too. "We'll do whatever you want."

He wanted to kiss her. Breathe her in and taste her skin.

"Take off your shorts, too." He shuddered at her words. It was the one thing he hadn't done yet.

She set her hands on his waist, but she didn't push them lower. If he wanted to fuck his wife, he had to be naked, and it had to be his own action.

"I know it's complicated," she whispered. "And we

haven't talked about it, but I just want to be naked with you. All the way naked."

Cold shivers raced beneath his skin as he pulled his shorts off. He hadn't put any boxers on under them, and now her hands stroked lower, teasing at the curve of his ass. He tensed up, and she made a pleased sound deep in her throat as she squeezed his muscles there.

He kissed her again, harder this time. "You taste like raspberries."

"We added more fruit to the sangria. And just ate the fresh berries, too."

She was delicious. And warm. And soft.

He pressed against her, ignoring the fact he wasn't hard yet, and kissed her again. "Berries, eh?"

"So good." She shimmied beneath him, bringing her heat into more insistent contact with his dick.

That was so good. So very good indeed.

She kissed his jaw, her lips soft whispers against his stubble there. "What do you want to do with me?"

"Everything."

He could feel her smile. "Lucky me."

"Sean?"

"Mmm."

"Should we talk?"

He laughed. It wasn't funny. They should. But it was such a sweet, Jenna thing to say. "Yeah."

"Can I be more naked for it?"

He slid to the side then rolled onto his back. She took off her t-shirt, then her bra, and finally, she stood on the bed above him and shimmied out of her panties, too.

He loved the way her breasts jiggled and bounced. They weren't big, but they were perfect. Two handfuls of soft, womanly flesh. As she straddled his waist, he tugged her forward so they dangled in his face.

"You talk first," he whispered as he kissed first one nipple, then the other.

"I want you to know how happy I am with where we are now." Her breath hitched. "Especially this very second. Very happy. I don't have any expectations."

"I do," he said. He pulled her breast into his mouth, sucking until she groaned and ground her hips against his belly. "I miss sex."

"Wanting something and expecting it are two different things." She eased her hips back, and for the first time in months, he felt the slick slide of her sex against his cock. "I'll give you anything you want," she breathed as she rolled her hips. "Anything."

He couldn't speak. If he could, he'd be babbling about how good she felt, how warm and wet and sexy this was. But his brain was stalling out in a haze of lusty hormones and misfiring signals. He set his hands on her hips and guided her on auto-pilot.

Her breasts swayed in front of his face. As her nipple brushed against his mouth, desire tugged hard inside him, and he ground their hips together. She pushed back again, and that tug turned into a fast-spooling bobbin of need.

His dick wasn't even fully hard, but that didn't matter. He threw his head back, every muscle in his body straining, and with a guttural shout, he came so hard he worried he'd blinded himself.

White, sparkling spots danced in front of his eyes. He gulped for air as Jenna fell on top of him, her mouth brushing the cords of his neck, then his jaw, and finally— finally, yes—his lips.

He kissed her like she was the air he breathed. He

inhaled her, consumed her, worshiped her. If he weren't so wrung out, he thought it was possible he might cry, and Fosters didn't cry.

Ever.

Maybe they might make exceptions for the return of orgasms.

"That was incredible," she murmured as she ran her hand down his torso and patted his abs. "Be right back."

She returned a minute later with a warm wash cloth. He watched through a daze as she cleaned him up.

Holy. Shit.

"I know, right?"

Had he said that out loud? He cleared his throat. "So that was…unexpected."

"I could tell. Your face went from turned on to climaxing pretty darn fast. It was totally hot."

"Not something I usually brag about," he said dryly.

She got up again and sauntered over to the laundry basket and got rid of the washcloth. "No," she said as she swivelled back to him. "I guess not. Which makes it kind of special for us."

She was a goddess. An understanding, ridiculously sexy goddess.

"I felt like a teenager again," he said, reaching for her. "Like it was hard to control."

"You'll get it back. The control. And when you do…" She grinned wickedly. "Maybe you'll have the, uh, recovery of a young man, too."

"I *am* a young man," he growled, kissing her hard on the mouth. "And I think my recovery is going to be just fine."

She glanced between them.

He wasn't all the way hard, same as before, but…he

was recovered. Thick and ready for touching again, he was pretty sure. He wrapped his hand around himself experimentally. Yeah, he was ready.

"What do you want to do next?" she asked breathily.

His heart hammered in his chest. "Maybe we could try that blow job now."

CHAPTER TWENTY-SIX

September

LABOUR DAY BROUGHT quiet to the peninsula. Cottagers and day-trippers from Toronto disappeared, and in their place came a weekly parade of fall festivals that thrilled Jenna. Apple picking, pumpkin celebrations, and everyone broke out the plaid shirts.

Not Sean, though.

"You know that I love you," she said slowly as she followed him from the bedroom into the kitchen early one morning.

"Yes."

"So I'm not saying this is a relationship deal breaker *now*, but—"

He stopped in front of the coffee maker and grabbed the fresh grinds he'd just measured out. "If you'd known that I didn't wear plaid flannel shirts, you wouldn't have married me?"

She tried to sound as serious as possible. "It's a possibility."

"What's wrong with what I'm wearing?"

She gave him an appreciative once over. There was nothing wrong with his tight black t-shirt and cargo pants that hung perfectly from his hips.

Nothing at all. "You know you look good. That's not the point. There's just something in the air."

He pressed the power button on the coffee maker and turned around, leaning back against the counter. "I think it's called frost. Go get me the shirt."

She pumped her fists in the air and did a happy dance all the way back to their bedroom.

When she got back to the kitchen, he had her travel mug filled and her bagel toasted. "I love you," she whispered as he fisted his hand around the red and black fabric. She wrapped her arms around his neck and kissed him.

"Was that for the coffee or the shirt?"

"For both. For the way you take care of me. For getting up with me so early in the morning too."

It was early, too. She wanted to make morning rounds at the hospital.

He walked her to the front door, grabbing his cane on the way. "I've got a busy day today too. I'm heading out with the search and rescue team. We're going to talk about endurance and cross country movement, and then they're going to do some timed exercises I planned for them in the woods."

And tomorrow was his last official day in the Canadian Forces, but they weren't talking about that just yet. He'd been studiously avoiding the topic, other than to tell her he'd be gone in the evening for the unit's regular training night and the official "mug out" send-off from the officer's mess.

"Good luck with the training. And stay warm in that super-handsome shirt!" She kissed him again, then grabbed her bags and her breakfast and headed into the still-dark morning.

Dawn broke as she drove out of town.

She put on a top 40 station and rolled down her window. There was frost in the air, Sean was right. She drank her coffee and thought about her case load as the cool morning air pinked up her cheeks.

Her first intake client, Brenda, was five days past her due date. Jenna would have to touch base with her after rounds. And she needed to follow up with her newest intake, too—a Syrian refugee, recently arrived in Canada, and terrified about navigating an unfamiliar health care system.

Jenna's limited Arabic had never felt so useful as in that first meeting.

But it wasn't enough. She'd have to help the mother find a native speaker translator who she would be comfortable having at her delivery. Maybe Jenna could put the word out in the midwifery forums and see if there were any Arabic speaking students who wanted to do a spring placement with her. As welcoming as Jenna could be, she was no replacement for someone who shared more of a client's culture and background.

She liked being this busy, though. It was no hardship. And while a small town practice offered its own unique challenges—like the hour-plus drive into work four or five days a week, and being a significant distance from a delivering hospital much of the time—she wouldn't give up its benefits.

Like being surrounded by friends.

Waking up to her husband's kisses each morning.

Having a close-knit support group at the end of an exhausting day.

The pies at Mac's.

And the chance to make a real difference in an under-served community.

It's why she'd flown halfway around the world, but she was needed here, too.

The day flew by, and then in the late afternoon, it got exciting.

After a no-news phone call with Brenda at lunch time, she called back at three and said she was having contractions. "They're not close together yet, but they're pretty intense. I think. I don't know."

"If you aren't sure yet, then it's probably still early, but you're on my way home. How about I stop in and see you in about an hour? And call me again if anything changes."

She wrapped up the rest of her clinic work, checked her calendar for the next day—which was wide open, as it wasn't one of her two clinic days for patient appointments. A good day to help a couple deliver a baby, for sure.

She updated her partners about the contraction news then headed for her car. Brenda lived on a farm halfway to Pine Harbour, and when Jenna got there, she found her client hanging laundry on the line.

"Last minute nesting?" she asked with a smile.

"Something like that." Brenda gave her a nervous look. "The first one wasn't so bad, but some of them have taken my breath away."

"That's a good sign, it might mean that they're productive contractions. I'll watch you through a few of them. Maybe we can adjust your breathing a bit to make them more manageable too."

The first one came as Brenda was hanging the last of

the laundry. She stopped and leaned forward, bracing her hands on her knees.

Jenna kept an eye on her watch. Only thirty seconds, although she was sure it felt longer than that for Brenda. And when it ended, Brenda slid right back into the conversation.

"They're definitely stronger like that when I'm standing or walking."

"Let's go for a little walk, then, and see how long it takes for the next one to come. But then I want you to go inside and get some rest."

It was almost ten minutes until the next contraction. In that time, they talked about breathing, and eating, and sleep. All the things a labouring woman needed to maintain her strength.

Inside the farm house, Brenda's husband was working on his computer, but he came to her side right away.

Jenna patted him on the shoulder. "Let's get her onto the couch. Your job is going to be enforcing a nap at the very least."

She took Brenda's vitals while they waited for the next contraction, and then she sat on the floor next to the couch and watched her client.

There was no magic ball when it came to estimating labour. But as a first-time mom, with weak contractions that lengthened with rest… Jenna didn't want Brenda to get too excited about having a baby tonight. "Maybe tomorrow," she said. "But it is possible for this early labour stuff to go on for a few days. Your uterus is figuring out the contractions. It's a waiting game now."

"Can you check me? Inside?"

Jenna furrowed her brow. She wasn't one to offer an

internal exam, but if a client asked for it... there were pros and cons, and she explained them to Brenda.

"I think if I knew what my cervix was doing, if I was dilated at all, that would help calm me."

Jenna nodded. "And if you aren't dilated at all, don't be disappointed."

They waited for the next contraction to pass, and then Jenna pulled out what she'd need from her travel bag.

Sure enough, the first-time mom's cervix was maybe one centimetre dilated, just a fingertip, and quite firm. Jenna discarded her medical gloves into a biohazard bag then covered Brenda back up with the blanket her husband had brought for her to rest under.

"Your cervix is still pretty high and firm. That doesn't necessarily mean anything—our bodies are amazing, and things can change quickly, but what we usually see with first time moms is that it takes a while. I do like the look of your contractions, though. Those are nice and regular. This is definitely early labour, but I'd expect it to come and go over the next twenty-four hours. So I recommend you get some sleep." She glanced at Brenda's husband, including him in that. "Both of you. And I'll come and check on you again first thing, or whenever you page me. Okay?"

She made sure her numbers were programmed in their phones.

"Get some sleep," she repeated. "Tomorrow you're having a baby."

After she stowed her bag in the trunk of her car, she called Sean.

He answered on the third ring, and from the background noise, she could tell he was still outside. "How goes the baby delivering?"

"Slowly. It'll probably be tomorrow, so I'm heading

home to sleep. Are you still out with the search and rescue team?"

"No, I'm at the meadow."

Again. He'd been spending a lot of time there lately. She smiled. "Okay. I'll see you when you get home, then."

"I…" He laughed. "I could use a ride home, if you want to stop and pick me up. I walked here."

"From where?"

"Home."

"Sean, that's five kilometres!"

"I made it, though."

She shook her head even as she smiled with secret pride. "I'll be there in half an hour."

He met her at the access lane, but when she pulled to a stop, he didn't get in the car. Turning it off, she hopped out and went around to him.

He kissed her quickly. "How tired are you?"

She shook her head. "I've got lots of energy."

"I want to show you something."

Even though he'd been going since early morning, he was pretty steady on his feet. She didn't miss that he was using his cane, though. Sometimes it was just a safety net now, but other times—like toward the end of the day, or when he was suffering from a migraine—he used it with every step.

Tonight was one of those times.

But he wanted to show her something, and she wasn't going to rain on that parade. He was a big boy. Her shock over him walking all the way to the meadow was enough doubt for one day.

Besides, he was wearing her shirt and holding her hand as they walked through a forest. It was pretty much her fall fantasy come to life. If there was making out up against a tree, her already great day would be made perfect.

She checked the signal on her pager and her cell phone, because sometimes reception on the peninsula was spotty, but she was fine.

Once they were across the snowmobile trail Sean slowed down. "Right here."

So they weren't walking all the way in to the meadow.

She turned in a slow circle.

But when she returned her gaze to where Sean had been standing, he was gone, moving around some scrubby brush.

"Careful," he called out over his shoulder. "Don't trip over the kitchen."

She pulled up short. In front of her was a thin rope stretching across the pine needles covering the forest floor. She followed it to a wooden stake in the ground then took the ninety degree turn to the next stake. Here there were two ropes, one extending forwards, more external wall, and the other cutting in again. "Big kitchen," she said quietly, her heart thudding in her chest.

"It's become a tradition in my family to build a house for the women we love." She jerked her head up and found Sean had returned. He had a bouquet of wildflowers in his hand, late summer blooms. Hardy flowers that had withstood the crazy heat waves and heavy summer storms. Bright orange, pale yellow, the odd purple dotting here and there.

He stopped in front of her and lowered himself to one knee as he held out the flowers. "I want to build you a house, Jenna."

She already had everything she needed. And he wanted to give her more?

They had a little house. She'd brought up buying it from Dean, but Sean had always been vague about when they might do that.

"I already asked you to marry me, and I thank God every day you said yes. I fell in love with you in a heart-beat, and my entire life changed. And when my life changed *again*, you never wavered."

That wasn't true, though. She'd wavered plenty. Second-guessed her crazy plan to follow him, worried she wasn't enough… She wanted to fall to her knees and kiss him. Tell him he didn't need to do this.

But she couldn't move, and the look on his face was one she'd never forget. He *wanted* to do this. He gazed up at her, his eyes bright and filled with promise, and it was like they were back in Spain.

Heady feelings and endless dreams.

He pressed the flowers into her hands, covering her fingers with his own. Strong, solid hands, attached to a strong, solid body. A quiet, solid man, made stronger still by all he had survived.

"I want to build you a house big enough for all our dreams," he said, squeezing her fingers. "A threshold I can carry you over."

Her heart flipped and she nodded. "Yes."

"Yes?" He grinned and stood again, using his cane to get up. He wrapped his arm around her waist, hooking his fingers into the back pocket of her jeans as he pulled her against him.

"Show me our future home," she said as he curved over her, as he leaned in for a kiss she already knew was going to steal her heart. His kisses always did. Soft, sweet plundering embraces that turned dirty on a dime.

This was no different. His lips coaxed and his tongue

teased, until she was up on her toes and he had to widen his stance to hold her as he kissed her with his entire body.

"Right, the house," he finally said with a quiet laugh as he held her close. "Got distracted."

"Yes. Show me before we lose the light."

He turned her around and pointed at the lines. From this angle, she could see them more clearly, and there were orange paint marks on the wooden stakes. "This is the kitchen. Big enough for a farmhouse table so we can have dinner parties, just the way you like them. Everyone helping with the prep. A wine rack here, and around the corner, a butler's pantry. Behind that..." He gestured with his cane, and she followed. "A mudroom that leads into a garage. A place to store hockey gear and your medical bags."

"Hockey gear?" She gave him a wide-eyed look. "Are you going to start skating again?"

He shrugged. "I was thinking about trying sled hockey. A lot of injured vets play it. But not right now. Either way, our kids will have stuff. Need to plan ahead."

"Kids?"

He pointed into the tree-studded sky above them. "Four bedrooms upstairs, with a library off the master bedroom that can be a nursery."

How many kids was he planning for them to have? "Fancy."

"You're a hard woman to please," he murmured, but his eyes were on fire now, and she loved it. "I haven't even gotten to the good part."

Him wanting to make babies with her was definitely the good part, but she wasn't letting on just yet that she was sold, all in, whatever he wanted.

The forest floor here wasn't level, and he took her

hand, tugging her to the top of the rise, where their tent was erected. How had she missed that? "This," he murmured as he moved around her. "This will be the view from our bedroom window. Even better, really, because we'll be up another storey."

There was a gap in the trees ahead of them, and through it, she could see their meadow.

"Oh, Sean—"

Brrrt. Her pager vibrated.

She tugged it off the strap of her cross body bag and read the text message from the answering service. Brenda's water had broken and they were heading to the hospital. "I have to go," she said, regret lancing each word. "Come on, I'll give you a ride home."

He cupped her face and kissed her. "I'll call someone else to come get me. Go."

"But—"

"I'm going to spend the rest of my life right here. Sending you off to bring babies into the world. Hearing the phone ring and knowing that our plans will need to change. And that's okay. That's more than okay. That's *wonderful*. I love you. Go. I'll be at home when you're done. Wake me up and tell me all about it."

CHAPTER TWENTY-SEVEN

THE LAST DAY of Sean's career in the Canadian Forces started in the best way possible—with his wife coming home in the early morning, before dawn, and crawling into bed with him.

"Baby arrive?" he asked, shaking off the heavy veil of sleep.

"Yep. Fast and furious. A little bit of excitement after the delivery with a blood pressure drop for mom, but they're all okay now."

Her hair was damp from the shower. It felt good to touch and he curled his fingers into it and tugged.

They hadn't had a chance to finish their conversation the night before. Hadn't gotten to what he'd hoped would follow the conversation, either.

"You tired?"

"I'll sleep soon." Something in the way she said it made him blink his eyes open.

She was wearing that plaid shirt she'd given him.

And, God willing, she wasn't wearing anything else. Her bare leg was curled up and around his body.

He was suddenly a big fan of red flannel.

"Hey," he said softly, pushing himself up onto his elbows. "You look…wow. I like the shirt better on you."

She rose, too. This was the most arousing image in the world—Jenna, rising on her knees beside him, smiling as she reached for the three buttons she'd bothered doing up in the first place.

She didn't even need to open her shirt and he was blissfully, thankfully hard. Ready and eager for his wife.

He pushed the blankets away and sat up, leaning back against the headboard. She crawled into his lap, straddling him, as the shirt fell open. He skimmed his fingers over her waist and curled them around her breasts. Cupping, squeezing, loving.

That he had this again was a gift. He would never take it for granted.

He'd lost much, and some he would never gain again. But he could hold his wife in his lap. Slide into her tight, wet heat, and hear his name on her breath as she sighed.

"Sean…"

He'd had so many plans.

Races to run.

Wars to fight.

And then he'd walked into that mess tent and fallen head over heels in love.

When he lost the ability to run, to fight, he'd thought he'd lose this too.

But *this*—Jenna, and their love—had saved him. It had given him a new set of dreams and goals.

He'd build her a house.

"So…" she said, her breath hitching as she rode him slowly. "You want to make babies with me?"

He curved his hands around her waist and lower,

cupping her bottom. His fingers stroked her ass lightly, teasing her crease the way she liked before he squeezed her cheeks tighter and urged her to pick up the pace. "I've been thinking about it."

She wouldn't be hurried tonight, though. "Maybe we could build this house first."

"Definitely by the time the second one comes along." Oh, he could tell she liked that. She shuddered in his arms and rolled her hips, pulling him deeper into her body.

He was going to be just fine.

Broken.

Put back together.

Missing a few pieces, maybe, but Jenna had filled those spots with new and way more interesting plans.

He had a wife and the promise of a family. A plot of land and a house to build. A set of skills for which he would forever be grateful.

"One thing at a time," she whispered as he tugged her forward so he could get his mouth on her breasts.

Sure, they'd take it slow. But they'd learned together that even small, careful steps could eventually get them where they wanted to go.

He tugged her shirt—his shirt, their shirt—down her shoulders, baring more of her as she rose above him. Through lust-hooded eyes, he watched her body roll in pleasure. Muscles moving beneath overheated skin. Flushed marks decorating the swells and dips he'd now memorized.

She was his, and he was hers.

He pushed up, suddenly craving that tight, desperate squeeze of her heat around him. Like he was too big for her, too much. Of course he wasn't, but there was now always that little bit of his brain that worried he wasn't enough. What turned him on worked in weird ways to balance that doubt.

"Oh yeah, just like that," Jenna breathed. She knew. She knew him to his soul. "God, yes, *Sean.*"

With a cry, she came around him, and he jerked his own release deep inside her.

His gorgeous, wonderful wife.

It was the last day of a chapter in his journey that had once been everything. His mission, his drive. Now it was just a bittersweet goodbye to what had been a good gig while he had it, and which had mercifully carried him to meet the woman who would be the rest of his journey.

His forever.

———

SINCE JENNA NEEDED TO SLEEP, Sean also spent much of the day in bed. He'd spend the night getting drunk for the first time in almost exactly a year.

He was not wrong—that is exactly how it was playing out at the Wiarton Armoury.

"This time last year we were heckling you for falling hard and fast for Liana," Sean said to Dean when his older brother brought him yet another beer. He was on his third now. He'd skipped all of his meds today, which meant tomorrow was going to be a fucking gong show in his head, but this was his mug out—drinking was non-negotiable unless it really wasn't an option, and that wasn't the case for him.

"This time last year we were having a *wicked* party at your place," Matt added shamelessly as he joined them.

Sean gave him the finger. It wasn't a lie, it was just…a different time in his life.

Now he made different choices—like nursing this beer and passing off the other rounds bought for him to those in attendance. Not that the officers, even the junior ones, were likely to get blitzed.

But the Fosters were in attendance tonight, and that changed things.

His brothers were all non-commissioned officers, and their messes—first the Junior Ranks Mess, now the Sergeants mess—were more raucous than the Officers' Mess.

But they were all here by invitation. And they were all bored out of their minds.

So was he.

"To the Queen!" Jake called out, raising his beer high.

Sean grinned. It was good to be back in uniform one last time. Before coming up to the mess, he'd spent an hour sitting with the CO and the padre. He took their lectures on the chin—he'd been too distant, too closed off, and could have accepted more support from the unit.

He hadn't wanted it. Couldn't see at the time that they meant well.

He was glad he came out of that haze when the unit was stood down for the summer.

After the formal goodbye meeting, he signed the last few pieces of paperwork for his release with the clerk, promised to return his uniforms within fourteen days, and headed upstairs to the mess.

"To the Queen," he murmured as he raised his own bottle.

The next toast was a quiet one. Dean pulled Matt in close, and Jake closed in on the other side, until they were in a circle of just the four of them. "To our baby brother," Dean said. "Full of surprises and capable of anything."

"I'll drink to that," Jake said.

"You guys have been…" Great. Far too patient. Rockstar brothers. There weren't words to properly describe how Sean felt. "I'm beyond grateful," he finally said. "For all the ass kicking, and driving, and food and shelter and beer."

"More of that in the future," Dean said gruffly. "Jake pushed the calendar appointment to my phone this afternoon. Construction begins in March?"

"Yep." Sean had a plan. Having a contractor for a brother brought costs down, but building a house was still a significant cost. It would eat up most of his savings.

But Chloe was helping him build a website, and Jenna had booked a week of holidays. They were heading to Florida in December, to his old winter training camp. This time, he was returning as a speaker and limited-run special coach. The fees for that would cover his income needs through to the end of the spring.

And so it would begin. The rest of his life.

"Hey," Dean thumped him on his shoulder. He pointed to the door, where their father stood. He wasn't in uniform —long retired now—but as a former member of this very mess, as a former CO of the unit, he was always welcome. "I didn't know he was coming."

Sean gave a single nod, and the room didn't spin. A small improvement that felt like he'd climbed a mountain. "Yeah. I invited him."

The look on his oldest brother's face was priceless.

"What?"

"Nothing." Dean raised his voice. "Over here, sir."

"Sons," the Colonel said as he approached. "I see you're bringing your beer-guzzling ways into the Officers' Mess."

"Only way to do a mug out, Dad," Matt said. "Mug. Of Beer. Well, I'd do a mug out with gin, too, but I don't think you'd approve of how that would end."

Jake groaned. "Don't say it."

Matt crowed as he lifted his beer in the air. "Pants off, all the way."

Their father immediately turned and scanned the crowd. "Good turn out tonight."

Sean cleared his throat. "How about you and I go have something that's served in a proper glass?"

That got more shocked looks from his brothers.

Good.

He was all about surprising them. First with the fact he'd owned a plot of land all this time, then with his business ideas. Now with his ability to act like an adult with their father.

"Matt, make sure your pants stay on until you head back to your own mess."

"Yes, Captain."

"Last day for that," his father said as he led the way to the bar.

Sean nodded. "Yep."

"How do you feel about that?"

He'd been thinking about this all night. "You know, sir. Jenna's taught me something pretty significant this summer. We don't always get what we want, you know? Thank you." He accepted a glass filled with what smelled like brandy. "But we can make what we get something worth wanting."

EPILOGUE

The following spring

SEAN FROWNED AT HIS WATCH. If they didn't appear in another sixty seconds, it would mean their miles per hour speed had dropped significantly on the last ten kilometres.

But just when he was about to reach for his phone, he heard footfalls in the distance, then voices. One light, the other strained.

Dean was more than done. Too bad the stubborn ass wouldn't admit it.

When Liana had approached Sean about training her for an ultra run, Dean had volunteered to pace her.

It was time for his brother to admit he couldn't keep up with his wife, not for hours at a time.

Sean tugged his visor off his head and wiped at the sweat forming along his hairline before he stood up. It was hard work, sitting in a camp chair and thinking about running techniques. He grinned at his little joke just as the happy couple turned the corner.

"What are you laughing at?" Dean growled as Sean

handed him a bit of beef jerky and a Dixie cup of pickle juice.

It wasn't watching his brother suffer through this trial run of his fifty mile training plan. Nope. "Nothing. Just happy, that's all."

His brother gave him a long, suffering look before nodding. "Good."

Liana tugged off her mini backpack and handed it to Sean. "This is starting to chafe against the inside of my arms."

He took a look at the buckle, and quickly unthreaded it, sending it the other way so the loose end would be on the outside instead. "Try that, but you want to keep your arms out a bit more, anyway. And we can order a different pack that doesn't have any buckles there, just elastic."

She nodded and took it back, slinging it over her shoulders with ease. Her breathing was back to normal too.

"How are the legs?"

"Hammy's tight."

"Both?"

She shook her head. "Just the right."

"Stretch it out a bit now before you turn around and head back."

Dean groaned.

"Just ten more, big brother," Sean said, slapping him on the chest. "And this time, stop slowing Liana down. Let her go ahead if you can't keep up."

Liana gave him an apologetic look. "That's on me. I like running with him."

When it came to running, Sean didn't have a lot of room for romance. "That's not going to work as we get into longer distances. The big guy here can be your pace bunny for the first leg, but we'll find you fresh bodies to run with for each subsequent chunk. That's how it'll be on a race day, anyway. Might as well get used to it. When the training group arrives next week, you'll get a taste of how a race actually goes, and it'll all make sense."

She nodded as she stretched her leg. Then she bounced on the balls of her feet. "I'm ready."

"Okay. Off you go. I'll meet you back at Mac's."

It would take them forty-five minutes at least, more if Dean slowed down, so Sean had time to stop in on his build site.

He picked up his camp chair and his backpack, and headed for his truck. He'd figured out a bunch of these check points up and down the trail. Their new house was the first one, five kilometres south of Pine Harbour. This spot was the next point, ten clicks out. He could get people started on a run then meet them at each point along the way.

It still blew him away that next week, ten elite athletes would show up for a week of training with him. That they'd all paid good money to have him put them through their paces and teach them more about cross-training.

He'd hired Olivia to manage the logistics that were beyond him now—no reason to induce a migraine if he didn't need to, and she could do all the cottage booking and catering ordering ten times faster than he could anyway. She'd done all of that for a film shoot two years earlier.

If Hope Creswell wasn't careful, Sean might just try to steal her assistant away.

He turned north, toward home—their new home, although they only had a foundation so far. And a new lane, properly graded. He drove all the way in, expecting to find the property empty.

Instead, he found his wife's car parked at the end of the drive, and that was even better.

He didn't see her, so he grabbed his cane. He didn't need it for short distances now. He could better anticipate the vertigo and compensate for the disorientation when it happened. But for a longer distance, it was just smart, and if she was exploring the meadow…

But she wasn't. She was curled up on the far side of the poured foundation, sitting on an outdoor blanket, with a book in her lap.

"This is a welcome surprise," he said after he spotted her.

"My afternoon was wide open and I thought I might come and see if you were here." She'd joined the practice in Walkerton as a full partner just before their winter vacation to Florida. Her job still consumed a lot of her days and nights, but the flip side of that commitment to whatever her clients needed was that every so often, she got a day to herself—and because he was the luckiest man on the planet, she chose to spend that found time with him.

"Liana wanted to go for a run." He gestured south. "They'll be running past here in ten or fifteen minutes. Do you want to go out for lunch?"

"Sure." She picked up her book, and her blanket, and they strolled back toward their vehicles together. "The laneway looks good."

It had been a disaster just a week before, with the excavation equipment and cement trucks tearing it up. But they were done now. The next thing to go in would be a well and a septic tank, and after that, they would be done with heavy machinery and he could grade in the last load of gravel to make the lane smooth again.

He checked his watch then glanced down the trail. A

few more minutes, and he'd see them running past. "We can come back here after lunch," he said. "Come with me in my truck."

She hopped into the passenger seat, and he turned the truck around, pointing the nose at the trail so he could watch for his trainee.

He was taking this job seriously.

But this was also a prime opportunity to make out with his wife in his truck, which had been on his Sean's-Getting-Better bucket list for a while.

He turned off the truck again and pushed up the middle seat, that most of the time he kept down as an armrest. He gestured for Jenna to come closer, and she lifted one eyebrow as she did just that.

"What are we doing?"

"A long time ago, I promised myself I'd show you how good it was to make out in a truck." He kissed her, one hand possessively cupping the back of her neck, the other unzipping her sweatshirt so he could stroke her curves a little as he tasted her mouth.

"It's really good." She chased his mouth, her breath hot and alive against his skin. He curved his hand over the barely-there swell of her belly.

A year ago, his world had exploded and he'd thought his dreams of a family with Jenna had turned to dust. She'd had hope enough for both of them, though. His throat got tight when he thought about how close he'd come to losing her.

Their trip to Florida hadn't just been the official start of his new career. They'd conceived a baby there.

"We might get caught," he said as he tugged her closer. He didn't care. Let them tease him for loving his wife this much.

"So?" She grinned as she climbed into his lap. "Remember? Life is short."

Oh, he remembered. He remembered everything. Bring on the crazy adventure.

THE END

That's three of the Foster brothers who have found love. Matt's story is next, in *Love on the Outskirts of Town*. And be sure to sign up for my email newsletter so you don't miss any of the Pine Harbour news!

www.zoeyork.com

ACKNOWLEDGEMENTS

aka The People Who Make Me Want to Get it Right

This book is way longer than it was supposed to be. So my first grateful thank you note is to my editor, Kristi Yanta, who rolled with the changes with grace. Because of her, this book is tighter, smarter, and better. I can't wait to work on the next Pine Harbour novel with her.

Dana Waganer did a very thorough proofreading pass. So many commas in the wrong places. So many typos. Any remaining errors are because I probably changed something at the last second.

I'm also endlessly appreciative of my husband. The Viking not only puts up with my head being in the computer most of the time, juggling work and our kids, dinner and laundry like a freaking pro, he also had to tolerate me writing about an officer this time around—a true hardship for any senior NCO. I'm sorry, sweetie. I'll be back to the NCOs in the next book.

Finally, a very special thank you to one of my midwives, Diane, who took time out of her busy schedule to have lunch with me and humour my questions about what a midwife who was trained in BC and working overseas would have to do to shift gears and work in Ontario suddenly. That lead to a dozen more questions, and we talked until I had pages of notes to draw from for Jenna.

Getting Jenna right was important to me because midwives are, to me, the most special health care providers.

Nine and a half years ago, my first born arrived seven weeks early because I developed severe pre-eclampsia. I went to the hospital to have some blood work done, and left a week later, a mom to a six-day-old baby I was leaving behind in the NICU. A baby who had been born by c-section and immediately whisked away, who I didn't get to hold until the day after I left the hospital. Through it all, and the weeks that would follow until he came home, my midwife Jennifer was a wonderful support as I adjusted to a start to motherhood I'd never expected.

Almost four years later, my second was born. He arrived just one week before his due date, and his delivery was night and day compared to his brother's. Again, I had midwives by my side. Diane and Marie cheered me on and promised me that this time could be different. And because of them, it was. My youngest was born with Feist playing in the background, in a few easy pushes, and after he was delivered, they put him right on my chest and I got to hold him skin-to-skin.

We don't always get what we want, but we can make what we get something worth wanting. That was the lesson I learned in my second delivery. That was what my midwives taught me. I still got sick in my second delivery. Still had a lot of drugs and interventions. But we fought for some elements of a delivery that mattered to me. None of that is in this book, because this story isn't mine. It's Sean and Jenna's. But the kernel of that lesson I learned still made its way into their story, and I don't mind that at all.

Finally, to my readers, thank you for loving Pine Harbour. Thank you for coming back over and over again for more of these stories that take me so long to write.

I love you all,
Zoe

www.ingramcontent.com/pod-product-compliance
Lightning Source LLC
Chambersburg PA
CBHW030358200726
48286CB00015B/1536